HEROES
OF THE
EMPIRE

BOOK 2: THE GENERAL

HEROES
OF THE
EMPIRE

ISRAH AZIZI

Page Turner Press LLC

Published in the United States of America by
PageTurnerPress LLC. Visit page-turner-press.com
Title: Heroes of the Empire/ Israh Azizi
Other titles: The General
Cover design by Damonza
Identifiers: Library of Congress Control Number: 2023915644
ISBN: 978-1-958688-04-5 (hardcover)
ISBN: 978-1-958688-03-8 (paperback)
ISBN: 978-1-958688-12-0 (ebook)
Printed in the United States of America
10 9 8 7 6 5 4 3 2 1
First Edition

For my father.

I'm as strong as I am because of you.

PRONUNCIATION AND CHARACTER GUIDE

Adelania (eda-lay-nee-ya) — former Ondalarian princess

Alesto (eh-les-toh) — Coralie's personal advisor

Aria (ah-ree-ya) — Boltrex's daughter

Asilles (es-sill-lees) — Ondalarian shieldmaiden

Astarolos (es-tuh-role-us) — king of the Old Empire

Aylis (EYE-less) — Savorian, Thorsten's former love

Bear (bay-er) — Velamir's former mentor

Boltrex Vaz (bol-TREX) — general in Verin

Bronus (BRO-nis) — Honzio's decoy and bodyguard

Cerel (SER-rill) —True Manos in the Grand Palace

Colein (coh-lane) — Chishma

Coralie (cora-LEE) — princess of Verin

Cores-na (core-es-na) — Kolesta-na's daughter

Cselnsor (SELLIN-soar) — General Winston's son

Dale (DAY-ell) — king of Verin, Coralie's uncle

Domavan (Duh-muh-ven) — Draven's captain

Draven Valent (DRAY-ven VALL-ont) — crown prince
    of Ayleth

Elwin (el-wen) — stable master

Evala (ee-vall-uh) — Lord Hisel's daughter

Evinshore (eh-VEEN-shore) — commander in Verin

Feldon (fell-din) — Tariqin commander

Finnean Colleda (FINN-ee-ahn COLE-eda) — Verin soldier

Gabriella (gah-BREE-ella) — Lord Hisel's daughter

Gallaxos (gall-axe-us) — Ondalarian prince

Galva Blayton (BLAY-ten) — Verin councilman, Galvasir

Grongar-ja (gron-gar-ja) — Uluzar/Savagelander

Hesten Hartinza (HES-tin HEART-inza) — Natassa's older brother, deceased

Honzio Hartinza (HON-zee-oh HEART-inza) — crown prince of Karalik Empire, Natassa's older brother

Irox (EYE-rocks) — deceased prince of Verin, King Dale's brother, Coralie's father

Jaxon Tana (JAX-en tan-nuh) — Shadow Manos, Velamir's closest friend

Jinong-ja (jih-nong-ja) — Uluzar chief

Joster (JAW-ster) — king of Ayleth, Draven's father

Jovinne Servan (JO-ven sir-vahn) — Coralie's bodyguard, Mordon's childhood nemesis

Julius (Ju-lee-us) — Chishma, Velamir's former classmate

Jyorm (JEE-yorm) — combat instructor for the Chishman Academy

Karakan (kara-KON) — Rumlok twisted into a savage beast

Kasdeya Vosta (kas-DAY-a VOZ-ta) — Natassa's former decoy and handmaiden, Krea's twin

Kira and Kerstor Sevelis (SEV-el-iss) — twins that developed a strategic combat move

Kolesta-na Zurg (coal-esta-na Zoo-org) — Uluzar, king of Ayleth's former courtesan

Koseer-ja (KOH-seer-jah) — Uluzar/Savagelander

Kostos (KOS-toz) — head advisor in the Grand Palace

Krealyn Vosta (KREE-ah-lin VOZ-ta) — Natassa's decoy and handmaiden, Kasdeya's twin

Lady Blayton (BLAY-ten) — Latimus's mother

Latimus (LAT-ih-miss) — Verin captain, Blayton's son

Lilly (lil-lee) — Jax's cousin

Lissa (LISS-ah) — Chishma

Lord Hisel (HISS-ell) — Karalik councilman

Lord Jasper (JA-es-per) — prisoner at the Grand Palace

Malus Hartinza (MAL-us HEART-inza) — emperor of Karalik Empire

Mari (MAR-ee) — late Verin princess, Coralie's mother

Moralis Vane (MORE-al-less vein) — Honzio's cousin, Galvasir

Mordon Vaz (MORE-dawn) — Galvasir, General Boltrex's son

Natassa Hartinza (NAT-ossa HEART-inza) — princess of Karalik Empire

Nestor (nes-TOR) — prisoner at Tariqin war camp

Nildon (NEEL-din) — Imperial Galvasir

Ovi (OH-vee) — Natassa's late mother

Povon-ja (POV-own-jah) — Uluzar/Savagelander in communication with Kasdeya

Prolus (PRO-lus) — the lord of Tariqi

Quintus (Qu-win-tis) — Chishma

Rasdor (RAZ-door) — True Sight, legendary Savorian hero

Revoz (REV-ozz) — Chishma, Shadow Manos

Rost (roh-ist) — merchant

Rumlok (RUM-lock) — wolf/bearlike creature

Salvador (SAL-va-door) — Vykus's henchman

Saphira (sef-ee-ra) — Winston's wife

Serana (sir-ronna) — Boltrex's wife

Silopar (SEE-lo-par) — Handler

Sim (Sih-em) — Vykus's cousin

Sirchoba (sir-cho-bah) — messenger bird

Sovor-ja (SAV-oar-jah) — Uluzar/Savagelander

Svorgin (sa-vor-gin) — Aylis's brother

Talon (TA-lawn) — Chishma, one of Winston's right hands

Thander (THA-en-dir) — Honzio's late guard

Theris (Thair-es) — Imperial captain

Thorsten Hartinza (Thor-stin HEART-inza) — Natassa's late brother

Tio and Tyras (TEE-oh tie-ross) — Salvador's younger brothers

Vandal (VAAN-del) — Velamir's horse

Velamir (vel-uh-meer) — Winston's adopted son, the Cavalier

Vykus (VI-kiss) — renowned mercenary king

Welix (WELL-ix) — advisor in Verin

Winston Raga (win-ston raw-ga) — Prolus's general

Yera (yeh-rah) — Sirchoba

Zenrelius (ZEN-rel-ee-us) — Ondalarian general

IMPORTANT LOCATIONS AND TERMS

(the) Awal (OW-aal) — the Tariqin Army, filled with deedans

Alaris (UH-lar-rus) — the afterlife, eternal bliss

Ayleth (EYE-leth) — one of the four kingdoms

(the) Borderlands — once a defensive stronghold against the Tariqins

Borel Inn (BORE-ell) — inn Honzio visits in Hearcross

Cadellion (KED-el-lee-on) — Emperor Malus's bodyguards, wielders of four blades

Calestor (KEl-es-tore) —Tariqin captain title

Chishma (chish-muh) — Prolus's elite soldiers and graduates of the Chishman Academy

Clovensgate (clo-vens-gate) — General Boltrex's old fortress

Deedans (DEED-aans) — soldiers in the Awal, rejected from the Chishman Academy

Devorin (DEH-vorin) — one of the four kingdoms

(the) Docks — lawless city containing mercenaries and illegal trading ports

Doer — common Shadow Manos ability, crafter and able to enhance poison with their blood

Galvasir (GAAL-vasir) — high-ranking soldier in the Empire

Hearcross (HEER-cross) — capital of the Karalik Empire

Jehen (juh-hen) — Savorian word for hell

Karalik Empire (KAARA-lik) — land of the remaining four kingdoms

Kilisham (kill-ee-shom) — common deedan weapon

Lagrima Sea (la-ree-ma) — body of water bordering Savoria

Lure — rarest Shadow Manos skill, able to bend a person(s) to their will

Mavaalin (MOV-aw-lin) — Savorian farewell meaning *wind in your sails*

Namaar (na-MAR) — town in Verin

Ondalar (on-DUH-laar) — one of the four kingdoms

Savagelands — also called Uluz, an arid environment housing tribal groups

Savoria (SAAV-oria) — large island conquered by Prolus

Seer — rare Shadow Manos ability, able to see, past, present, and future

Shadow Manos — an individual marked with a phoenix birthmark, withholding a type of shadow

Shikista (shi-kis-ta) — castle in Ayleth

Sok (so-uk) — main city in Devorin

Tariqi (TO-RIH-qee) — realm consisting of nine kingdoms, eight of which used to belong to Karalik Empire

True Manos — Imperial healer

Vedale (veh-day-el) — Imperial Day of Oaths

Verin (VER-in) — one of the four kingdoms

Yadigar (yah-dee-gaar) — fortress in Verin

Zamanin Sulari (ZAAMON-in SOOL-ari) — waters of time, a swift traveling serum

Zat (ZAAT) — crimson wine-like drink

Zelont (ZEL-lont) — Imperial for *monster*

A DEPICTION OF
KARALIK EMPIRE
AND SURROUNDING
TERRITORIES,
AS DRAWN BY
IMPERIAL CARTOGRAPHER
MASTER GALLIEN
Savoria
Port
Lagrima Sea
Fort
Castle
Ondalar
Port of Ayleth
Ayleth
Karakan
Castle Shikista
Elondin
Wallington
The Pit
The Ja Sea
The Savagelands
The Ja Desert

The Red Bridge
Port of Savoria
Realm of Tariqi
Mines
Topragar Fortress
Kalea Acadamy
Awal Military Base
The Qistool
Fortress Yadigar
Red Eagle Forest
Verin
Castle Verin
Namaar
Raqu Manor
Verintown
Flondin Woods
Tariqin Border Camp
Devorin
Savastown
Sok Town
Hearcross
Mines
Karalik Palace
Whispering Woods
The Docks
nds

PROLOGUE

Fear gripped Mordon with such strength, he could almost see it, almost touch it. The stares of the spectators burned as he approached Jovinne Servan. He dragged his feet with each step, and his eyes flashed to the seats placed at the far end of the barracks. His father peered at him, brows lowered, green eyes glinting with warning. The people around his father blurred into faceless images. They didn't matter.

"Ready to be defeated, Vaz?" Jovinne said in a low voice as Mordon entered sword range. "I'm going to send you scurrying with the rest."

Mordon tore his attention from his father and forced his panic down as he faced Jovinne. That was the last fight—or mock battle, as the instructors called it—in the yearly competition to test the children's newest skills. Mordon *had* to win. Besides training in the barracks, his father had instructed him personally, using tactics that felt like torture methods for Mordon: holding bricks, maintaining endless positions that tested his core strength, arm strength, and even the mental strength within him.

Do not let him push you. Do you understand? his father had told him after watching a training session during which he'd been paired with Jovinne. *He's big, but you're bigger. He is strong, but you're stronger, and no matter what, you will not fail. He hit you today, and you backed down. Retreating is for cowards. Are you a coward?*

Tears had stung Mordon's eyes. He shook his head. *Good.* Boltrex nodded. *I have no use for cowards.*

Mordon had wanted to protest, to beg for Boltrex's understanding, but when he looked into those cold green eyes, he only found anger and bitterness. What he would do to have his father's eyes light with love for once . . .

"Begin!"

At the instructor's shout, Mordon shot forward, lifting his wooden sword and slashing it through the air. Jovinne's training blade halted his blow and shoved him back. Mordon stumbled, his heart pounding in his chest as Jovinne circled him. Mordon kept his sword high, swinging it into a guard position—a Galvasir stance. Murmurs and soft gasps reached his ears.

"Who do you think you are?" Jovinne spat, his eyes narrowed. "It seems you need a reminder that will knock you from your pedestal."

The fear Mordon had tamped down flared back to life. He sensed the threat in the implication. Jovinne had his methods of belittling him. His two-year age difference also gave him the upper hand and experience Mordon didn't have. Mordon suddenly felt younger than ten years, his frame crouching, swallowing into itself. His stance weakened. Jovinne attacked, flying forward.

Mordon desperately parried until he found himself on the floor. Jovinne held his sword over Mordon's, dragging it down. The wood splintered as Mordon tried with all his might to hold Jovinne's weapon at bay.

"Guess what I heard?" Jovinne sneered. "You're illegitimate. That's what my father told me. The bastard son of a nobleman that General Boltrex took pity on."

"You're a liar," Mordon growled. He wished his voice were deeper, more intimidating. "Take it back."

"The only thing that should be taken back is you. Back to rot in the hole the general saved you from."

Mordon roared and propelled his sword up with a strength he hadn't known he possessed. Jovinne flew back, but Mordon didn't stop. He rushed Jovinne, smashing his wooden sword against him over and over. He heard the instructor calling to stop, but his voice sounded so far away. A loud crack brought Mordon out of his haze. He stared at Jovinne, surprised by the tears streaking the boy's face as he cradled a limp arm. Pained wheezes escaped him. Mordon's sword slipped from numb fingers, clattering at his feet. Chairs screeched across the floor, and people swarmed around them. A firm hand grabbed hold of Mordon's arm and jerked him away. His father pulled him out of the barracks, and soon, they were in the castle.

"Go to your chamber. *Now*," Boltrex ordered, his voice harsh.

Mordon wanted to ask about Jovinne's insinuation, but when he opened his mouth, no sound came out. He didn't have the courage to hear his father's answer. Mordon entered his chamber and fell onto his bed. He cried into his pillow until his chest felt hollow. Terror clutched him not because of the others' judgments or his impending punishment, but fear that Jovinne's words were true.

1

MORDON
KARALIK EMPIRE
KINGDOM OF VERIN
CASTLE VERIN

"IT'S NOT POSSIBLE," Mordon whispered.

He clutched the tower crenellations, pulling himself up. Coralie placed herself under his arm, taking some of his weight. Mordon's focus didn't waver from the inconceivable sight. A pale man with graying hair and dancing blue eyes stood before them. He was dressed in dark apparel. A thick cloak was draped around his shoulders, and his scuffed boots were planted firmly before the staircase leading down the tower—the only way out. His followers, deedans, swarmed behind him at his order, barricading the exit. Mordon blinked once, twice, blood clamping the lashes of his right eye together as he tried to comprehend what he was seeing. Standing before him was a dead man. At Mordon's whisper, Winston glanced at him, his lips tilting up in satisfaction.

"You know what they say," Winston replied. "Nothing is impossible."

Mordon shook his head, mumbling, "I killed you. I know I did."

Mordon's attention trailed to his father and Velamir. Velamir's eyes were wide, and his hand shook at Boltrex's throat, his dagger tip trembling. Mordon's anger simmered. He despised Velamir for even daring to touch his father. A foolish puppet who worked for Prolus attempting to kill the general of Verin? It took guts, Mordon would give him that. Boltrex didn't move, his jaw clenched, his face carved from stone. Mordon glanced back at Winston, that burning in his chest sizzling at the smile he wore—the same smile that had greeted him at the tavern.

That night flashed through Mordon's mind. He had procured the poison from Quinn, a man who traded illegal materials acquired from the Docks, or so he'd told him. It wasn't hard for Mordon to slip into the tavern, inebriated as the inhabitants were. A heavy pouch of coin and the barkeeper had sealed his lips. Just as Mordon was debating how to poison Winston, the man himself called for a midnight refreshment. Mordon had dumped the poison into a mug of frothy buttermilk and hurried to the room after the barkeeper directed him to the correct door. He'd taken a pitcher of water as well and entered the room with his head down.

"Here you are, sir."

He felt Winston's eyes searing into him, and his muscles bunched as he kept himself slightly bent, an uncomfortable shiver drifting over him. Winston beckoned him forward.

"You don't seem the type to work at a tavern."

Mordon extended the tray, keeping his lips closed. Winston took the mug without question and slurped the contents down. He peered at Mordon over the rim.

"Set the tray there." He nodded at the small table beside the bed.

Mordon did so and then clasped his fingers behind him to hide their clenching, their itch to reach for his dagger.

"I've been expecting you."

The words sent Mordon's head flying up.

Winston nodded. "Boltrex sent you, didn't he?"

"I don't know what you mean."

But Mordon did know what he meant. His father's explicit instructions had guided him all the way to Namaar, the final flag being Winston's corpse. But the conversation halted at that moment, replaced by a sudden fit of coughs. Winston placed the mug on the tray, thumping his chest.

"You're finished now, old man. Tariqi will never succeed," Mordon whispered, a seething smile forming on his lips.

He grabbed the mug and ducked out of the room, leaving Winston thrashing behind him. He glanced at the other doors. The barkeeper had told him Winston had four companions. Mordon wasn't eager to stick *around and encounter them. He crossed down the first steps when he heard a door creak open. Without looking back, he'd stumbled out of the tavern as fast as he could.*

Winston couldn't have survived. Unless . . .

"Quinn was your man, wasn't he?" Mordon growled. "Was it all an act?"

Winston's hearty chuckle was so loud, it nearly masked the sound of battle below them. "You can rest assured I was poisoned. But I knew I would be. I had the antidote with me."

"Quinn?" Velamir interrupted, snagging Mordon's attention. "You mean Quintus?" He shot Winston a look. The initial shock of seeing him had seeped off his face. "I don't understand."

"Chishma obey orders, Velamir. They don't ask for details. But if you must know, yes, it was planned. Quintus knew, Lissa knew, Jaxon . . ." When Winston hesitated, tension stiffened Velamir's posture. "Jaxon didn't know, but I'm surprised he didn't figure it out."

"Why would you do this?" The betrayed tone of Velamir's voice was clear.

"It was a test, Velamir. A test of your loyalty. I trust you will not fail me." He gestured to Boltrex. "Finish your mission, lad."

The roars below the tower grew louder as the Tariqins pushed against the keep doors. Mordon stepped forward, but Coralie placed a firm hand on his chest. He glanced down at her. She stared back, keeping him at bay with a blink of her dark almond-shaped eyes. He relented, suddenly feeling so tired. Warm blood trickled down his face and arm, the result of his battle with

Velamir just minutes before. But he couldn't afford to back down, not when his father remained a breath away from losing his life.

"Release my father," he warned Velamir through clenched teeth.

Velamir retained his hold on Boltrex, pressing the dagger closer and closer to the veins in his neck.

Boltrex laughed, deep and rumbling. "Are you still following him? After such a lie, after what he concealed from you, are you still obeying his orders?"

Mordon watched the struggle on Velamir's face. A battlefield of emotions raged over his features. Winston stepped closer, his minions following suit. Coralie lifted her sword with her free hand. Mordon tightened his arm around her shoulders, fighting the urge to push her behind him.

"Before Chishma Velamir takes your life, I wanted you to know, Boltrex, that I was behind the attack on Clovensgate."

Mordon's father blanched, and his tan skin paled at Winston's words.

"The Savagelanders broke through your fortress walls, killed most of your men, but I was the one who finished the battle."

"How could you?" When Boltrex spoke, it was with a voice Mordon didn't recognize, one filled with grief and unspeakable sorrow. "How could you kill a woman and children? How could you burn them at the stake? Serana wasn't only my wife; she was Saphira's sister. She was *your wife's* sister. Her children weren't only my children; they were Saphira's relations. You killed your own family."

Coralie inhaled sharply, and Mordon realized his fingers had curled around her shoulder, digging into her flesh. He flexed his hand, releasing her. He needed to vent. He needed something to break, somewhere to scream, someone to punch. Preferably someone whose face resembled Winston's. That vile man had killed his mother and siblings. He'd never been able to meet them because of him. He'd never been able to speak about them because of him. He had *forgotten* them because of him. But that all changed when Winston continued.

"I didn't kill your family."

Boltrex peered at him, his mouth slack. His confusion mirrored what Mordon felt inside. "What?"

"The woman and children I placed at the stake were put there to torture you. I knew it would haunt you." Winston smiled. "I wanted you to think they were dead."

"I don't understand. Where are they? What did you do with them?" Boltrex shoved against Velamir's hold, but Velamir tightened his grip despite appearing just as rapt by the conversation as the rest of them.

"Aria's whereabouts are unknown to me. Alaric . . . is a different matter. And Serana is alive. She is in our main camp, coming with Prolus's army. She's one of us."

Boltrex sputtered before shouting, "You're lying. You're lying!"

Winston sniffed, his mirth dissipated. It seemed playtime was over. "Believe what you want. Velamir, it is time to finish this matter."

Boltrex slammed his hand upward, catching Velamir off guard and shoving the imminent threat of the dagger away. They grappled with each other until Boltrex smashed Velamir's head to the side. Mordon's tension built as he watched. He wanted to intervene, but a moment later, Boltrex froze with his hand plastered on Velamir's face, keeping his head positioned to the side. His eyes widened as he stared at Velamir's neck.

Mordon peered closer, his vision darkened by a thick sheen of blood. He wiped a sleeve over his face. The slash Velamir had sliced into him earlier continued to well with crimson drops. Mordon focused on the scene before him. A long scar trailed down Velamir's neck. Boltrex's lips trembled, and a foreign look came over him. Mordon couldn't believe what he was seeing. He didn't want to believe it. His father, Boltrex, was staring at Velamir with longing and pain. A man who'd just held him at knifepoint, intending to take his life, and yet he was looking at him like he *meant* something. A hollow ache filled Mordon's chest, and he swallowed back his revulsion.

"Alaric," Boltrex whispered. "My son."

A spear could've wedged through Mordon, and it wouldn't have hurt as much as those three words. Mordon stuttered, but he couldn't speak, couldn't voice his thoughts. He tried to blink, but his lashes remained clamped together, glued closed by the sticky blood. He forced his eye open, and when wetness trailed down his cheek, he wasn't sure if it was his blood or tears. Winston took a step forward.

"Don't listen to him, Velamir. Complete your mission."

Boltrex released his hold on Velamir, who retreated a pace, his dagger lowering as he watched Boltrex with uncertainty. Mordon had thought he'd lost his humaneness long ago, that the heart within him was there purely for survival, but no, that tearing, the ripping within him, told him it was still there. It split in two while Boltrex reached out with shaking fingers, inches from brushing Velamir's face.

"Enough!" Mordon finally managed, his shout echoing into the wind. "This is all a lie!"

Winston's voice followed his, directed at Velamir. "If you truly were his son, would you have wanted a father like him? One that so easily replaced a family he believed dead?" He waved at Mordon. "So easily moved on with his life with another son?"

"Shut up, old man," Mordon snapped, his throat hoarse. It wasn't real. It was another terrifying dream he'd eventually forget. He would soon wake up like all the other times.

But the nightmare continued. Boltrex's eerie chuckle sent shivers over him.

"She came to me. Saphira." Boltrex's eyes settled on Winston, who stiffened at his dead wife's name. "She feared you, what you were doing, what you were becoming."

An awful silence stretched around the tower. The sounds of fighting slashed through the long expanse of time as Boltrex and Winston stared each other down. Mordon's heart thumped, warning him, telling him he wouldn't like what was coming.

"She begged me to help her. She knew your desire for power would endanger everything she held dear, everything you used to treasure with her. I wouldn't be surprised if you caused her death."

Winston flinched, and Mordon knew Boltrex had struck a nerve.

"I helped her the only way I could. I protected what she loved most from the one who used to hold her heart—from you." Boltrex exhaled a shaky breath. "So, you see . . . Mordon isn't my son."

Mordon shook his head, his arm dropping from Coralie's shoulders as Boltrex's next words slipped out, hard as a slap, cold as ice.

"He's yours, Winston."

Mordon recoiled, his chest tightening like a snake wrapped around him, strangling him, snatching his breath. He turned away and leaned halfway over the gap in the crenellations, the armed and furious soldiers below blurring as a gray haze curtained his vision.

"Mordon." Coralie's soothing voice filtered through the haze. Her comforting hand pressed to his back.

Mordon isn't my son. Isn't my son. Isn't my son. The words ricocheted in his mind. An image of Boltrex with his stiff lips tilted up remained scarred in his head.

"How?" he whispered and then spun around, shouting, "How could you?" at Boltrex. "This is the reason. The reason you pushed me away, the reason why, despite how hard I tried, I wasn't good enough for you! Because blood is more important. Because I'm not your son." His voice cracked.

Winston's calculating gaze bored into him. Boltrex opened his mouth to speak when blaring horns cut through the moment. On top of the sloping hill, leading down to the ransacked town and castle, stood a large cavalry. Yellow flags wafted in the air. And with the rising sun, the Ondalarians came.

2

THE HORNS CONTINUED as the thundering cavalry streamed over the hill. Velamir glanced at Winston, the man he had once thought of as a father, a mentor, someone he trusted. All of that had been trampled to dust by just a few words from Boltrex. Velamir's throat bobbed, and a tightness in his chest held back a thousand emotions. The old man in the dungeon had told him his true name was Alaric and that his father was alive. Boltrex stared at him with a sheen of tears in eyes the same color as his. Velamir shook his head and stepped forward, lifting his dagger again.

"Why should I believe you?"

Boltrex pointed at Velamir's scar. "You were three years old. Your mother was trying to put you to bed, but you wouldn't stay still." His voice trembled as he spoke, his gaze far away. "I followed you out of the room, pretending to play a game of chase. You bumped into a glass pot, and it fell on you. You were so tiny. So small." Boltrex gaped at Velamir with disbelief, like he couldn't believe he stood before him, grown and whole. "It shattered, cutting you right there." He gestured at Velamir's neck. "I feared like I never had before, thinking I would lose you. I didn't then, but I did anyway," he whispered. "I lost you all." Boltrex's head bowed, a single tear trailing down his cheek.

Velamir lowered his blade, body shuddering at the newfound revelation. The man he had hated, despised, and wanted to kill was also the man he'd missed all his life. "Father." The word slipped past his lips, like it belonged to someone in another life.

Boltrex placed a hand on his shoulder, gripping it with a firmness that told him it was real. A sob ripped from Boltrex's throat. "My son."

"Enough!"

Velamir turned to the source of the shout. Mordon had retrieved his fallen sword, his stance strong despite his wounds. His black eyes were furious orbs, and they focused on Velamir and Boltrex. The brokenness of his features showed how much the revelations had fractured him.

Mordon waved his sword at them. "What role did I play in your game? You used me. And for what? To get back at Winston? Why didn't you tell me?"

Boltrex released Velamir, running a large hand over his face to wipe the runaway tear. "Mordon, I—"

"I don't want to hear another word." Mordon's hunched posture, like that of a hulking beast, formed shadows on the stone below him.

Velamir stared at him, recalling the pity he'd felt for him when they'd fought. Mordon's jaw was clenched, his arm still lifted, sword in hand. Coralie stood beside him, face anxious as she glanced at the deedans. She gripped Mordon's arm. Her long fingers seemed to keep him together as well as hold him back.

At a deedan's movement, Velamir's attention darted to Winston. The deedan whispered in his ear, and Velamir caught the flash of alarm on his face.

Why? Why did you do this to me? Velamir thought as Winston's pale eyes snapped to meet his. His old mentor's jaw tensed.

"Make your choice, Velamir," Winston said, his voice harried, an urgency charging beneath it.

"Never again," he breathed, and then in a harsher tone, he said, "I will never be your pawn again."

Winston's face dimmed. "So be it." He turned to the deedans. "Kill all but the large lad." His eyes trailed to Mordon.

The deedans approached, half toward Mordon and Coralie and the rest flanking Velamir and Boltrex. Velamir's fingers flexed around his dagger hilt as he slid his foot to the side, slipping his boot under the grip of his fallen blade. He flicked the sword up and caught it in a firm fist. Boltrex bent, retrieving his weapon, and nodded at him. Velamir inhaled, eyes flicking for an opening in the opposition. A blur of red and black rushed forward, swinging at him with a kilisham, the common weapon in the Awal. Velamir ducked and stabbed in an instant. The deedan gasped, his immobile body sliding farther onto Velamir's sword. Velamir withdrew his blade with a grunt, and the deedan collapsed, crimson staining the stone beneath him.

That was all it took for the others to fly forward. They unhooked their kilishams from their belts, the tail of each whip tipped with a sharp point. Velamir and Boltrex stuck together, ducking and riposting. Avoiding crackling whips and watching each other's backs. It was a strange moment, but it felt right fighting with the man who had once been his enemy. Sweat burned Velamir's face and crawled down his neck and back, coating every inch of him as he fought with everything he had. He was covered in blood and gore when he heard Mordon scream Coralie's name.

Velamir spared a glance in their direction. Coralie's motionless form was splayed across the ground. Mordon dropped his sword and fell to his knees beside her. "Coralie!" he shouted again, the agony in his posture silhouetted by the sun shining above them.

A fist connected with Velamir's chin. He grunted, teeth sinking into his cheek, and blood burst onto his tongue. Velamir shoved the deedan back, fighting to reach Mordon and Coralie. He dropped into a crouch just before a sword sailed over his head. Mordon touched Coralie's face, his blood-streaked hand leaving a trail of red behind. Velamir had nearly reached them when deedans grabbed hold of Mordon. They attempted to pull him away. Mordon clutched Coralie's hand, fighting against their grips. Then a hilt slammed against the back of his head, and he was out cold, eyes rolling as he collapsed beside Coralie, fingers still clasping hers.

Velamir froze mid-stride at the sound of his name. He turned, his heart thumping at the sight of Boltrex pushing his way to him. Velamir's lips parted, the taste of blood lingering in his mouth as he watched Boltrex freeze and drop to his knees. Winston stood behind him. Time slowed as he ripped a dagger from Boltrex's back with a sickening squelch. Boltrex coughed, and a trickle of blood trailed over his lower lip. Velamir blinked, motionless for only a second, and then he charged forward.

"There's my warrior." Winston smirked. He backed away as Velamir drew closer, signaling the deedans. "Let's move."

The remaining deedans closed in, blocking Velamir's route to Winston. Some of them drew away, following Winston down the tower staircase. Velamir spotted Mordon's limp form being dragged with them. Velamir shot forward, locking into combat with the deedans in his path. The nameless faces dropped around him until only three remained. They looked wary and were as sweaty as he was. Velamir wasn't sure how long he could last, but he couldn't allow Winston to escape.

One of the deedans shot out, his whip curling around Velamir's ankle. He yanked on the kilisham, and Velamir fell, crashing to the ground with a loud groan. Another deedan approached, lowering his weapon toward Velamir's chest at a frightening speed. Velamir rolled to the side, and the kilisham shuddered as it smacked the ground. Velamir kicked the first deedan, disentangling his foot from the whip, and then slashed his dagger across the other deedan's throat. Blood splattered onto his face, the drops salty on his tongue. Both men dropped. Velamir spat the blood from his mouth and finished the first deedan.

The remaining deedan trembled. Velamir almost pitied him, but he knew the man wouldn't hesitate to kill him if he could. He couldn't afford to be weak. Velamir adjusted his stance, falling into an attack position. The deedan copied his movements, flicking his wrist. The kilisham shifted, making a grating noise as the whip snapped into a long immovable blade. A tense moment stretched out, and then the man dropped his weapon and ran, retreating down the steps. Velamir stepped forward to follow when he heard a wheeze. He glanced back. Boltrex lay in a small pool of his own blood. Velamir inhaled a harsh breath and rushed to him. He kneeled down, his hands hovering in the air, uncertain how to proceed. He looked over the bodies, seeing Coralie unmoving a short distance away. He needed Jax.

Boltrex shook his head. "No," he breathed. "Stop Winston."

Velamir clenched his jaw. "Don't move." He ran as swiftly as he could, stepping over bodies and taking the stairs three at a time. He searched the first hall. No one in sight. Velamir's need for assistance warred with the fury burning in his core.

Winston had destroyed everything. He'd painted a picture of the world to Velamir—a world that didn't exist. A world he'd twisted to hell. And it was his turn to burn.

3

THE STONE CHAMBER doors shook. The woman beside Natassa jumped, reaching out to grip her arm. Natassa winced as the woman's fingers tightened around her skin, numbing her to the point that she almost dropped her sword. She reached with her free arm to pat the woman's hand.

"It's going to be all right," she told her with a reassuring smile.

Natassa repeated the words to herself. She needed the encouragement as much as the rest of the chamber. She needed to be brave. She *had* to be. The Tariqins were getting closer to breaking through the doors with each slam, and there was no one to come to their aid.

Natassa glanced at the only guards in the room. They circled King Dale, and they wouldn't move from their position. Natassa clenched the sword in her hand. The weapon was heavy, so different compared to the knives her brother had trained her to wield. Natassa willed herself to face what was coming. Despite not being ready, everyone in the chamber was armed. But when was anyone ever prepared to fight for their life? Someone sidled up beside her, the familiar presence comforting.

"Kasdeya?" Krea asked. "How are you faring?"

It took Natassa a moment to recall her new name— her false name. She was no longer Princess Natassa Hartinza, daughter of the most prominent figure in the Empire, but a mere handmaiden, or rather, a disgraced handmaiden, and twin sister to Krea. The shift was difficult to adapt to.

Krea stared at her, her hazel eyes, oval face, and pink lips, along with a dozen other features, so similar to Natassa's that it wasn't hard to pass as identical twins.

Natassa's lips trembled as she forced a smile. "Fine."

Krea's concern shattered when the chamber doors crashed open. Deedans poured in, holding their weapons high with a collective roar that grew louder when they became certain of their impending victory at the sight before them: distressed elders, screaming children, and a group of women who did not know how to properly wield a sword. Natassa was part of the last group. Her breath caught in her throat as the Tariqins continued to pour inside, bloodlust in their eyes. A deedan at the front directed the group.

"Kill the king!" he shouted, pointing his weapon King Dale's way.

Natassa had only a moment to swallow before the chamber was thrown into chaos. Deedans rushed at them. She had to move, had to act, but her limbs were frozen. She was glued to the floor, panic spearing her stomach, as a deedan zeroed in on her and advanced. He flicked his hand, and his weapon shifted into a long sword. He swung it, but before Natassa could blink, Krea was there, blocking his blow. His shock would have been comical if not for the life-and-death situation. Krea used his surprise to her advantage, slicing her sword across his throat. Red droplets showered them, and Natassa cried out at the slick feeling. She touched her skin, rubbing the blood and holding back her revulsion as the deedan collapsed.

"There is no time for that." Krea slipped a knife into Natassa's free hand. "Stick close to me."

As they gathered together with the women closest to them, they were tossed into another bloody fray. Screaming filled Natassa's ears, and her lungs ached, telling her she was a part of the noise. Her arms and hands shook, but she slashed and stabbed when she could. She had never known how terrible battle could be. The fear—no, the *terror*—that she inhaled with every breath. In a split second, she was torn from the group by a hand gripping her arm.

"You're a pretty thing."

Natassa fought against the hold. The man's other hand came up, and she saw he carried a blood-covered sword. His twisted lips curled, and he tugged her closer, wrenching her wrist. She winced, her sword nearly falling from her fingers as sharp pain shot up her arm.

She slashed her knife at him. He dropped his own sword and caught her hand. His face darkened as he stared at the knife point inches from his eye. He thrust her arm away and backhanded her face. His gauntlet sliced into her cheek. Stinging agony stole Natassa's breath, and searing heat bloomed over her skin as blood dribbled down her face.

Natassa remembered the sword she still held, and with one last ounce of energy, she stabbed him in the chest. Her attacker gasped, staring down at his leather armor. Her sword had pierced through it and into his chest. He clasped his hands around the sword and wound, taking a shaky step forward. He tripped over his discarded weapon and smacked the ground. Natassa grimaced at the sound as her sword emerged from his back. Then the man was motionless. Natassa pressed bloody fingers to her lips, bile rising in her throat. She'd just killed someone.

Natassa glanced around the room, ignoring the queasiness roiling inside her stomach. More deedans pushed closer, dominating the weak group desperately trying to hold them off. King Dale's bodyguards lay still around him, and a deedan was poised for attack above him, about to bring a sharp blade down into the king's chest.

Natassa hardly knew what she was doing.

Her legs moved of their own accord, propelling her forward. She ran, screaming at the top of her lungs to catch the deedan's attention. She pushed through bodies engaged in combat and launched herself onto him. He stumbled to the side, his arms flailing as he attempted to throw her off. Natassa kept her arms wrapped around the deedan's throat. He collapsed and took her down with him. She was squashed beneath him, a choked breath escaping her as the air was knocked from her. The deedan swore and pulled himself up. Anger coated his face. He lifted his blade before faltering, face contorting, then dropped to his knees. Natassa shoved him away, and when he crumpled, she saw the arrow in his back. She glanced up, spotting a man hurrying toward her, bow in hand.

"Defend the king!" he shouted.

A group of women surrounded the king and Natassa scanned him, searching for stab wounds. She didn't see any blood, but worry consumed her at the way he sat glued to his seat. The archer who had helped her offered his hand. His blond hair was damp with sweat, matted curls sticking to his forehead. When she clasped his hand, a streak of gold flashed before her eyes, and she saw herself rising. A shout, the sound of a blade sliding into flesh, and the blond man falling. Natassa shook her head, and the vision disappeared.

Gut instinct told her to act. As soon as he pulled her up, she snatched the dagger from his belt and shoved him out of the way. A deedan's sword swung through empty air. Natassa slammed the dagger into his belly. He paled and gripped his stomach before retreating into the horde of deedans edging closer to the king and the remaining survivors. The blond man gave her a nod of thanks, but Natassa saw a flicker of confusion in his gaze. There was a clamor at the front of the chamber. Deedans panicked, their attention drawn to the entryway.

"For the Empire!"

Imperial soldiers rushed inside the chamber, locking into combat. Natassa's relief was immense as the deedans focused all their power on their new opponents. A head rose above the others by the entryway. Disheveled black hair, a piercing gaze, and frightening prowess. General Zenrelius. The tension that had left her returned in a flood. Natassa watched him shout commands while leading his soldiers into the deedans. The Tariqins were no match. Not long after, the room was littered with Prolus's lifeless warriors. The remaining deedans escaped through the doors.

"After them!"

At the general's shout, the Ondalarians pursued the runaways. The battle was over, and worry for the wounded replaced the sheer panic running through her veins. Cries for help rang on all sides of the room, and everywhere Natassa looked was nauseating red blood. General Zenrelius drew near her. His deep voice echoed in the chamber as he attempted to settle everyone down and determine how to proceed. Natassa ducked her head, and icy fear settled in her bones. She hoped he hadn't seen her. She had no doubt he would recognize her. Not as Natassa's maid, as she was portraying herself, but as the princess. A hand gripped her arm, and she was startled. Natassa glanced up.

The blond archer's brow furrowed. "You all right?"

She nodded. "Yes. Thank you. For saving me back there."

His blue eyes narrowed as he stared at her. "How did you know?"

She knew what he meant. How had she seen the

deedan attacking him? It was impossible from the angle she had been at. Natassa shrugged, hoping to appear inconspicuous. When she didn't answer, he introduced himself.

"I'm Jax."

"Kasdeya."

He sank down beside the deedan he had killed. "It would be a shame to waste this." He grimaced and wrapped his hand around the imbedded arrow shaft. It made squishing noises as he pulled it from the skin, tissue, and muscle.

When he finally extracted it, his face contorted, and he slapped a hand over his mouth. All Natassa's disgust and horror over the past hour caught up with her, and she coughed, then heaved whatever remained in her stomach. Seeing the splatter of vomit, Jax joined her, throwing up until they made eye contact, hands on knees.

"Killing isn't my strong suit," he admitted and wiped his mouth.

"It was my first time," Natassa whispered.

His ocean eyes welled with pity, and she turned her head, unable to hold his gaze. She wondered how many more lives would be taken before it would end.

4

MORDON
KINGDOM OF VERIN
CASTLE VERIN

ORDON WINCED AS searing pain lanced through his skull. It felt like someone had smashed his head in with a rock. He groaned, prying his eyes open. He peered past the brittle blood coating his lashes and saw nothing but darkness. His boots dragged over the ground as rough arms hauled him forward.

"Move faster."

The command was sharp and near. Winston.

Mordon panicked, his thoughts twisting over each other. What had happened? He jerked against his captors, fighting like a caged lion.

"He's awake, General."

The men kept their grip on him despite the struggle. Mordon shoved at them and pushed to his feet. He was in a tunnel of some sort, but he couldn't figure out how he had gotten there.

"Hold him still." Winston neared. Mordon could make out his outline in the dark before him.

"Let me go," Mordon said. "Or kill me. Because if you don't, I will be your nightmare."

Winston chuckled, the sound echoing down the tunnel. "Mighty words from a captured man. We can negotiate once you're at camp. Perhaps King Dale will pay a ransom for you . . . Oh wait, you aren't his general's child, which makes you nothing to Verin."

The mention of King Dale brought Coralie to the forefront of his thoughts. Her limp figure was branded into his mind. Mordon's fists clenched, and he jerked against his captors again. He'd already lost his life, his father—everything he used to be. He couldn't lose her too.

"Coralie." Her name slipped past his lips. "What did you do to her?"

Mordon made out the shadow of Winston's arm as it lifted. Then the deedan to Mordon's right swung a fist. Blinding pain exploded in his skull when the blow connected. Mordon's head snapped to the side, and darkness washed over him once again.

A cool breeze brushed his neck and blew long strands of hair into his face. Mordon inhaled the air, noting the difference in it. The smell of smoke accompanied the scent of grass, and despair rent the wind. He lifted his head, biting his lip when he felt the crick in his neck. Mordon blinked, peering through the thick hair obscuring his view. His arm ached, and when he tried to move, he stiffened. His hands were bound behind him. He glanced over his shoulder, finding that he was tied to a tree. His legs stretched out before him, lashed together at the ankles. Winston and the surviving deedans crouched around a hastily made fire, along with a man Mordon hadn't seen before. He wore a thick robe and fingered a vial among the many that adorned his belt. He glanced at Mordon as though sensing his gaze. His mouth stretched, and the sun caught the shadowed patchwork of lines above his upper lip. When his smile settled, Mordon realized what it was. The Shadow Manos mark—a phoenix. Mordon jerked against the trunk, trying to wrench his arms free.

The crackling fire danced, flickering like the evil in Winston's eerie eyes. The Shadow Manos returned to the discussion around the fire. Mordon stopped thrashing to appraise the sky. The sun was high overhead. He couldn't have been gone long. A few hours might have passed since he was in the castle. He had time to escape and return, but he couldn't tell where he was. A long expanse of empty grassland stretched around them, indicating either Mordon had been unconscious for far longer than he assumed or Winston had propelled his secret force to travel at a breakneck speed.

"They will seal the entrance," the Shadow Manos said in a low voice.

Winston grunted. "Our chance was ruined." He tore into what looked like a jerky of some kind. "That blasted Zenrelius spoiled our plans."

"What will you tell Lord Prolus?"

Winston's back stiffened. "What I tell him is none of your concern."

"Forgive me, General."

"We leave in ten minutes. Knock him out again and see to his wounds. I will deal with him at camp." Winston glanced at him, and Mordon met his calculative stare with a sneer and defying glare. Winston leaned forward to whisper to the Shadow Manos.

Mordon concealed his panic deep within as the Shadow Manos stood and strode toward him. He inspected Mordon, probing at his wounds with decisive hands. Mordon gritted his teeth when he prodded the long gash in his arm. Then the Shadow Manos gripped Mordon's face with clawed fingers and jerked his head up. He laughed. It was short and derisive.

"That's not a bad look," he said, and the cut along Mordon's face burned as the man stared at it. "Trust me, you're better off in the world ugly."

Mordon wrenched his face out of the harsh grip and nodded pointedly at the mark above the man's lip. "Did you learn that from experience?"

The Shadow Manos tsked. "Careful. I wouldn't insult the person tending your wounds."

Mordon's apprehension built when the Shadow Manos made his way to the fire to heat a brutal-looking needle in the flames. When he returned, he smirked before piercing Mordon's flesh. Mordon's stomach tightened as he held in his agony. The needle drifted in and out of his skin, binding the wound closed. When the Shadow Manos tied off the string, Mordon sank against the tree, sweat coating his brow. The Shadow Manos extricated a vial from his belt and snapped the cork off. He held it out to Mordon, who turned his chin away.

The Shadow Manos shrugged. "It's to relieve the pain. I could've given it to you before, but . . . oh well."

When Mordon refused to take it, the Shadow Manos called for reinforcements. A deedan held his face while another grabbed his shoulders, keeping him firmly pressed to the tree. The Shadow Manos pried Mordon's mouth open and shoved the vial's contents down his throat. Mordon coughed as the liquid burned a trail through him. When the Shadow Manos pulled back, Mordon wheezed, tasting the dreadful bitterness lingering in his mouth. He blinked at the figures standing before him. Their faces blurred and morphed together.

Then he saw her. A girl with black hair twisted into braids. She approached him with a confident stride that seemed vaguely familiar. Something told him he was hallucinating, but he found he couldn't care less. Mordon's last conscious thought remained on her—on the girl with courage greater than he'd ever known.

5

VELAMIR
KINGDOM OF VERIN
CASTLE VERIN

VELAMIR RELEASED A frustrated breath. Winston was long gone. But he couldn't think about that. He had to find help. Boltrex in a pool of blood and Coralie's prone figure rushed to his mind. Velamir raced through the corridors, searching in vain. He couldn't find living people, let alone a True Manos. Bodies with gaping wounds and empty eyes stared up at him as he moved past. The sounds of clashing swords drew near, and Velamir's fingers tightened around his sword hilt, preparing for what was coming. He stepped into the next hall, where his battle with Mordon had begun. The door leading down to the dungeon was slanted, creaking open and closed. Booted steps rushed up, and Velamir tensed, raising his blade. Men poured through, and then relief crashed into Velamir at the sight of Finnean.

"Velamir?" Finnean sputtered. "You're alive."

Finnean's shock was plain to see. He sheathed his short swords, sliding them in place behind his back as he approached Velamir. Sweat and blood trailed down his face, tangling in his beard. Short strands of black hair stuck to his forehead. Velamir lowered his weapon and clasped Finnean's forearm in greeting.

"What happened?" Velamir asked.

"We would be dead if it weren't for the Ondalarians," Finnean told him. "I came to look for you. The Tariqins didn't leave an inch of the castle untouched, not even the dungeon."

Worry gouged Velamir. "Did you see an old man down there? Is he all right?"

Finnean nodded, face grim. "He won't live long. He was stabbed."

"Send for aid," Velamir said after a moment of stunned silence. "He needs treatment."

Finnean shook his head. "We have so many wounded. Why should we waste time on a prisoner?"

"Do it." Velamir glared at him. "And send a True Manos to the south watchtower while you're at it. Boltrex and Coralie are in a critical state."

Velamir left Finnean sputtering behind him. He raced down the dungeon steps but slowed for a few seconds to adjust to the darkness. The smell of unwashed skin and rodents pierced his nostrils. Velamir grasped a torch hanging on the side wall and brought it over to the cell door. The old man lay curled into himself, fingers clasped over a gutted stomach. Velamir swallowed at the sight and looked away. He searched for the spare keys and found them hanging on the weapons rack. The metal rattled each time he fit one into the slot. He swung the cell door open and hurried inside, dropping beside the old man.

"Aid is on the way," Velamir said, wincing at the wound when he saw it up close. "Hold on."

The old man muttered indistinctly under his breath. Velamir wasn't sure if he had heard him. He reached out and placed a tentative hand on the sparse rags covering his shoulder. The old man jerked, hazy eyes turning wild as they focused on Velamir.

"He's coming, Boltrex! He's coming. I saw him. He did this." The old man sobbed as he pulled his hand away and stared at the blood dripping from his fingers. "He did this."

The man had recognized Boltrex in him from the start . . . Even when Velamir had been in the cell across from him and hidden partially by darkness, he'd seen who he was. Velamir took his hand in a gentle grip and placed it back on his stomach.

"Press here. We need to keep pressure on it."

The old man closed his eyes, and when he opened them again, they were panicked. "No, no, no, you need to go. He's coming for you, Boltrex. He will kill you. I told you to be ready. I told you who he was."

Velamir frowned, wondering how much of the words were true and how much was the old man's delusion.

"I wrote to you." The old man stared at Velamir. "Why didn't you listen?"

I wrote to you. Velamir wondered why that sounded so familiar, and then he recalled sneaking into Boltrex's chamber. The small chest that contained the letter and drawing. The old man had sent it. He'd realized who Winston was. That must've been the reason he was in the dungeon. Winston had trapped him in there somehow so he wouldn't speak.

I was put here for a crime I didn't commit.

But how had he done it? And why would Winston come to kill him? Out of pettiness? That didn't sound like him. But then again, Velamir had never known the true Winston. He'd only seen the side Winston had been willing to show him. The old man sputtered, and blood burst from his mouth. Red droplets trailed down the side of his cheek and onto the cold dungeon floor.

"Hold on," Velamir pleaded.

"It's too late." He labored over a tortured breath. "Fulfill my final duty, Boltrex." His dirt-crusted fingers pulled away from his stomach and dipped into the hole of his ragged tunic. He struggled with something behind his neck. A moment later, he pulled out a long chain with a pendant nestled at the end. He placed it in Velamir's hand and closed his fingers around the pendant. "Take it to Devorin to the Elders," the old man told him. "Only then is my mission finished."

"The Elders?" Velamir opened his hand and stared at the symbols on the pendant. They were letters, but he didn't recognize the word they formed or what language they represented.

"Place it in the room of martyrs—" The old man gasped, chest heaving. "The room of memories. Promise me."

"Help is coming. Don't give up."

But the old man shuddered, and then a final breath eased out of him. Velamir bowed his head over his still form. Steps echoed behind him, and a True Manos stepped inside. He took one look at the body and then crouched down, closing the old man's eyes. Velamir stood, guilt turning in his stomach. He was somewhat responsible for all the lives lost. If he had known what Winston was planning . . . If he had chosen a different path at the start of his journey . . . *If.* It was a dangerous word, one that spoke of limitless possibilities. But what was done was done. Velamir pocketed the pendant. He could still do something right.

Two piles of corpses rested outside the Stone Chamber, and they, along with Velamir's fear, grew as more and more were brought forth. Red-and-black uniforms filled one mound, while the other contained Verin green. Yellow-clothed soldiers carried the bodies out, with an occasional green-garbed soldier appearing as well. Velamir stared at each body as he passed, hoping he wouldn't recognize any of them. He stepped inside the chamber. Wailing and loud shouts met his ears, and he grimaced at the sight of so many wounded people—some with missing limbs, detached fingers, scrapes, and cuts. Too many for the few True Manos to handle. Velamir glanced around, his sense of desperation growing. Someone shoved against him and grunted.

"Watch your step." The deep voice came out in a growl. There was a mixture of arrogance and power within it.

Velamir spun around, coming face-to-face with the speaker. A tall man with dark hair and golden armbands circling his armored biceps scowled at him, and lethal black eyes evaluated him. The man's jaw clenched as though sensing something in Velamir—something he didn't like.

"A good warning for us both," Velamir said, not appreciating the stare down. "Close encounters could end with a gut wound."

The man blinked. "Are you threatening me?"

Velamir moved to reply when an arm flung around his shoulders. He stiffened and glanced to see Latimus beside him smiling from ear to ear. It was a strange expression to see, given the circumstances, but Velamir couldn't help the elation that filled him at the sight of an ally of sorts, alive and well.

"Velamir comes across rough, but he means well. Forgive his brashness." Latimus maintained his sickeningly fake grin.

Velamir lifted his shoulder, shrugging Latimus's arm off.

The man's brows lowered as he watched them. "Is that so?"

Latimus nodded. "We are all on high alert because of the attack. Velamir tends to be extra jumpy."

Velamir frowned, but before he could speak, Latimus turned that false smile onto him. "This is *General Zenrelius.*"

Velamir tilted his head and stared at the general. An uncomfortable silence floated between them. Finally, Velamir said, "I've heard about you."

And he had. Although he'd been raised in Tariqi for a good portion of his life, there was no avoiding the name Zenrelius. The strategic general. The legend. Many had reason to fear him, but as Velamir stood before him, he simply saw a proud man. And any man could be killed just as easily as the next.

"Not enough, it seems," the general shot back. "If you did, you would know close combat doesn't faze me and I wouldn't be gutted even if they outnumbered me ten to one." Zenrelius laughed, but it lacked humor. "If there were to be gruesome ends involving me, it would be my opponent's body impaled on my sword."

"Strong sword," Velamir remarked.

"*Foolish foes* would be the correct answer. Anyone willing to make an enemy of me is asking for a lifetime of torment." A spark of warning flamed in his eyes.

Latimus interrupted the strangling tension. "We are fortunate to have General Zenrelius on our side. Verin still stands because of him."

"I know it is not feasible to imagine Ondalar and Verin allying, but Prolus is Ondalar's enemy, and as the saying goes, the enemy of your enemy is your friend." Zenrelius smiled, thin and cutting. "At least for now."

Velamir wondered what had happened between Verin and Ondalar to cause a break between the kingdoms, but it was fortunate for the Empire that they had allied. Velamir recalled Latimus's words from weeks before.

We would have fallen to Prolus long ago, but an Imperial's heart doesn't give in. Even when all the odds are against us. We're strong enough to stand together despite our differences.

Someone called to the general, and he turned after nodding once at Velamir and then Latimus. As he strode away, Latimus slapped a half heart to his chest in salute, his eyes wide with admiration as he stared at the general's retreating back.

"He can't see you," Velamir said dryly.

"How could you speak to him so rudely? A peasant would have more manners." Latimus shook his head. "But I should know better than to expect respect from you. Velamir the Great! The Cavalier does the opposite of what everyone assumes."

"Quit it."

"What?" Latimus shrugged before changing the subject. "Something I *am* surprised about is how the Tariqins managed to find the Stone Chamber. The doors blend in with the walls of the corridor—undetectable, untraceable—and yet they made their way here as soon as they broke through the keep."

"When did they break inside the keep?"

"Nearly the same time the Ondalarians came."

Which meant Winston couldn't have come in from the front . . . When the Ondalarians arrived, he'd already been up on the tower. "Is there a secret tunnel in the castle?"

Latimus frowned. "I would assume so."

Who would know the castle better than someone who had lived in it? Winston must have ordered the Tariqins to the Stone Chamber to take the king's life while he handled other matters. Velamir kept his thoughts to himself and instead said, "We need to find it and seal it."

6

"**H**OLD IT HERE," Jax told her.

Natassa clasped the cloth on the older woman's head. Crimson soaked into the material, and Natassa's stomach flipped. She breathed in, steadying herself. Jax moved fast to help as many of the injured as he could. Natassa smiled as she watched him work. He was gentle and patient with the wounded but also firm and had a critical eye. The woman she was assisting released a pained gasp.

Natassa crouched down, softening her hold. "It's going to be fine."

The woman's hands trembled. "I need to look for my son. What if—"

Natassa made a calming gesture. "We will find him, but first, we must ensure your well-being. Your son wouldn't want you putting your life in danger by searching for him, would he?"

The woman met her stare and finally gave her a resolute dip of her chin. Natassa made room as Jax returned. He gave the woman a sip from the same vial he was using for everyone. He saw Natassa looking and spoke up.

"A tonic for pain. I would normally administer more, but I don't have enough. This will have to do."

She nodded, then watched him stitch the woman's forehead closed, trying not to be squeamish at the sight. When Jax finished, he moved to a basin and cleaned the needle. Another woman approached, carrying fresh cloths and a new basin of water. Natassa thanked her and took it. She went to deliver it to Jax, but he was gone.

She glanced around and spotted him pulling someone into a hug. Natassa's heart lurched to her throat, pumping with a hope she had been pushing far into the back of her mind. Jax pulled away, waving his hands animatedly as he spoke. The other man nodded. He looked up then, as if he could feel her gaze on him. Relief wafted through her with such strength it surprised her. Natassa fancied she saw the same relief in his countenance. He patted Jax's arm and walked past him, his steps sure as he made his way to her. Natassa's cheeks heated, and she turned away, busying herself with arranging the new cloths into a neat stack.

"I'm glad you're safe." The words drifted over her like a soothing balm.

He stepped closer. Warmth emanated from him. Natassa pasted a smile on and readied herself before turning. He was close, far too close. She was not prepared for those emerald eyes that delved into her features, and she was most definitely not ready when they darkened as he focused on one side of her face. She let out a shaky breath, somehow more nervous at the sight of his enraged expression than the wounds she'd been looking at earlier.

"Who did this?" There was a low, dangerous tremor in his voice.

She was confused until his hand lifted inches from her cheek, nearly touching the large gash splitting her skin. She couldn't feel it since Jax had given her the pain tonic straightaway. He hadn't even allowed her to ask what it was or to deny it.

"It's war," she said, shrugging. "No one comes out unscathed. There are many with worse wounds."

"Jax," Velamir growled over his shoulder. "I need some cloth."

Jax slid behind them and grabbed a cloth from Natassa's stack. He hid a smile as he deposited it into Velamir's waiting hand.

"Velamir, my face can wait . . ." Natassa's voice trailed off as she spotted the tear in his sleeve.

The torn fabric was plastered to his arm, glued to his skin with blood. She reached out, wrapping her fingers around his arm but not touching the wound. Velamir glanced down. He appeared stunned, as if noticing there was a slice across his bicep for the first time. But then she realized he wasn't focused on the gash in his arm but rather her hand. He wore a foreign expression Natassa couldn't decipher. She snatched her hand back, uncertain.

"That needs to be stitched."

Natassa jumped. She'd been so focused on Velamir that she hadn't realized Jax had been analyzing the wound over her shoulder. He placed a gleaming needle into her palm, and she shook her head.

"What? I can't—"

"I have too many people to see. I'm sure you can take care of one."

"But—"

"Vel can handle a little pain."

Her protests died as Jax moved off. Natassa winced and looked at Velamir, surprised to find him watching her with a small smile playing on his lips. She cleared her throat and spotted a newly vacated wooden chair. She led the way and motioned to it.

"Sit here."

Natassa went in search of the basin and cleaned the needle as she'd seen Jax do. After preparing everything, she returned to Velamir's side. She washed the wound as best as she could, trying not to glance at Velamir as she did. She didn't think she could continue if she saw him in pain. To his credit, he didn't make a sound. She lifted the needle, bracing herself as she brought it closer and closer to his skin. She paused an inch from the wound.

"I've never done this before," she admitted, daring a glance at his face.

His expression was calm and unwavering. Her hand trembled, and he reached out, catching her curled half fist in his larger fingers.

"I trust you," he said softly. "Now, trust yourself."

The words were like a compress, covering the gaping

doubt and worry until she saw only his eyes. She'd never been looked at like that. Like she was capable. She pulled her hand from his and slid the needle into his flesh. Natassa could still feel his eyes on her. It seemed like it took forever to weave the needle through his skin. As she stared at the stitches, she remembered Thorsten. How pale he'd been on his deathbed. His forehead had been sutured with catgut. She could visualize the dark thread like he was still lying before her. Something wet dropped onto Velamir's arm as she tied the thread closed.

"Don't cry."

The words startled her, and she blinked, alarmed that she'd allowed her emotions to get the best of her without even realizing it.

"I'm sorry. I remembered my brother."

She expected him to remain silent, but he spoke, the words seeming to slip out. "Tell me about him."

Natassa couldn't meet his gaze, afraid he would see how much losing Thorsten had shattered her. She tore a long piece of cloth and wrapped it around his bicep. With careful movements, she tied it closed over the stitches. "He was everything to me. I didn't have anyone else."

When she chanced a glance at Velamir, she saw he was frowning. A spark of alarm trailed through her. He thought Krea was her twin. Of course, he would be confused that she didn't consider her as important as Thorsten.

"Krea will always be part of me," she hurried to say. "She's practically my other half. You know how it is with twins . . . two parts of one whole. But Thor—"

She paused and cleared her throat. "Thor was my rock. He stood in the path of all my troubles. When the chisel came down, he let it take parts of him so I could be safe. I watched it carve him into a hardened soldier. When I lost him . . . it was the worst thing in the whole world."

Her hand drifted to her wrist, and her fingers splayed across the bracelet there, playing with the black pearl at its center. "He gave this to me," she said with reverence. "His final wish was for me to be free."

"It's good your princess left you here. You no longer serve her. You no longer serve anyone."

That was what he believed. Natassa tamped down the guilt that rose in her chest. She hated lying to him, but she no longer had the comfort of trusting anyone. "We all serve someone, Velamir. If not a person, then a cause."

She began to move away, but Velamir reached out, wrapping his hand around her wrist. She froze as warmth shot up her arm.

"It's my turn." His tone brooked no argument.

He stood, motioning for her to take his place. Natassa settled in the chair, shifting as he peered closer. His fingers grazed her chin. Her eyes widened, and her breath caught. Velamir didn't seem to notice as he turned her face to better see the wound. He dabbed a cloth against her cheek, pressing gently. He brushed her hair back, and a surge of panic burst through her. She couldn't allow her mark to be exposed. The golden phoenix would reveal who she was. Her eyes met his, and he returned her fear with a comforting glance. She needed to distract herself from all these sensations, so she blurted the first thing that came to mind.

"Tell me about your family."

He seemed surprised before settling into deep thought. It took a minute for him to answer, and when he did, it was sharp. "I have no one."

Natassa flinched, regretting the question.

His features shifted, sorrow turning his eyes a deep green. "No one but myself. It's better to trust in yourself than to rely on others because, sooner or later, they will let you down."

Shouts drew her attention, and Velamir pulled the cloth back. Natassa stood, and he fell into step beside her. As they neared the commotion, they joined a cluster of people formed around a prone figure. Horrified whispers raced through the group.

"We need a True Manos!"

Someone pushed the figure over, and Natassa made out the face.

It was King Dale.

7

CORALIE STOOD IN a large field, where flowers of every kind overwhelmed the surrounding grass. She walked forward, and the swish of fabric rustled with each step. She glanced down. Her dress was deep garnet, the shade of blood, the mourning color in the Empire. A rush of wind blew toward her and flipped her braids back. A figure stood ahead of her. The sun shone above, casting rays of light around him. He wore armor but no helm, dark waves of hair streaming over broad shoulders, and his body was planted in the assertive stance she would've recognized anywhere.

"Mordon," she breathed.

Each step was painful, her thick dress heavy on her shoulders. But no matter how much she walked, he seemed to get farther away. Coralie lifted her skirts and ran, her bare feet pounding the grass, crushing the flowers, her footfalls weighed down by anchors trying to bury her in place. But she didn't give up. She was getting closer; she could feel it.

"Mordon!"

He turned and watched as she approached. He examined her dress, a somber look filling his eyes. It was the color, she realized. Someone had died, but she couldn't remember who. Mordon appeared as she remembered him—tough and solid as a mountain, unshakable. But as she drew closer, she saw the scar cutting down his face, like a crack at the mountain's center. A small crack, but a crack all the same, and it was usually the broken pieces in the foundation that brought the tallest of walls down.

"Mordon?"

He stared at her, regret evident in his features. Sudden howling rose from the hills behind him. Coralie looked past him at the shapes hurtling toward them. They gained speed, and she realized what they were. Rumloks, creatures Prolus had twisted into vicious beasts inclined to kill the nearest breathing thing. Teeth razor-sharp, eyes glowing like demons.

"Mordon!" Coralie rushed up beside him, then reached for her sword but met empty air. "Do you have a weapon? We need to go. We can't fight them."

She searched for a route back. The sun was gone, and the valley darkened as shadows drew over them. Coralie sputtered, scanning wildly for an escape.

Mordon grasped her arm, bringing her attention to him. "No," he said simply.

She frowned, waiting for him to continue.

"I'm sorry, Coralie."

He touched his chest plate, and Coralie noticed the design on it for the first time. A mask with protruding horns. Prolus's symbol.

"No," she whispered. "What is wrong with you? Why are you wearing that?"

"I have no choice."

The rumloks gathered around them, growling and ready to pounce. Coralie felt the sting of betrayal like a dagger plunged into her middle. When she looked back at Mordon, his face was set, determination gleaming. Coralie shook her head, a rush of heat filling her. Sweat poured down her face.

"Princess? Your Highness, wake up." The soft voice cut through her mind.

Coralie blinked her eyes open, and bright light made her close them just as quickly. A cool cloth rested upon her head. She opened her fluttering eyes again. She was in her bedchamber, and her windows were opened wide, allowing sunlight to filter in. She attempted to sit up. A moan slipped out, and agonizing pain stabbed her skull. She touched her head, recalling the dream. It had felt so real . . .

"Lie still," a woman said.

"Mordon! Where is he?" Coralie turned to her, partly surprised by the familiar face. It took a moment for Coralie to recall her name. "Kasdeya? What are you doing here?"

Kasdeya leaned over her, pressing a hand to Coralie's shoulder. She didn't resist as she was pushed back onto soft pillows. She rested her head, exhaling a sharp breath as another wave of pain racked through her body. Kasdeya removed the cloth before replacing it with a wet one.

"I volunteered to assist with the wounded," she told Coralie, smoothing the cloth over her forehead.

Coralie dropped her chin slightly to affirm she'd heard her. She was struggling to keep her eyes open. "The battle? What happened?"

"The Tariqins retreated." It was a vague answer.

"I spotted Ondalarians advancing toward the castle. Prolus withdrew because of them, didn't he?" Coralie pressed, blinking at the hazy form of Kasdeya above her.

Kasdeya nodded, her lips turned down. Coralie knew she was holding back so she wouldn't overwhelm her, but Coralie didn't take pleasure or comfort in being unaware. It was a time of war—a war Prolus wouldn't back out of. Coralie had to be prepared. She almost laughed at the thought of Ondalar assisting them. The last kingdom she had expected had saved them. Another pressing question came to mind.

"How long have I been unconscious?"

"A few days."

"Days!" Coralie exclaimed, wincing as she tried to rise again.

Kasdeya must have been anticipating such a reaction, because she was pressing Coralie back down an instant later. "Your wounds are severe. You had deep cuts on your back and some on your legs and arms, not to mention a head wound. They festered, and you had a fever that broke last night. You almost died. You need rest."

"Thank you for tending to me." She lifted a weak arm and wrapped her fingers around Kasdeya's wrist. "Mordon? Is he all right?"

"You mentioned him before." Kasdeya frowned. "I'm afraid I don't know who he is."

"General Boltrex's son."

"The Tariqins have captured the general's son."

Coralie released Kasdeya with a harsh exhale. Her worst fear had been realized. It made her wonder how much of her dream was true. But no. Mordon would never join Prolus. Never. She held that resolve within herself as she glanced at Kasdeya.

"And my uncle?" A panicked note struck her voice. "King Dale, how is he?"

Kasdeya seemed reluctant to answer. "He is gravely ill."

Coralie sagged into the pillows. What little strength she did have seeped out of her.

8

Mordon
Kingdom of Verin
Tariqin War Camp

MORDON STRUGGLED AGAINST his bonds. The rough rope dug into his skin, searing marks into his wrists like the growing frustration within. The vast size of the Tariqin camp astounded him. Hundreds of tents, thousands of deedans, and countless Chishmans. Mordon caught sight of many Savorians as well. They wore a mix of green and gray, and over-sized belts sat above their hips, holding tools much like the Chishmans used. A hard push sent him stumbling forward past a set of cages. Mordon grunted, shooting a glare at the deedans behind him, then sniffed and grimaced at the rancid smell emerging from the cages. Snarls and low growls alerted him to the rumloks trapped within.

The deedans shoved him along until finally depositing him in an empty tent.

Mordon swore under his breath as he struggled to loosen the ropes binding his hands. He glanced around, searching for something to assist him. There, at the edge of the tent, peeking in from under the canvas, was a small rock with enough of a point to aid in his escape.

Mordon crouched, turned, and edged his way backward. His eyes remained trained on the tent flap for signs of movement, where at least two deedans guarded the entrance. His fingers brushed the rock. He wrapped it in his fist and started working at the rope. His shoulder and back muscles strained as he used all his strength to undo the binds. A sharp sting made him wince, and warm blood trickled to his pinky. He exhaled, his thoughts running wild as he toiled. He wondered what had happened at the castle. To Coralie and Boltrex and . . .

"Velamir," he hissed.

Velamir, the Chishma who had snuck into Verintown, winning the hearts of many and then destroying them with his betrayal. Velamir, who'd stolen his father from him. Mordon had sacrificed everything for Boltrex, and still, he'd chosen Velamir, a face that had been nameless a month before. A growl built in Mordon's chest as he recalled the soft look Boltrex had worn when he'd seen Velamir's scar. Mordon had always yearned for a look like that. A bitter tear escaped his eye, infuriating him. He pressed his face into his shoulder, rubbing it off with a rough motion.

He wouldn't let Boltrex hurt him anymore. The time of obedience was finished. Mordon would make his own choices. He would oversee his own fate. But first, he had to escape the camp. The rope fibers had begun to slacken when low voices filtered through the tent canvas. Mordon stood.

"I will see the prisoner."

"But, General . . ."

The tent flap shifted, and Winston entered, a bowl full of something steaming in his hands. Deedans filed in behind him. Winston smiled. A look that should have made him appear welcoming only disgusted Mordon and made him wonder how that pathetic man could be his father. With blue eyes, graying hair, and a much smaller form, Winston looked nothing like him.

"Can't go anywhere without your guards?" Mordon smirked, eyeing the deedans.

"Oh, trust me, they are here for your protection, not mine. I wouldn't want you to do something you might regret."

Mordon laughed, lifting his head to stare at the tent ceiling while continuing to work the ropes as discreetly as he could.

"What did you think of the camp?" Winston asked, then answered the question for Mordon. "Quite impressive, is it not?"

"Let's cut to the chase." Mordon pinned him with a glare. "What do you want with me?"

"I have only your best interests at heart," Winston said and motioned the bowl toward him. "Starting with this meal." He jerked his head at a deedan. "Unbind him."

The deedan approached with hesitance in every step. Mordon continued staring at Winston until the deedan closed in. Then he snapped the last thread of the rope apart and grabbed the deedan's collar before flinging him from the tent. He kicked out, smacking the bowl from Winston's gloved hand, then slid the Tariqin general's dagger free and placed it at his throat. It all happened in a blink. The deedan's scream ended with a thump as he landed outside.

Mordon stared at Winston coolly, nicking his skin with the dagger edge. Half a dozen swords were trained on Mordon as the remaining deedans struggled to maintain hold of the situation. A ghost of a smile traced Winston's lips, which only served to infuriate Mordon further.

"The soup wasn't to your liking?"

"I'm not one of your puppets," Mordon said. "End the small talk and tell me what you want."

"You do understand that with one twitch of my hand, you could be gutted, don't you?"

Mordon chuckled at the threat. "I may be killed, but I will be taking you with me." He pressed the weapon closer to Winston's neck.

Winston's teeth gleamed. "Bravo, lad, bravo. I admire such courage." He glanced at the deedans. "You may leave."

Mordon felt the air fill with uncertain reluctance, but at another wave from Winston, the deedans sheathed their blades and ducked out of the tent.

Winston glanced back at Mordon. "Now, we can discuss business. I usually prefer doing so without a dagger at my throat."

The implication was clear, but Mordon didn't lower the blade. "I won't be doing any business with you."

"I only want the best for you . . . *Son*." The word inflamed the tension.

Mordon seethed. "I'm not your son."

Winston dared to stoke the flames. "Oh, you're Boltrex's, then? The man who cast you off, who used you?"

Mordon's free hand fisted.

"I've searched for someone I could trust, someone who could assist me, and the fates have smiled upon me," Winston said. "My own son."

"Don't play games with me. You only care about Prolus. You grovel before him."

"That's where you are wrong. I've wanted to kill Prolus for a long time, but the perfect moment hasn't arrived. That time is coming, and when I remove him, you will be at my side."

Mordon chuckled. He stepped back, releasing Winston, who rubbed his neck. "You're insane."

"My intellect is intact. I was hoping yours would be as well." Winston pointed at the tent entrance. "If you want to leave, if you want to return to those who turned their backs on you, go ahead. Just know that you will miss a great chance to prove yourself, Cselnsor."

Mordon started. "What did you call me?"

"That was the name I gave you. *King's blood*. You have Savorian blood in your veins, lad. You inherited it from me. My ancestors were kings. You have every right to rule. And when you wed Princess Natassa, no one will doubt it."

Mordon didn't know how to begin asking the list of questions forming in his mind. Winston was utterly insane. How did he plan to pull off that plot to overthrow his leader? How on earth did he think he could arrange a marriage between the emperor's daughter and Mordon? What gave him such arrogance, such surety of his success?

Winston's shoulders sagged, and Mordon wondered if he was trying to look weak and defeated. Was it a ploy to make Mordon pity him and fall into his trap? The top of Winston's head was level with Mordon's neck. Satisfaction wound its way through him. If nothing else, at least height was still an advantage Mordon held.

"What are you talking about, old man? The princess is betrothed to Draven."

"For now." Winston smiled, his face crinkling. "The prince is on a leash. We can eliminate him when he no longer proves useful."

Mordon absorbed that knowledge. Draven's lack of loyalty to the Empire didn't surprise him. If it would mean saving his skin, Mordon had no doubt Draven would sell his own father. But the thought of marrying Princess Natassa sent an uncomfortable feeling down into his gut. Until then, Mordon had only seen one person walking down that road with him.

"Think it over, lad." Winston moved past him, stopping by the tent flap. "If we ruled, how much could we change?"

He ducked out, and Mordon stood in contemplative silence. Winston was aware he could escape. He'd even offered him freedom, but he knew Mordon wouldn't take it or else he wouldn't have allowed such an opportunity.

Mordon couldn't return to the castle until he was prepared. He would bide his time, grow his strength.

He'd fought against the dark side of himself for too long.
Maybe it was time to stop.

Maybe it was time to accept it.

9

Kasdeya
Kingdom of Ayleth
Castle Shikista

"Four," Kasdeya whispered, reading the date on the letter.

The message had been sent four days before, and she'd received it that morning. Kasdeya stepped beside the elaborate vanity and closer to the arched window. Sunlight highlighted the words on the creased paper.

Vosta,

Good work. Grongar-ja is pleased to know you have succeeded in entering Ayleth. We have heard the prince is in Prolus's hands. Remove him, take the throne for us, and you shall be rewarded. Use the roots we sent. The sap within them is poisonous.

Povon-ja

Kasdeya glanced at the original letter lying

open beside the container. Savese translation sheets sat alongside it. Kasdeya took the container, probing inside for the desert roots. Poison—how well she knew it. She felt the smooth round stems and then tucked them back inside before slipping the container into her wardrobe. She would have to find a better spot for it.

Kasdeya stepped back, glancing around the chamber. The castle was so different compared to the Grand Palace in Hearcross. The chambers were round, even the throne room, and they circled the base in a tight spiral to the top. The various shades of purple were starting to hurt her eyes.

She sighed. It had been a long month. Deceiving Natassa, being abducted by Vykus, finally coming to Ayleth, marrying Draven . . . The last part had been easier than she'd thought it would be. Draven had encouraged their wedding, marrying her as soon as they arrived at the castle. Kasdeya's stomach heaved at the thought of the celebration and the royal binding nectar she and Draven had drunk. Panic had consumed her during the ceremony. If a person didn't have royal blood in their veins, the golden liquid would turn green. She'd drunk it slowly, hoping her lips wouldn't taint the color. Draven had snared the goblet from her before she could see and stared into her eyes as he took a long sip. He'd said nothing leaving her certain that the nectar shifting color was just a ploy to trick commoners into believing that they could never possibly attain the level of royals.

A giggle filtered into the room. Kasdeya's head snapped to the connecting door. She took hesitant steps toward it. Draven's silky voice passed through the door, growing clearer when she placed her hands on the wood and pressed her ear to it.

"It's been too long, my prince." The voice was sultry.

"Far too long," came the reply.

Kasdeya's fingers curled along the wood, her nails scraping down in slow, vicious rakes. *The cheater.* They'd been married for all of seven days, and he couldn't stay loyal. *What else were you expecting?* She would enjoy killing him, enjoy watching him fight for air, enjoy watching the life die in his eyes. For so long, she'd been justifying her actions and reassuring herself that everything she did was to improve her life, but sometimes, guilt wormed into her thoughts, traveling through the muddy areas of her mind and finding its way to the center, eating at her conscience. Like when she remembered Natassa's betrayed face or Krea's horror or Thander's corpse. But when she killed Draven, she would only feel bliss.

A soft sigh wafted through the closed door, grating on her nerves. She couldn't care less what he did, but when he carried on with his lovers where she might encounter their affairs, *that* irritated her. Kasdeya wrapped her fingers around the handle and threw the door open. It smacked the wall with a satisfying thud. Draven glanced at her, his blond hair rumpled. A scantily clad woman was draped in his arms. Her eyes widened as she focused on Kasdeya.

"Get out," Kasdeya spat.

Draven nodded at the woman, and she scurried away, pieces of her skimpy dress tumbling off. Kasdeya faced Draven. She wanted to punch the arrogant smirk off his face. Why was he smiling? He'd just been caught in the act.

"How dare you?" she snarled and then softened her voice, trying to act like the princess she had been portraying these past days. "How could you do this to me?"

Draven ran a hand into his hair, smoothing the strands back. "I must have missed something. I only recall what you did to me."

"If you want to carry on with your lovers, at least have enough respect for me to do it somewhere else."

Draven approached the decanter and poured himself a glass of zat. "I don't understand why you are so upset."

"My father will hear of this."

Draven spat the zat out, tilting his head back and releasing a loud laugh. "Emperor Malus has his fair share of courtesans. If anything, he will pat me on the back and congratulate me."

"You are wretched."

"Wretchedly handsome? I agree."

Kasdeya shook her head. He was a lost cause. She shouldn't have confronted him. She hadn't gained anything from it. Stay silent, stay hidden. That was her armor.

Kasdeya turned, storming back into her room. She was closing the door when a hand caught the wooden frame and thrust it back open. Draven stepped inside. He grasped her wrist, wrenching her against him. She thought of everything she could do to escape his thick arms. Duck, kick his knee, scratch his face, elbow his exposed ribs, grab his earlobes and yank down hard. Each idea brought her glee, but she couldn't execute any of them without blowing her cover. She managed to contain herself and allowed him to press her against the wall, knocking over the stand holding her hairpins and brushes. As they clattered on the ground, Kasdeya forced a fearful expression onto her face.

"What are you doing?"

He lowered his head to her neck and inhaled. Kasdeya froze for what seemed like an endless moment. He exhaled, his hot breath shooting over her skin. Then Draven raised his head, staring at her with red-rimmed eyes.

"There was something about her," he said, his voice unguarded, the false smoothness gone. "She smelled like the garden. My mother would take me there when I was a boy."

Kasdeya frowned. What in the world was he talking about?

"She had this look on her face, this determination that drew me in. I wanted to see how long she would fight me, how long she would resist. I wanted to break her courage. I wanted to break her. I wanted *her.*"

He blinked, and the haze in his expression faded as he focused on her. Apprehension grew in Kasdeya at the storm cloud gathering on his face. He shoved her arms against the wall. "Natassa."

Kasdeya grimaced when his fingers tightened into shackles around her wrists. "What?"

"I want Natassa."

The words sent a shock over her. "I don't understand," she whispered. "I *am* Natassa."

He laughed, releasing her, and stumbled back. "You're not her. You're not Natassa!"

He swiped an arm across the vanity, tossing the perfumes and jewelry off. Kasdeya watched, frozen with growing alarm, as he threw things and shouted. But fear filtered through her for the first time when he headed for her papers. To the translated letter.

She launched forward, wrenching his arm back as he reached for the parchment. He flung her onto the bed with a grunt, his fingers catching her face. Kasdeya's teeth cut into her lower lip and blood burst from the incision, burning her tongue and trailing down her chin. Draven took up the papers and tore them without looking at them. The scraps drifted to the floor like snowflakes. Kasdeya's breaths escaped her in a ragged rhythm, and relief flooded her.

"I knew you weren't her from the moment you rushed at me in Verin. But I decided I didn't care. You would be easier to use. Now I regret it. I wish I had taken her. She could've screamed and fought, but at least I would have her."

Draven leaned over her, jerked her chin up, and stared at her with cold gray eyes. "You aren't a princess. You tainted the goblet. Any doubt I could've had disappeared during the ceremony."

Kasdeya's heart sank, and her fingers dug into her dress, curling around the knife sheathed at her thigh.

"You don't have any power in Ayleth. You are a servant as you were, as you always will be." He released her chin and left the disheveled room with rough steps, slamming the door closed and creating the barrier between their chambers again.

Kasdeya spat away the blood on her lips and took the pillows in her hands. She ripped them open, screaming in anger.

He knows, he knows, he knows.

10

WIND WHISTLED THROUGH the small gaps in the wood boarded across the window. Coralie shivered, cold despite the roaring fireplace and blankets pooled over her legs. Winter had dug its ravaging claws into Verin. Snow covered the burned town, and the moat had frozen over. Coralie had seen the remnants of the once-grand Verintown from her window before it was barred. She'd sat in numb shock on the stone sill as flakes of snow obscured her precious home inch by inch.

Her anger built as the snowstorms continued to rage.

Prolus would pay. For all of it.

"The people are planning on setting out. They no longer feel safe in the castle." Her personal advisor's voice flooded into focus.

"Advisor Welix is filling the council. There are now ten members."

Coralie sat up on the bed, flinching when pain slithered down her back. It felt like ages had passed since she'd obtained them, and still the wounds stung. She pinned Advisor Alesto with a sharp gaze while he fidgeted.

"Who gave him the right? And why am I only being informed of this now?"

"Your H-Highness," Alesto stuttered. "You were under much duress. Pardon me, but King Dale's days are numbered. Advisor Welix stepped up to the task and did his best to return the castle to its proper state. Besides, I did come to your quarters many times, but . . ." He shot a glare at the corner of the room, where Coralie's new bodyguard stood. "I was turned away."

Alesto had been removed from the council years ago at the vote of the members. They'd found his ideas of reform revolting. Coralie, however, found them refreshing. Usually. He could be off putting at times. But she'd recruited him as her personal advisor as soon as she came of age, and he'd been dedicated to her ever since, despite his disapproval of some of her actions.

He returned his focus to her. His eyes were brown and wide, as if in a constant state of shock. It made him appear much younger than the forty years wearing down his slight frame. The green councilman robes he never seemed to take off nearly swallowed him whole. But his skin remained the same—unblemished, unlined, and a healthy golden brown.

"I want to be informed of everything from now on."

Coralie glanced at her bodyguard. "Jovinne, you will not prevent this."

He nodded, though his face remained stony.

Coralie's mind raced over the developments. If Advisor Welix had chosen the new council members, that meant they would vote for his calls. She had to act at once. There was no time for further recovery. She glanced at Kasdeya, who was speaking with her twin by the large closet containing the many dresses Coralie never wore.

It was easy to tell the twins apart since she'd been watching them over the past days. Krea was forthright and warm, easy to talk to, and empathetic. Kasdeya, on the other hand, seemed to hide within herself. She was reserved but didn't hold back kindness from those in need of it. They also had physical differences. Kasdeya's hair hung at an awkward uneven slant at her shoulders, and it always covered her face. Her lips were often down-turned, whereas Krea could usually be found smiling.

"Kasdeya," Coralie called, interrupting their conversation. "Bring me my armor and sword."

They turned to look at her as Alesto stiffened and Jovinne took a step away from his post.

"You aren't fully recovered, Princess. Whatever you have in mind, I suggest you wait," Alesto advised.

"I don't have the luxury of time." Coralie circled the ring around her thumb. "Prolus will return, and we cannot rest our hopes on Ondalar to save us again."

Alesto shook his head. "The storms will hold them another month. General Zenrelius and his troops remain. They still side with us. We can form an alliance. There's time."

"Not enough," Coralie snapped. "Not for Verin, not for politics, not for planning. Not for Mordon." Her voice softened at his name. She'd been plagued by doubts every night. Nightmares that had drenched her in sweat. She couldn't bear the thought of him being tortured, used, hurt. *Killed*. She had to get him out of there. "We must strike fast, where they are least expecting."

They leaned closer, interest sparking in their eyes. But her next sentence doused their hopes.

"Bring me Velamir."

Alesto's face crumpled. "The traitor? The spy? They will not barter for him. Prolus won't give us anything, let alone General Boltrex's son."

Coralie recalled the Shadow Manos, Jax's plea, his promise to help the Empire. *I know Velamir would say the same thing,* he'd said. *He has always chased the right path.*

"He won't, but Velamir will." Coralie's lips twisted. "He will give us Winston's cold dead heart."

11

THE BLOW TO his jaw sent Mordon reeling. He righted himself, brushing fingers over his lips, then glancing at the wet blood staining them. He shook the daze from his eyes, focusing on his four opponents. The shirtless deedans surrounded him, fists raised. They were grim, with hardened faces. There was nothing personal about the way they'd been beating him. They had orders, and so did he.

Cages formed a perimeter around the practice location. Cold air brushed his bare chest. Flakes of snow traveled around them, and ominous clouds loomed overhead, projecting yet another snowstorm. But that hadn't stopped the deedans from bringing him out of the tent that served as his prison. Winston's idea of training was far different from what Mordon was used to.

I accept your offer, Mordon had told him.

Good, very good. Winston had smiled. *I must hold you prisoner until you prove yourself worthy enough of Prolus's esteem. He doesn't trust anyone, you know. Show your value and loyalty.*

Mordon's breath puffed out visibly before him. The icy snow bit into his sweaty skin. A deedan rushed at him, throwing a punch at his stomach. Mordon caught his fist and thrust him away. His heel dug into the snow as he spun before backhanding a deedan creeping from behind. Something connected with his temple, and he grunted, the pain rocketing his skull. Then another blow found its way through his raised arms, burying into his face. The crack of bone was audible and reverberated through Mordon's mind. He spat blood, touching his broken nose. The deedans continued pounding him, urged on by the cheers of gathering Tariqins.

Mordon stumbled through the snow, farther and farther back, until another blow threw him against rattling metal. He grasped for purchase in the loops in the metal. His fingers caught sharp edges. His skin split, and he winced as drops of blood coursed down his fingers. Before he could blink, a deedan lifted his booted foot and slammed it into Mordon's midsection. The metal door gave way with a squealing crash. Mordon fell backward, collapsing into a pile of snow. He lay there in the cold, white slivers drifting around him, soothing his broken nose with frozen numbness.

When he lifted his head, stars shot across his vision.

Gasps traveled through the onlookers. Then he heard a low growl. The sound seemed to multiply, coming from every direction. Gleaming red eyes peered at him. He'd fallen into a rumlok cage.

Mordon's breath came quicker, and his head thumped back down in the snow. A rumlok approached him. It was large, with black fur and rippling muscles. It sniffed Mordon, probing his hair before lifting its head and howling at the other rumloks. Mordon stared into the beast's fiery eyes, seeing something in them—something calculating but not bloodthirsty. It sniffed Mordon again, and he heard a voice drift hazily through his mind. *Hastar?* The word came once more, and Mordon knew what it meant. *Master.*

He blinked, his consciousness fading into a curtain of black.

He awoke to hands drifting along his arms, touching and prodding. Mordon sat up, nearly knocking his head into a woman's. He was lying across a long board hefted into the air by what appeared to be barrels.

"You're in the healing tent." The woman's voice brought his attention back to her. There was something familiar about her tone.

Her hair was tied back, with a few black strands escaping to frame her face. Brown skin, purple eyes. Yes, he knew her.

"We meet again, Lissa Raga," he said and, as an afterthought, added, "if that is really your name."

"Lissa will do." She smirked. "The last time we saw

each other, we were on opposing sides. It's a wonder how things can change."

Mordon scoffed and immediately regretted the movement when agonizing pain shot up his nose. "What are you doing here?"

"What does it look like? Tending to your wounds." She placed a blood-soaked cloth onto a table covered with disturbing-looking tools.

"Seems a low job for a Chishma. Shouldn't one of your Shadow Manos be doing this?"

Not that he wanted a Shadow Manos around. He recalled the man who had shoved the tonic down his throat. He would be content never seeing him again.

Her eyes narrowed. "Some of the best Shadow Manos trained as Chishmans perform healing very well. In fact, without their tonics, you wouldn't have recovered from your wounds so quickly."

Mordon huffed, remembering the scars on his face and shoulder. Marks Velamir had carved into him.

"They have better things to do than waste time on you." She lifted a flask with blue powder nestled inside and shook it. "*Abuz.* Blue death. Chishma Revoz introduced it to me. He was the Shadow Manos you met on the way."

Mordon eyed the glistening powder, and distaste curdled his stomach. He had a name to match with the disturbing Shadow Manos's face.

"We believe we have so much time left. But then I look at this." She tapped a nail against the flask. "So many different poisons. You could be gone before you can blink."

"What does it do?" Mordon asked, curious.

"Wouldn't you like to know?" Lissa set the flask down with a *thunk*. She glanced at him and burst into laughter, then pinched his cheek. He turned away, grimacing. "You look so disappointed. Fine, I will tell you. Consume this, and you will appear dead for an entire week. It knocks you out. When you wake up, there is the possibility you won't remember your name or who you are." She stepped closer. "There's also the ravaging torture to your stomach. Someone who was experimented on said it felt like ice clawing up his insides."

"Is that what Winston used?" Mordon asked. "When he faked his death?"

Lissa shook her head. "The risk was too great. He wasn't willing to chance forgetting himself. The poison he ingested that night would have killed him if he hadn't had the antidote. But he *did* ask Chishma Revoz to look into poisons that imitate death. This was the best one Revoz found."

Mordon was still finding it hard to accept that Winston had poisoned himself. It was foolish, risking your own life for some petty revenge.

Lissa leaned over him, bracing her fingers on his nose. "I'm going to reset the bone on three. One—"

"So, you escaped from Castle Verin only to start setting bones? You were demoted because you failed." Mordon smiled at the rage darkening her eyes. "Am I wrong?"

Her hands were lightning, snapping his nose into place before he could blink. Mordon groaned, his shoulders jumping. His eyes watered, and tears spurted down his cheeks. "You said you would count to three."

"You wouldn't have been ready, anyway." Her lips twisted as her eyes ran over him. "It's a pity for a man this fine of form to be so daft. Falling into a rumlok cage, what were you thinking?"

Mordon touched his nose gingerly. "To be precise, I was kicked in there."

The tent flap moved aside, and Winston entered. He nodded at Lissa, and she backed away from Mordon. She seemed to stiffen at Winston's arrival and exited a moment later.

Winston approached, a large smile fastened on his face. "There is no longer any doubt you are of my blood."

"What do you mean?"

"Only a person with Savorian roots can connect with a rumlok, which is why all the Handlers are Savorian. While rumloks, especially the ones in this camp, will kill any living being that sets foot in their cage, they will not harm a Savorian gifted with blood from the old kings. This proves you are a descendant."

Mordon remembered the strange voice he'd heard in the cage. Had the rumlok been speaking to him? Another rumlok flashed in his mind. The one he'd fought in Verintown. Its claws had rested on him, ready to end his life, but it hadn't. He'd thought it strange then, but his confusion was answered. Even in their demented state, a rumlok didn't kill the ones they bowed to. The truth was clear as day. He was Savorian. Winston was his father. And he would have to learn to bear that truth.

12

NATASSA STARED AT the slash running down Coralie's back while the princess sat on a stool before her. Coralie's posture was stiff, and Natassa could tell she was rigid in an attempt to ignore the pain. The wound had improved, but there was inflammation around it. Natassa would have to find Jax. The Shadow Manos had holed himself up somewhere in the castle—experimenting, last she'd heard. Natassa was surprised no one bothered him. In fact, the amount of respect he'd earned astonished her. Since he'd help the injured, it seemed no one cared about his mark, about who he was. Natassa lifted her fingers to her forehead, sifting underneath the hair to touch the phoenix mark her father had tried to burn away.

"How does it look?"

The question startled her. Natassa took a second to focus. "Better."

That seemed to satisfy Coralie. The princess stood, outstretching her arms with a wince. Her maid approached to clothe her in a dress with slits to the upper thighs revealing the thick trousers garbing her legs beneath. The upper part of the dress molded to Coralie's body like a second skin and was followed by a metal chest plate. The fabric was black, reminding Natassa of a cold night. Coralie's maid handed her a dagger, which she strapped to her waist. That was followed by her sword belt. The sword slid into the sheath with a lethal rasp. The look suited the princess. She appeared bold and fearless. Natassa admired her confidence and strength. Coralie was the type of princess she had always strived to be.

"I know what you're thinking. You must have advised Natassa against such foolish decisions."

Natassa started upon hearing her own name. She shook her head, and Coralie chuckled, pulling on a pair of riding boots.

"I know I'm still wounded, but I cannot leave Verin in the hands of people who will lose it." Coralie winced as she straightened.

"I'm worried about your injury, but I would never stop you. It's madness to throw yourself back into the heat of the fray, but then again, where could a heart go—"

"Without a little madness," Coralie finished the line with her.

They stared at each other for a tense second, and Natassa's pulse thrummed as panic spread over her.

"Where did you hear that?" Coralie asked.

"A book," Natassa blurted. "A book that Princess Natassa had."

Now that she remembered, she was sure it had been Coralie who had recommended the book to her all those years back during a celebration at the Grand Palace. Coralie frowned and parted her lips to speak, but a knock at the door broke the conversation.

"Velamir is here to see the princess." Jovinne's voice was muffled behind the door of the adjoining chamber.

Coralie's attention changed route, and she entered her main chamber, leaving the closet behind. Natassa hurried to follow, but then hesitated. She reached out, fingers flat against the wooden frame of the door. She held it open the slightest bit, uncertainty rooting her in place. She wasn't sure why. It was Velamir, not a stranger. But he'd been avoiding her.

She'd learned from Krea that he spent his time in the barracks. Natassa had gone there once, watching from a distance while he shot at targets along the wall. He'd done it again and again with tension in his shoulders. There was an agony in every arrow loosed from the string. Something was weighing on him.

"What happened, Your Highness?"

The voice sent shivers over her. It was Velamir, but the tone was different. Spiteful.

"Decided I was too dangerous to roam freely?"

"You are speaking to the princess of Verin. Watch your words," Jovinne snapped.

"It's all right," Coralie said. "I know what you're feeling, Velamir. You want nothing more than to exact retribution from Winston, from Prolus."

Natassa peeked past the door. There he stood, arms crossed over his chest. Dark circles marked the skin beneath his eyes. He looked thinner. Natassa's heart ached. She couldn't see him like that. Velamir wasn't hopeless. He was the one who gave hope.

But maybe that was just the Velamir she'd planted in her mind.

"The day I gave Jax a chance to prove himself, that offer extended to you." Coralie faced him, her stance firm. "You have what it takes, Alaric."

Natassa frowned, confusion mounting. Velamir flinched.

"I want you to enter the Tariqin camp."

The rest of the conversation devolved into buzzing as blazing pain lit Natassa's mind. She stepped back into the closet, crouching and gripping her thighs as she tried to hold back the shadows. But they broke through her mental shield and a vision glazed over her eyes.

She was in a tunnel, holding a pack, boots echoing ahead of her. The vision flashed forward, and she saw herself beside Velamir. They were sitting on a log, a roaring fire before them and snow cascading down around them. He took her hand, closing it in his, and gave her a smile so gentle it melted her heart like the fire melted the cold. Natassa stood and stumbled. Looking down, she found shackles around her ankles and wrists.

"No," she whispered.

She was in a small circular room. An old man with a large white beard sat with legs crossed and stared at her with kind eyes.

"Don't be afraid," he said. "We will help you."

She looked down again. The chains were gone.

"You have found us," the old man said. "You found the Elders."

His face shifted, swirling like sand before forming into another marked with numerous runes. Dark eyes, black as tar, gazed at her. A smile curled his lips, and he lifted a finger, pointing at her. "I see you. I see you, phoenix."

Natassa gasped, and she was in the closet again on her knees. Her nails dug into her clenched hands, tearing at the skin. She couldn't breathe.

The closet door opened, and Krea stepped inside. She stilled when she saw Natassa trembling, then rushed to her side. "What happened?"

Krea's concern caused tears to spring to Natassa's eyes. She shook her head.

"Natassa, what's wrong?"

"The shadows are messing with my mind, Krea. I see visions all the time. I don't know which ones are true and which are false."

Krea rubbed her back.

"I saw my father dying," Natassa said. "Last night, when I was trying to sleep. He was stabbed in the heart." A sob rattled through her. "Despite everything he's done, he's still my father."

"You shouldn't feel guilty for wanting his death, Natassa," Krea told her. "No one could blame you for wishing for it."

"But I didn't feel guilty. I was relieved." She laughed, tears escaping her eyes. "I was relieved." Natassa looked up, meeting Krea's mournful gaze. "I have to leave."

"Where will you go?"

"To Devorin. I believe I can find help there. Perhaps a way to free myself from the burden of these shadows."

Krea looked skeptical. "Tariqin scouts are watching the castle. They will catch you." Then her eyes widened. "The tunnels! Princess Coralie and Velamir were just speaking about them. Velamir will leave the castle through them."

Natassa grasped Krea's arm. "Thank you."

Krea nodded, a tiny smile lifting the corner of her mouth. Natassa recognized that determined gleam in her eyes and was shaking her head before Krea could speak.

"You cannot come with me, Krea. You've done enough."

"I made an oath to protect you."

"I release you from it," Natassa said swiftly. "You are free."

Krea turned her hand over, showing Natassa the thin scar lining the center of her palm. "Till the last drop of my blood, I will fight. Till my last breath, I will protect the royal heart." Krea whispered the same words she'd said at the ceremony so many years ago. "I'm bound to the crown. I swear my solemn oath. I will protect her skin and bone. I will sacrifice for her, starting with blood of my own."

During the ceremony, Krea had sliced the blade across her palm. Her blood had dripped from her wound into the Fountain of Oaths, along with Kasdeya's. The fountain had been betrayed many times. Oaths were broken. Not only Kasdeya's, but those of so many others who had sworn themselves loyal to the crown.

But Natassa couldn't fault them when even she wouldn't follow her father's orders.

"I won't break my oath till my last breath, Natassa," Krea said, her posture defiant.

Natassa held her gaze, trying to convince her to stay behind with a steady look, but she was only met with sheer fortitude. "This could end badly."

Krea squeezed Natassa's hand. "I'm with you, even if it's to the grave."

13

HONZIO'S EYES WERE on the goblet, riveted by the red liquid that dripped off the rim, staining the careless fingers gripping it. He glanced at his father. Emperor Malus waved a hand at the servants, urging them to hurry, as if the food covering every inch of the table wasn't sufficient. The servants, mostly Savorian, carried in more trays and replaced platters. It was enough food to feed all of Hearcross, and yet only three people were situated around the table.

Honzio peered at Head Advisor Kostos, watching him bury a fork into a thick chunk of perfectly sautéed meat.

A shaking Savorian girl refilled his father's goblet. Seeing the servants left Honzio haunted by the promise he'd made. His fingers wound around the napkin resting by his untouched plate. He'd broken that promise, along with the one he'd given Thorsten. *Take care of her*, his brother had said. But Honzio had failed to protect Natassa. Instead of being sheltered with the Elders in Devorin, she was trapped in a den of snakes. She was married to Prince Draven, and he couldn't do anything to save her.

"Reports, Advisor," Emperor Malus spat before sinking his teeth into a seasoned slice of potato.

Kostos snapped his fingers, and his assistant propelled forward, placing a stack of papers on the table beside him. Kostos flicked through the pages and tapped one. "Savagelander representatives have stated their wish to re-navigate the peace agreement. They find it unsatisfactory."

Emperor Malus sniffed. "The only unsatisfactory thing I see is the drab decorations in the palace. We've been in mourning long enough. Change the furnishings. Add a little gold."

Kostos nodded. "I shall have a word with the staff."

Honzio's stomach dropped, and what remained of his appetite dissipated. Thorsten hadn't been dead two months, and their father was determined to remove his memory from the palace.

"And do something about that outfit. I don't want to see mourning colors within these walls." His words were directed at Honzio, but Advisor Kostos responded.

"Mourning colors will be removed at once, Your Majesty."

Honzio glanced at the sleeve covering his mangled arm. The fabric was deep ruby, the color of the zat his father drank, the color of blood spilt in the name of the Empire. Honzio was helpless to do anything except obey, even in simple matters, like choosing his own wardrobe. His speech was generally comprised of a few common phrases: *Yes, Father; Right away, Father; As you wish, Father; At your command, Your Majesty.* All of them lumps of brittle rock he forced past his lips.

Advisor Kostos lifted a letter from the stack. "From Ayleth."

Honzio's father scoffed. "What could that be about?"

Kostos unfurled the letter and cleared his throat. "Your Supreme Majesty, I was quite disappointed when you didn't attend my wedding. Princess Natassa felt your absence keenly. But I understand your situation. Keeping a falling empire together is strenuous work." Advisor Kostos coughed and took a sip from his goblet before continuing. "I do not want to bore you with trivial matters, so I will get to the point. It will be Vedale soon, and Natassa misses her home. We decided what better time than the Day of Oaths to reunite her with her dear family. Who knows, maybe we can make a few new promises? Until then, Crown Prince Draven Valent."

Honzio frowned. No one would miss living in the confinement of the Grand Palace, least of all Natassa.

Emperor Malus sputtered, his fingers wet with juicy remnants of meat. "This is ridiculous. How dare that little brat convince him to make the journey here? I told her I never wanted to see her again. This marriage was supposed to keep them away. Both of them!"

A guard entered from the side door. He paused near the table and awaited permission to speak. The emperor continued rambling until Honzio caught his eye and motioned to the guard.

"What is it?" Malus snapped.

"The Savorian hasn't broken. We've tried the ropes, the pikes, and whipped him." The guard kept his gaze down.

Malus sneered in distaste. "Bring him to the throne room, along with the racks. I will personally see to his torture."

Honzio swallowed his disgust. The Savorian recently transported from the prison of an Imperial town was alleged to know the location of the Golden Crown. Emperor Malus craved the long life, all-encompassing power, and knowledge of all things that the Golden Crown granted. He wouldn't stop torturing the Savorian until he spoke or died, whichever came first.

The guard bowed in answer to Malus's order. "Your Majesty, I also have news from the city. We have located an underground base. Runaway Savorian slaves were holed up inside."

Honzio's heart pounded, and he stared at the guard, hoping his fear wasn't written across his face. They'd been found. He'd tried to convince the Savorian woman, Aylis, that she wouldn't stay hidden for long, but she'd refused his help. He could still see her—posture defiant, feet planted, eyes narrowed. Like a true warrior, she'd stood her ground. Honzio wasn't her enemy, but he hadn't been able to convince her of that.

"You know the law. Runaways are referred to as dead. Destroy the place and whoever's inside," Emperor Malus commanded.

"But, Your Majesty—"

"What?" A vein throbbed in Malus's temple.

"The mercenary Vykus has been spotted. He's the reason we found the base. He already ransacked it."

Honzio's heart dropped like a stone to the bottom of his stomach as worry for all those innocent children consumed him.

"He captured most of them and left the rest dead."

Emperor Malus shot up and swiped his hands across the table. Platters of food clattered to the ground. "Go after that bastard! He should have been dead long ago. I'm Emperor Malus, and as long as I draw breath, my possessions will not be stolen from me."

The guard nodded and hurried away.

Malus released another wordless shout and turned furious eyes around the room. "I want an announcement made in the city. Tell the people I will turn the ground upside down looking for that supposed mercenary king. Those who have information on his whereabouts will be rewarded." He leveled Honzio with a look. "Be there when the declaration is made. Hearcross should see that the Hartinza line does not back down easily."

He waited expectantly, and Honzio nodded. "Yes, Father."

Malus was right about one thing: Honzio was a Hartinza. He wouldn't give up. Not when the Imperials relied on him. Not when the Savagelanders tried to slither in. And not when Draven was attempting to take the throne.

He would fight back.

14

KASDEYA HELD HER breath while gripping the edge of her vanity as the maids pulled her corset closed. One of them pressed her knee to Kasdeya's lower back to keep her in place. She stared at her figure in the vanity mirror. Good, but not good enough.

"Tighter," she whispered.

They yanked the corset so firmly, Kasdeya thought it would snap. A surge of satisfaction drifted over her as she gazed at her defined curves and amplified hourglass shape. The maids finished dressing her and applied rouge on her cheeks and lips.

Kasdeya peered at herself in wonder. With purple shadows over her lids to highlight her hazel eyes and powders to pinken her cheeks and emphasize her cheekbones, she looked like a princess. All she needed was a crown. Her gaze slid past her reflection to the maids. For years, she'd been in their position, catering to Natassa. Krea slaved on. Kasdeya suspected her sister enjoyed life as a decoy, and so she hadn't sought a higher purpose. Kasdeya's fingers curled into a fist.

I entrust your sister to you, her mother had said on her deathbed. *You are the strong one, the smart one. I know you will find a way to live.*

To live, not merely survive, as her mother had. Kasdeya would never beg in the streets again. She would continue building the fortification that would ensure her status. She could've taken Krea up with her, but her sister had chosen the fool's route.

"I couldn't protect her, Mother," Kasdeya whispered.

"Pardon, Your Highness?"

Kasdeya waved the maid away. "That's enough for now."

The chamber door flew open without warning. Kasdeya swiveled around. Draven burst inside, hair wild, his noble attire rumpled.

"Out."

The single word sent the maids scurrying from the room.

He peered around until his animalistic gaze landed on her, and then he froze. His lips parted as his eyes roamed over her, tracing her dress and lingering on her assets. He took one step, then another.

He exhaled. "Natassa?"

Kasdeya laughed, crossing her arms. "Unfortunately for you, it's just me, the princess of Ayleth."

Draven snapped out of his trance and stormed over to her. He wrapped steel fingers around her arms tightly enough to add to the assortment of bruises he'd left before. He shook her. "How dare you hold a party in my name?" His zat laced breath shot warmth into her face.

"You're drunk," she replied calmly. "And I thought it was custom for Ayleth's princesses to host parties for their husbands' birth celebrations."

"You are not my wife," he slurred, leaning over her. His eyes were red, veins of blood leaking into the gray orbs. He roared, punching a fist behind her.

She stiffened at the sound of shattering glass. Kasdeya looked back, seeing Draven's battered hand with sharp fragments sticking from his knuckles as he pulled away. Glass clattered from the mirror and landed on the vanity.

"You are not my wife," he said again. "You're a . . . a conniving woman. Trying to reach for things too high for her. My throne is mine and mine alone."

"Conniving? Are you speaking of me, Your Highness?" She pushed his chest, and he stumbled back. The blood from his knuckles trickled in fast drops onto the floor. "You are the greatest schemer I've ever known. Perhaps I have plans, goals, but so does everyone. Perhaps I am rotten inside, but deep down, everyone is. We can pretend all we want outside this room, but in here are our true faces. Draven and Kasdeya."

He blinked, reaching for the bedpost to steady himself.

She approached him, smirking. "You think you're so great. So powerful. But you know the truth. All that arrogance and pride is just a cover." She stood on her tiptoes and pressed her lips to his ear. "You are weak under that disguise. Nothing but an empty weakling."

He hunched over, breathing fast. With a move so

sudden, he reached out, grabbing hold of her shoulders. Draven forced her onto the bed, crushing her beneath him. "Shut up! Shut up!" His fingers dug into her back, tearing at her dress. Kasdeya smacked her forehead into his. She blinked past the pain, struggling to see. Draven groaned, and his hold on her slackened, but he recovered fast and used his weight to keep her pinned. Kasdeya brought a leg up and kneed him in the groin. The skirt made the move difficult, but she managed to curl her legs around his and flip him over. Since she was on top, Kasdeya slapped him several times. His skin was clammy and cold, like a fish.

She wrapped her hands around his neck and squeezed. Draven's eyes bulged, and his veins throbbed. He thrashed, and his big arms nearly flung her off, but Kasdeya retained her hold until he fell limp. She exhaled, lifting shaking hands to brush back strands of her damp hair. She stared at him, the grand prince of Ayleth.

"How pathetic," she said.

Draven was so drunk, he wouldn't remember anything when he woke. Unless . . .

Kasdeya smiled.

Unless he never woke.

She turned to the vanity and reached over, finding a long shard of glass. She brought it to Draven's neck and poised it over the tender skin there. She could kill him, finish him, and then King Joster would be the only thing remaining between her and the throne. A mentally ill king wouldn't be hard to remove.

She laughed, the sound ringing around the chamber. Was she losing her mind? Kasdeya couldn't tell. All she knew was that it was a chance she couldn't miss. She readied herself, eager to see blood pouring from Draven's neck. But she froze when the chamber door flung inward and guards poured inside. Kasdeya hid the shard up her sleeve and summoned the helpless act she'd used on Natassa so many times.

"Princess, a maid informed us you needed aid," a guard said as they took in the scene with wide eyes.

Kasdeya's heart beat erratically as she pictured what they were seeing: the blood dribbled across the bed and floor, the mirror shards scattered around the room, not to mention the state of her dress, and she wouldn't doubt her face was a mess.

She thought fast. And manufactured tears. "He went crazy." She sobbed, clambering off Draven. "Take him to the infirmary."

They hauled the prince up. One of them shot her a suspicious glance. Kasdeya's breath stuck in her throat when she saw fingerprints marking Draven's neck. She scrambled for words. "He broke the mirror and began choking himself."

The guards took Draven out, and maids entered to pull off the ruined sheets and sweep away the glass fragments. Kasdeya drew the shard from her sleeve, staring at her fractured image in the broken piece. Hair spilled out of her intricate updo in wild snares. Her makeup was ruined and her dress ripped.

"Do you need anything, Your Highness?"

Kasdeya looked up at the maid. The girl seemed scared, as if sensing Kasdeya was in a fragile mood. "Peace. I want peace."

The maid nodded and left, following the others out of the room. Kasdeya glanced at the wall above the vanity where the mirror used to hang. She stepped closer, placing the shard on her vanity and staring at the wall in a daze. She stared for so long, a crack started to make itself known in the wall.

"I'm seeing things now. What's next? Mother?" she called in a sweet voice. "Mother, is your ghost arriving? I could use some motivation."

She looked at the wall again and frowned. The crack remained. She pried at it and gasped when it slid loose. A hidden panel. Inside rested a thin book. Kasdeya reached for it and flipped through the faded yellow pages. The text was written in Savese.

"A secret journal," she mused.

Kasdeya brought it to her table and opened a drawer. She pulled out her tablets that contained the translation guide. Hours later, she had deciphered the first page.

Kolesta-na Zurg, daughter of the wolf. My mother named me. I was born in the tribe of wolves, daughter of a chief, and yet today, I've become the lowest I've ever been. The king of Ayleth's courtesan. Every hour, every second, is torture, but I endure. I must. For my people, the Uluzar, for my mother. We will succeed in our plan even if it takes years of service on my part. The king may believe he rules, but he will someday see who truly howls.

Kasdeya set the translated sheet down. A slow predatory smile tugged at her lips. She had found something valuable, and if it contained the secrets she thought it did, the Savagelanders would reward her immensely. She simply had to determine how much it was worth.

15

VELAMIR LEANED AGAINST the doorframe of Jax's chamber. The directions to the tunnels were illustrated on a hand-drawn map Coralie had given him earlier. His stomach tightened at the thought of the approaching mission.

"I can't believe you were going to leave without me," Jax grumbled as he tossed items from around the room into a sack. "If the princess hadn't forced you to take us, you would have gone alone."

When Velamir didn't answer, Jax dropped the sack and approached him. He stood before him, lines creasing between his brows.

"Vel? What is going on with you? You haven't spoken to me properly for so long. Ever since—" He halted before forcing out the words: "Ever since the fight with Mordon on the tower, you've been different. What happened up there?"

Velamir broke away from Jax's stare and took a step into the room. "We spent years in that academy. Years of service and dedication, only to be tossed into a manipulative game."

Jax was silent, waiting.

Velamir turned. "Winston never died, Jax. He planned everything. He faked his own death."

Jax paled and retreated a pace. He placed a hand on the bedframe as if to steady himself. His mouth opened, then closed without uttering a word.

Velamir continued, his frustration slipping free. "Lissa was aware of that, and so was Quintus."

Jax flinched at Lissa's name, and Velamir's sympathy broke through. Despite all the warnings and witnessing her ruthless nature with his own eyes, Jax was still in love with her.

"But why?" Jax managed.

"Because he wanted revenge on Boltrex." Velamir paused. "On my father."

Jax froze, shock plain across his face. "Your *father*?"

Velamir nodded, still unable to believe it himself. "All this time, Boltrex was my father. And Winston admitted that my mother is alive as well. That she's in the Tariqin camp. If it's true, I need to get her out of there."

Jax remained speechless as Velamir continued.

"Coralie is sending us for a different reason. Her main focus is to free Mordon, but she believes I can accomplish destroying Winston too. She doesn't trust us fully, though, which is why the others are coming along."

Jax shook his head, brows raised. "You and Mordon are brothers?"

Velamir winced at that disturbing suggestion. "No. If what I heard up on the tower is true, he is Winston's son."

Jax sank onto his bed, staring at the wall across from him with dazed eyes. Two strips of leather crossed his chest to form an X. Sharp tools and small vials had made their home in the slots there. Another belt rested over Jax's hips, and circular objects hung from the side.

"What are those?" Velamir motioned, hoping to draw Jax out of his troubled state.

Jax glanced down. He unhooked one and held it out. "This is Sedelon."

"Sedelon?"

Jax's concern faded to admiration as he stared at his creation. "Yeah. You know the story of the woman who married the first lord of Tariqi? She was very influential. Her own husband wanted to kill her. That's how the Chishma came about. Only, his plans never succeeded. It was her son who became her end." Jax raised a brow. "You don't remember the story, do you?"

Velamir shrugged. He vaguely recalled the tale. The thought of sitting in those classrooms filled with lies and following blindly along made him feel sick. He'd spent years he could never recover there.

"Anyway, she was cast as the villain of the story in Tariqi, considering Prolus was her son. That's why I named it after her." He hooked the invention back onto his belt. "Because now I see the other side. She wasn't trying to be a ruthless monster. She was just trying to survive."

Velamir whispered, "Aren't we all?"

Two guards peered at Velamir with narrowed eyes—the same look most of the castle residents bestowed upon him. He was accustomed to it, and he couldn't blame them. How could they trust him when he represented the Tariqins they hated so much? Coralie was risking her people's loyalty by keeping him and Jax alive. Although Jax seemed to have won most of the citizens' favor.

"I'm here to see the general," Velamir told the guards.

They shared a glance, and one said, "General Boltrex will not be disturbed."

"On whose orders?"

"Mine."

The guards moved aside to reveal General Zenrelius standing in the open doorway of Boltrex's chamber. He stepped forward and closed the door behind him. The general wore a golden tunic over long breeches tucked into well-made boots. His beard was groomed, and his hair was combed back. The golden armbands at his biceps called for attention as they shone in the light of the hallway candelabras.

"As far as I know, your orders are only effective in Ondalar," Velamir said.

Zenrelius gave him a thin smile. "Since Ondalar has come to Verin's aid, we are continuing to help in any way we can, whether it be to act as general in the wounded one's stead or protect the ailing king from Tariqin vermin."

Velamir could sense the general's true aspirations within his words. He wanted control in Verin and was operating under the guise of assisting the kingdom to attain it. Had that been the Ondalarian king's plan when he sent his general? But no . . . As Velamir stared into the man's dark eyes, he detected a cunning there. Zenrelius played by his own rules and made his own moves, like starting small by sacrificing his soldiers like pawns and using them to cross the line that would win him the game.

"Last I checked, we have a king and a general and no need for filler figures."

A flicker of rage raced across Zenrelius's features so fast, Velamir almost missed it. "We?" Zenrelius scoffed. "Who is *we*? Since when did Verin house traitors in their midst? And what do you want with the general at this time of night? To assassinate him, like you attempted before?"

Velamir's fists clenched. The man didn't miss a thing, and he'd clearly done his research. "Why would I murder my own father?"

Zenrelius's brows shot up. "Father? But I heard Winston Raga was your father. A once-respected man who sold out the kingdom to the Dark Lord."

"You seem to be hearing a lot. Someone once told me don't believe the things you hear. They are usually lies and slanders spread by people who have nothing better to do than gossip."

As he spoke, he heard the same words in Bear's voice. His Savorian mentor had said that to him when he was a child. Velamir's heart ached at the remembrance of him. Bear had betrayed him, too, in a way. He must have known Winston's plan. That would explain why he'd been so uneasy when they parted ways all those weeks ago.

Zenrelius stepped closer. "A word of advice: There's always a grain of truth in rumors. If you keep your ears open, you will be prepared for whatever storm comes your way. But if you close yourself off, sheltered in a box, you will be destroyed. I learned that, and with time, you might as well." He paused. "That is, if you live that long."

Velamir opened his mouth, but Zenrelius held up a hand.

"We've said what needed to be said. I forbade visitors from seeing the general because he took his tonic. He will fall into a heavy sleep soon. But by all means, continue. I have no reason to stop you from seeing your *dear father*."

The general brushed past him. Velamir drew in a deep breath and returned his attention to the door. The guards didn't prevent him from entering the large chamber. A boarded window kept out the cold and was further covered by thick curtains. Silver engraving etched the moldings along the walls. A large bed formed the center of the chamber, a narrow table holding a goblet and linen beside it.

Velamir approached the bed slowly. Boltrex's eyes were closed, and sweat trailed from his brow. Velamir stopped beside the bed, staring down at him. A silence lingered until Velamir cleared his throat and the words he'd been keeping within himself the past week slipped free.

"I wanted to kill you," Velamir whispered. "For a time, that was the only thing urging me forward. And now, to know you were the one missing from my life . . ." His jaw clenched, and he took a linen from the stack beside the goblet. "It's not easy for me to accept you. I don't know if I ever truly can."

Velamir stared down at the man he had considered an enemy. His mission called to him. Jax and the others were waiting, but he couldn't have left without seeing Boltrex. He wanted to remember him differently, not as the man he hated, but as the man he could've loved. Boltrex's tunic was open at the chest, and Velamir could see a harsh burn marring the skin there. It was faded with time, making him wonder how Boltrex had received such a severe wound. Velamir reached out, wiping the sweat gathering at Boltrex's brow. A hand shot out and circled his forearm. Velamir stiffened, and Boltrex's eyes opened. They were a hazy green, lighter than usual under the influence of the tonic. Boltrex mumbled. His other hand fumbled at his hip, searching for a sword that wasn't there. Then he focused on Velamir, and the tenseness in his body faded.

"Alaric."

Velamir pulled his arm free and placed the linen back on the table. "How's your wound?"

Boltrex grimaced at the mention of it, and Velamir recalled Winston driving the dagger through his back with the curdling smile of victory on his face—the smile of hatred, the smile of a man Velamir didn't know.

"It's tolerable," Boltrex rasped. "But the wound that

troubles me isn't there." He dragged his hand over his chest, over his heart. "It's here."

Velamir stayed silent.

Boltrex's eyes fluttered as he struggled to remain conscious. "At one time, Winston was like a brother to me. We went through hardships, faced many obstacles together. Until we fell in love with the same woman. That was when a chasm formed between us."

Velamir listened. Part of him wanted to leave, but another part needed to know the truth. The truth about who Winston was.

"Saphira was King Dale's niece. She was beautiful and bold. Those who laid eyes on her were struck." Boltrex's expression was distant, his voice soft. "She cared for me, and once her feelings were clear, Winston noticed. He despised me for it. He ended up in King Dale's good favors and won her hand in marriage. I was distraught, furious. But I was forced to cope with it. When I saved Castle Verin from a Savagelander attack, King Dale acknowledged my assistance by marrying me to his other niece, Saphira's twin, Serana." He spoke her name in a longing whisper.

"With time, I grew to love and cherish her. She had loved me even while knowing I had feelings for her sister. Winston moved from the castle after his marriage to live on his estate with Saphira. The few times I saw her, she looked lost and unhappy. I knew something was wrong but didn't interfere in their life. I was content at the time with Serana and the baby we were expecting. Your sister, Aria."

Velamir grew uneasy at the mention of a sister. The

tale Boltrex told seemed to be about someone else, someone unknown to Velamir. In his mind, he couldn't possibly be a puzzle piece that fit into all of it.

"Years passed, and I suspected Winston of treachery but never had proof. You were born, and Winston had a son shortly after. Cselnsor was his name."

Velamir's head lifted. That was the same name that had been engraved on the chest in Winston's manor. The one Winston had seemed so despondent at seeing. Velamir understood why. It had belonged to his son.

"I learned through a letter from a close friend that Winston worked for Prolus. I had planned to use the letter as proof of his betrayal, but my friend was framed for treason shortly after. The letter of a traitor was meaningless. I had no choice but to keep silent, only barely managing to save my friend from the noose. Although, he might have preferred that to the long miserable days he'd suffered in the dungeon. Saphira came to me around that time. She snuck into the castle and confirmed my friend's words. Winston was a traitor."

Velamir touched his neck where the pendant rested. He considered giving it to Boltrex. It had belonged to his friend, after all, but then his fingers curled around it. He'd promised to take it himself.

Boltrex carried on, his face years away. "I told her to stay in Castle Verin with her uncle, but she refused. She forcefully gave me her son, made me swear to keep him safe. I didn't know what to do." His regret was clear. "Once she left, I received news that my fortress had been attacked. When I got there . . ." His throat bobbed. "I was too late. It was the worst day of my life."

Though Boltrex was stoic as he forced the words out, a tear escaped his eye. Velamir's jaw tightened as he listened in silence. How could Winston have been so heartless? To place a woman and children on a stake? To convince Boltrex of his family's death? What kind of person would do something like that?

A sick person. Winston was sick.

"I believed Savagelanders were behind the attack after seeing their uniforms on some of the dead. I was compelled to leave the fortress, knowing their forces would return to claim the place for good. I remained in Castle Verin from then on. I raised Saphira's son as my own. No one said anything, most assuming him to be you. I considered the possibility and almost changed his name to Alaric. But I couldn't. No one could replace you, Son. No one." Boltrex glanced up at Velamir. "Every time I looked at him, I remembered the son I'd lost."

Velamir couldn't hold his gaze and stared at the wall instead.

"So, I changed his name to Mordon. On the outside, I remained a strong general, but within, I was burning, suffocating. The ones I lived for were gone. I wanted to die and recklessly endangered my life many times. How humorous it is that I wanted to die for so long, and now that I've found the will to live, I'm lying here with a mortal wound?" He chuckled and then grimaced, placing a hand on his side. His eyes grew distant. "If there's a chance she's alive . . ."

Velamir knew he was speaking of Serana. He stepped closer. "Princess Coralie has tasked me with infiltrating the camp. If she's there, I will get her out."

"My boy, what a man you've become."

Velamir fidgeted, uncomfortable with the praise.

Boltrex's brow furrowed. "Mordon bears no responsibility for the way these events have come to pass. He's lost. He needs to be shown the way. They say Winston took him captive. Alaric, you must take him from there. He is your family too. You are cousins."

Velamir had never liked Mordon, but he hadn't hated him either. In fact, during those last moments with him, he had come to pity him. Besides, Coralie had ordered him to rescue Mordon from the camp. Her eyes had flashed when she made the request, and Velamir had recognized the underlying desperation in them. "I will."

"Good," Boltrex said softly as the fog returned to his eyes. He blinked again, fighting the impending sleep. "Your sword. It was always meant to be yours."

Velamir frowned at the cryptic words. He glanced at his sword, grasping the hilt.

"It was always . . ." Boltrex's voice trailed off into incoherent mumbles.

Velamir remained by Boltrex's bedside and watched him lose the battle to sleep. A knock on the door startled him. Velamir turned, and a guard peered inside.

"The Shadow Manos is asking for you."

Velamir nodded. It was time to leave.

CORALIE SAT ON the stool beside her uncle's grand curtained bed. His chest rose and fell with labored breaths, and sweat dotted his hairline. Her brows lowered as she examined him. Instead of recovering, he only seemed to get worse. *He won't survive this sickness*, a True Manos had told her earlier. Her uncle was dying. It was not a question, only a matter of when.

Coralie stood and left the chamber with a need to shake off the restlessness burdening her. She entered the barracks, taking her sword with her. She knew Jovinne was near, her silent shadow, watching over her but not encroaching on her privacy. She practiced moves she had done a thousand times before. Her sword slashed through the air, cutting down invisible enemies.

Coralie let her worries fade and focused solely on the blade in her hands. The intricate metal was beautiful to look at and yet so deadly, it could take a life in a blink. Many blamed weapons for the bloodshed and death in the world, but Coralie knew they were just tools. The real villains were the people who wielded them. Deep down, everyone had a darkness. The true battle was fighting against it and doing what was right. One could use these tools to conjure fear and destruction or to protect and inspire justice.

Coralie thrust her sword forward into a target. She heaved harsh breaths, perspiration soaking her over-heated skin. She snatched her blade free and strode out into the open courtyard cast in the night's shadows. Snow drifted around her, falling onto her face and cooling her skin. The guards opened the main gates for her, and she stared at the raised drawbridge before taking the stairs up the ramparts to view the damage to Verintown. She placed her palms on the cold stone between the crenellations and peered at the burned town below, untouched by healing hands, like an abandoned ghost of the lively place it had been before.

A gust of wind lifted her braids as she looked over the snow-covered ruins. No one was trying to repair it. Advisor Welix, who was attempting to take her uncle's place and act as regent, had given no orders. He didn't see a reason to fix the town when the fires of the Tariqin camp rested mere days' walk away. Another attack would come soon, so why rebuild? But Coralie had seen the remaining soldiers, the citizens. Their morale was depleted and growing worse and worse because of the surrounding wreckage. That needed to change, because the next time the Tariqins attacked, they had to be ready, or they would be extinguished as easily as a single candle flame.

Coralie looked up at the moon, admiring the pink glow around the edges with a pang of wistfulness. A pembin moon. It seemed fitting for it to come at such a time of darkness. Coralie smiled and fiddled with the ring enclosing her thumb.

SIX YEARS EARLIER

Coralie couldn't survive the ball a moment longer. The perfumes and sweat of congregated people mingling in the air made it harder for her to breathe than her tightly fastened gown. Verin's balls hadn't been that terrible on her past visits. She grimaced and closed her eyes. Only, it wasn't a mere visit. It was a permanent welcoming. King Dale was hosting it for her, his new ward. Coralie's chest tightened, and she broke away from the crowded ballroom, escaping onto a nearby balcony. The breeze fanned her heated face. She gripped the balcony's cold railing. Night darkened the town below. Her view was lit by the torches the guards held as they circled the town, watching for signs of danger.

"You must be the guest of honor."

Coralie spun and searched wildly for the speaker. Her eyes landed on a man hidden among the shadows. He stepped closer, and the moon's light fell on his face. He was tall, with black hair and dark eyes, and he was more of a boy, maybe around her age. One of his dark brows raised.

"Do I meet your approval?"

Coralie blinked, realizing she had been staring too long, but did not feel embarrassed. "You are lacking in some regards."

It was his turn to blink. "Lacking?" he repeated.

"For one, your hair is far too short, and your nose has a dent in it."

He ran a hand over his cropped hair and then touched his nose. "This is the style everyone wears in the Empire, and my nose was broken a few weeks ago."

"What happened? Did you run into a wall?" Coralie smirked.

"More like a fist." He chuckled. "Someone was making comments about my father, and well . . . let's just say he won't be saying anything else." His face darkened, and he stepped back into the shadows again. "What are you doing here? The party is for you."

"I don't like parties."

He scoffed. "That's a first. All the girls I know like them."

"You know many girls, then?"

"Jealous?"

Coralie made a disgusted noise. "Of course not. I don't even know you."

He gave a dramatic bow. "Mordon, at your service."

Coralie curtsied in reply, although she did not want to. He seemed to enjoy making a joke out of serious matters. She had never met a more aggravating person. "I am Princess—"

"Coralie."

"It's rude to interrupt people," she told him, glancing down. He had a bucket by his feet. "What's that?"

"A little prank. Nothing that would excite a princess."

Coralie crossed her arms. "I will be the judge of that."

He smiled, his teeth shining in the dark. Coralie's chest felt strange, like something warm fluttered inside. She longed to press a hand over the spot to quell the feeling but kept her posture rigid and hands folded demurely before her.

"As you wish, Your Highness." Mordon dragged the bucket closer to the balcony edge.

She stared into it and glanced at him inquisitively. "Eso paint? What will you do with that?"

His smile stretched wider, and he motioned for her to watch. He lifted the bucket and waited a moment before tossing some of the paint over the edge. Coralie gasped and leaned over the railing, watching the green liquid splatter onto a well-dressed nobleman. He looked up, howling his rage. Mordon grabbed her wrist, jerking her back. His mischievous smile made him appear even younger.

"Are you insane?" Coralie exclaimed, eyes wide. "Eso paint won't come off for weeks." But even she couldn't help the smile fighting to break free.

"I told you it wouldn't be amusing to a princess. Especially one like you."

"One like me?" Coralie placed her hands on her hips.

He shrugged. "Elegant, pretty, too good for everyone else." He kept rambling on until he noticed her smiling, then frowned. "What?"

"You think I'm pretty."

"Sure, I'd have to be blind not to notice. Besides, being pretty doesn't mean anything when there's nothing here." He tapped his head. "And especially when you don't have courage."

She huffed. "I have plenty of both."

"Really?" He stepped closer, holding up the bucket. "Then I challenge you to toss this on the next person who comes by below. I bet my ring you could never do it."

Coralie glanced at Mordon's hand. A ring with a noble insignia circled his pinky finger. He gave her a crooked grin as she snatched the bucket from him, longing to slap his smile off his face. Coralie spun away toward the railing. One of her uncle's captains stumbled to a halt right below. He swayed, and she wrinkled her nose. He was drunk and perfectly in line with the bucket.

"It's now or never," Mordon whispered.

Coralie took a deep breath. She couldn't back out. She thrust the bucket forward, and a large amount of paint flew out, falling like a waterfall onto the captain. He shouted and rubbed a hand over himself, smearing the paint further. He looked like a crazed man, patting himself and turning in wild circles. Coralie giggled. She couldn't help it. Her laugh grew and grew, and when she glanced at Mordon, he was staring at her. He was laughing, too, a broad smile on his face.

"Hey, you!" the drunk man called up.

Mordon placed a hand over her lips. "Shh."

His hand was gone before she could register it. They crouched and waited a few minutes. Mordon looked up, and Coralie followed his gaze. The pembin moon glowed down on them.

"They say the pembin moon is really just the shadow of Astarolos, the king of the Old Empire. He had riches, a title, everything he could've wanted except one thing. The woman he loved."

Coralie knew the story, but there was something mesmerizing about the way Mordon told it.

"He made a deal with the shadows to attain her, but he became cursed and eventually a shadow himself. He returns twice a year in the pembin moon. They say the curse will break if he says her name, but because of his pride, he refuses. He was king; he should only need himself to be free. He can't accept his savior as anyone else."

Coralie spoke softly. "So he'll remain cursed for the rest of eternity."

Mordon glanced back at her, looking surprised. He watched her intently until the warmth in her chest returned and she stood.

"I should get back," she said, brushing her skirt. "My uncle might be searching for me."

"Wait," he called, and she turned back. He slid the ring from his pinky finger. "You earned it."

Coralie smiled and accepted it before trying it on all her fingers, but it was too large. She ended up placing the ring on her thumb and closing it in her fist. She peered up at him. His lips tilted upward slightly. Coralie started to smile back, but then he looked over her head, and his *eyes darkened. She turned to see General Boltrex watching them from the balcony doorway. Mordon strode past her without a word. Coralie was left startled by the abrupt change in his demeanor, but she brushed it off, looking down at her new ring. It wasn't very expensive, and yet it meant more to her than all the jewels she owned.*

Coralie closed her fist. The ring fit snugly around her thumb. The playful boy she'd met that night had disappeared, becoming the brooding, rage-filled man she knew. But she hoped she might find him again under all the layers he covered himself with. She *would* find him again, even if she had to wait all of eternity. She stared at the pembin moon and whispered his name.

17

"What are you looking at, *dsell?*"

Mordon jumped at the voice, tearing his gaze from the pembin moon and the thoughts and doubts restraining him. He glanced at the sweaty Savorian who had spoken. The Handler's blond hair hung in oily strands to his mid-back, tangled and wild. A long sack the length of a body rested at his feet. Mordon held one of the same size over his shoulder.

Mordon shrugged. "Nothing."

"If we don't feed the rumloks on time, we will end up being their meal." He gave Mordon a sidelong glance as he hefted the bag. "Or at least I will be."

Mordon ignored the implication and followed the Handler to the third and final cage. Chains around his boots cuffed his ankles—

an assurance that he wouldn't attempt escape. The cold was bitter enough that even with his boots, his feet felt like two blocks of ice trudging through the snow. Despite days of menial tasks, he hadn't been deemed loyal enough to have the shackles removed. Mordon glanced at the man slogging before him. Out of everyone in the camp, Mordon had been around him the most, and he still didn't know his name. He'd asked him once, but the man hadn't told him.

Handler is good enough, the Savorian had replied. *The man I was before died with my homeland.*

Mordon understood him. He had no hope for a future and a hatred for the past. Mordon had been the same way and still was except in one aspect. He was looking forward to the future—a time when he would prove himself to everyone who had doubted him, who had put him down, who had made his world torture.

"Coming, *dsell*?" the Handler asked, placing a ladder at the edge of the cage.

Mordon quickened his pace, wincing at the pain in his frozen toes. "Stop calling me that."

"It suits you." The Handler grinned. It was a rare sight, and though it contained several missing teeth, it brightened Mordon's spirits. Mordon had asked the Savorian what the word meant, but he'd refused to tell him. Finally, another Savorian had explained it to him, an older man the others called Bear.

It means crazy, lad. He's saying you've lost your senses.

I will make him senseless if he keeps doing it.

Bear had exchanged a look with the Savorians gathered around. *They're all calling you that. Consider it a word of praise, lad.*

"You're dozing off," the Handler said. "Move unawares, and the next thing you know, a rumlok bites your arm off."

The Handler climbed the ladder and hefted the sack over with a grunt. A guttural noise and the snapping of teeth followed. Mordon stepped closer to the cage, peering through the metal holes at the feasting rumloks. They ripped into the dismembered body like they'd been starving for days. The intensity of their movements kept him riveted in place until the Handler motioned for his sack. Mordon's muscles strained as he tugged the sack off his shoulder and lifted it up to him. The sack was thrown in moments later. Sprinkles of blood escaped the confines of the cage and speckled his face. Mordon wiped the red beads off.

The Handler came down from the ladder. "They're something, aren't they? *Kuriled.*"

Mordon glanced at him, and the man explained, "*Cursed.* That's what we Savorians call these creatures. They are not rumloks any longer. Not to us."

"How were the rumloks in Savoria?"

The Handler shrugged and scratched at the scar on his cheek that stretched into a big H, the long spidery lines of which faded to a light pink. All the Handlers had the same mark. Mordon assumed it was to distinguish them from the other Savorians.

"They didn't eat people, for one."

Mordon found it disgusting that the rumloks were fed humans—ones who had displeased Prolus, in particular. But, he had to admit, it wasn't a bad method to get rid of useless people, and it kept the beasts fed.

"They would eat rabbits and usually fish. They were friendly." The Handler smiled. "And they protected the family they bonded with until death."

"How did they become part of the family?"

"Rumloks bond with the first human that feeds them. They have a connection. Here." He pointed at his head. "You can speak with them."

Mordon thought of the red-eyed rumlok, the large one with black fur. He spotted it in the throng of rumloks surrounding the human remains. Had he really heard the voice, then? But how was that possible? He wasn't the first to feed it, and he hadn't even fed it during that time.

"They were like friends," the Handler said, a touch of longing in his words. "But the ones here are animals. They're lost."

"Because of the concoctions in their food," Mordon surmised. "Isn't it?"

The Handler nodded. "They are fed the vile stuff from a young age. It makes their minds weak, which allows them to be controlled by any Handler."

"So, why do you drink the vials?" Mordon asked, nodding to the Savorian's belt.

"Because it isn't normal to control rumloks this way. We have to use unnatural methods to attain their minds." He glanced around them. "None of this is natural. These things, the potions, they come from Devorin. They say the ice witch makes them."

Mordon frowned, and the Savorian's eyes darted around once again. They were alone except for the caged rumloks and the thick shadow of night. Soft flakes of snow flitted around them, tangling in the Savorian's light lashes and highlighting his wide icy blue gaze.

"The queen of Devorin."

Mordon laughed. "Why would she help Prolus? She's Imperial, loyal to the emperor."

The Savorian retained his stony look, and Mordon's laugh faded. "A person would do anything to maintain their standing."

The queen of Devorin was a subject of gossip among many in the Empire. Mordon hadn't cared to discuss her, but even he knew of her mysterious air. She was queen, but no one knew *who* she was or what had become of her husband. Devorin was a kingdom whose secrets were covered in more than layers of snow. As far as Mordon knew, Emperor Malus didn't care what she did as long as she paid the yearly taxes. Could she truly have been helping Prolus? After all the new truths Mordon had learned, it didn't seem far-fetched.

The black rumlok turned toward Mordon and prowled close until only the wall of the metal cage separated them.

"That one's hard to break," the Savorian said. "Since his birth, his mind has been difficult to control, no matter how many potions he's fed."

Mordon stared at the beast. *Can you hear me?*

A surge of embarrassment washed over him, and he shot a quick glance at the Handler to ensure he hadn't noticed his attempt to communicate with the rumlok.

"That's why he's in the third cage with the worst ones," the Handler said.

The rumlok snorted, a gust of air fanning from his nostrils. His red eyes gleamed at Mordon.

Your order.

The words came faintly, like a soft whisper in his ear. Mordon stiffened and glanced again at the Handler, but the Savorian remained untroubled.

Your order.

Mordon banished the thought. All their talk of rumloks and obedience was getting to his head. Although, he wouldn't have minded having one of his own. It would be useful when he was king someday. While he wouldn't feed them humans . . . Mordon smiled, thinking of Prince Draven. He could make an exception.

The sound of claws and scrambling snagged his attention, and his eyes grew wide at the sight of the black rumlok climbing the cage and taking a leaping jump over. The Handler shouted beside him, fumbling for a vial at his belt.

Stop! Mordon screamed internally. *Stop.*

The rumlok pounced on the Savorian, whose cries broke off as he stared up at the beast atop him in horror.

Your order?

The voice was clear as day. The rumlok's head swiveled to meet his gaze.

Get off, Mordon told him in his head.

The rumlok hesitated, its muscles bunching as it leaned over the Handler. Saliva escaped the big beast's mouth, but he looked again at Mordon and then slowly pulled back.

Good boy, Mordon thought. *Back in the cage. Now.*

The rumlok whined pitifully, then jumped back

over the impossibly high cage wall. Mordon waited to ensure the rumlok wouldn't try anything else and then approached the Handler lying on the ground.

"H-how?" the Savorian stuttered, staring at him with wide eyes. "You were controlling it."

Mordon extended a hand down to him. "You can start repaying me by giving me your name."

The Savorian glanced at his hand and then back at him before clasping it. "Silopar."

Mordon hauled him to his feet. "Welcome back, Silopar."

18

Karalik Empire
Hearcross
The Grand Palace

Honzio stared at the corpses sprawled around the tunnel entrance. The hatch was open. The large rock that had covered it before rested feet away, splattered with blood. The soldiers shuffled uneasily, the flickering torches they held lighting the dark alley. Honzio couldn't blame them for their anxiety. It wasn't every day one saw lifeless children.

Honzio's decoy, Bronus, pulled himself up and out of the tunnel. He shook his head. "Two men, one woman. All dead."

Honzio grimaced, closing his eyes. There had been thirty-two people in the safe house. Honzio had counted eight children and one woman among the bodies aboveground. That tallied twenty people Vykus had taken.

And all were lives Honzio had lost. All were people he'd failed to save. He opened his eyes to find the soldiers staring at him. He straightened. It wasn't the time to put his emotions on display. He had to be the silent, brooding prince they knew.

"Bury the bodies."

"With all due respect, Your Highness," Captain Theris said, "the emperor ordered us to destroy what was left and erase all traces of these runaways."

Honzio glanced at Bronus. His bodyguard signaled for him to back down. Honzio gave him a slight nod. He couldn't go against his father. Not yet. He couldn't risk his father retaliating if word got back to him.

"Fine. Be quick," Honzio said, swallowing the bile rising in his throat.

The soldiers moved fast, dragging the bodies to the hole and dropping them in like sacks of potatoes. They wanted to wipe their hands of the situation. Captain Theris dropped his torch into the hole, lighting the bodies with an irretrievable flame. Honzio turned, unable to think of those innocent children who had suffered and even then, after death, would remain nameless, faceless, and forgotten.

Honzio strode away, walking until he no longer heard the crackling flames and the smell of burning flesh. A glance behind him revealed no one had followed. He exhaled and thumped his head against the alley wall. He stayed like that for a long moment, hating himself, until a distant moan caught his attention. Honzio pushed off the wall and approached the origin of the sound with tense steps. He spotted a crumpled form at the end of the alley, though the dark night obscured most of the body from view.

He kneeled beside the figure, reaching out with his good arm to turn them over. A long braid concealed the person's face. Honzio's fingers were hesitant as he brushed the braid aside. Prominent cheekbones highlighted with smears of blood, full lips, and a pointed chin. It was Aylis. Her eyes were closed. Honzio pressed his head to her chest, checking for a heartbeat. It felt like an eternity had passed before her chest finally rose, and she inhaled a harsh staggered breath. Honzio straightened, scanning her for wounds as best as he could in the dark. His good hand trailed over her until he touched something wet—blood.

Honzio placed his arm under her and lifted her halfway from the ground. His teeth clenched, and the muscles in his arm strained with the effort. He couldn't do it alone. Honzio glanced at his mangled right arm and swore. He was half a man and a useless one at that.

"Your Highness?"

Honzio froze at the voice. He turned, and relief seeped in at the sight of his bodyguard. Bronus peered at him, torch in hand.

"Take this girl and deliver her to the palace in secret. Bring her to my chambers and retrieve Manos Cerel."

Bronus nodded and hefted Aylis in his arms as easily as if she were a feather. Honzio gritted his teeth, attempting to crush the envy that sprouted within him. The soldiers' distant voices grew closer.

"They are searching for you," Bronus said.

"Go. I will see you at the palace."

While Bronus disappeared into the next alley, Honzio regrouped with the soldiers. Upon returning to the palace, Honzio was summoned by the emperor. He entered his father's vast chambers, where Malus lay sprawled across an enormous divan. A chained Savorian woman poured him a glass of zat. Tears rolled down her face, and fingerprints marked her skin. Honzio's fists clenched, and he heaved in a breath. *Ignore it.* It was nothing he hadn't seen before. The thrumming anger in his chest reluctantly subsided.

"Give me the news," Malus said.

"We announced the price for Vykus's head. There will be hunters after him."

Malus took a swig of zat. "And the shelter?"

"Burned." Honzio had to force the word past his lips.

"Excellent." Malus jerked on the Savorian woman's chain, pulling her closer. "Pour another."

Her hands trembled as she poured zat into his goblet, and a sob burst from her. Honzio clenched his jaw but otherwise forced himself to remain a statue.

"I hate the sound of tears." Malus slapped her across the face. "And you cannot even pour the zat properly!"

She cried out, collapsing on the divan. The drunken emperor hovered over her, evil intent in his eyes. Honzio stepped forward, taking the chain from his hands.

"She should be disciplined."

The emperor held Honzio's gaze for a long moment before nodding. "Twenty lashes and her thumbnails."

Honzio jerked her up roughly, putting on a show for his father. He dragged her from the chamber while her cries stirred the guilt circling his queasy insides. He pulled her through the halls. Bronus encountered him and nodded, wordlessly conveying what Honzio needed to know. Honzio handed him the chain.

"Take the restraints off and tell the cooks to give her kitchen duty."

The girl's crying ceased at Honzio's words, and she stared at him with glistening eyes. She glanced back several times as Bronus propelled her past Honzio and down the hall, his grip gentle. Honzio stared after them. He hadn't done much, but at least he'd done something for her.

Honzio entered his own chamber. The mask that formed a solid shield around him fell. There, he could cut the act and be as broken as he wanted. And then he remembered he wasn't alone. Aylis lay on his bed, her still form covered by thick blankets. Honzio took a hesitant step in her direction, but then a scrap of paper caught his eye, and he approached his desk instead.

I closed and stitched her wound. She should be up soon. I left a tonic. —Manos Cerel

Cerel was one of the few people in the palace Honzio fully trusted. She had kept many of his secret endeavors confidential. Honzio sank into the cushioned chair before the desk, and his hand drifted to a drawer. He sifted under official papers until he found what he was looking for: a miniature painting of himself, Thorsten, and Hesten. Natassa had been so young when she painted it. He'd been newly injured and bitter. She thought the painting would make him feel better. Honzio closed his eyes, remembering how he'd flung it across the room when she'd given it to him. Later, when he'd gone to bed, he found it on his pillow. She hadn't given up on him.

At the sound of muttering, he glanced at Aylis. She gripped the thick blankets with a vengeance. Her brows lowered as she continued to mumble in her sleep. It sounded like a name. Honzio scooted his chair closer and leaned in.

"Thorsten," she murmured. "Thorsten."

Natassa had told him how much Thorsten loved Aylis. It seemed she returned the affection. She was sort of pretty, even with the scar cutting her lip. He could see why Thorsten had favored her. But he had a problem on his hands. He had to keep her hidden from the prying palace eyes and especially from his father. She groaned and thrashed under the blankets. Honzio stood, leaning over her. Her eyes opened, and an icy coldness rushed through him. She grabbed hold of his collar and yanked him closer until they were inches apart. Her pale blue eyes gleamed a warning.

"*You,*" she hissed.

19

Natassa followed the voices, taking careful steps to ensure she didn't fall or make a sound. She could make out Krea's faint outline beside her in the dark. So far, Velamir and his companions hadn't noticed them. She spotted the glow of torches ahead; they had drawn too close. She stilled, grabbing Krea's hand in a silent cue to stop.

"The guards posted at the end of the tunnel will begin sealing the entrance once we pass through." The voice belonged to Finnean.

As someone responded to him, worry pooled within Natassa. If the guards spotted them, they wouldn't allow her and Krea to leave. The voices ahead faded. Natassa released Krea's hand, and they resumed the trek forward. A strange feeling in her gut told her something was amiss. She peered into the darkness, searching for an orange glow. As she focused, her breathing became loud to her own ears. Natassa stared ahead, eyes widening when she glimpsed silver light. It flashed toward her. She slammed against the tunnel wall. A gasp slipped past her lips as she struggled to break free. Someone gripped her wrist and pinned it above her head. Cold metal brushed her neck, and her breathing grew shallow. The person held a dagger to her throat.

"Let me go," she ordered, her heart pounding with fear. "Release me!"

Her captor inhaled, and the dagger lowered. But their looming presence didn't retreat, and her arm remained trapped above her head. Muffled shrieking sounded in the dark, and worry for Krea struck her.

"Kasdeya?" The warm cadence oozed over her.

"Velamir?"

He didn't reply, but Natassa knew it was him. Since the fear in her stomach had settled, she sensed other things, like the familiar scent of cedar and musk that emanated from him.

"Jax!" he called. "Come out. We caught the pursuers."

The glow of torches appeared, revealing a turn in the tunnel ahead. Latimus and Jax came into view. As they moved closer, the torches bathed the tunnel in warm, bright light. Latimus frowned at the sight of her, and Jax's mouth opened in a surprised O. Natassa glanced over Velamir's shoulder. Krea was clasped in Finnean's arms, one of his hands over her mouth and the other restraining her. Finnean dropped his hold, and Krea glared at him.

Velamir peered down at Natassa, his green eyes glowing. His nearness was overwhelming, reminding her of the vision she'd had—the one where he'd taken her hand and smiled at her so warmly that just the memory of it increased the already rapid pace of her thumping heart. She fought the urge to hug him, to confide her fears, her doubts, and even the new feelings sprouting up within. But she could never do that. Not when he didn't even know who she was. She had deceived him, and nothing could be built from lies.

"What are you doing here, Kasdeya?"

The whisper of her false name struck her like an arrow. He leaned closer, and air escaped her lungs, leaving her breathless. She broke contact and looked up at her caged arm.

"Can you let me go?" She tried to add force to her command, but the words came out softly.

He dropped her wrist like it were a branding iron and retreated a pace. Her frozen lungs remembered to breathe.

"I apologize." His eyes probed hers for answers. The stubble that covered his jaw was growing out, as was his hair. The torchlight highlighted the brown strands. He was so different compared to the men she'd known, the admirers who'd gathered around her, seeing her as a means to heighten their status. Even with the law prohibiting marriage to the emperor's children unless one was of noble blood, they lingered, flocking around her, lavishing attention and exaggerated compliments onto her. Their words and true intentions had been plain to see in the greed on their faces and their soft uncalloused hands pressing together as they thought of their plans. But all that finally ceased when the rumors of her father pledging her to Prince Draven had spread.

Velamir's heart was void of evil intent, of plots and deceit. She had seen it in the way he cared for her when he rescued her from Vykus's mercenaries. He'd treated her well when he thought she was nothing but a handmaiden. Would that change if he knew who she truly was?

The loud clearing of a throat broke the moment. Natassa blinked, darting a glance at Jax and Latimus. The latter was clearly the source of the noise.

"We . . ." Natassa said, "we followed you."

"We are aware of that." Latimus's tone was dry and irritated.

Velamir shot him a glance and motioned for Natassa to continue.

"We heard you speaking with Princess Coralie and learned you would use the tunnels to leave the castle. We knew we wouldn't be allowed through the gates. We had to follow you to find the tunnel."

"Where are you heading?"

"Devorin," Natassa blurted. "I—" She stopped, casting a panicked look at Krea. "I mean, we have family there."

Krea nodded. "Our great-aunt. We used to live with her before becoming the princess's decoys." She said the lie so easily, Natassa almost believed it herself.

Velamir glanced between them. "Why now? Wait until the war settles. It's too dangerous."

"We may die before it's over. We must go."

Velamir looked at Jax, who shrugged. He turned back to Natassa. "Stay with us. We can part ways when we are near the mountains."

Natassa shook her head. "We will go on our own. We would be a burden to you."

But Velamir insisted, "It's safer to travel in a bigger group."

"We will hinder your mission."

"Please, don't fight this."

Natassa saw Krea nodding and sighed. "Fine. Just until we approach the mountains."

A flicker of a smile tugged at Velamir's mouth.

"Are you actually considering this?" Latimus's whisper was cutting.

Velamir faced him. "I'm not considering. It's decided. Kasdeya and her sister will accompany us."

Latimus sneered. "You aren't in charge here, Velamir. This isn't the time for one of your heroic acts. We should cast a vote."

"Then you would find yourself outnumbered."

Finnean and Jax nodded, showing where their allegiance lay.

"Spare yourself the embarrassment," Velamir finished.

Latimus's scowl broadened, and he gave Natassa a dirty look. But without another word, he turned his back on them and marched forward. Natassa shook off the tension from the encounter and fell into a walk beside Krea. The group set off, and when they'd finally reached the end of the tunnel, Velamir exchanged words with the guards stationed there.

It was dark outside, but the pembin moon lit their

path. They walked for hours. Natassa's feet ached, and the cold seeped into her skin. The cloaks Krea had obtained for them provided little warmth, even less so when flakes of snow soaked into the fabric. She wrapped her arms around herself, fighting off shivers. A grunt came from behind her, and then Latimus spoke.

"If only we had horses, it would have made the trip bearable."

"The princess wasn't willing to risk exposing the mission. We would have been noticed if we had taken our horses," Velamir told him.

Natassa stumbled to a stop at the sound of a squeal, then froze entirely, listening. The shrieking continued, and she separated from the group, following the noise to a tiny form by a tree. Her shoes sank into the snow as she approached it. She kneeled beside the animal. It was a fuzzy little thing, with tufts of fur running along its small body. Its eyes were shut tight above a pointy beak. Natassa's heart wrenched for the poor thing. She unhooked her cloak, smoothing it over the snow before reaching for the animal. Its fur had frozen into points, and when she held it, her fingers grew numb.

"Shh, you'll be okay." She placed the bird into her cloak and wrapped it tight.

"Empire's sake, what is that thing?"

The crunch of snow neared as the others approached. Latimus reached her first, his face twisted with disgust. "That's the ugliest creature I've ever seen."

"It's a Sirchoba," Jax whispered, awed.

"A messenger bird?" Latimus raised an eyebrow.

"But they're extinct, and that looks nothing like the drawings."

"The Tariqin Shadow Manos were experimenting with different breeds of birds in hopes of resurrecting the Sirchoba," Jax explained. "This is a hatchling. Its wings haven't sprouted yet. That's why it looks like that. But I've never heard of one surviving."

"Damn Tariqins. They have a hand in everything." Latimus shook his head and cursed. "What's dead should stay dead."

"Or maybe now they'll have the chance to live," Jax said softly. "They were killed on sight in the early years, persecuted along with Shadow Manos because they were seen as their symbol."

Natassa looked down at the Sirchoba. Its cries had quieted.

"What's it doing in the Empire, then?" Latimus asked. "Prolus must be using these birds. If one of his twisted Shadow Manos's experiments has survived, it's up to us to destroy it."

Latimus unsheathed his dagger, and Natassa recoiled, gripping the Sirchoba tighter. Latimus's eyes locked on the bird in her arms, and he took a step forward. Velamir blocked his path, and Natassa stiffened as a dangerous tension formed over the group.

"Latimus." The name was whispered in a seething tone. "Take a walk."

Latimus hesitated, as if weighing the odds, before trudging off.

"Let's take a short break here," Velamir told the rest of them.

The tension slowly drained as Krea and Finnean fell into a conversation and pulled Jax into their group. Natassa stared at the sleeping Sirchoba before glancing up. Velamir's emerald gaze connected with hers, and the stiffness in his brow smoothed. For a moment, it was just the two of them. Finnean's mumbled conversation with Krea dimmed. Jax's rare laugh faded. Latimus's anger receded. It was just them. Two people trying to find their way in a world full of evil. Their paths were uncertain, but maybe if they stopped trying to fight alone, they could overcome it. Then the Sirchoba awoke, screaming out a cry, and the moment broke apart. She looked down at the bird and smiled when one of its tiny claws poked through her cloak.

"Do you know what they eat?" she asked Velamir as he kneeled beside her.

"Jax will know."

A heavy wind blew over them. Natassa shuddered. Velamir leaned closer before tugging his cloak off and pulling it over her shoulders. She opened her mouth to refuse but then stilled at the sudden warmth enveloping her. Velamir closed the clasp, his fingers brushing her chin as he did.

"But you'll be cold."

He smiled, the corners of his mouth rising in a soft look that matched the kindness in his eyes. "I can endure the cold if it means you won't freeze."

A rush of boots snared their attention. Latimus approached, concern on his face. "We need to find shelter. There's a storm closing in."

Finnean spoke up. "I know a cave nearby."

They followed him. Natassa bundled the Sirchoba into her pack, leaving an opening. Wind pressed on her back, and the snow grew thicker, obscuring the way forward.

"Hurry!" Finnean called. "The cave is just ahead."

The air became treacherous, gathering gusts of snow around them and concealing their path with a curtain of white. Hail pelted them. Natassa winced as the hard ice grazed her cheek. Her boot sank into a hole under a mound of snow, and her ankle twisted. She gasped, sinking to one knee.

"Kasdeya!" Krea leaned over her, worry creasing her features.

The group paused, glancing back at her.

Natassa blinked to clear the snow coating her lashes. "I'm fine!" She grimaced and pulled her leg free. She took a step, and the agony shooting up her ankle nearly made her fall again.

Velamir approached her with quick strides. "What happened?" He shouted to be heard over the wind.

"I tripped. That's all." She took another painful step and forced a smile. "Let's continue."

Her hair whipped in the air, and her cheeks felt chapped by the cold. She ignored the sting in her ankle and took a few more steps. Velamir closed the distance between them, then hefted her into his arms. The Sirchoba screeched, and Natassa gasped, but her arms slipped around his shoulders on instinct. He continued forward, carrying her as if she weighed nothing. Natassa knew protesting wouldn't aid her in any way, in fact it would only prolong their time in the harsh weather.

She pressed her face to his shoulder, seeking refuge from the vicious wind. "Thank you."

He nodded, his chin brushing her hair.

The snowstorm followed them inside the cave, and wafts of cold wind continued to tear at them. Jax started a fire by sprinkling what looked like ashes over the cave floor and then pouring a vial over it. Flames sprang into the air with a viciousness that almost seared Finnean's brows off.

Jax winced. "Watch out for the sparks."

Latimus chuckled. "Finnean would look like a Savagelander shaman without his eyebrows."

"And you would look better bald," Finnean shot back. "Let the flames claim what little hair remains."

Latimus scoffed. "I have plenty of hair! Besides that's a distinguished look, have you seen the king of Ondalar's portrait? I would be honored to resemble him even slightly."

Finnean snickered. "You've been an obsessive admirer of Ondalar recently. If I didn't know better, I would never guess you were born and raised in Verin."

Velamir placed Natassa gently beside the fire, then pulled back to speak with Jax. The Shadow Manos approached her and removed her boot. He checked the swelling and gave her a tonic.

"You'll be fine in a few hours."

Latimus broke away from his word-sparring with Finnean. "We have to wait for her?"

Velamir pinned him with a glare. "We have to wait for the storm to settle. Get some rest."

The Sirchoba darted out of Natassa's cloak, making

a mad dash around the fire. It squawked and pecked at Latimus, attempting to snatch the jerky in his hands. Latimus shouted and tossed the dried meat to rid himself of the creature. Natassa couldn't hold back her laughter, and the others joined her.

Latimus scowled. "How long is their life span?"

20

CORALIE
KINGDOM OF VERIN
CASTLE VERIN

CORALIE STARED AT the girl before her. She appeared uncertain, her posture lowered in a way it never was. Coralie's gaze trailed from the flowing dress she wore to the sword sheathed at her side. Her black hair was braided back, and her eyes were a common brown with dark brows furrowed over them. A girl who'd fought with everything in her, so why did she falter?

Coralie spoke to the girl through her eyes. *You've come this far. You will do whatever it takes. Whatever it takes.*

Her attention dropped to the circular metal in the girl's hand, which she held with a fierce grip. She was scared to lose it but also afraid to bear its weight.

A knock startled Coralie, and she looked away from the mirror.

"Your Highness?" It was Jovinne. "Advisor Welix is holding another meeting. They are speaking of escaping the castle and going to Fortress Yadigar."

So they're running, she thought.

"I will be out in a moment," she told Jovinne.

His footsteps retreated, and Coralie glanced back at the girl. But she wasn't a girl anymore. Coralie lifted the metal crown that she hadn't worn since her parents' deaths and placed it over her head. She stared into the mirror, the corner of her lips tilting into a smile.

She was Verin's princess, and it was time she acted the part.

The doors flung open, and the thick wood banged against the adjacent stone walls. Conversation ceased, and all eyes focused on her. The guards posted at the council room entrance held their spears uncertainly. It was so quiet that the silence seemed loud. Coralie waited at the entrance, wanting every single person sitting around the war table to see her clearly. The council was much diminished compared to its previous state.

Ten council members, including Galva Blayton, Commander Evinshore, and a few new faces, along with General Zenrelius, were seated. Advisor Welix sat in her uncle's chair—in the king's chair. A flicker of rage threatened her calmness, but she tamped it down. Coralie walked forward, her boots thunking against the floor. She moved slowly, taking her time as she glanced over each face. Jovinne's large presence behind her increased her dominating authority.

She stopped beside Advisor Welix, pinning him in place with her firm gaze. The advisor closed his hanging mouth, darting a quick glance at the others. They rose in respect, placing half hearts over their chests. Zenrelius simply bowed his head. His hands remained still at his sides.

"Your Highness," the advisor managed. "We weren't aware you would be joining us."

"And why is that?"

"As princess, you must have better things to do." He laughed uneasily. "You've been at your uncle's side these past days."

"At least you understand who I am."

Advisor Welix paled. "Of course, Your Highness. Please, join us."

He waved to a guard, who scurried over with another chair. The guard placed the chair beside Galva Blayton's. Welix smiled, his mouth tight. Coralie didn't move an inch.

"Is something wrong?" Advisor Welix asked.

"You're in her seat," Jovinne said.

The advisor looked down, then rose slowly, as if suddenly realizing it. "I apologize, Princess." He gestured to the chair and brushed past her to take the seat he had intended for her.

Coralie swept toward the head chair. She stood in front of it, staring down at the council members. "It seems much has been occurring on this council. Is it not an Imperial law? In fact, in the Book of Codes, page fourteen: In the ruler's absence, the heir shall take the place of regent until the ruler returns or is deceased.

In the case of the latter, the heir assumes the ruler's place permanently."

A councilman nodded. "That is correct, Your Highness."

"Good, I'm glad that's clear. Now," she said, sitting and waving a hand before her, "let's begin."

General Zenrelius spoke first. "We were discussing Verin's next plan of action."

Coralie nodded. "I want to make sure something is understood. The ones who want to breathe their last on this soil and defend our home will remain here. We aren't running anywhere."

Zenrelius smiled, his teeth flashing white. "I'm pleased to know I was mistaken about the inhabitants of Castle Verin. I thought you were all cowards." He glanced at Advisor Welix, who stiffened.

Coralie straightened her shoulders, staring down at the table. "We hold a piece of the Empire. Without Verin, the Empire would be missing part of its heart. Without Verin, it would cease beating." She glanced around. "So, if there is a coward here, I suggest you leave now."

After a long pause, Commander Evinshore said, "Your Highness, what do you suggest we do? Prolus is too strong. He's undefeatable."

"Prolus . . ." Blayton began. "He's been around for so long. He's lived far past the natural age. Some say he already has the Golden Crown and that he's immortal."

"Whoever is spreading those rumors is trying to strike fear into our hearts," Coralie said. "Prolus is flesh and blood. He's just a man."

"We promised the people safety," Advisor Welix

said. "The citizens would be the ones leaving the castle. We cannot go back on our word."

"Prolus has spies waiting for your next move. A party of that size out in the open—you think he will not notice?" Zenrelius told him. "They will be killed."

"They will be killed either way," Welix snapped. "Wouldn't that be better than being holed up in the castle?"

Another advisor agreed, "I say we allow the citizens to leave."

"We might as well tell them to carry a large banner signaling their presence. They will be doomed," Evinshore said.

Zenrelius exhaled an exasperated breath. "We need a proper plan, one with the least risks."

"As general of Ondalar, you must have a great number of tricks up your sleeve," Welix muttered. "But this is Verin. We will decide our strategies ourselves."

"And that is how you will meet your end," Zenrelius said bluntly.

Voices rose as heated debates sprang up among the council members. Coralie remained silent, focusing on the map at the center of the table. The arguments continued to build as a plan formed in her mind. Then Coralie stood, unsheathed her dagger, and stabbed it into the map, snaring everyone's attention.

"Unless we distract Prolus by doing the unexpected." She pressed her finger to the map beside her dagger. "We take back Namaar."

21

MORDON
KINGDOM OF VERIN
TARIQIN WAR CAMP

ORDON'S CHAINS RATTLED as he took a step forward. Men stood before him and behind him in the line, crushing him in the center. Deedans were positioned on either side of them. The snow fell faster, warning of a storm, and Mordon's breath left his lips in pale clouds on the cold air. He stared at the man in front of him. With blond hair and a tough build, the Savorian was bound in chains as well, his hands and feet. At least half of the line was Savorian. He listened to bits and pieces of the muffled conversations drifting past. Tariqin was simple to understand. It was similar to the Imperial language. A sprinkling of different words and the thick accent made up the differences between the languages. Mordon recalled

Velamir and his accomplices. They'd been trained well. He didn't remember them having an accent.

The pavilion ahead rose above the other tents, the solid black of the canvas contrasting with the white snow. Prolus's personal space. It was the closest Mordon had been to the Dark Lord. A man he'd heard horror stories about as a child. A man he'd heard wasn't even a man, but a demon. A demon he was supposed to defeat. A demon he was supposed to stand against.

"Move."

He glanced at the deedan peering at him with dark eyes. Mordon continued forward, trying to remember the last time someone had tried to order him around. A smile found its way to his face. *Ah, yes.* He'd broken their jaw. He was nearing the front of the line and could overhear the Chishmans speaking.

"Group four." The voice was sharp and precise.

Mordon soon found himself face-to-face with two Chishmans. One was standing farther back, taking notes, while the other stared Mordon down, or rather, stared him *up*. He was dressed in Chishman robes. The fabric rippled oddly, intriguing Mordon. The Chishma wore a hood over his face, but Mordon could make out most of his features: a thick beard splattered with gray, black eyes, and what appeared to be a thin yet strong frame. Mordon heard people calling him Chishma Talon.

After a measuring look, Talon snatched Mordon's arm in a firm grip. Mordon tensed, but Talon only pushed his sleeve up and scribbled with ink across his skin.

"Group five," Talon announced and released him.

Mordon stared at the number and then followed the

others making their way to the large cooking pots nestled between the food stores. Fires crackled, biting into wood and cooking the stew in the pots. Mordon joined yet another line. He stared over the heads of everyone else, catching sight of Lissa handing out bowls of stew. Her lips were turned down in disgust and Mordon let out a small laugh, but his mirth faded as he stared at her. If he focused a little harder, he could almost see Coralie there—her tall, muscled build instead of Lissa's smaller one. Long braids, thick brows, and that confident smile she flashed so rarely, to him at least. He missed her. Even though his heart was blackened and the rage inside him could have lit the entire camp on fire, he missed her with whatever good remained in him.

"Cooking duty?" Mordon couldn't help the barb when he reached Lissa.

Her eyes shrunk to small slits, and she grabbed a clay bowl before reaching for the large spoon in the pot. "General Winston says you've changed, that you are with us." She huffed a laugh. "No one changes that easily."

"Are you sure? Velamir and that little weasel of a Chishma changed quick enough. Or did they only do so when their lives were on the line?"

"That weasel of a Chishma has a name. Jax saved your life. Besides, you had them imprisoned there. It wasn't like they could get away."

"But you got away," he pointed out. "If they really wanted to, they could have found a means of escaping."

She thumped a spoonful of stew into the bowl and extended it to Mordon. Her gaze snagged on his arm as he reached out to take it. "Instead of concerning yourself with me, prepare yourself for the testing."

At Mordon's quizzical look, she laughed. "In a day or two, there will be a test. The ones who pass will enter the Awal and become deedans. The ones who don't . . . they become rumlok food."

"How hard can it be?"

The line grew agitated behind him, so Mordon gave Lissa a lazy salute, pressing his hand to his forearm as he'd seen the Tariqins do. She ignored him, her eyes already on the next man. Mordon recognized a few faces among those eating. He sat beside Silopar, and the Handler acknowledged him with a nod.

A flurry of cold wind blew over them. One of the Savorians coughed. He looked young, hardly a man. A boy that age shouldn't have been in chains or forced to fight. Mordon swallowed a mouthful of the stew. The warmth rushed down his throat, soaking his bones with a current of heat. The Savorian boy spoke to Bear. His words sounded rough, the language clearly Savorian. Bear laughed and clapped the boy on the shoulder.

Silopar leaned over to Mordon and translated. "He asked to hear the story of Rasdor."

"Rasdor?"

"A legendary Savorian hero. He was our first king."

Bear's deep voice rumbled over them, and though Mordon didn't understand a word he was saying, it was somehow soothing.

Silopar translated for Mordon. "Savoria was divided into separate sections. Each section had its own chief, much like the Savagelanders. One chief had a son. But that day—a day considered one of blessing—was horror for the chief, for his son was blind, with eyes white as milk, white as the paleness of his skin. The chief, in his agitated state, called for his first commander to exchange children with him. The commander was forced to give the chief his own newly born son and take the blind boy. The commander resented the boy, treating him like a creature from Jehen."

Mordon frowned. "Jehen?"

Silopar scratched his beard. "It's like . . . like the underworld, a place you go when you die. If you were a sinner."

"Like hell."

"That's the word." He nodded, then hurried to translate the rest of Bear's tale. "The white-eyed boy grew. He would often escape the commander's torments by lingering by the sea. He would remain alone there for a long time. On one of those days, the chief's adoptive son took over the sector. He killed the chief, the commander, everyone. You see, he was sick."

Bear pointed to his head and then heart.

"He was poisoned," Silopar said. "His thoughts and actions were evil. He took over each section, gathering power-hungry men like himself under his rule. Because the white-eyed boy had been by the sea, he escaped death. Later, he returned to the sector and found everyone dead. He scoured the faces with his hands, recognizing the woman who'd raised him by touch. When he realized she was dead, he cried out. Some say he let out a roar so powerful, it shook the sea and the wind, and a flash of power poured from his eyes. The boy who had taken his place at birth felt it as well, and he grew fearful, his actions becoming even viler than before. He was intent on keeping his rule, and so his attacks grew more vicious."

The Savorians around Bear were riveted by the tale, and a few of them smiled.

"The white-eyed boy tried to recruit whoever would listen. Most shied away from the boy, asking how he could help or lead them when he couldn't even see. So, the boy went alone. He stood before the wicked chief's armies. He faced them with his courage and resilient heart. And when the people saw his bravery, they stood with him as one. Sometimes, it takes just one brave choice to change the fate of the world.

"The wicked chief grew afraid, but he didn't retreat. The white-eyed boy requested a battle—the battle of kings, the battle of blood. They fought, and though the boy was blind, he saw with his heart. Their blood soaked the ground. It was long and painful, but finally, the boy won. He became the first king. Rasdor. *True Sight*, they called him. He united Savoria."

The wide smiles around the group slowly faded, and Mordon glanced at Silopar, who shrugged. "We may have been united, but that Savoria is long gone. We are waiting for another Rasdor to come. To save us."

Mordon stared into his empty bowl. The story had stirred something in him, and he felt a connection to Rasdor. He'd been blind his whole life, believing his father to be someone else. The snow grew harsher, and a gust whipped at his hair. Mordon stood and faced the coming storm.

22

"A LETTER FOR HIS Royal Highness." The servant bowed, extending a folded piece of parchment. Feeling his father's heavy gaze on him, Honzio took the letter without thanks and nodded for the servant to leave. After the door closed, Honzio scanned the name signed on the back of the letter and tucked it inside his thick overcoat.

Beads of light filtered through the large window at the back of the consul chamber. His father had been meeting with city residents throughout the day, allowing them time to speak but avoiding a confrontation with the Savagelander delegation who'd been lingering with growing impatience. Honzio took a seat before his father, emulating the emperor's lazy posture, and poured himself a glass of zat from the large decanter. He took a sip, holding back a grimace. It was strong and bitter, not the watered-down norm, but the kind only an emperor could afford. Honzio swallowed, knowing his father was watching him with his beady eyes. He peered at the map spread across the desk, eyeing the calculations and taxes owed from the kingdoms.

"Who was it from?"

Honzio's head snapped up to meet his father's dark gaze. The emperor stared at him over the rim of his glass. Honzio instinctively touched the front of his overcoat where the letter was nestled, and it crinkled beneath the material.

"Moralis." At his father's blank expression, he added, "Galva Vane, Mother's cousin."

Malus's expression soured at the reference to his late wife, as if he'd tasted something revolting. The emperor chugged an entire glass of zat and motioned for Honzio to pour him another. Honzio watched him with unease. Addiction to drink wasn't uncommon, but when it was consumed the entire day, every day . . . it was difficult not to take notice. There was a time when one had to step up and rule, but it seemed his father felt he had every right to indulge in his vices whenever he wanted. Honzio's eyes followed the red liquid as he poured zat into his father's glass.

"The Savagelanders have been waiting to speak with you for a long time. Aren't you going to meet with them?"

Malus wiped zat off his lips and retrieved his glass from Honzio. "Why should I meet with savages who showed up without a proper appointment? I should kill them for daring to step foot in the palace."

Honzio winced. "Perhaps you should make peace with them, Father. Hold them off for a while, at least until we handle Prolus. The Dark Lord's army is invading Verin now. It won't be long until they take the kingdom. Make peace—"

"I won't be making anything except crushed bones from their bodies. I won't have peace with those vermin." Malus's eyes narrowed into slits of suspicion. "Why do you insist? Are you plotting behind my back?"

His father couldn't see past himself. In his mind, everyone around him was trying to bring about his ruin, and that made them targets.

"I'm trying to save the Empire. I'm trying to keep the Imperials together."

The emperor stood from his chair, leaning over Honzio. "Is that your job?" His voice was eerily quiet.

Honzio stood as well, fuming through his flared nostrils. "Well, what is my job, Father? Besides being your puppet."

An uneasy silence followed the question. Honzio didn't flinch away from his father's cold gaze. The emperor's face cycled through different expressions— icy rage, confusion, shock. His hand lifted, each finger enclosed by an enormous ring. It had been a long time since his father had struck him, but the memory of the cold metal against his skin hadn't diminished with time.

The door to the chamber flew open, and the emperor's hand dropped. A chamberlain rushed inside, his face pale, chest heaving. "Your Majesty, I could not stop them."

Who?

Honzio's question was answered when men in gray-and-black uniforms rushed inside. They moved in a blur. Honzio blinked, trying to comprehend what was happening. The door was slammed shut, the chamberlain's throat sliced, the guard who'd been posted at the door flung in a bloody heap before the desk.

"Cadellion!" Emperor Malus shouted, his attention on the side door as he called for his bodyguards.

One of the Savagelanders broke the door's handle and hoisted a desk chair underneath it to lock the door in place. Fists pounded against the door, and muffled shouts of anger sounded from behind it. They'd blocked the Cadellion off. Honzio's hand inched to the dagger on his belt.

"I wouldn't try it, princeling."

From amidst the small group of Savagelanders, a man stepped forward. His upper lip curled to reveal a row of teeth sharpened to points. His hair was braided back, with pieces of what looked like bone scattered throughout. His eyes were coal-black, matching his hair. Unlike his men, his uniform had silver stripes instead of gray, and the spikes on his shoulder pads were higher.

"I assumed you to be smarter than your father. Don't prove me wrong," the Savagelander cautioned.

Honzio's hand lingered over his dagger.

"How dare you barge inside in this manner? You Savagelanders ask for peace but cannot even respect my rule." The emperor's voice contained fury.

"We learn to take what does not come, Your Majesty." He addressed the emperor with an extra heap of sarcasm. "We are not accustomed to waiting for what we want."

"You damn well will wait if I tell you to. Now get out."

"You know how capable we are," the Savagelander said.

The two lifeless bodies were proof of that. Honzio's heart thumped against his ribs. He'd never seen Savagelander violence that close.

"I could kill you now if I wished, but I will give you one more chance. And as we've reminded you Imperials many times, we are called the Uluzar, not Savagelanders. You can make up as many names for all the territories as you want, but they will turn against you in the end. The Empire is falling."

The pounds on the side door grew harder and more frantic. The Cadellion would be in soon.

"You have two weeks," the man warned. "If you do not sign the treaty, we will raze the palace to the ground. If I do not do as I say, may no one call me Grongar-ja."

His men roared in approval, thumping their chests four times. Grongar-ja's attention fell on Honzio, and it seemed as if he were speaking only to him when he said his next words.

"Choose well."

The Savagelanders stormed out of the chamber as quickly as they'd come. Moments after, the Cadellion burst inside.

"After them, you fools! After them!" Malus coughed, then wheezed, his hand flying out and knocking his glass over. Zat soaked the map. The emperor clutched at his throat, and Honzio took a hesitant step forward.

The Cadellion raced after the Savagelanders, but Honzio had a feeling the wild men would evade them. He looked at his father, who was slamming a fist onto the table.

"Curse them!" he hissed, and then the fight in him wore out, and he muttered something incoherent before falling face-first onto the desk.

Honzio approached with caution and pressed his fingers to his father's neck for a pulse. The emperor breathed in, a loud snort erupting from his nose. Honzio found himself disappointed.

He glanced at the map stained red. The liquid continued to spread, covering the Empire. Honzio sighed and stepped away from the table as servants rushed in and tended to the bodies. He whispered a prayer for the dead and left the chamber. Once he found a secluded area, he reached into his overcoat.

Cousin,

We have conversed often of late. I find myself confiding in you. You are a close friend of mine. I even consider you a brother. I've been a mess since my fiancée broke our arrangement. She decided to accept the offer of marriage from Prince Gallaxos. I can't fault her for that. He's an Ondalarian prince. How could I compete with him?

Never mind my love life. I wouldn't even mention it, but I had to share my sorrow. I need a distraction to take my mind off it. I'm coming to Hearcross.

Until then,

Moralis Vane

Honzio folded the letter back, smiling as a sudden thought struck him. He made his way to his chamber and paused before the door, unsure how to enter without startling Aylis and confusing the guard at the door. He knocked once, lightly, and then entered, freezing at the sight of Aylis staring into the mirror, a brush in her hand. Her hair swallowed her in a golden halo and fell to her waist. She set the brush down and faced him, her expression grim.

She'd savagely grabbed his collar the night before, demanding an explanation. She'd taken the news hard. She was the sole survivor to have escaped imprisonment and death and would carry the burden of the losses on her shoulders. Honzio could only hope she wouldn't do anything foolish.

"What if someone else had come in?" Honzio said as he closed the door. "You should stay in the adjoining room." He nodded to the connecting door that led to quarters meant for his wife. The wife he didn't have and likely never would. After all, who would want to marry a lame-armed man? If anyone were to marry him, it would be for his crown, and he wouldn't constrict himself to a life like that.

"If someone caught me, it would give me a reason to fight. What more could I ask for?"

"Why would you risk your life when you haven't reached your objective? You're looking for someone." Honzio approached her. "I heard as much when you were sleeping."

Her eyes went wide, but she shook her head. "You don't know what you are speaking about."

"Svorgin."

At the name, she froze.

"Svorgin, I will find you." Honzio nodded. "You said many things as you thrashed about, but those four words the most."

She looked as though she wanted to argue, but her shoulders slumped in defeat. "I've been searching for him for so long. He is my brother."

Honzio waited for her to continue.

"He was captured. I followed the slavers, but I lost him. I've been trying to find him ever since."

"If you want to find your brother, keep yourself alive, understand?" At her nod, he smiled. "Good, then listen well. I have a plan."

23

KASDEYA RUBBED HER eyes, her vision blurry and body aching after hours spent hunched over the journal. A satisfying pop echoed as she straightened her back. She rolled her neck next. The light from her lantern was all but gone, but the sun had risen, making up for the darkness.

She went over her notes kept in a separate book. Kasdeya planned to give it to the Savagelanders if they proved themselves trustworthy enough not to swindle her. Kolesta-na, the wolf's daughter, had done much during her time in Ayleth, including killing King Joster's brothers with poison and everyone else who shared the king's blood. She'd poisoned the food sent to the king's harem and even tampered with the queen's meals.

She gave the queen a special poison, one

that curled its way into the womb, leaving the consumer barren. Kasdeya laughed aloud at several mentions of the queen, a fragile Savorian woman who seemed to shatter at everything, according to Kolesta-na. Kolesta-na accomplished everything with subtlety—silent and effective, a woman Kasdeya would have appreciated meeting.

She pored over the last notes she'd added. Kolesta-na's hopes bled through the pages. She had believed she would leave the castle, return to her tribe, and live long enough to birth the next chief. Kasdeya admired her determination but not her naivety. Once you entered palace life, you could only move up.

Kasdeya continued reading, not surprised to find the details of Kolesta-na's pregnancy. Out of all the women touched by Joster, she was the only one to become pregnant. A Savagelander, or rather—as Kolesta-na continued calling herself—an Uluzar. Kasdeya translated an entry that marked the halfway point. When she read the deciphered sheet, her eyes widened.

It's been months since I escaped. Yes, I escaped. I saw the future, many futures in my visions. I will have a daughter. Bright as the moon, a treasure in the eyes of my people. If I had stayed in the castle, my child would've been killed. Joster only cares for the male heirs. Mari helped me. A kind woman, far better than most in Ayleth, especially for a noblewoman. She's been married to Prince Irox for a while. They were unable to have a child, and she pitied my state and allowed me to stay in her home. I heard the queen is pregnant. I doubt she will survive the pregnancy, let alone the birthing. We shall see.

Kasdeya blinked. Her eyes felt heavy and swollen, but she persisted, turning to the next entry. After transcribing it, she noted that it was dated two years later.

They caught me. I'm a prisoner once again. Prisoner to Joster. He locked me in his wife's old room. She was granted grander rooms after the birth of the heir. She survived the birth and has more fight than I thought. I found a place for my journal, although no one will read it even if they find it. Imperials believe Savese to be barbaric. I was forced to part with my moonlight, Cores-na. My baby. Mari will raise her as her own. She promised me. I have no choice but to trust her. Joster believes I miscarried. He has a son now, a boy younger than my Cores-na. The child looks so innocent, so peaceful. I saw him for a moment before they brought me to the room that serves as my prison. Poor child. Who knows what life will hand him with such a wicked father. My end is near. I pray that my Cores-na will be found by her true family one day. The wolf women are born with birthmarks on their necks, have been for centuries, and if they aren't, the symbol is burned there. A half-moon. My girl had one, a perfect crescent. She has the blood of wolves in her. My job is complete. Even if I fall, I won't be the last to howl.

The last lines were scribbled hastily. Kasdeya's mouth parted as she translated the final word. She needed to know more. She flipped to the next page, but it was empty and so was the page after. Kasdeya turned the pages, desperate, but only blank sheets stared back at her. She closed the journal and sat still for a long while. Mari had taken Kolesta-na's daughter as her own. Mari,

Princess Mari. King Dale's sister-in-law and wife of his youngest brother.

Cores-na.

Coralie.

Coralie wasn't the true daughter of Mari and Irox, which meant she had no blood relation to King Dale. She couldn't be his heir. Kasdeya smirked. She could topple a kingdom with that knowledge.

Kasdeya cleared the table, ensuring everything was hidden, and then went to bed, but no matter how tired she was, sleep wouldn't claim her. She finally stood and walked to the connecting door. Her fingers lingered on the handle before turning it. The door creaked when it opened, and she stared into the dark room. The curtains were drawn closed, and a motionless form sprawled across the giant bed. Kasdeya entered, her bare feet silent on the stone. She stopped a foot away from the bed. Draven's eyes were shuttered close, his jaw rigid even in sleep. For once, a woman wasn't hanging over him. He lay alone, tangled in sheets resembling the web of lies he spun.

Kasdeya sat on the edge of the bed, glancing at his bandaged hand. Bruises the size of fingerprints marked the skin of his neck. She'd done that. She looked at him— truly looked at him—trying to see that innocent little boy Kolesta-na had seen all those years ago. Kasdeya reached out, brushing back a strand of white-blond hair. He might have been that way once, but he was far from innocent. He was too far gone, and so was she. But in all stories, there was only one villain who remained standing and rose to the top. Kasdeya pulled her hand back.

She wouldn't be the one who lost.

24

CORALIE STOOD SILENTLY in the shadowed entry-way to the kitchens, listening. A pang flitted through her at the empty sight that met her eyes. A place once filled with merry laughter, a team of cooks and their assistants moving in chaotic harmony, the smell of delicious meals being prepared, the clang of pans, the *thunk* of knives—it was all gone. What remained was a handful of terrified people clustered together.

"It's only a matter of time before the next attack," a woman said, her face contorted with fear. "I've lost my husband and sister. I can't lose my boy."

Nods circled their way through the group. Another woman lifted her chin. "The servants are down by more than half. All the work has fallen to us now that any sword-trained man or woman has been sent to the barracks."

"It's not fair! Why don't we leave the castle? Why are we trapping ourselves here?"

"We must wait for the council's order. They say the princess has joined the table."

"My family is more important to me than obeying royalty."

"You're right," another woman said. "She's young, the princess. She isn't wise enough to understand that we cannot overcome this."

If her people were speaking about her in that manner—and so openly—Coralie had much to do. She stepped into the chamber, her boots echoing along the stone and turning heads. Abashed gasps, open mouths, and shamed faces greeted her. They dropped into curtsies, placing half hearts over their chests. Coralie beckoned them to rise. She didn't want their regard, not when it wasn't real.

"Prin—Princess," one of them stammered, stepping forward. "How can we assist you?"

Coralie scanned her features, recognizing her as the under chef of the previous lead cook. Many castle servants had died during the attack. She must have taken the cook's place as head. "How much food do we have left in the stores?"

Relief flooded the woman's face. She'd thought Coralie would bring her to account for her words. "Enough to last a month."

Coralie nodded. "Good." She turned, heading back toward the door and Jovinne's shadow. She took measured steps, but at the relieved breaths behind her, she paused and turned slowly. "I know you don't believe I am capable of leading this kingdom."

The women appeared like frozen statues, until the one who had spoken to her before winced. "Princess, we—"

Coralie lifted her hand, silencing her. "But I give you my oath: Until my last breath, I will protect Verin, and I will fight to avenge the deaths of the warriors who gave their lives for this kingdom—your families. The council has decided. Those who wish to leave may prepare. But I cannot abandon the home my uncle has entrusted me with to the hands of the Dark Lord. I will not allow Verin to become a place of darkness. I promise you."

Coralie left the women in a stunned silence. Jovinne's heavy boots sounded behind her in the castle halls— halls that had once been patrolled by guards but held only the memory of ghosts.

"How many have readied to leave?" she asked without slowing her brisk pace.

"Seventy-eight, Princess."

"Leaving an estimated seven hundred in the castle," Coralie said under her breath.

"We also have Ondalar's troop, the general's men," Jovinne reminded her.

Coralie frowned at the mention. The enmity between Verin and Ondalar was too deep to be mended so easily. She doubted Zenrelius would aid them again, not without some form of compensation. Coralie paused, turning to look at the door at the end of the hall—solitary, like the man within. She'd spoken with Boltrex and had been overwhelmed by the information he confided with her about Winston, his family, all the things he'd contained for so long. Things he wouldn't have shared unless he felt it was necessary. He'd told her the queen of Verin should know. *The queen.* That word had shaken Coralie to her core. Boltrex had already accepted her uncle's impending death and saw her as queen.

The guards were doubled at the gatehouse, their watchful eyes peering into the distance. They were prepared to lower the drawbridge for the people leaving the castle. They only needed her order.

"Is the group ready?" Coralie asked.

"The soldiers you chose are awaiting your command," Jovinne responded.

Coralie absorbed that information as she stared at the gatehouse, remembering something General Boltrex had told her.

During the attack, when we were falling back into the castle, we raised the drawbridge. I couldn't see during the battle, but the next thing I knew, a swarm of deedans were rushing after.

Someone lowered it, Coralie had whispered.

As if sensing her thoughts, Jovinne spoke. "It could have been that Velamir fellow or the Shadow Manos."

Coralie shook her head. "It's not possible. Velamir was on the tower with Mordon, and before that, he was in the dungeon. Jax was guarding the Stone Chamber."

Her blood chilled. Another traitor in their midst. Faces rushed through her mind. It could be anyone. Someone who had taken the time to earn their trust and fade into the background, unnoticed.

"Princess!"

A True Manos approached. "Princess," he repeated, panting from his rush. "Your uncle, he's dying."

25

MORDON
KINGDOM OF VERIN
TARIQIN WAR CAMP

MORDON CROSSED HIS arms, watching with a sneer as the observers shouted their praise for the young Chishma sitting at the table. Light-haired, with brown eyes and a large build, Quinn was his name. At least that was the name he had given Mordon in Namaar. The name had been as bogus as Winston's death. Another man took a seat before Quintus and extended his arm.

"Are you sure you want to do this?" Quintus asked, an arrogant smirk carved into his face.

The Tariqin nodded in return. "You've been doing this for a good hour. Can't keep winning."

"We'll see," came his confident reply.

Mordon scoffed, tearing his attention away. Arm wrestling was a game for the weak—a show of dominance when one was too afraid to enter a real battle to prove their strength. Mordon glanced over the large group in the oversized tent. All eyes were riveted on the match, Savorian and Tariqin both. A thump sounded, and the Tariqin swore. Another loss, then. Quintus laughed, full of himself. Mordon held in the urge to plaster himself in the chair and demand a match.

The tent flap moved aside, and Chishma Talon entered. When the others caught sight of him, a tense silence overtook the group.

Talon announced, "Group four."

As the group walked up to him, Talon checked their inked arms for the correct number. The tent emptied until only fifteen people remained—Mordon's group. Mordon leaned against the wooden tent post, willing it not to crack. He closed his eyes, imagining himself in Castle Verin with Coralie. What would he say to her?

I'm captivated by you. I've been captivated ever since I can remember.

He imagined her reaction. Those warm brown eyes rounded in shock and startled confusion.

"What're you smiling for, pretty boy?"

Mordon's eyes snapped open. Quintus, who was without a partner, had shifted his attention to Mordon. At first, Mordon didn't know how to respond. He'd been called many things before—mostly insults—and it was no secret that he was considered handsome. But he'd never in his life been called *pretty*. And there was no chance of that with the scar cutting down his face. Quintus was mocking him.

"What did you say?"

"What *should* I call you?" Quintus leaned forward. "Perhaps, you prefer *traitor*. After all, you left your hometown. Or maybe *naïve* because you fall so easily for lies. Perhaps *coward* works best since you haven't tried to best my strength. Which do you fancy?"

Mordon was before him in three strides, his hands gripping the chair facing Quintus so tightly, his knuckles turned white. "You would know best. You seemed skilled at making up names."

"Chishmans do anything to complete the job they are entrusted with. You wouldn't know about loyalty. You left your precious castle too easily for that."

"I was wounded and dragged out. I didn't leave."

"So, you would go back? Or are you here as a spy?"

Mordon sat in the chair. "My old life is over."

Quintus extended his hand, an elbow planted on the table between them. "We'll see if you last the testing."

Mordon flexed his fingers and took his hand. The remaining observers watched their rivalry closely. Quintus tried to incite him, but Mordon blocked his words off. His old self would have attacked Quintus, but the old Mordon had gotten nowhere except deeper in a pit he'd dug for himself. The match started, and Quintus pushed against Mordon. Mordon allowed him to get the upper hand, his arm tipping to the side, edging nearer and nearer to the tabletop. Quintus was already grinning, a triumphant smirk lighting his face. A smile crept along Mordon's lips too. He held his arm there, inches from losing, his muscles bulging, the veins in his arm plump with blood. Quintus's winning grin faded when he spotted the look on Mordon's face. His mouth opened to speak, and Mordon took that moment, slamming Quintus's hand down on the other side. A wave of cheers lit the tent, and someone clapped him on the shoulder.

Mordon stood, staring down at Quintus. "As they say, don't start a fight you cannot win."

"Really, Quintus, tiring the potential recruits?"

Mordon turned.

Lissa swayed over to them. "I thought you were supposed to be building their morale."

Quintus laughed. "And I used to think you were a skilled Chishma. People assume, and they end up wrong."

Lissa glared, but before they could continue bickering, Talon reentered.

"Group five."

Mordon left with the others, barely noticing as Talon checked his arm. Outside the tent, the sun was bright, and for once, it wasn't snowing, which was a mark in his favor. Lissa walked beside him. He glanced down at her.

"Planning on joining us?"

"While it would be fun watching you fall up close, I prefer viewing from a distance," she replied. "General Winston asked me to give you some guidance."

"I'm all ears."

Snow crunched beneath their boots. The others moved slowly, their paces unsteady, some appearing fearful, while others seemed resolved. The spot chosen— a wide snow-covered field—was a good distance from the camp. A dark figure stood there, with Chishmans swarming around him. A wave of unease washed over

Mordon at the sight of the horned mask and the devilish smile pasted on it. *I've wanted to kill Prolus for a long time*, Winston had said. Mordon laughed. Quintus was focusing his accusations of betrayal in the wrong direction. Mordon wrenched his gaze from Prolus, observing the large netted wall leading up to a tall platform looming ahead.

"The snow is covering a hole in the ground," Lissa told him. "It's right before the net. If you don't jump, you will fall in." She paused for effect. "And be skewered on the spikes below."

"Good to know."

"If you reach the top of the platform, you can stay there and be accepted as a recruit, or you can attempt to become captain of the group by crossing the rope to the next platform."

"That shouldn't be hard to accomplish."

She huffed a laugh. "If more than one person manages to make it to the second platform, there will be weapons awaiting them. The one who survives becomes captain."

Talon addressed the group and informed them of most of what Lissa had told him, except for the bit about the hole. At the loud whistle, Mordon took off, staring with unwavering focus at the approaching netted wall. His eyes darted toward the ground, where the irregularity could be spotted by someone looking for it. He took a leaping jump and wrapped his hands around the net. He grunted, pulling himself up. Pained cries rang out below him, followed by the slick sound of pierced flesh. Mordon didn't look down or stop to help. He couldn't risk himself for someone else. Mordon climbed, and sweat slipped down his clenched jaw. His muscles were aching when he reached the top. He hauled himself over and placed his hands on his knees, regaining his breath.

He was the first to reach the top, but a few others were gaining on him. A man clambered onto the platform beside him—a Tariqin. He surveyed Mordon, and it seemed as if he were contemplating shoving him off. Mordon held his gaze until the man looked away to focus instead on a Savorian nearing the top. The Tariqin placed his boot on the man's hand as soon as it touched the platform. He ground his heel in, and the Savorian wrenched away with a grunt. The Savorian gripped the net with only one hand, hanging by the last of his strength. The Tariqin stepped back with a satisfied smirk, rushed to the rope, and crossed hand over hand to the next platform.

Mordon moved to follow him, but then hesitated. He glanced back at the Savorian hanging there, at the desperation coating his face. It reminded him of himself, when he had hung from the castle crenellations. When Velamir had saved his life. He didn't know why Velamir had done it, and the question haunted him. *Why?* Mordon would never forget the fear that had clung to him as he hung there. The terror had plastered over him like a second skin.

Mordon dropped to his knees and reached down to help the Savorian. He heaved the man onto the platform. The man stared at him with confusion before his face shifted to gratitude.

"Thank you, *mosori*," the man repeated over and over.

Mordon waved him off, wincing. *Mosori. Brother.* He was no one's brother, no one's ally, no one's savior. It was a lapse in judgment that had made him save the man. A mistake. Mordon stumbled to the rope. He wrapped his hands around the rough fiber and dropped off the platform. He crossed the rope, gaining on the Tariqin in the distance. His shoulders ached above him.

He was nearly to the other side when the Tariqin lifted a sword—one of the weapons Lissa had told him about. The man neared the edge. He was going to cut the rope, Mordon realized, and dread filled him. He glanced at the ground a world away. Nausea curled in his middle. He would never survive a fall from that height. Panic urged him on with a speed he hadn't known he possessed. The rope severed. Mordon jumped. His fingers found purchase on the platform's edge. He dragged himself up and swept his feet out, knocking the Tariqin flat on the wooden boards. Mordon searched wildly for a weapon. He spotted a pile of swords and moved to retrieve one. But the Tariqin got there first and kicked them off the edge. Mordon cursed and faced the man who was holding the only remaining weapon in his fist.

They circled each other on the platform. The Tariqin swung at him, left, then right before striking overhead. Mordon evaded each blow. The sneer on the man's face and the way he held the sword reminded him of his childhood rival, Jovinne. Mordon rushed forward, disarmed him with a quickness that seemed to surprise the Tariqin, and the sword fell from the platform, clanging into the pile of metal far below.

Mordon and the Tariqin grappled. Jovinne had

shown him that if he wanted to stop being bested, he would have to be stronger, meaner, tougher than the others. Jovinne was part of the reason Mordon had become the dark person he was, and he hated him for it.

He *hated* him.

Mordon twisted the Tariqin's arm until he heard a satisfying crack. The Tariqin screamed, and his arm dangled at an unnatural angle. Mordon smiled as the man fell to his knees and stared in horror at the bone protruding from his arm. Then he glanced up at Mordon, a mix of desperate emotions contorting his face.

"Please," he begged.

Mordon's lips twisted. He pictured the Tariqin digging his boot into the Savorian's hand. He saw himself, young with a broken nose and a broken self. All the sympathy he might have had was gone—gone with the child he once was.

"Go to hell," he spat and shoved the man over the platform.

26

NATASSA LINKED ARMS with Krea as their group passed a frozen stream. She stared at Velamir's back as they walked. He was at the front, along with Latimus and Finnean, while Jax ambled behind her and Krea. Velamir moved with confidence, like he knew he had the strength to handle whatever came at him, and yet there was no arrogance, only a calm, collected power circulating him. Like the glimpses she recalled from the storm: strong arms beneath her legs and back, pulling her tight to his chest to conserve warmth, and the stubbled jaw above her, brushing her forehead.

"I've never seen anyone look at someone the way Velamir looks at you," Krea said in a low tone. "He's so stoic, but the moment you show a sign of discomfort, he reacts as if it's a feeling of his own."

Natassa swatted her. "You're imagining things."

"I think you should tell him." Krea stared at her intently. "The truth."

Natassa froze. The *truth*. How much weight that one word contained. She recalled a saying she'd heard in the palace.

We can fabricate a thousand lies to conceal one truth, but in the end, it is simply a fabrication, a cover, and when that curtain is swept away, the truth will be revealed in the form of the sun bursting through. And we will be blinded by that sun and burned by the lies we told.

Natassa yearned to tell Velamir the truth, but she feared what he would do if he discovered she was a princess of the Empire, when he believed her to be a handmaiden who'd been trapped into servitude. She couldn't bear to lose his respect, to lose the warmth that shone in his eyes when he looked at her.

"I can't," she told Krea.

A sharp ache pierced her head. *Attack*, a voice murmured. *You're under attack.*

The Seer was telling her; her shadow was warning her. She glimpsed a man in leather armor peering over the approaching hill. He held a bow in his hands, the arrow trained on Latimus. Natassa moved fast. It was almost as if she weren't in her body, but watching from afar as her form hurtled forward, shoving Latimus aside. The arrow loosed.

"Hey!" Latimus shouted, but she remained focused on the coming arrow.

Natassa twisted her body, and the arrow flew past her to land in the snow by Jax's feet. She glanced up, catching sight of his shocked face. His lips parted, and then knowing flashed across his features. He knew what she was—a Shadow Manos, like him. But he didn't know she was also much, much worse.

"Gather together!" Velamir shouted.

Natassa reached into the bag hanging from her belt, fingers wrapping around the dagger within and earning a squawk from the Sirchoba nestled inside. Swords unsheathed, and the group closed in together, forming a tight circle. Men erupted from behind the hill, pouring down and surrounding them. Natassa scrutinized their armor, and dread burst over her, along with the memory of a tattooed wrist. A snake. A spy.

"Savagelanders," Natassa breathed.

The Savagelanders angled their swords as they took up battle stances, the metal glinting, matching the steel in their eyes.

"Steady," Velamir said. "Steady."

A shrill whistle cut through the commotion, and the Savagelanders froze. Sudden beats like the pounding of her heart came closer. A man appeared over the hill, runes tattooed into his face. Leather tassets hung over the trousers clothing his legs, and he was shirtless, appearing unfazed by the cold weather. His eyes struck Natassa with a paralyzing familiarity. Black as night, dark as ink, murky as her vision. It was him. The shaman. Natassa pressed closer to Krea. The shaman neared, beating a large circular drum with a bone. He twirled and twirled while he chanted in Savese. A wave of dizziness almost made her collapse as her shadows' voices poured into her mind, translating the chants.

From the sands of Jahar,

of wolf's blood,

bright as a thousand stars,

streaming in golden flood,

the hero returns

to bind the clans.

The phoenix burns.

The heir stands,

wielding power,

in strong hands.

Wolf's blood,

golden flood,

the prophecy nears.

The clans unite.

They know, the Seers,

they have the sight.

Bow to the prophecy,

bow to the hero,

bow to the might.

The chants trailed off, and the Savagelanders fell to their knees as one. They bowed their heads, fingers curled into fists that they pressed to their lips. The shaman continued spinning, tossing Natassa into another fit of dizziness. She slumped against Krea, who sent her a worried glance.

"Natassa?"

The whisper of her name startled Natassa into regaining her composure. A quick glance around ensured that the others hadn't heard. They were focused on the shaman barking something in Savese. The Savagelanders pulled back, sheathing their weapons.

"What in the four kingdoms is going on?" Latimus muttered.

While the Savagelanders no longer appeared to be a threat, Natassa was uneasy in their presence. The shaman crept closer after abandoning his drum. As he approached, Natassa's eyes scanned over the runes carved into his skin.

"We will help you," he said in broken Imperial.

A shiver ran through Natassa as his gaze broke from Velamir to glance over at her.

"Weapons, food, supplies? What do you need?"

After a long moment, Velamir cleared his throat. "What do you have?"

"Follow," he whispered and headed toward the hill.

Finnean's eyes narrowed. "Velamir, this might be a trap."

"Stay here and keep watch on the Savagelanders. If they attack, call a warning," Velamir told him.

Finnean nodded, though he appeared conflicted about the decision. Latimus and Krea stayed behind with Finnean, while Natassa and Jax followed Velamir after the shaman. When they crossed the hill, a solitary tent came into view. The shaman stopped before it. A long wooden table stood beside the tent, laden with wares. It seemed too deliberate, as if the shaman had known they were coming. On the table were potions, insects, metal, arrows, and an assortment of other goods. Natassa perused the items until her gaze fell upon a set of knives. Tears stung her vision. She blinked them back.

"They're yours."

The coarse words made her jump.

The shaman appeared beside her. His eyes focused on her, or rather, *through* her. "I've been expecting you, phoenix."

Natassa glanced furtively over at Velamir and Jax, but they were too engrossed in conversation about the table's contents to notice what the shaman had said.

"I don't know what you mean," Natassa replied.

"You are cursed, bound by fate, and until you fulfill the prophecy, you will not be free."

The words stung. He knew what she was doing: running away to the Elders, desperate to escape the shadows plaguing her.

"Accept it, contain it, overcome it, release it." The instructions flowed from his throat in a rasp. "You know what you must do." The shaman stretched his hand out, a shaking finger pointed at her chest. "Even if you don't, your heart does."

Her heart. Natassa splayed her fingers over the treacherous organ. The weight of metal pressed into her other hand, and she looked down, seeing the shaman pushing the belt of knives into her grasp.

"Take it, phoenix," the shaman urged. "You will find your path soon."

Velamir stepped forward. "We've found a few things." Jax hefted weapons and other materials over his shoulder, and Velamir carried a small box. "But we don't have enough to pay you."

The shaman shook his head. "I would sacrifice myself for the hero. Take as much as you need."

Velamir seemed confused, and he protested, "I cannot."

"You will, wolf's blood."

The prophecy . . . The words the shaman had chanted upon his arrival. Blood of the wolf. Could it be possible? She had put Velamir's face as the hero of legends in her mind, but could he truly be *the* hero?

Velamir nodded his thanks, and as they left, Natassa glanced back, meeting the unsettling gaze of the shaman. The Savagelanders allowed them to leave peacefully. Finnean's relief was clear as he took his place beside Velamir at the lead. Latimus fell into step beside Natassa, and she stiffened, wondering what other insults he had prepared for her. She waited for him to speak, but long seconds passed.

"You saved me back there," he blurted, and then, so softly she almost missed it, he said, "Thank you."

Natassa smiled, surprised. He returned to the front, and a rush of happiness filled her. The group was starting to accept her. But the elation faded when the conflicting dread swiftly returned to her again.

Would they still accept her if they knew the truth?

27

KASDEYA EYED THE king before her. The old man slumped over the chessboard, and greasy hair hung over his lined forehead. It probably hadn't been washed in weeks. The king didn't care about himself—that much was clear—but it seemed no one else cared about him either. Kasdeya had seen the way servants ignored him, the way advisors bypassed him for Draven. He had no company but himself. If only he were sane enough to see that—to see that the castle he'd once prized was falling from his grasp. His wrinkled hand swept forward, and he swiped a pawn off the board before replacing it with his rook. He set it beside the board with the mix of other defeated pawns. A smile cracked his face in two, and he looked like a small child.

A small insane child, Kasdeya amended.

"I took your last pawn!"

She tapped a piece. "There's one more."

The king's lips drooped, and he looked at her, confusion wrinkling his face further. "Who are you?"

Kasdeya laughed. She couldn't help it. It was the fourth time he'd asked. The attendants serving tea sent her curious stares, but she ignored them. Kolesta-na had hated this senile old man, but Kasdeya was finding it impossible to loathe him. It was humorous, really, how quickly he forgot everything.

When Kasdeya had first arrived at the castle, he was still aware, lucid. It hadn't taken long for her to catch on to the gifts Draven sent him, like imported zat she knew must be laced with something that made him forget his past, everything he'd done, the way he'd sacrificed people like the pawns he took from the board in front of them. Kasdeya envied him sometimes. She wished she could forget. Forget her abusive upbringing, her mother's empty gaze after her father's death. She wished she could forget the promise she'd made at her mother's deathbed—her promise to protect Krea—and Natassa's face when she placed the dagger against her throat. She wished she could forget the betrayal that had cracked through her features.

She wished most of all that she could forget how to feel.

She had thought she'd killed her emotions the day she poisoned Natassa for the first time, but they had returned in a tumultuous wave since reading Kolesta-na's journal. She'd started to feel something for the cruel prince she had married. It was more than hate and pain and wishes to kill him. Because, every time she looked at him, she saw someone's son, an innocent boy who had been twisted by the life he'd been forced to live. Just like her.

Kasdeya leaned toward King Joster. She sent him a wink. "I'll tell you a secret."

He frowned.

"I'm going to be the queen of Ayleth." She reached out, countering his move with her knight and swiping the piece into a spot that threatened King Joster's rook. The king's confused expression faded as he watched her knight eagerly. He moved fast, steering his rook from danger. If there was one thing Joster hadn't forgotten, it was chess. It seemed his knack for playing games would follow him to his death.

Kasdeya sipped her tea, and her eyes drifted to the third and empty chair at the round table. She had been waiting for this day for so long. The day her plan would be set in motion. But since it had come, instead of antic-ipation, she felt empty and almost . . . regretful. She steeled her spine, and her hand clenched around the cup, eyes still rooted to the chair. As if sensing her thoughts, the rabbit himself entered, heading toward her snare. He paused by the chair, glancing at his father with an annoyed tilt of his lips before turning his attention to her.

Draven stepped closer, and she reluctantly stood to greet him. Then he did something she didn't expect. He tugged her toward him, almost hugging her, his hand splayed across her lower back. The touch sent a ripple of shock over her. The servants watched. Was he doing that for them or to toy with her? Who was he spinning the show for? Her speculation vanished when he leaned closer and placed his mouth by her ear.

"You look stunning today."

She'd heard it from countless others and even from Draven himself in the past, but that was before, when she had just wanted to use him. She looked up, catching hold of his pale gray eyes lit by the sunlight streaming through the grand windows. She held his gaze, then frowned when he smirked. His crooked grin tilting up in that heart-snatching way had never affected her before.

It doesn't bother me, she told herself.

So why was her heart thumping so fast?

"Careful there," he said, his voice low. "If you stare any longer, I'll get the impression you want to kiss me."

That jerked her right out of her thoughts. She stepped back, glaring at him. "Your head is looking better. The bruises are fading."

His grin withered, and he touched the marks she'd made when she slammed her head into his. He motioned to her chair, and she sat. He pushed the chair in and then took the seat meant for him.

"Chess?" he said, his gaze roving over the board. "I didn't know you played."

"One tends to learn a bit about everything when trying to survive."

Draven lifted his brows and leaned back, resting his hands on either side of the board. Kasdeya signaled to an attendant to refill their glasses. The attendant approached with a small cart, stopping behind Draven. The girl's hands shook as she filled Kasdeya's and the king's before reaching for Draven's cup. Kasdeya narrowed her gaze. The girl couldn't fail her.

The attendant darted a nervous glance at Kasdeya as she selected another teapot from the cart and poured it into Draven's cup. When she placed the cup before him, Draven looked up at her and graced her with a wink. Kasdeya gritted her teeth, a sudden surge of envy crashing through her. Why did she care? Why *should* she care? The man hated her. He dallied with other women in the room right beside hers. He was a wicked monster who deserved a dagger in his chest. So why did she want to take the attendant by the hair and drag her around the room?

Kasdeya returned her attention to the chessboard. Endless minutes passed as she and Joster exchanged moves. It was nearing the end of the game, but Draven still hadn't drunk from the teacup, leaving Kasdeya's emotions stretched taut. She wanted to scream.

Abruptly and seemingly at random, Draven stood, then waved his hands at the attendants. They all left, closing the door behind them, leaving Kasdeya alone with the king and Draven.

"I've been waiting a long time," Draven said, his voice silky, flowing like a waterfall. "A long, long time for this."

His gaze hardened, and he wrenched his father up and dragged him to the wall, then slammed him against it with a vicious heave. Kasdeya's heart thumped as she watched with growing alarm. Draven wrapped his hands around the king's neck like she'd done to him only days before.

"It's long past time for you to die."

The king gasped for breath while clasping Draven's forearms, struggling to escape his iron hold.

Kasdeya stood. "Draven."

The prince's head whipped toward her, long blond strands escaping his perfectly combed hair, gray eyes wide and unfocused. He released his father, and Joster slumped to the ground, wheezing.

"I was ten years old," Draven said, and Kasdeya wasn't sure whom he was speaking to. "I went to my mother's chamber, and I saw . . ." His jaw clenched and lids closed before flying open again. He yanked the king up by his collar. "You held my mother against the wall. And then you struck her." He lifted one hand and slammed it into Joster's face. "Again and again and again."

Each word was accompanied by another blow. Blood trailed down the king's lips, but Draven didn't stop and Kasdeya could only watch with growing apprehension.

"I tried to prevent you, but I couldn't. I wasn't strong enough then." Draven's voice strained around the words. He was crying. "You punched her here." He shoved a fist into the old man's stomach. "You killed her, slowly squeezing the life from her."

He wrapped his hands around Joster's neck once again, digging his fingers into the king's vocal cords. Joster gasped, and his eyes bulged. Life faded from those eyes as Draven continued mumbling. They collapsed to the ground, Draven leaning over the king until he stopped fighting, stopped breathing. Kasdeya slipped a hand into her skirt, reaching for the knife strapped to her thigh.

Finally, Draven looked up at her. Wet trails shone on the sharp contours of his face. He stood and approached her, and she held the knife in a tight fist, preparing herself. Draven stopped before her, staring at her for a long moment before glancing at the table. His shaking fingers curled around the teacup. He lifted the glass to his mouth and downed the contents in one gulp. Kasdeya's lips parted, eyes trained on his hand as he placed the cup back with a clatter.

"I killed him," he whispered, seemingly almost in disbelief. Then he looked at her, a sinister smile spreading across his face. "I killed him."

A tear fell from his lashes, and he closed the remaining space between them. Kasdeya raised her knife, ready to plunge it into his belly, but he crushed her into his arms, oblivious to the weapon. He pressed his face into her shoulder.

The knife slipped from her hand as he shook against her. She heard the last thing she'd ever thought she would hear from Draven: long heart-wrenching sobs. Her shoulder grew wet through the fabric. She reached up with shaking hands and gently touched his back. He pulled her closer until they were plastered together. She swallowed the ache clogging her throat. Tears stung her eyes, and she cried with him. She cried until he couldn't stand any longer, pulling her with him to the ground. She cried as he convulsed and foam appeared on his lips.

She cried and cried and cried.

28

HONZIO STRETCHED HIS legs out beneath the table. Voices, clattering plates, and thumping mugs made up the muffled background noise as his concentration was monopolized by the note in his hand. Neat loops across the paper read:

The Borel Inn is convenient enough. I will see you there.

Moralis

Honzio closed the note in his grasp. He had been waiting in the inn for ten minutes, but there had been no sign of his cousin. Bronus tilted his head in question from across the table. Thick cloaks covered them from head to toe, obscuring their faces and weapons beneath. Honzio wasn't taking any chances with the possibility that someone could recognize him and report back to his father. He shook his head at Bronus. They wouldn't be leaving yet.

"Are you sure you can trust him? Your cousin?"

The voice startled him, coming from the seat to his left. He turned to look at Aylis, or rather, at the shadowy parts of her features he could make out under her hood. Her lips were pressed thin, and the cold in her blue eyes burned him even from the darkness they hid in.

"He's helped me in the past," Honzio replied, his thoughts drifting to the years when he'd been a boy and subjected to the emperor's way of teaching. Beatings and meager amounts of food were small parts of a grand scheme Malus believed would form Honzio into a great leader. Moralis had helped him escape several of those lessons, and that was how their bond had formed. "You can trust him. As much as you trust me."

Aylis turned away, looking at the wall beside her. "I don't trust you."

She whispered the words, but they still reached Honzio's ears. They didn't bother him. After all, she'd agreed to his plan and had allowed him to blindfold her as he led her through the secret passageway out of the palace. She had to trust him on some level, or maybe she was more desperate to find her brother than he'd thought.

The door of the inn opened, and a gust of wind accompanied it. A man dressed in fine clothes and polished boots strode in with a sword belt around his hips. The innkeeper took stock of the newcomer and approached far faster than he'd done for Honzio. But then again, Honzio hadn't arrived dressed like coin. The innkeeper spoke to the man, and a deep familiar voice washed through the inn.

"Drinks on the house!" the man said, and a wave of cheers rose up.

Honzio swore under his breath at the attention he was drawing. He spotted two others behind him, both equally armed.

Aylis peered over Honzio's shoulder. "Who's that?"

The man's attention fell on them where they sat in the corner of the inn, and he set off toward their table. With his easy grin and the dark brown hair curling around his ears, it was like seeing Thorsten again. Every time Honzio thought of his little brother, he couldn't escape the pain that accompanied the memories, and to see an almost replica of Thorsten increased that pain tenfold.

"That," Honzio said as the man stopped in front of their table, "is Moralis."

Aylis released a soft gasp, and Honzio glanced at her. Her face paled until it was white as a sheet, as if she'd seen a ghost. Honzio nearly reached out to steady her but held himself back.

"Cousin." Moralis's grin stretched wider as he held his arms out.

After a moment of hesitation, knowing the eyes of the inn were plastered on them, Honzio stepped into his cousin's strong embrace. Moralis clapped him on the back several times. Honzio appreciated the enthusiasm, but the action crushed his mangled hand into his chest and he winced.

"I wanted to meet here for a reason," Honzio said

in a low voice, adjusting his hood with his good hand. "So we wouldn't draw attention."

"It was an excellent choice, but I don't think there's anything to worry about. Emperor Malus will know of my coming soon enough."

"It's not you I'm worried about."

Moralis motioned for his men to stand in front of the table to conceal their small corner from view. Bronus moved down the booth, allowing Moralis to sit. The Galva's eyes found Aylis, and he rose halfway, extending his hand to her. Aylis stared at his face and then at his hand. A look Honzio could only describe as petrified marked her features.

Honzio cleared his throat. "Moralis, this is Aylis. Aylis, this is Galvasir Moralis Vane, my cousin. He hails from Ondalar, as I've told you before."

Aylis finally reached out with shaking fingers and placed her hand into Moralis's. He lifted her fingers to his lips and brushed a kiss over them. "A pleasure, my lady."

A rosy blush spread across Aylis's cheeks. The sight irritated Honzio for reasons he didn't want to dwell on. He cleared his throat again, and Aylis snatched her hand back. Uncertainty crested on her face.

Moralis tore his attention from her and looked at Honzio. "What did you wish to speak to me about? You said you had a plan to pull me from my misery."

Honzio released a strained laugh. "Yes, I . . ." It had seemed so easy when he'd thought of the plan, but it was much harder to imagine it all unfolding. "I know you like to perform chivalrous deeds, so I thought, what better way to do that than to help this lady?"

Moralis nodded, sweeping a glance over Aylis, concern webbing his eyes as though searching her for a mortal wound.

"She's running from her family in Ayleth. They mistreated her and wanted to apprentice her to their local blacksmith in exchange for their debts." Honzio felt Aylis's eyes on him, her pointed stare growing more heated along with his lies. He hadn't told her what story he would tell. "She asked for my help, and this felt like the best way to assist you both."

"What is *this*, exactly?" Moralis asked.

"I want Aylis to pose as your fiancée." The words tumbled out of Honzio's mouth. "At least until her family stops searching and I find a place for her."

Moralis looked dumbstruck. He opened and closed his mouth several times, glancing between Aylis and Honzio. Finally, he pulled himself up straighter and nodded. Honzio could see the strong boy from their youth in his face. "I will do whatever you need."

"Aylis will be called Lady Aylis Ceves from Devorin, your intended. You will say your previous engagement was unsuccessful."

Moralis grimaced. "That much is true."

The inn door flew open again, and a clamor drew their attention. Honzio was on his feet, but not before Bronus and Moralis. His bodyguard joined the other guards, holding a protective line before them. Honzio stared over their shoulders, and a spurt of fear traveled down his spine at the sight of black and gray. The lightly armored Savagelanders—or Uluzar, as Grongar-ja had called them—swarmed inside, pushing aside men who'd been enjoying the free drinks Moralis had paid for. The customers scurried from the inn, their terror written plainly on their faces. Honzio scanned the Uluzar in search of Grongar-ja. Relief filled him when he didn't find him. A few of the Uluzar approached them, the last patrons remaining in the inn.

"We will occupy the inn for the night," one said. "We are the delegation from Uluz, or the Savagelands, as you say."

The innkeeper hurried to pour zat for the roaring Uluzar. Moralis stepped forward, and Honzio recognized the angry look on his face. He was going to do something foolish. Honzio grabbed his arm and shook his head.

Honzio raised his voice and said to the Uluzar who'd spoken, "We'll leave." Their group moved toward the door. At a sudden shriek, Honzio spun around. An Uluzar had a firm grip around Aylis's wrist. Rage flared in him and he stepped toward them, but Moralis was faster, smashing his fist into the Uluzar's face. The Uluzar released her, and Moralis pulled her behind him.

"You may be a delegation and not a war party, but I will not hesitate to kill you if you dare touch my intended again."

My intended. The words burned hotter than the rods his father used to use on him. Honzio's fist clenched as he eyed Aylis's hands wrapped around Moralis's arm.

Doubts plagued him after they managed to escape the inn without a bloodbath and parted ways. It could've been him. He could have pretended to be her fiancé. If he'd been more of a man. If he'd been whole. But no one wanted a one-armed man. No one wanted a weakling who could barely defend himself. This was better, for Aylis, for Moralis, for himself, he thought as he watched them disappear into the night.

29

THE WEATHER REMAINED frigid despite the midday sun hovering over them. The tall mountain ridge was visible in the distance. Devorin. The lofty peaks marked the kingdom, and regret poured over him. Kasdeya would part ways with them soon. He slipped a hand into his pocket, fiddling with the box nestled within.

A good choice. The Savagelander shaman's accented voice washed through his memory. *A pledge bracelet. We give it to the ones we love. The stone at the center will remain dark if not honored, broken, or at death. But it will shine red if your promise is true.*

Velamir didn't know what had urged him to take it. He glanced back. Kasdeya and Krea playfully nudged each other as they walked up the slope to where Velamir stood. Kasdeya's hair blew in the wind. Her sister said something inaudible to him, and she laughed.

The angelic sound sliced into Velamir's chest, and his fingers clenched around the box. She looked like a portrait at that moment—her face lit with joy, her cheeks flushed from the cold, her arm locked with her sister's. Velamir saved the moment in his mind, hoping he could remember it whenever darkness overwhelmed him.

"She's beautiful," Finnean said. Velamir startled, then followed his gaze and saw that Finnean was staring at Krea. "They will leave soon. We might never see them again. And even if we tried to find them, we would first have to survive the war." His resolved expression told Velamir he didn't believe they would.

"We will." Velamir clapped a hand on his shoulder. "We will live to see the good days and a land at peace." He felt as though he were assuring himself as much as Finnean.

The others joined them, with Latimus and Jax at the back of the group arguing over the health benefits of a root Latimus's mother used. Velamir led the way across a long plain. Snow coated the trail, and trees grew closer and closer together until they found themselves in an icy forest.

After a while, Finnean climbed a tree and reported down. "I see the fires of the camp."

"We're almost there," Velamir said.

Their faces shuttered. The trek had been challenging, but it would be nothing compared to their mission. Each crunch of Velamir's boots built his apprehension. What would he find at the camp? Was his mother—if she was truly there—still alive? Or had Winston killed her to destroy what was left of Boltrex? And Mordon. If he was still breathing, he'd most likely been enslaved or tortured. How would Velamir save him? How would he convince him to trust him? A soft hum cut through his distorted thoughts, stealing his focus—a calming melody that shattered his fears and built something else in their place. He glanced back at Kasdeya. She gazed at the trees around them as they walked, her mesmerizing voice entrancing him. Velamir had heard the song before. A hazy image of a singing woman with a wide smile and gleaming red hair formed in his mind's eye.

"The Song of Eshelor. It's a tale from the Old Empire," Finnean told Velamir as he fell into step beside him. "I haven't heard it in years."

Krea joined Kasdeya, and lyrics morphed with the melody.

> *On a night of tears,*
>
> *a boy was born.*
>
> *His father's fears*
>
> *were realized.*
>
> *The boy was scorned.*
>
> *He lost his mother,*
>
> *his father too.*
>
> *He lost his name,*
>
> *and all those he knew,*
>
> *but the sky whispered, the wind whispered, and behind closed doors,*
>
> *they whispered a name:*
>
> *Eshelor*

Velamir smiled for a reason he didn't know. The song made the world less dark despite being so disheartening itself. It must've been the way it was sung, with such hope, such passion. His grin widened when Finnean and Latimus joined in. Latimus's voice was as good as Kasdeya's. He exchanged a surprised glance with Jax, who nodded with a smile. Jax had heard Latimus sing when they'd stayed at his home. Velamir never remained for the dancing sessions, uncomfortable being around Lissa.

Jax's expression sank. He was thinking of her, too, Velamir guessed. He banished the worry for his friend and focused on the trail ahead and the next lines of the song.

> *Into a man the boy grew,*
>
> *and gained a family anew.*
>
> *He rose to great heights*
>
> *before he fell.*
>
> *His family was killed,*
>
> *their corpses defiled.*
>
> *He lost his name*
>
> *and those he loved,*
>
> *but the sky spoke, the wind spoke, and through gaps in doors,*
>
> *they said a name:*
>
> *Eshelor.*

Velamir listened to the story within the lyrical prose. He saw a man who'd lost everything as a child lose everything again. On his knees, crying out for a reason, for an explanation. He saw himself, and all those times he would wonder, *Why?* Why couldn't he have been someone else? Someone who had a safe home instead of wondering if he would survive until the next week? But deep down, Velamir knew he wouldn't be content with that kind of life. Because it wasn't about him; it was about all the people suffering in the Empire, in Tariqi, in Savoria, in all the world, and he had a chance to help them. And he had to take that chance even if it meant he would die for it.

> *The man had lost.*
>
> *He'd given up*
>
> *on living, on the price it cost.*
>
> *But he found the will again.*
>
> *He found his family in the world,*
>
> *in the flowers and trees, in his memories.*
>
> *He stopped the blame,*
>
> *and for them, he found his name,*
>
> *and the sky shouted, and the wind shouted, and through open doors,*
>
> *they yelled a name:*
>
> *Eshelor.*

The last verses vibrated in the wind. There was something different in the air, something different on the others' faces. Peace, contentment. Even Latimus seemed to have mellowed. Velamir faced forward. He felt lighter and stronger at the same time. But there was something nagging at him. It was the shaman's voice and his dark knowing eyes. Velamir didn't understand what he'd meant by his words but the weight of them rested on his shoulders.

The time will come, wolf's blood. You will wield the strength of kings, and you must not fail your destiny.

30

Advisor Welix accosted Coralie on her way to her uncle's chamber and, without allowing her a chance to protest, pressured Coralie into following him into the empty library.

"My uncle is currently taking his last breaths. What could be so important that you dragged me in here, Advisor?" Coralie demanded.

Instead of answering, Advisor Welix produced a parchment faded with time and extended it to her. Coralie took it, wary of its contents. She scanned over the words, her heart thumping in shock as they sank in. It was a document detailing an adoption procedure taken by Princess Mari and Prince Irox. *Her* adoption. But that couldn't be true . . .

Coralie shook her head, looking up to

meet Advisor Welix's knowing stare. "Where did you find this?" she asked, her voice rising with anger.

"Please remain calm, Your Highness. This is proof that you are not heir to Verin's throne. You will taint the chalice."

Coralie refused to believe a scrap of parchment she'd never before seen in her life. She tore the paper before Advisor Welix's wide eyes. Welix sputtered, appearing distraught at the sight of his ruined blackmail. How long had it taken him to craft it? A document so precise and even the way it appeared to be aged would require hours of patience, and the fact that he presented it to her at a moment when she was at her weakest, with her uncle breathing his last, made her doubt him further. Someone that calculated and malicious could easily have lowered the drawbridge. Could Advisor Welix be the traitor? What had Prolus's minions promised him in return? His life in exchange for giving up his home? Coralie's stomach turned in revulsion.

"I cannot believe you would sink this low, Advisor, simply to take control of Verin." Coralie's lips turned downward in disgust. "We will speak about this abhorrent display later."

She didn't wait for his response and stormed out of the library. Minutes later, Coralie swept into her uncle's chamber, blinking in the sudden darkness. The curtains were closed, and the candles waned. A somberness filled the air. Council members were gathered around her uncle's bed, their heads bowed. Was she too late? Coralie rushed forward, falling to her knees beside the bed. She gripped her uncle's waxen hand between both of hers. His eyes fluttered open, and he winced as if in great agony.

"I will be with the princess. Alone," he said, his voice coarse and laden with pain.

The council members hurried from the chamber. Blayton was the last to leave, a worried line between his brows.

After the door shut, Coralie said, "I'm here."

He coughed, and a thick trail of blood escaped his mouth, alarming her. She took a cloth from the table and dabbed around his lips. Crimson bloomed across the fabric.

"Coralie. I know . . . you will make a good queen."

A lump formed in Coralie's throat. She blinked back a sheen of tears.

"Don't listen to the cruel words of others." Her uncle coughed again, and more blood escaped, streaking onto the silk pillows propped behind his head. "You were brought up for this role. Verin will do well under your rule."

His words were strange, as if he were trying to convey something else. King Dale smiled up at her fondly. Then he wheezed, and resignation lit his eyes. He lifted a bloodstained hand and touched her cheek. "You will be all right."

His smile dimmed, and his hand dropped beside him. Coralie sat in shock for a long while, numb and cold and empty. The streak of blood on her cheek tingled, but she didn't wipe it away. She pressed her head to his chest and stayed by him with her face plastered to his linen shirt until his skin grew cold.

Warm fingers slid over her shoulder, and she jerked up.

"What are you doing here?" She said harsher than she'd intended, but she didn't regret it.

General Zenrelius didn't seem fazed by her tone. "I thought you might need comfort." He scanned her uncle before returning to her. "His pain is no longer, his glory remembered."

Part of her had hoped none of it was real, but at those words, something inside her shattered.

"I know what it's like." Zenrelius said softly. "I lost my sister."

Coralie searched his gaze. His eyes seemed to glow, the dark orbs shining with something deep. "I know."

The death of Queen Adelania had started the rift between Ondalar and Verin. She was the daughter of the Ondalarian king at the time, and he'd blamed Dale for her demise. The animosity only grew after that. Coralie didn't know Zenrelius had been close to the queen. After all, she must have been at least ten or fifteen years older and left Ondalar when she was young to marry Dale. Zenrelius would have been a boy when she died. But the stark pain and agony was evident on his face. Coralie's pity rose, and she didn't fight it when he took her hand. His lips brushed over her fingers, and the cracks in his features seemed to grow wider. He drew her closer, and Coralie placed her head on his shoulder.

Something told her to stay away, but at that moment, she couldn't see reason. It might have been because of the raw pain on his face; when she looked at him, she saw Mordon in his features—in the black of his hair, strength in his stance, in the callouses marking his palms. Zenrelius reached up and placed his hand in her hair, his fingers weaving through her thick braids.

But Coralie snapped to her senses and pulled back. If Zenrelius was startled by her abrupt retreat, he didn't show it. His face returned to the calm mask she associated him with.

Coralie looked back at her uncle. "There's no time for tears," she whispered, brushing the back of her hand across her face.

She stepped toward the bed and took hold of the white sheet. Despite Advisor Welix's attempt to dissuade her from taking the throne, she would be queen, and it was up to her to defend Verin. Prolus had taken everything from her—her parents, her life, her love—and he was coming for the rest of the kingdom. She covered her uncle's face with the sheet and leaned over to place a final kiss on his forehead. Her lips met cold fabric. No, it wasn't the time for tears.

It was time for revenge.

31

"Y OU'VE PROVEN YOURSELF worthy of these colors."

Mordon stared at the black and red fabric splayed across the table in the middle of his tent—one of only thirty tents with a black stripe running down the side, marking him as a captain. He was no longer a prisoner but a leader in the Dark Army. Mordon had never thought he would see the day. Guilt swirled in his gut as he pictured the faces he'd once been loyal to: King Dale, Boltrex, the soldiers who had fought alongside him in Verintown. He dunked his hands into the bucket of water beside the table, then scrubbed his face, ran his fingers through his short beard, and splashed water over his head. The cold water seeped into his scalp and dripped onto his bare shoulders. A piercing stare examined him as he washed his hair.

"Won't you put it on?" Winston asked.

Mordon's gaze fell on the clothes. Hair hung in his eyes, obscuring his vision. He flung the dripping strands back and reached for the uniform, but he stalled an inch from the fabric. Could he truly do it? Could he become a captain for Prolus even if it were temporary? Could he pledge himself to the Dark Lord? Mordon grabbed the uniform. He pulled on the trousers and tunic before he took the provided leather and tightened the straps across his chest. He looked down, staring at Prolus's symbol marking the front of the leather. The smiling mask seemed to jeer at him.

Winston approached, lifting a gold pin engraved with sharp slashes of letters. *Calestor*, it read, the Tariqin form of *captain*, so similar to Cales, the Imperial version. Winston pinned it onto Mordon's chest and peered at him with pride. He should've felt something at that look, but it only reminded him of a moment years back when he'd returned to Castle Verin after his duty at the Borderlands. He'd been given a new suit of armor along with the title of Galvasir. It had been months since he'd seen Boltrex. His father hadn't given him emotional words or an embrace or even a smile. He'd only stared at Mordon and tipped his head. His eyes held a glint that Mordon had read as pride, but it was gone so quickly he might've imagined it. Then Boltrex's lips had twitched—not a smile, but almost. That had been one of the best days of his life. The day he'd been closest to earning his father's approval. Boltrex, he reminded himself. *Not Father. Boltrex.*

Mordon straightened in his new uniform. Boltrex was dead to him. Winston, his true father, stood before him, accepting him with open arms. So why did he feel nothing?

"You look like a true Calestor." Winston smiled and then added, "Calestor Cselnsor."

Winston had instructed the other men to call him by that name. Mordon was gone, trampled to ash like Verintown. Wasted and forgotten. At least by Winston.

"You've chosen your men?"

Mordon nodded, thinking of the people he'd picked to complete his group. All Savorian, including ones rejected from other groups, and Silopar as well. He'd considered some of the Tariqins but decided against them. They looked at him like they didn't trust him in the least. He couldn't place confidence in a person likely to stab him in the back rather than obey him.

"The Chishmans have returned from scouting."

Mordon didn't respond, hooking his sword belt over his hips.

"They've seen people evacuating the castle."

Mordon's head snapped up at that.

A calculating gleam lit Winston's blue eyes. "The storms have lessened. We are awaiting Prolus's order to eradicate the group."

"I thought you wanted to kill Prolus and take his place."

"We, Son, *we*. *We* will kill him. *We* will take his place. Don't forget you are with me. But now is not the time. Enjoy the freedom you have and the revenge you will taste when we take the castle. Boltrex and Velamir will be there."

And Coralie, Mordon thought. She would fight the Dark Army even if she were the last one standing in the castle. He had to do something, find some way to convince her to surrender.

Mordon cleared his throat. "Excuse me." He pivoted on a heel and left the tent. He knew his departure was as abrupt as it felt when he caught sight of Winston's bewildered look, but he needed a moment alone.

He made his way to the rumlok cages and nodded at the deedans standing guard. They hesitated before one of them unlocked the metal door with uncertain fingers. Mordon entered the cage, and then the door clanged shut behind him. Growls and sniffs greeted him. He scanned the rumloks, and a smile graced his face when he caught sight of thick black fur approaching him through the sea of gray and white. Intelligent red eyes gleamed, focusing on him. He crouched, and the rumlok charged forward and tackled him to the ground. Mordon groaned, wrapping his arms around the rumlok's midsection, and rolled with him. The rumlok buried his nose in Mordon's face and hair, catching his scent. Mordon laughed and patted the thick muscle rippling along the rumlok's side. He closed his eyes, focusing on the whispers. The rumloks' voices invaded his mind, and he could feel them circling him.

"Down," he breathed. "Get down."

When he opened his eyes, the animals were gathered around him, their heads bowed. They had accepted him. It had taken days of trying, but it seemed they had given in.

Distant shouts snatched his attention, and Mordon clambered up and strode back to the cage door. The deedans allowed him through. He headed for the camp's entrance. Half his group was guarding the open area between two posts. Mordon grimaced. Of course things had gone awry when his men were assigned guard duty. As he neared, he spotted ragged-looking men attempting to force their way through. Curses were thrown back and forth between members of the camp and the newly arrived bandits. The bound prisoners behind the bandits remained quiet.

"What's going on here?" Mordon shouted, and all eyes swung to him.

He spotted a familiar man at the front of the bandits. Calm, calculating brown eyes and a mohawk adorning his head. Then it hit him: the mercenary leader, the one Coralie had commissioned a portrait of to warn the people in Verintown.

"Vykus," he said bluntly.

The man smiled. "My reputation precedes me as usual."

Weeks ago, Mordon wouldn't have hesitated to spear a blade through his gut. The man had stolen more from Verin than he could count.

"Are these your men?" Vykus asked, gesturing to the Savorians. "They don't seem pleased that I brought more of their countryfolk. Tell them to stand down, or they will have to answer to Prolus when he hears of this."

A tall man stepped up behind Vykus, bald, with tattoos crisscrossing his skull.

"We are guarding the gate. Prove you aren't a foe, and I will consider letting you cross," Mordon said.

Vykus let out a barking laugh. "He will consider.

Consider! Who do you think you are, boy? I haven't seen you a day in my life, and I can tell you that I am far more important to Prolus than . . ." His eyes dipped to the gold pin at Mordon's chest. "Than some Calestor."

"We will see. State your business."

"I brought recruits."

Mordon surveyed the prisoners. They were younger than he'd first thought. "They're children."

"Let me reword that. *Slaves.* I'm delivering slaves." Vykus grinned upon hearing the disgruntlement of Mordon's men.

Mordon's jaw clenched as he met Silopar's gaze. The Savorian Handler shook his head. Mordon could read the emotions on his face easily. *Don't allow him to continue using us.* But what else could Mordon do? He wasn't a hero. He wasn't some kind of saint. And he sure as hell wasn't the king the Savorians were waiting on to rescue them.

"Let them pass."

A groan shuddered through his men, and it seemed to pain them to step aside for the mercenaries.

Vykus smiled. "Good choice." He brushed past Mordon.

Mordon glared at his back, watching the mercenaries shove the slaves forward. Silopar came to stand beside him. "They will be safer here, your countrymen. Would you rather have left them at the kindness of the mercenaries? In the cold? With no food and no shelter?"

"You had no choice," Silopar said. "I understand."

Mordon could see that he did, but there was also disappointment in the Handler's face. Mordon headed to

Winston's tent. He was supposed to report to the general at midday along with the other Calestors.

When he arrived at the tent, the deedan guarding it told him to wait. "He has a visitor. Vykus has returned."

Mordon moved around to the back of the tent, pressing close to the canvas in hopes of catching wind of the conversation within.

"You failed your mission. It would not surprise me if Prolus has you killed for this," Winston was saying.

Mordon heard an amused laugh, and Vykus replied, "If it wasn't for your Chishma, I would have been successful. You vouched for the boy in Namaar, and now he ruined a masterfully crafted plan. You should have been more careful."

"Velamir will pay for his treachery, but we expected more from you, Vykus. Not only did you lose your captives, but you also scurried to our camp instead of reclaiming them. We will never find another chance to abduct Emperor Malus's daughter."

He heard a thump and pictured Winston's fist hitting the table.

"I lost many men, and besides that, my wanted poster has been circulating throughout Hearcross. I could either risk my head or the gold I was promised, and as much as you might find this hard to believe, my head has more value to me." A pause. "And I need more of the traveling potion."

"You're out so soon? I told you to use it sparingly and only when at dire risk."

"With all the people hunting me down, it seemed dire enough."

"Zamanin Sulari is a new invention, and it's very pricy."

"You didn't seem to consider it so valuable when you tested it on my men," Vykus shot back.

"I wasn't going to use it on my own soldiers when I wasn't sure of its capabilities. But now that I know its strength, it is no longer expendable."

"Unlike my men." Vykus's chuckle boomed through the canvas. "Well, one of my *expendable* men saw a group of people in the forest on our way here."

A disturbed tone marked Winston's voice. "Who were they?"

"How should I know? I didn't see them myself, but my man said they were nearing the camp and the description he gave of one of them sounded strikingly familiar to your boy Velamir."

"I have heard nothing from the Chishmans scouting the forest."

"Set up precautions before it's too late."

"Do not think to advise me," Winston snapped. "I know what I'm doing. If Velamir is truly coming, the Chishmans will inform me."

"Now about the pay . . ." Vykus changed the subject. "I brought the slaves. I should be compensated part of the agreed amount. And I lost many men in this venture. No thanks to your traitor Chishma."

"Prolus will decide your pay, if he even sees you fit of earning one."

"He'd better, or I will find a more advantageous employer."

"I wouldn't do that if I were you," Winston said

with an icy edge. "You know what Prolus does to traitors, don't you?"

"I wouldn't be a traitor. This is business. I do what I want, and I don't care what anyone else has to say."

Winston continued as if he hadn't heard Vykus. "He skins them alive. He tortures them in the most gruesome ways until he feels they have paid for their crimes."

"It's a good thing I am not his soldier, then," Vykus said. "Be careful, Winston. I would hate to see you skinned."

Vykus's loud laugh rent the air outside the tent, and Mordon watched the mercenary leave as he processed what he'd heard. Velamir was coming. Mordon ran a finger along his scar. He'd been longing for a reunion.

32

NATASSA PICKED UP a branch and stacked it over the wood in her arms. Ever since they'd stopped an hour before, a sinking feeling had settled deep in her bones. She'd used her shadows. Hoping to give the others courage and peace for the journey, she'd driven those feelings into them with her voice and the silken power drifting through the song. Natassa had been drained after, but she didn't regret what she had done. The team had grown closer, more bound.

She sat on a fallen log and placed the stack of wood beside it, then brushed a twig along the snow, creating lines and marks, crafting a face. An ache filled her, and she longed for a paintbrush or a palette of colors, to paint to relieve the tension in her shoulders. But that time was gone, stuck behind in the palace and entrapped with the ghost of her former self. Natassa froze when she made out the face she'd sketched in the snow. A firm jaw, a strong chin, and a long slightly bent nose. Natassa grimaced and wiped her hand across it, slashing away the evidence. She was leaving soon, and she would have to forget Velamir when she did.

A perfect tree stood a short distance ahead of her. It was about the same size and girth as the one she used to practice on in Hearcross with Thorsten. A sudden sting of tears made her blink. She stood, edging closer to the tree. Natassa touched the belt at her waist equipped with her new set of knives. She deftly drew one free and propelled it into the air. It sailed into the wood with a satisfying *thunk*. Natassa released a breath that clouded the air before her. She withdrew another knife and aimed. It landed beside the first. She could almost hear Thorsten applauding her and then picture his thick brows lowering.

Firm your stance, shoulders back.

Natassa's lips trembled as she smiled. She missed him. She missed him so much. What she wouldn't give for one more day, even one more moment with him. Natassa exhaled a shaky breath as she slipped another knife free. She lifted her arm, her fingers on the end of the knife, holding it lightly. She released, and it flew toward the tree, the metal glinting in the icy daylight. An arrow slammed against it, dragging the knife into the snow. Natassa gasped and whirled around. Velamir stood in an open space between trees, his bow in his grasp. She was struck like she'd been the moment she first saw him—riding to her rescue like a hero in legends.

"You're good," he said, motioning to the tree.

"My brother taught me. I prefer it to close combat."

He angled his head, examining her. "You were the princess's bodyguard, weren't you?"

Natassa glanced away, cursing herself silently. If she wasn't more careful, she would give herself away. *I think you should tell him.* Krea's words drifted over her. *The truth.*

"We were more like body doubles, there to take the fatal blows."

"She didn't deserve you." His voice was bitter, and she guessed he was remembering the way Kasdeya had treated them.

Natassa ducked her head. *Had* she deserved her bodyguards? Their lives had been at risk so often, and yet she was always focused on other things. She hadn't been worthy. No wonder Kasdeya had betrayed her. Natassa's fingers curled over her belt, and she glared at the snow. She had to stop relying on other people for protection.

"Will you teach me?" She glanced up at Velamir. "To shoot?"

He stared impassively for a long moment, as if struggling with himself, and then he nodded. He closed the distance between them. *Breathe, Natassa,* she told herself. Velamir stared at her as if memorizing every feature, every breath she took. Natassa wished she could paint him again—a real painting, not like the one she'd done in Hearcross. That one was missing the strands of gold in his dark hair, the flecks of amber in his emerald eyes, the determined tilt of his head, and the beard cresting his strong jaw. Natassa's eyes traveled over his face, taking in all the details. His thick hair was beginning to fall over his forehead.

"The bow."

She glanced down and realized he was holding his bow out to her. Her blush deepened, and she took the weapon, unable to meet his gaze. Instead, she examined the bow. It was heavier than it looked. Gentle fingers touched her chin, lifting her head. Her eyes darted to Velamir's.

Humor creased his face. "You must look at your target if you want to learn."

Natassa marveled at how drastically different he looked when he smiled. He directed her chin toward the tree and then dropped his hand.

"There," he said. "Your target is between the two knives you threw."

Natassa released a small laugh. "There is barely any space. I won't be able to hit it."

"Not with that mindset."

Natassa straightened her back and lifted the bow. Velamir stepped behind her. She was more aware of herself the closer he came. Of the beating in her chest, the rapid breaths escaping her lips, the warmth blooming across her skin. She attempted to ignore him. She squinted instead at the almost nonexistent gap between her knives.

Velamir held out a long arrow shaft. Natassa took it, muttering her thanks, then fumbled to place it on the string. Velamir reached out to help, but she protested, assuring him that she could manage. She slid the arrow on and lifted the bow. She pulled back, her lips tightening in a grimace. Natassa's arms quivered. How did Velamir do it so easily?

She released, and her shot went wild, careening into the snow far from the target. Natassa peeked at Velamir, but he didn't look amused or pitying.

"Again," he said.

"Perhaps I shouldn't."

He closed the remaining space between them, with his chest pressed to the back of her head. Natassa froze as his arms circled her. He moved her gently, adjusting her stance before pulling forth another arrow and fixing it to the string.

"Lift the bow."

She did as instructed. The shaking in her muscles stopping when Velamir's hands drifted over hers, guiding the bow and holding her steady. Natassa's heart thudded so fiercely she feared it might escape her chest. She feared Velamir heard it too.

"Focus on your target." His breath ruffled her hair, and his chin brushed the top of her head.

He pulled the string back, his fingers enclosing hers. Natassa allowed him to direct her. She felt something thumping against her ear and realized his heart was beating as fast as hers. The thought comforted her somewhat, and she smiled.

"Release," Velamir murmured.

The string sprang forward, and the arrow flew, twisting through the air. Natassa gasped when it hit the spot between the knives. She clapped her hands and glanced up at Velamir. Her giddiness stilled when she saw the warm look in his eyes. She blinked, fisting her skirt as silence descended. "You were always shooting in Castle Verin."

He touched the scar trailing his neck. "It's something I do when I feel frustrated. It . . . It brings me . . ."

"Peace," she finished for him, and his gaze tangled with hers.

It was the same thing she felt when she threw her knives or painted.

"Yes, whenever my anger or tension builds, I focus on a target. When I'm shooting, nothing can stop me. The way forward is vivid and clear." His voice dropped to a gruff whisper. "It's as clear as you are to me now."

Natassa's breath caught. He reached out with tentative fingers. In a movement so gentle, so tender, Velamir brushed back the hair fluttering over her lashes. Her eyes drifted closed. He grazed her ear as he moved the hair behind it, and his hand came to rest on her cheek. He trailed a finger over the skin there. Natassa didn't dare to open her eyes, afraid he would see how much a simple touch had affected her.

"Velamir!"

Natassa's eyes flew open, and she broke away from Velamir. His hand dropped to his side, regret looming in his features.

"I'm here, Latimus," he called without taking his eyes off her.

The crack of twigs and brush of branches neared, and then Latimus stepped into view. He scanned them with a frown before speaking.

"Finnean caught some rabbits, and Jax is waiting for the wood. He's out of the magic fire."

Natassa contained a laugh at his description of Jax's concoction. She went to recover her knives and the wood she had placed by the log. Velamir retrieved his arrows and tucked them into his quiver. As they trekked back to the group, they encountered Krea with her own stack of wood. She shot Natassa a smirk that told her she had seen some of the encounter with Velamir, if not all of it. Natassa ducked her head, concealing a bashful smile, and fought the urge to place a hand over her racing heart—a heart bursting with an unnamed emotion. A heart she feared she was losing.

33

HER EARS TWITCHED at the distant buzz of voices. Kasdeya had been existing on the edge of reality for hours as she tried to fight the drug-induced sleep. The dreams, or rather, nightmares, gushed through her mind until she couldn't tell what was real. She saw herself embracing Draven and then plunging a dagger into his back. He stumbled, holding his own weapon: a blade soaked red. Kasdeya looked down, gasping at the crimson spreading across the front of her dress. She dropped to her knees, and Draven wound up on the ground beneath her, foam bubbling from his lips.

I poisoned him, she thought. And then she saw something she wished she could take back: an image of herself uncorking the anti-dote and pouring it past his lips. His dazed

eyes focused on her with a rush of searing fire. Kasdeya felt the anger all the way to her bones and wished with all her might she could reverse time. The doors smashed open, and guards poured inside. Kasdeya had ordered the attendant to send them in after twenty minutes. She had been so sure Draven and Joster would be dead, and the story of them being killed by Chishman assassins lingered on her tongue. But nothing went the way she'd planned.

The guards circled her and Draven in the terrible nightmare. Their concerned shouts sounded like gibberish, but her focus remained on Draven and the menacing hate emanating from him. Then his mouth moved.

It was her, he'd said. *It was her.*

She screamed at that moment, and when the guards grabbed her, she'd thrashed against them. Something sharp pierced her skin, and darkness enveloped her.

"Ready the carriage. We're leaving as soon as she awakens."

The voice was so familiar it brought an ache to her chest. She hated it with such a passion, and she hated that it had become something more.

"But, Your Majesty . . . she tried to kill you."

Your Majesty. He was king. He'd made it. Kasdeya struggled to open her eyes, but a heavy weight rested over her lids. The sounds faded, and so did she, back into the torrent of nightmares.

Until they stopped, releasing her from their torturous hold. Kasdeya lay still, the silence a peace she'd never known. There were no thoughts plaguing her, no monstrous memory haunting her. They had all been pushed back to the depths of her mind, like a hidden chest beneath a floorboard. Then a wave of fear splashed through her. She couldn't move her hands.

A gasp slipped past her lips, and her eyes shot open. Kasdeya sat up. Rough cords bound her wrists together. She was in her room—the room meant for Natassa. Her chest rose and fell in harsh breaths as she struggled against her bindings. Night's claw-like hands filtered through the large window behind the bed, draping its darkness over her. A rustle of pages stole her attention, and her head snapped toward the sound. Draven sat beside the bed, reading from a book by candlelight.

Panic struck her like lightning. It was her book filled with translated text, the one loaded with secrets. How had he gotten it? Draven tucked a strand of white-blond hair behind his ear.

He glanced up, meeting her harried alarm with gleaming gray eyes. "I would tell you to hide your belongings more securely in the future, but"—he snapped the book closed and moved to stand over her—"it won't happen again. *Ever* again."

He wasn't just speaking about her hiding things from him. He was hinting at that uncertain bond, that shaky bridge that had formed between them. Their shared pain that had linked them together. He was severing that fragile connection for good.

"What would you have done when I was dead? Ruled Ayleth?" He laughed, and the chuckle vibrated with a darkness that rivaled the night. "You think your *masters* would've allowed that?"

Masters. The word ravaged her chest like sharp

talons. All her life, she'd been owned by someone. By Prolus, by Savagelanders, even by destiny, which had fated her to be born a peasant when she could've been so much more. Something wet slipped down her face. A tear. A cursed tear. Draven stared at her, at the tear, as that stony exterior of his neared. Kasdeya closed her eyes. She didn't want him to see her vulnerable. Not again. She longed to slash the tear from her cheek, but her bound hands prevented it.

What had she done to deserve this life? She'd only wanted to be secure in the high ranks of power and wealth. Another tear followed, and she took a shaky breath instead of releasing the scream begging to burst out. Stiff fingers brushed the tear from her skin, and her lids flew open. She stared into eyes that could wither summer to winter. Kasdeya knew everything he was capable of, but in that moment, as he wiped her tears, she wished he could've been different.

"Draven," she said, her voice raspy. "Give me a chance. Give *us* a chance."

His hand froze on her cheek. He stared at her, surprise evident in his face. He searched her features, and those steel eyes warmed. That rigid jaw softened. In that moment, she could see all his pain and hurt written across his face like the patchwork of fabrics her mother had used to make a raggedy blanket when she was little.

"My mother told me a bedtime story when I was young. It was the same one every night." His hand moved again, drawing circles on her cheek. He sat beside her on the bed. "About a woman who'd loved, who had given everything. Who'd cut her own heart out." His other hand tightened into a fist. "I knew she was speaking of herself, of her loyalty to my father. The woman in the story was betrayed in every way possible. My mother would make me promise every night after she finished the tale. *Promise me*, she'd say." His eyes grew hard, and his hand slipped past her cheek into her hair, gripping it tight. *"Promise me that will never happen. Promise me if you're ever betrayed, you won't allow it to happen again."*

Kasdeya winced as his grip on her hair tightened.

"I won't let you." His eyes fastened on hers, and he tugged her head toward his. "I won't give you another chance to betray me."

Kasdeya shook her head, a gasp slipping out as he stood and tore the cord around her wrists free.

"Move." He jerked her up by her arm.

"Draven!" She tripped, but he didn't stop. His grip was vicious. "Please." The sob burst out of her, followed by a cry that she would have never allowed in the past.

He ignored her pleas as he tossed her out of the chamber and shoved her through the hall. Kasdeya stumbled, spent and empty. The stares of the servants drifted over her as she was thrown out of the castle. A gilded carriage awaited them in the courtyard. The stars and guards were there to witness Draven's brutality as he dragged her, and tossed her inside the carriage. Then the door closed with a thud.

Kasdeya huddled inside alone, unable to stop the shaking that racked her form. Her hair hung in front of her eyes in a ragged mess. She heard Draven shout at the guards, and the carriage rocked forward, traveling at a clipped pace. She reached out with a shaking hand and moved the brocade curtain aside. Draven rode at the front of the group, his back rigid, guards swarming around him.

Kasdeya released the curtain and placed her head against the seat. Her stomach revolted as the carriage moved faster, and she threw up. She drew in a shaky breath, grimaced, and wiped her lips. Then her hand drifted to her thigh, and her fingers slipped through the folds of her skirt over the knife sheathed there.

Hours passed and her hand didn't waver until she found the courage to do what her father had done so long ago. She unsheathed the knife and lifted it ever so slowly. She closed her eyes and brought it to her throat.

"I'm coming, Papa," she whispered.

The knife bit her skin.

34

Velamir

Kingdom of Verin

THE SILENCE EMPHASIZED the crackle of the fire, and the surrounding trees curled their long branches over them. Velamir opened his flask and poured water over his hand. The oily coating of rabbit meat dripped off his fingers. He leaned back against a trunk. Latimus's arms were crossed over his chest, his eyes shut. Kasdeya and her sister had bundled together to conserve heat. Jax was feeding the Sirchoba the remaining rabbit meat. The bird snatched the strands of flesh with a sharp beak.

It was the first time in a long time Velamir had felt peace. He wasn't sure the undercurrent of weariness and uncontrollable tensing of his muscles would ever leave him, but it was the first time he'd eaten a meal without thinking of death, without worrying about whom he would kill next. His thoughts had been taken prisoner by another force. He glanced at Kasdeya resting against her sister's shoulder, her lips curving upward as Krea spoke.

It was strange that she didn't know how to shoot. She had been the princess's bodyguard at one point. Velamir's fingers closed into a fist at the memory of her telling him she'd been more of a shield. She was worth so much more. Didn't she know that?

She certainly didn't know how his heart quickened when she smiled or how his attention was drawn to her by any slight movement she made. She didn't know her own courage, but he'd seen it many times. When she'd warned them of the Savagelanders' presence or when she'd stood before the Karakan, hair blowing wildly, birthmark gleaming like the sun, stance as firm as a mountain. She was beautiful.

Kasdeya's eyes caught his, and a flush crept over her cheeks. It was the most endearing shade of pink he'd ever seen. Sometimes he would catch himself watching her, hoping to see it. She ducked her head, tearing her eyes from his. Velamir smiled, and heat closed over him like a blanket. Not from the crackling fire, but the memory of her skin, soft as silk.

But she would be leaving him. She would be leaving the group. And he would only be hurt if he grew too attached.

Krea leaned forward, an excited grin on her face. "Let's play a game. General's Three."

Velamir had never heard of it. Latimus perked up, and Finnean leaned forward.

"How do you play?" Velamir asked.

"It's fairly simple. The person beside you secretly tells you a word, and you must announce three words that describe the mystery one. If the person on the other side of you can guess the original word from the three, they score a point, but if they cannot, they will be skipped."

Jax spoke up. "Why's it called General's Three?"

"It's a village game about General Zenrelius. When he was young, he came across a group of Chishmans that had infiltrated the Empire. He told them to leave, but they didn't listen. They say it was the first time he ever wielded a sword he bloodied. He was eleven." Krea paused for dramatic effect.

Latimus whooped. "I already love this game."

"I'm not surprised." Finnean rolled his eyes.

"When the Chishmans came closer, he told them, 'I gave you a chance. Is one word not enough? Do you need three?' Or so they say." Krea laughed. "The villagers, I mean. I do not know if it's true."

"It's not," Velamir said, his voice darker than he'd intended, and everyone's attention swung to him. The Ondalarian general with his golden armbands and scowling face unsettled him. "A boy of eleven years could never defeat one Chishma, let alone multiple. Even Zenrelius."

An awkward silence descended, and then Finnean spoke. "Well, let's play, shall we?"

Krea nodded. "Jax, choose a word and tell it to Finnean, but don't let the rest of us hear."

Jax's face scrunched as he thought. Finally, he leaned closer to Finnean. Then it was Finnean's turn to think of three words. He stared at Krea as he did. She returned his stare. Velamir felt like he was interrupting something.

"Bright, scattered, unreachable."

Krea tapped her chin. "Hmm." She answered a moment later. "Stars."

Finnean laughed. "Correct, though I was wrong about one word. I said they were unreachable, but the brightest star somehow sits right before me."

Latimus made an exaggerated gagging noise, but Krea's eyes widened and she grinned. "Why, thank you, kind sir."

Velamir glanced at Kasdeya. She watched her sister with a small but somewhat sad smile. The game continued. Jax was unable to guess Latimus's word and was forced to skip his turn, leaving Latimus to provide a word for Velamir. He approached Velamir and stood for a moment, wearing a contemplative look. Then he glanced at the others, lingering a moment on Kasdeya. He leaned close to Velamir and said in a low voice, "Love."

The word took him aback. Velamir sat frozen for a long second, watching Latimus retreat to his seat with a smirk. Velamir blinked. Was it that obvious?

"Well?" Latimus waggled his brows. "Can't think of anything?"

Velamir glared at him. "Give me a moment. We waited nearly thirty minutes for you."

Jax and Finnean chuckled at the exchange while Velamir drifted off. What did he know of love? His first thought was of a family. Parents, siblings, a tangible bond. But he'd never known that love. Winston was the only parent he'd known, and he had betrayed him, raised him into a monster. Kasdeya patted the Sirchoba's head as the bird nestled in her lap. She glanced up, watching him as she waited for him to speak.

"Fragile," he said softly. That was how he felt right then. After all the betrayal and bloodshed in his life, was he even capable of love? Of being loved? The embers of the fire sparked, filling the silence. "Relentless. Battlefield."

Latimus snorted, but Velamir remained focused on Kasdeya. She frowned, ruminating. "I am not sure." She peered at Latimus, perhaps wondering what kind of word he would choose. "Crown? They're made of fragile jewels. People go to war for titles?"

Before Velamir could reply, Latimus chuckled. "It was actually *love*, but it seems Velamir cannot find the right words."

"Love?" Kasdeya said. "Is that how you view love? As a battlefield?"

Velamir's hand trailed over his sword hilt as he looked down. Then he slowly lifted his gaze, finding hers. "I believe the greatest battle would be fighting for the ones you love."

The stillness that followed could only be described as timeless. At least to Velamir. The other voices and conversation faded. He only saw her—her widened hazel eyes and stunned features that glowed in the firelight. He would've shot a thousand arrows if she asked. For her, he would make the sky rain with them. He blinked, and the moment passed.

The game continued, but Velamir couldn't focus, his thoughts drifting off.

"What do you say, Vel?"

"Huh?" He glanced up to find Jax's attention riveted on him.

Jax spoke quickly. "I got the word right. *Talent.* We were wondering what we would do if we weren't on this mission. If we weren't . . . hadn't been . . ."

Chishma, Velamir finished in his mind.

"I would open a shop, craft things," Jax said. "Maybe search for my cousin Lilly to see how she is."

"I, for one, would've made a great ambassador." Latimus grinned. "Perhaps I still will, once this is all over."

Velamir couldn't hold in his laughter. "You? An ambassador?"

Latimus shrugged. "I can be convincing." He stood, brushing off his tunic, and then puffed his chest. "I, Latimus Blayton, on behalf of King Dale of Verin, have come to discuss trading routes."

The others joined in Velamir's laughter, unable to hide their mirth at Latimus's silly expression.

"What?" he said, but his mouth tilted up in a smile too.

"If I had a choice," Finnean began, and Latimus sat back down, "I would live somewhere peaceful and never pick up a weapon again. Maybe get married to a beautiful woman." His eyes slid to Krea. "Have a passel of children. Who knows?"

Krea sighed. "That sounds like a dream to me."

"More like a nightmare. Imagine all those children." Latimus shuddered. "Horrible creatures."

Finnean ignored Latimus and gave Krea a sad smile. "And that's all it will ever be. A dream."

And when they were on the verge of entering an enemy camp, death was nearer to them than any dream of a different life.

35

MORDON FLUNG THE tent flap aside despite the guard attempting to deny him entry. He stepped inside, and Winston looked up, startled. The death grip he had around a dagger stabbed into the table loosened. It seemed Vykus's words had troubled him more than he'd let on.

The deedan behind Mordon spoke fast. "General, I could not stop him."

Winston waved him off. "Leave us."

Mordon waited until he heard the tent flap fall, his focus remaining rooted on Winston. "What are your plans for Velamir?"

Winston released the dagger, stepping around the table. "Velamir?" His eyes lit in understanding. "Ah, you heard my conversation with that ruffian."

Mordon didn't falter, his posture firm as Winston drew nearer.

"You are very clever, Cselnsor. However, I would prefer if you spied on the enemy rather than your own father."

The enemy. Mordon was starting to wonder who *wasn't* his enemy.

When he didn't respond, Winston frowned, returning to the table to pour himself a glass of zat. He took a long sip, then smacked his lips in appreciation. He held the glass out to Mordon. "Would you like a drink?"

"I would like to know what you're planning."

"Stubborn, I admire that. I was tenacious like you when I was young." His amusement faded. "I put a lot of work and years into Velamir. If he truly is coming, there could be two reasons for that. He's either coming for his mother, in which case we will be prepared."

Mordon scowled, remembering how Winston told Boltrex his wife was still alive. Mordon hadn't seen a woman that resembled Serana in the camp. He'd memorized a portrait of her as a child—the only image of a mother he'd had. But Velamir had taken that too.

"But if he's realized his mistake and wishes to repent and rejoin Tariqi . . ."

"What of Prolus? He will forgive a traitor?" Mordon was tired of everything falling into Velamir's lap. Why was he so easily forgiven? Mordon was sure if Boltrex found out he'd become a Tariqin Calestor, he'd behead him himself.

"He overlooked your past and allowed you into the army," Winston pointed out.

"I was tested and could have easily died."

"There's no use speaking of it. For now, Velamir is a traitor and will be captured on sight. There's only one way for him to get through this camp unscathed, and that's if he chooses the right path." His voice dropped. "My path."

Mordon's brow furrowed. "We don't need him. Once a traitor, always a traitor. He will turn again."

Winston peered at him, as if trying to see through his hard exterior. "Why do you care so much about Velamir?"

"I want to get even with him. At least give him a scar that rivals mine."

Winston's mouth cracked into a hard smile. "If he doesn't choose us, then you are free to do as you wish."

Mordon's fingers formed a fist. He wanted to push harder, but he knew he had to stay calm. Winston retreated to his seat.

"I want you to guard the prisoner tent with your men. At least until we solve this Velamir situation. It has a red stripe down the center, on the western side of the camp."

Mordon grunted in acceptance. "Fine. But when is the camp going to move?"

"Soon, Cselnsor. We will know everything soon. Keep low and do as I tell you. I don't want Prolus's attention on you any more than necessary." A smile sharpened his features, almost like an afterthought. Mordon didn't like the scheming look on his face.

"You were going to marry me to the princess, but it seems that plan has gone awry."

The smile slipped off Winston's face, and his features

turned cold. Mordon could almost see his thoughts drifting to Vykus. "We don't need her. You have the blood of royalty in you. Your mother was a princess, and I have highborn blood. If we must prove your worthiness to the people, you can drink from the royal chalice. I have no doubt it will be pure."

"And why me? Why don't you take the throne for yourself?"

Winston took another swig of zat, his lips lingering over the rim of the glass before answering. "I'm older now, lad. My time will be over soon. You, on the other hand, have years ahead of you. I would rather see the world under the rule of my son than some useless fool. Do you see the Empire now? Do you think that one-armed prince could make anything of it even if Malus were out of the way? Do you think Prolus could? Prolus is just a shadow, a face no one knows. Tariqi has been living in shadows for far too long. We need someone we can see. Someone who can wield the power without hiding. Someone—" He halted, his gaze far off.

I would rather see the world under the rule of my son. The words sent a thrill over Mordon. He imagined another face saying them—a face with thin lips, dark green eyes, and a harsh scar. How he wished Boltrex would've spoken to him that way, with such belief and certainty. But his wishes were like water. Just when he thought they'd be granted, they slipped through his fingers. But Winston's words were dangerous. Anyone could've been listening outside the tent like Mordon had and could report to Prolus. Either Winston didn't care or he was very reckless.

Mordon cleared his throat, and Winston snapped out of his daze.

"Be off, then. And keep your eyes open."

"Oh, I will," Mordon said under his breath and left the tent.

36

CORALIE WATCHED AS the stone slab slid closed, sealing the tomb and her uncle's final resting place from view. Her eyes were dry and her head high. If she were to take his place, she would do it as he would have wanted—without tears, without regret, but with determination and the strength to shoulder Verin. Coralie placed a half heart to her chest and bowed her head.

"*Guleder, Amka, toh kih Alaris.*"

Goodbye, Uncle, until Alaris.

She would see him again in Alaris. In a land of tranquility, where no one hunted each other, where no one was assassinated. In the land of never-ending serenity. But until then, she would make the most of his memory. Coralie lifted her head and turned.

A sea of crimson met her. The dark red robes pinned her in place, reminding her of the dream she'd had all that time ago. Coralie scanned the faces around her, the uncertainty, the doubt. They needed a leader to guide them. They needed a flame to draw to.

Coralie cleared her throat, but there was no need to do so. All eyes were rooted to her already. She caught General Zenrelius's gaze. He gave her a reassuring nod, and his thin lips lifted in an encouraging smile. A pulse of comfort drifted through her, and she nearly forgot what she was doing. She broke contact and returned her attention to the onlookers.

"Verin's future appears dark, I know. There's no victory in sight. You're scared."

An uneasy rustle shifted through the crowd.

"My uncle, King Dale, used to tell me it was normal to fear, because how could we be brave without a little fear? Every one of you is brave." She lingered over each face. "The Dark Army will return. It's just a matter of when. We won't allow them to take Verin without a fight. I will be right there at the front, spilling every drop of my blood to stop them. Will you stand with me?"

A man yelled, "I'm with you!"

More shouts joined his, and Coralie smiled. Advisor Welix approached her with a frown, and it was obvious he was working to control himself before the crowd. She hadn't spoken to him since the incident in the library. He held the royal chalice. A servant stood behind him, carrying a radiant crown.

"Your Highness." Advisor Welix extended the chalice, a warning gleaming in his eyes.

A slice of panic stabbed her. What if there was truth to the document Welix had shown her? What if she wasn't the heir? What if Mari and Irox hadn't been her parents, as hard as that was to believe? If she refused to drink from the chalice, not only would it show disrespect to the old traditions, but it would also sprout suspicion. Her fingers shook as she extended her hand, and she stared at the limb like it belonged to someone else. Coralie wrapped her tentative fingers around the chalice. Time slowed as she brought it to her lips. Hundreds of eyes focused on her. She took a sip, the bitter liquid stinging her throat. She forced herself to swallow. Her eyes drifted down to the fluid swirling within the chalice. Her stomach twisted inside out as she waited.

The color didn't change.

Noise rushed back to her ears, and a wave of cheers rose. The chalice was taken from her numb hand and the crown placed into her hair. She held her chin up, while the crown pressed down on her head with the weight of jewels adorning it. Advisor Welix appeared distressed, but it wasn't the time for a confrontation. She stared at her people and found Zenrelius's disconcerting gaze on her once again.

"Long live the queen!" he shouted.

The chant was taken up by the rest of the chamber and echoed in Coralie's ears long after she'd left. It stayed with her as she entered the Great Hall, reminding her of who she was from that moment onward. She sat on her throne while the few minstrels remaining in the castle played a somber melody. Her people floated around the Great Hall like wraiths, their faces withdrawn. A proportioned amount of food was served to conserve what was left in the storeroom.

Coralie's eyes lingered on the entrance of the Great Hall. Many had walked through those doors. She recalled Velamir when he'd entered with the woman he called his sister. Her suspicions of him had started then. Was he sticking to the mission she'd entrusted him with? Or had he rejoined Prolus and his false father Winston? Had he surrendered Latimus and Finnean into the hands of enemies? Coralie's thoughts twisted into tangled ropes. The knots were so tight that, no matter how hard she tried, she couldn't loosen them. She could never escape her doubts completely.

A shadow covered the ground, and she glanced up. General Zenrelius stood before her on the first step leading up to the throne. His black gaze was impervious. He was well dressed in a fitted gold embroidered overcoat and boots shined to perfection. Most of his apparel was black, with hints of crimson throughout. He offered his hand, peering at her intensely. There was an aura about him that made her want to draw near . . . that made her want to earn the approval broadcasting from his eyes.

"Will you honor me with a dance, Your Majesty?"

Coralie stared at his hand and then looked up to meet his gaze, her dark brows lowering. She shook off the strange feeling his presence invoked in her. "I just lost my uncle. We are in mourning, General."

"Look around you. Haven't your people grieved enough? Dance, laugh, show them you're unafraid.

Show them you still have fight left in you. Show them you are more than a shell of a queen."

His sharp words probed deep, like a spear piercing her chest. He thought he knew her. He thought he knew her people. But he was Ondalarian, and he'd been Verin's enemy since he was young, since he'd lost his sister. Perhaps not as much of an enemy as Prolus, but an enemy all the same.

"You're right," she said, and he looked relieved. "I am the queen of Verin, and you have no right to advise me."

He stiffened but extended his hand farther. "I'm offering for the good of Verin, not to claim any authority. Give your people hope. The best way to do that is to prove you believe it's there yourself."

Coralie looked past him at the mourning people and dark hall lit by sparse candles. A plague of grief infected the room—a plague that could only be lifted by smiles and, as Zenrelius had said, *hope*. Coralie glanced at his earnest face, and finally, she nodded. She placed her hand in his, their hard-earned callouses brushing. He led her off the steps to the middle of the hall. A red sea parted for them, and curious eyes fastened on them.

"I know if my uncle were here, he would not want us to grieve." Coralie raised her voice so that everyone would hear. "He would want us to honor his memory with warmth, with friendship, with a promise to never stop smiling no matter how hard the world gets." She looked at Zenrelius, who watched her with appreciation. "And so, I will dance for him and smile for him and hope because of him. And I ask all of you to do the same."

Some people looked disgruntled, but a few smiled too. Coralie nodded toward the minstrels, and they struck up a livelier tune. Zenrelius stepped closer, placing his fingers at her lower back and taking her hand, pressing it to his shoulder. Coralie's eyes were level with his chin. They began to dance, both attempting to take the lead at once. They stumbled and laughed at their awkward movements before Zenrelius relented, allowing her the lead.

"You don't have to do all this," Coralie told him. "To encourage me, to stand by me."

"You remind me of her," he said, his features softening. "My sister. She was a strong queen."

Coralie looked up, meeting his eyes. The sharp blackness in them pulled her closer. And then there was Mordon at the forefront of her mind. How he'd wanted to dance with her during one of the castle celebrations. She'd refused him, and he'd retaliated by dancing beside her with another girl. He'd twirled the girl recklessly, and she went spiraling out of control, crashing into a group of onlookers. Coralie's partner had gone to help her, and Mordon took his place. He'd clutched her waist, pulling her close, and Coralie had gripped his shoulders, trying to contain her delight at seeing him work so hard to gain her attention.

That wasn't so difficult, was it? His dark chuckle had vibrated through her bones.

She missed him, and that yearning only increased when she was near Zenrelius. Mordon was there in the way the general stood, in the way he stared, and when they danced, she twirled like a swirl of vibrant colors. She laughed like the darkness would never come. Because she was with Mordon.

But she wasn't. Her smile faded as Zenrelius's features came back into view. His dark eyes were warm as he watched her, but then his brows lowered in concern.

"I wish I could be the reason for such a smile. Who were you thinking of?"

"No one. Just memories."

"I hope this will become one of those memories."

Coralie's eyes flicked up. What if there was another reason Zenrelius was assisting her? What if he was trying to entrap her, to earn her good favor? He must've had his eyes set on the throne. After all, as an illegitimate son, he would never receive a higher position than general or advisor unless he married into it. It might have been impossible for the emperor's children to marry less than nobility, but for a prince or princess of the four kingdoms, there was no law prohibiting such a marriage. Coralie eyed Zenrelius, trying to seek out the mastermind plotter behind the beguiling smile.

"I was, in fact, thinking of my betrothed," she told him, and his smile slipped.

"Betrothed?"

"It's not well known, but my uncle signed a betrothal agreement."

Coralie wasn't sure if there truly were any documents prepared by her uncle, but she hoped that declaration would keep the general at bay.

"You care for him, then?" He sounded bitter, but that might have been her imagination.

Coralie pictured Mordon—his windswept dark hair, his smirk, his courage, the softness in his eyes reserved just for her.

"Yes," she whispered.

Zenrelius was silent for the rest of the dance. When it was over, he led her back to her throne, where Jovinne stood. Her bodyguard was rigid and wore a scowl. Coralie wondered what had upset him.

Zenrelius took her hand and placed a kiss over her fingers. "Thank you for the pleasure of a dance, Your Majesty."

He released her hand and strode away. Coralie retook her seat. More couples spread out across the floor, and laughter floated through the hall. Coralie glanced at Jovinne. His angry look had receded into a stoic one.

"Do you have an order, my queen?"

"Tell the soldiers to mount up," she said. "It's time to march to Namaar."

37

Honzio

Karalik Empire
Hearcross, Capital of the Empire
The Grand Palace

H ONZIO PEERED AT the courtyard below through the arched gilded frame that matched the nine other windows lining the throne room wall. The gatehouse opened, and Moralis rode in with Aylis beside him and two guards riding behind them. A twinge of envy bloomed in Honzio's chest when Moralis reached up and lifted Aylis off her horse with ease. His arms were strong and steady. The sunlight shone on her hair, but it was no longer the golden halo he'd become familiar with, but as black as a raven's wing. She'd been angry when he told her to dye it. Although blond hair wasn't uncommon in the Empire, her natural shade—gold as the coins glinting in the treasury—was distinctly Savorian. Aylis looked up, and a shadow crossed her features as she took in the palace. Her face continued to darken until Moralis held out his hand. Aylis stared at it for a moment so fragile, Honzio knew it would shape her future.

If she took that hand, she would be entrusting her life to Moralis. She was daring to enter the palace again. A palace that had once served as her prison, and she would risk facing the same fate if her identity were revealed. But if she didn't take it, she would lose her chance of finding her brother. Honzio knew that if he'd been in Moralis's place, she would have rejected him in a heartbeat. He was a monster to her. A one-armed jailer who'd done nothing while her people were enslaved and killed. But Thorsten had, and she saw Thorsten in Moralis. Her face softened, and she entwined her fingers with Moralis's, sealing her fate. Regret bloomed across his chest. *It's for the best*. That was the only way he could help her. By entrusting her to someone capable enough to protect her.

"Prolus's forces are many, but they are coming from a land of ruin. His men are weak, malnourished." The voice came from behind him. Advisor Destin. "If all the kingdoms band together, we should be able to repel him."

"We have a special school here in Hearcross," another councilman said. "Experienced men who have been training their whole lives to become members of the Cadellion. We should send them, along with as many soldiers as we can spare, to aid Verin."

Honzio turned, eyeing the group as nods rounded

the circular council table. His father's gaze was fierce, and he glared until further talk ceased.

"The Cadellion has one purpose: to protect the emperor. Is the emperor in Verin?" Silence answered his question. "If I send the soldiers, I will leave Hearcross susceptible to attacks from mercenaries such as Vykus." He sent Honzio a look. "I still have had no reports on him."

"Vykus's trace has been lost," Honzio replied. "He's no longer in Hearcross. That's all we know."

"He would be dead if you had made an effort and handled the situation with the care a crown prince should have."

Honzio clamped his mouth shut. Any attempt to defend himself would further antagonize his father. The other council members shifted in their seats. Only Head Advisor Kostos seemed unfazed as he sifted through papers stacked before him.

"We have received reports that King Dale has passed on to Alaris."

Emperor Malus slammed a hand against the table. "First Joster, now Dale. Who's next?"

"The difference is Ayleth has Draven to replace his father, but Verin has no one. Without a sound leader, Prolus will take Verin with ease, Your Majesty." The advisor's mustache twitched. "The only remaining heir is his niece, Princess Coralie."

Emperor Malus released a bellowing laugh and slapped the table. "His niece, a *woman*." Malus's laughter skidded to a halt, and his face twisted in a sneer. "Just our luck. She must marry immediately. We can't have a kingdom led by an emotional woman."

"Agreed, Your Majesty," Advisor Kostos said. "But she is in mourning. It is against tradition for her to marry so soon."

"Bah! We are at war. Rules can be bent. In fact, we should have a joint wedding."

Honzio shared in the apparent confusion of the councilors. What did he mean by that?

"I don't understand, Your Majesty?" A councilman leaned forward in his chair. Lord Hisel.

Emperor Malus met his gaze squarely. "You owe taxes that have yet to be paid, Hisel. But I may be willing to overlook that. Your daughter, what is her name?"

Honzio didn't think Hisel could turn any paler. "Gabriella, Your Majesty?"

"No, the other one. The one with the large bosom and wide hips. Childbearing hips."

"Evala?" Hisel sputtered.

"Give her to me in marriage, and I shall forgive your debts."

"But she is only fifteen years of age," Hisel protested.

"It's best to take them young. Then you can mold them how you wish."

Don't do it, Honzio thought as he stared at Hisel, whose mouth opened and closed, words building but unable to spill out. *Don't do it.* But then Hisel's face settled in resignation, and Honzio closed his eyes. His father had won. He always won.

"The marriage may be solemnized when you wish it, Your Majesty."

"Good." His father's voice grated against his ears. "I'm young yet and can produce a proper son, one worthy of my place."

Honzio turned to his father, only to find the emperor already staring at him with beady intent.

"A son who is capable of riding and fighting and obeying without question."

Honzio flinched. *A son who isn't lame*, he might as well have said. He'd never wanted to launch himself at his father more than he did at that moment, but he held himself back.

A herald rushed into the throne room, announcing, "Galva Moralis Vane and Lady Aylis Ceves!"

All eyes were rooted to the entrance as the couple strode in. Honzio's gaze skimmed over Moralis, landing on Aylis. She strode forward, not like a lady but a soldier. Confident and calm. Any unease was carefully tucked away. She met Honzio's gaze for a moment, and he tried to convey his silent support to her.

"Moralis," Malus bit out, "you've paid us a visit after all these years and at the most inconvenient time. Don't you see I'm in a council meeting?"

Honzio heard the underlying warning in his father's tone. Malus knew of Moralis's ploys as a boy, how he'd helped Honzio escape from punishments, how he'd given Honzio his rebel streak. Malus was wordlessly telling Moralis he wouldn't allow it to happen again.

Moralis shrugged, an amiable smile on his face. "It's a habit, I'm afraid."

"It's a good thing habits can be broken. Why have you come?"

"To see my cousin, of course." Moralis's eyes flashed to Honzio. "Come now, Honzio, is that any way to greet a relative?"

The council stiffened with unease. Malus's fist clenched around his goblet. Any mention of Honzio's mother, even indirectly, could cause someone's death. Moralis was a living symbol of that—someone who carried Ovi's blood, someone who was unapologetic about who he was. Honzio admired Moralis for it. He wished he could be as brave.

Moralis released Aylis's hand and held out his arms. Honzio unglued his feet from the marble floor and walked into his cousin's embrace. Moralis clapped him on the back, greeting him like they hadn't just seen each other the day before.

"Honzio! It's been too long." Then, in his ear, he said, "Malus doesn't look happy to see me."

"When is he ever?" Honzio muttered back.

"Good point." Moralis laughed and pulled back. He glanced at Aylis, then took her arm, gently pulling her closer. "My fiancée, Aylis Ceves," he announced.

Emperor Malus lifted a brow. "Ceves? I thought you were with the Piree girl."

"It didn't work out. But I'm glad about that, or I never would have met the flower of my heart." His eyes scanned Aylis with such warmth, Honzio almost believed the farce.

Aylis ducked her head, her mop of black hair falling forward in a sleek wave.

Moralis tweaked her chin. "She's shy."

"And where does this Ceves woman hail from? She has such untamed locks and rather plain features."

Honzio stiffened in time with Moralis. Aylis lifted her head, and Honzio was taken aback by the stark hatred visible in her eyes.

"Loose hair is the fashion in Devorin, and I find her quite beautiful," Moralis said, a muscle jumping in his jaw. "But, of course, good taste is hard to find these days."

Anger continued to emanate from Aylis. When Honzio turned, he realized it wasn't the cruel remarks that had triggered her, but the row of Savorian slaves waiting for orders behind Malus. Aylis stepped forward, but Moralis grabbed her arm, drew her to him, and whispered in her ear. Whatever he said must have convinced her, because she nodded tersely.

Moralis gave Emperor Malus a strained smile. "If you'll excuse us, we've had a long day."

Malus waved them off, and Honzio nodded at Moralis. His cousin returned the nod and placed a hand on Aylis's back, guiding her from the room. They were near the door when she glanced back, a fierce passion crossing her face as she looked at the slaves.

It dawned on Honzio after the doors closed behind them what that look had meant. It was a promise.

38

"I**T'S BEAUTIFUL**," N**ATASSA** whispered as she peered at Jax's journal.

Jax jumped, covering the page with his hand—probably an instinct born from years of belittling. He glanced at her, then slowly drew his hand from the page to play with the stub of his little finger instead. A flush burned his cheeks, and she smiled at his awkwardness.

"I like to draw sometimes." He shrugged. "Simple things."

"This is far from simple. It's so intricate."

"Thanks," he muttered, eyeing the drawing again as if trying to see what she found so special about it.

A large bird was depicted on the page. Flames curled around it, and its wings flared out. It almost looked like a phoenix, only it had molten amber eyes, unlike the dark soulless ones she'd usually seen represented in phoenixes. Claws scratched her sleeve, and the Sirchoba clambered up her arm to sit on her shoulder. It squawked, beak pointing upward.

"It's the Sirchoba," she realized.

Jax nodded. "My impression of an adult one. The Sirchoba were like the extended hands of the Shadow Manos. Gifted Shadow Manos could use the Sirchoba to send messages quickly."

Natassa looked at the Sirchoba perched on her shoulder. Perhaps she could communicate with it. She had spoken to the Karakan weeks ago, but it had nearly killed her, which made her hesitant to try again.

Krea and Finnean folded the bedrolls, exchanging smiles and low chatter, while Latimus cleared the fireplace, removing evidence of their stay. Velamir hadn't returned yet. He'd told them he would scout the distance to the camp. She couldn't stop worrying. What if he'd been caught? What if he had fallen into a trap?

"You're a Shadow Manos," Jax said, and her head snapped toward him.

They sat on a thick log, where barren tree branches shadowed the sky from view. A chill swept over her, and she tightened her cloak around herself, much to the disapproval of the Sirchoba, who chirped at the movement.

"Yes."

"I'm sorry," he whispered.

She could feel so much agony in those two words. She saw him then—a boy who'd become twisted by things he couldn't control, and instead of helping him, the world had shunned him for it. Natassa reached out, setting a hand over his.

"You're not alone, Jax."

Tears sprouted in his vibrant blue eyes, and her heart ached. "But I will be," he said. "It's every Shadow Manos's fate. In the end, after all the torture, the shadow leaves, and you die. Alone."

His words sent a rush of panic down her spine. It was a horrible thing to imagine. She'd thought her shadows might be helping her, but what if they were just selfishly looking for an essence? A being to inhabit? A presence to live within until they found a new body and mind into which they could twist their slithery fingers? She forced the fear out. She would find the Elders, and they would help her. They would save her from those demons intruding her, and once she was free, she would aid as many Shadow Manos as she could.

She squeezed his hand. "There's always hope. We can give up, or we can hold on to it. We can grasp it until the stars burn out and the world collapses. Because even in the most desperate times, in the most uninhabitable places, it's there." She leaned down, plucking a tiny bright yellow flower from the dark shadows of the log surrounded by blades of dying grass and snow. She placed it in Jax's hand and closed his fingers around it. "It's there in the spots you least expect. We simply must be brave enough to look for it."

A small tenuous smile grew on his face as he stared at his fist. "I hope you find your aunt safe in Devorin."

The lie she'd told lodged in her throat, and she

forced a nod. "And I hope you accomplish your mission without difficulties."

With the thud of approaching boots, Velamir came into view. "The camp is close. It begins in the clearing past the forest."

Natassa met Krea's gaze, and her friend nodded. She glanced at Velamir. "Then this is where we part ways."

He seemed to struggle for words before his lips thinned and he gave a curt nod.

"Krea and I will cut through the mountain path until we reach Devorin."

Velamir nodded again, brisk and forced. She waited for him to say something, but he was silent as he shrugged a pack over his shoulder.

"Good luck," Latimus told her. In a lower tone, he said, "I'll look after him." It was not followed by the usual smirk or demeaning look. He meant every word.

"Thank you," Natassa said, earnest. "Take care of yourself."

"I will. Try not to run into any foul beasts."

"They'll most likely run from *her*," Finnean said.

Natassa laughed, ducking her head. "We'll keep out of trouble." She glanced at Krea, but her friend wasn't smiling. Natassa returned her focus to Finnean. "Goodbye, Finnean. I hope to see you all again."

"You will," Finnean told her. "If not in this life, then in Alaris."

Natassa heard a sob, and surprise rattled her. Krea pressed fingers to her mouth, shakily attempting to hold back tears. She spun around and walked over to a distant tree to collect herself. Finnean sent Natassa a sympathetic look, and his own emotions were plain to see. He followed Krea, and she turned when he came, allowing him to take her into his arms.

Natassa looked away from the scene and spotted Velamir standing on the edge of their small camp. He was the only one she hadn't said her goodbyes to. She approached him but stopped a few feet away, uncertain.

"Velamir," she said softly, and his back tensed. "Thank you for helping us. Without you, we couldn't have come this far. You will be in my thoughts. You and the others."

He remained silent, and a crack of hurt shuddered its way through her. She retreated a pace and was turning when he finally spoke.

"Don't follow the main road. Mercenaries ambush it."

He turned around, staring at her with those fiery green eyes, and she knew with certainty that she wouldn't be able to bear it if he got hurt—or killed. She closed the distance between them, gripping his arm.

"Be safe. We will see each other again," she said the words firmly. "And I want to see you whole and well. Promise me."

He placed his hand over hers, squeezing her fingers lightly. "I will try. For you."

His features shifted, and Natassa could see there was more he wanted to say. Her breath hitched, and a sudden well of tears blurred her vision. She closed her eyes, hoping to keep them at bay. "I send you to war. Return with peace. I send you to death's door. Return with sword sheathed." Her voice broke. It was the poem

Imperials said when sending their loved ones to battle. "I send you with one decree—to just return to me."

Tears had fallen from her eyes despite her attempt to hold them back. Velamir stepped closer, lifting a hand to brush the wet trails away. His coarse fingers were gentle as he tucked her hair behind her ears, exposing her birthmark. He leaned closer.

"Fly, phoenix," he whispered. "Spread your wings and soar."

He pressed a light kiss to the mark, and it touched Natassa's heart. She'd detested the mark for years because of the fear of others. Velamir proved himself to her then. Despite who she was, despite being afflicted with such darkness, he accepted her when not even her own father had. Natassa held his gaze until he stepped back, his face contorted as if it pained him to release her.

She turned to Krea, who was awaiting her. She clasped her friend's hand, needing the support. Natassa walked onward, and no matter how much she wanted to, she didn't look back. It was the hardest thing she'd ever done.

39

Velamir

Kingdom of Verin

ELAMIR STARED AFTER Kasdeya and her sister, watching their forms grow smaller and smaller between the trees. A sense of familiarity struck him, along with the image of a woman gripping the shoulders of a young girl, steering her away. He'd been beneath the coverlet. The woman had flaming red hair that contrasted with the girl's black locks. The image blurred, but he knew she had turned once, eyes scanning, searching. Velamir wondered if she'd been looking for him. Had it been his mother? Had the little girl been his sister?

It didn't matter. They were gone, fragments of a life that he couldn't recall. But Kasdeya . . . he would remember her. He would remember what she'd made him feel— something besides guilt and anger, horror and pain. She'd been part of his life for such a short time, yet she'd made her mark on it. Though, he was fooling himself if he thought a memory would truly suffice when he would rather see her smile, hear her voice, smell the flowery fragrance of her hair . . .

A hand landed on his arm, jerking him back to the present. Jax stood there, sympathy in his gaze. Finnean and Latimus drew in, and they formed a circle.

"What's the plan, Captain?" Latimus asked, a smirk on his face.

Velamir gave him a wry look. "We enter the camp, hopefully stay out of sight, find Mordon and General Boltrex's wife, and somehow manage to kill Winston. Then we get out."

Finnean nodded. "Sounds simple."

Latimus scoffed. "Yeah, *simple*. And if we get caught? What then?"

Velamir eyed each of them. Jax stared back, resolute. Finnean's face was grim, with thinned lips and black brows lowered. Latimus was still smiling, but it wasn't his signature sarcastic grin; it was the one he used as a front to convince others he was confident.

"If you want to back out, I suggest you do so now. Once we enter the camp, there's no knowing where the road will end."

"I'm with you, Vel," Jax said. "For the better."

Velamir grasped his friend's shoulder in a firm grip and nodded.

"I was lost for the last year of my life," Finnean said seriously. "Haunted by my past, my mistakes, the death of my brother. You gave me a purpose, Velamir. If I've found my way again, it's thanks to you. I'm with you."

Latimus was quiet for a long moment. "We've been through much, and you hated me for a good portion of that time." He gave a short laugh. "I betrayed you, Velamir. Even if it was for the good of Verin, you consider me a traitor. I don't know if my words mean anything now, but I want you to know I will fight at your side and I hope someday you will forget what happened. Perhaps we can form a semblance of friendship again."

It wasn't an apology, but it was close. And coming from Latimus, it meant a lot.

"Let's live through this first," Velamir said, "and take what comes after."

With the words that needed to be spoken said, they set off. Velamir took the lead, his bow in hand and fingers twitching for the arrows in his quiver. Finnean and Latimus clomped through the forest, trampling twigs and snow under their boots. Jax and Velamir were quieter. Years of Chishma training had bred stillness into them. Velamir scanned the branches above them, below them, before them, his eyes never lingering on one spot for long. And then he paused, stiffening. The others froze behind him.

"What is it?" Latimus asked.

Velamir shushed him. There, in the tree on their right side, he could see the tip of a boot. The branches shielding the person from view shifted. Velamir reached for an arrow. One breath, two, three. And then all at once, his arrow was strung on, metal point aiming at the figure. His fingers brushed his cheek as he pulled the string back farther.

"I know you're there," Velamir called. "I suggest you come down nice and slow."

The person didn't respond, and Velamir didn't hesitate. He released the arrow, and it buried itself into the branch a hair from the boot. The stranger yelped and lost his balance, crashing with a heavy thump onto the ground. He groaned.

"Or fall," Latimus said. "Fast is good too."

Velamir strode forward and grabbed hold of the person's collar to haul him up. He was met by a shock of brown hair and dark eyes. The man was young, younger than Velamir. It took him a moment to place him.

"Julius."

Recognition flickered across Julius's face, and he scowled, but not before Velamir caught a trace of fear flash through his features.

"*Zelont*," Julius hissed.

Velamir's arms tightened at the old nickname. He dragged Julius's collar against his windpipe. The man gasped for breath, and all signs of animosity disappeared.

"Not so strong without your ringleader, are you?" Velamir spat in a low biting tone. "How is Quintus, anyway?"

Jax peered at their old classmate. "Your nose looks better. Last time I saw you, it had been bashed against Velamir's knee."

A curl of satisfaction wormed through Velamir at the memory. Quintus and his two lackeys, Julius and Colein, had relished harassing him and Jax. He glanced at Julius's nose, recovered but bent, a sure reminder of the *zelont* he loathed every time he saw his reflection.

"Quintus has risen high in the ranks, commanding four Calestors and their squads. And do you know why?

Because he isn't a traitor like you." He sneered. "He is a loyal Chishma."

Velamir shoved Julius against a tree trunk, earning a grunt of protest. "He may be loyal, but let's see about you. What do you know of the prisoner in the camp?"

"Even if I knew, I wouldn't tell you."

Velamir's hand flicked back, and he snatched an arrow, then leveled the tip beneath Julius's chin. The man's throat bobbed.

Velamir lowered his voice to a careful whisper. "Tell me what you know."

Julius's head lifted higher in an attempt to evade the arrow. Velamir followed him, the arrow tip piercing the underside of his chin. A speckle of blood appeared. Julius swore and closed his eyes.

"All I know is that she's kept in the red-striped tent on the western side."

Velamir's hold slackened at that. He'd been trying to learn Mordon's location. Who was the woman prisoner? Could it be his mother?

He glanced at Jax. "Do you have some rope? We'll hold Julius captive and use him to negotiate if it comes to it."

Jax nodded, and then his eyes flew wide. "Watch out!"

Something sharp pricked Velamir's chest. He spun back around. Julius's hand was extended, and the end of the dagger in his grasp had just barely pierced through Velamir's leather chest armor. But that's as far as it had gotten. The dagger dropped, and Julius followed, collapsing on the ground. Blood pooled from his neck into the slushy snow. Finnean grimaced, wiping his sword onto the Chishma's robes. Warm blood trickled down Velamir's chest from the minor wound he'd sustained. It could've been worse. Much worse.

"I owe you a life," he told Finnean.

"I was the one who owed you. Do you think I forgot how you stayed behind in the Karakan's lair so I could escape? Consider both our debts paid."

Velamir smiled. "Thank you."

His smile grew strained as he looked at Julius's body. Though the man had tried to kill him, he'd been his classmate, a face he'd seen for years. And he was gone, just like that. Velamir pushed the regret aside and shoved the body behind a fallen tree, then gathered branches and large rocks to cover Julius from view.

"It won't keep him hidden for long, but we will be gone before he's found."

When they reached the camp, Latimus and Finnean remained with the packs on the forest's edge while Velamir and Jax crept their way along the western side. They were the quieter pair and moved quickly, able to more easily evade the patrolling deedans. Velamir inhaled the scent of cooking meat, along with fire smoke. Jax crouched beside him, glancing warily at their surroundings. Velamir spotted the red-striped tent in an instant. It was so near the tree line that it struck Velamir as odd, as if it were placed there to be found. Velamir moved past the tent he was hiding behind and saw a figure approaching the prisoner tent. He stuck his hand out, stopping Jax. It was a woman dressed in Chishman robes.

"Lissa," Jax breathed.

Velamir's gaze sharpened, and he recognized the thick curtain of dark hair, the familiar stance. She held a tray of food in her arms. She nodded at the guards, pouring them something from the pitcher on the tray, and they allowed her in.

"Wait till she leaves," Velamir whispered.

The guards laughed and drank whatever Lissa had given them. Minutes later, they slumped motionless to the ground. Velamir's eyes widened.

"She poisoned them," Jax said.

"What is she doing in the tent?"

Without further thought, Velamir rushed forward with Jax right behind him. He stepped over the limp forms of the guards and pushed inside the tent. Lissa was bent over a blindfolded woman, hands outstretched. Was she attempting to strangle her? Velamir grabbed her arm and wrenched her back. Lissa was startled. Eyes wide, she moved fast, twisting out of his grip and ducking under his arm. She seized his wrist and bent it behind his back. Velamir grunted, grimacing.

"Stop!"

Lissa's vicious hold slackened. Velamir glanced at Jax, whose brows were drawn together over eyes focused on Lissa.

"What are you doing here?" he asked her.

"What are *you* doing here?" she shot back.

"Trying to rescue her." Jax pointed at the blind-folded woman.

"So am I."

Lissa released Velamir, and he approached the

blindfolded woman and gently untied her hands. She mumbled around the gag in her mouth. Velamir felt sick. Winston claimed she had joined him, not that he'd had her gagged, blindfolded, and imprisoned. Another lie, he realized. It was all a lie. He pulled the blindfold off, and she stared at him with hazy gray eyes. That wasn't right. *Brown eyes.* The thought came to him suddenly. His mother had brown eyes, and her hair was red not the dark, nearly black locks the woman had.

"My son." Her voice sounded distant, like in a strange dream. She reached out to cup his cheek.

At a strangled gasp behind him, Velamir turned. Lissa stared between him and the woman, shaking her head.

"Why were you trying to save Velamir's mother?" Jax finally asked.

"Because that's not Velamir's mother. She's mine," Lissa told him. "She's losing her mind, but the one thing she never forgets is that she wanted a son. Not me."

Jax's hand lifted as if he wanted to comfort her, but then it dropped. "You were with Winston from the beginning. You knew he was alive."

"I had no choice. He was threatening to kill my mother. I tried to escape after the testing, after we were bound together. I realized I couldn't live a life where I would be forced to see Velamir every day and pretend I felt nothing for him." She glanced at Velamir, and he shifted uncomfortably. "But Winston told me he would kill my mother. He took her from . . . from a brothel."

At Jax's surprised face, she nodded. "Yes, my mother worked in a brothel, and Chishma Talon stopped by one day. When she birthed me, he took me. I was only allowed to see her rarely, and those times were never enough. Winston used it against me. He used her to use me."

Velamir never knew what Lissa had faced. He'd only seen her as a manipulative, conniving woman, not as the hurt, broken girl before him. Jax seemed to think the same, because he stepped closer to her, his feelings etched on his face. She held up a hand, stopping him.

"I heard rumors you were coming to the camp. I was going to use it to my advantage and leave with my mother."

Velamir filled in the rest. "And Winston would've assumed *we* helped her escape."

"I'm sorry," she said to Jax. "I've always been selfish. I would give you up to Winston without blinking an eye if it meant I could save her."

He appeared resolved. "I understand."

The woman—Lissa's mother—croaked, and she gave her some water.

She wasn't his mother. Velamir was alarmed by the disappointment that overcame him.

"We need to leave before someone notices the guards," he said. "You and Lissa go to the forest."

Jax shook his head. "I'm not leaving without you."

"You must."

"It's too dangerous," Jax said.

Kasdeya's voice filled his mind. *Promise me.* And his own words: *I will try. For you.*

"I'll join you before you even realize we've been apart," he told Jax.

Velamir slipped out of the tent into the cool evening

air. Before he could take another step, cold metal bit his throat. He turned, meeting black eyes in a face covered by a thick beard. Long hair brushed the man's shoulders, and a puckered scar cut down his brow, passing over his eye and ending at the bottom of the beard, leaving part of it hairless.

"Just as expected," Mordon growled. "Welcome, *Cavalier.*"

40

AT THE SIGHT of the curving trail ahead, Coralie pulled her horse to a stop. Zenrelius reined his horse in beside her, raising a fist.

"Halt!" his second shouted.

Horses stilled behind them. The general examined the path. His brows were drawn together when he turned in his saddle to meet her gaze.

"It's steep. We must go slowly."

She nodded. "Namaar is just after."

They needed to rest before attacking; they'd been riding for hours. Zenrelius had split his cavalry in half, taking two hundred and fifty men with them and leaving the rest at the castle. Darkness was encroaching on them. They couldn't stop for long. If one of the scouts saw them nearing the town, they would be warned of their approach. Although, if Advisor Welix was the traitor as she suspected, he might have sent word of their coming long ago. He'd been present at the council along with all the other members as they had discussed the best way to extract the Verintown civilians to Fortress Yadigar without Prolus noticing. Coralie had asked the group of people again, advising them against leaving, worried the plan might fail. But they had insisted, willing to risk death than await Prolus's next siege. Coralie did her best to alter the original plan. Instead of sending them after her troop as strategized, she'd sent them off first, in the secrecy of darkness, with only a few trusted people at her side as witnesses. She'd informed the civilians to travel the less traversed path to the fortress, to lessen the chance of them being spotted by the Tariqin spies. The main focus remained the same; she would distract Prolus, and the civilians would get to shelter.

"Ten minutes," Zenrelius told his second, seeming to read her mind.

Coralie dismounted, and the general followed her lead. Jovinne stepped beside her, handing her a water flask. Coralie drank. The cool liquid soothed her parched throat. She sniffed and wiped her mouth, then handed his flask back. Jovinne accepted it and pressed closer.

"Forgive me if I am being rash, but should we trust him?" He pointed with his chin to Zenrelius, who was speaking with his second. "We have few soldiers of our own here."

Coralie was risking a lot by depending on the general. She didn't have enough armed soldiers to chance taking more, so she'd left them behind at the castle. Zenrelius could kill her and the soldiers with her and say they'd died in the skirmish. It would be so easy for him to take over. Half her people already worshipped him since he'd come to their rescue.

"I trust him," she told Jovinne instead of her true thoughts.

He frowned but relented with a bow of his head. Zenrelius approached her, his thick boots thudding over the land.

"You left Blayton in charge of the castle." A question rested within the statement.

"He is a capable leader. I have faith that he can take care of matters until I return." She'd had to resort to choosing between the few faithful people remaining after demoting Advisor Welix. Welix had provided quite the show after that decision, and the councilmen loyal to him had shaken some of the belief her people had in her with gossip of her inexperience and brash actions. Coralie had ignored the slanders and placed guards on Welix to watch his every move.

Zenrelius tilted his head. "Blayton planned on leaving with the civilians. I heard that his wife ordered all their things in the castle to be packed."

"He wanted to ensure his wife's safety but, after further consideration, decided to remain."

"Isn't that strange?" Zenrelius's eyes probed her face. "He seems to hunger for power. You offered him a chance to lead, and he jumped for it. He behaved the same during council meetings before you began attending."

That struck Coralie as odd. Advisor Welix was

leading the meeting when she'd arrived the first time. Blayton was a reserved person and spoke only when necessary. Could Zenrelius have mixed them up? Or was he trying to turn her against her own council?

"I don't recall asking you to share your opinions about my subjects with me, General."

"I apologize, Your Majesty," Zenrelius said. "I have overstepped."

He pulled away and entered a conversation with some of his men. Coralie released a pent-up breath. She had been harsh, probably overly so. It would be foolish to brush aside the aid Ondalar offered, no matter how suspicious she was.

A woman from the cavalry approached Zenrelius. Asilles was her name, an Ondalarian shieldmaiden. She appeared a few years younger than Coralie, but she looked strong, wielding the custom golden chest guard and apparel of the shieldmaidens. Her sword was well made and hung over her hip, and a collection of daggers lined her back. Coralie found herself somewhat envious of her arsenal of weapons. She'd heard of the shieldmaidens' skills, but she'd yet to see one in combat. Coralie watched them converse, Zenrelius's mouth tight as the woman did most of the talking. Some of the words sifted to her.

"Dangerous . . . too risky . . . why . . ."

It was enough to know Asilles didn't agree with Zenrelius. Coralie couldn't risk the girl changing his mind. There was too much at stake, and she needed all the soldiers she could get.

"Let's move," she called.

Asilles glowered. Her dark eyes and hair matched Zenrelius's, but she lacked the compelling draw of the general. Coralie was certain they were related, third cousins perhaps. She'd heard shieldmaidens were illegitimate daughters of the Ondalarian king and high lords.

Zenrelius shouted for the company to set out, and Coralie remounted her horse. The Ondalarian warhorses were much larger than the lancer horses Coralie and her men used, forcing Zenrelius to narrow his group down to two riders heading down the curve at a time.

The town came into view, and Coralie urged her horse faster. She didn't see any deedans above the gate. Wind blurred past her, bringing tears to her eyes and flinging her braids behind her. Coralie unsheathed her sword as she crashed through the gate. Her horse's hooves dug into the ground as she propelled him in a circle, scanning for enemies. Only corpses met her eyes. Burned corpses.

Coralie slipped out of the saddle. She patted her horse's side as unease filled her. Booted footfalls echoed while Zenrelius and his men scoured the area. Coralie nudged a corpse over. The blackened face peered up at her, part of the cheek curled back to the bone. She flinched. He was too charred for her to make out his face, and his clothes had withered away, disguising his uniform. Had he been Tariqin? A deedan?

"My queen!" Jovinne was pale as he pointed down at a motionless form. It was the only body that wasn't burned. The head was severed from the neck and rested a short distance away. Coralie swallowed a rush of bile and leaned closer. A gasp slipped out. The face was

Galva Nildon's, one of her uncle's prized fighters. It was then that she realized they were standing in a graveyard. A graveyard full of Verin's dead. The soldiers who had fought and died defending Namaar from the Dark Army. Why had the Tariqins left the corpses? As a mark of victory?

She looked up, meeting Zenrelius's tense gaze. "This is Galvasir Nildon."

"Something's wrong," he said, sword in hand. "If these are Verin's soldiers, where are the deedans?"

The very thing Coralie was wondering. A clamor broke out at the entryway, and a man on horseback shoved past the cavalrymen. He dismounted, panting and covered in blood. His horse was foaming at the mouth and coated in sweat. The man rushed to her with what appeared to be the last of his strength. He dropped to his knees before her, panting, gripping her hands with bloodstained fingers. She recognized him. Elwin, the stable master, had left with his family, along with the group heading to the fortress. What was he doing there?

"Your Majesty . . ." He expelled harsh breaths. "They came. They killed everyone."

Icy shock filled her. *No. No.* What was he saying?

"We didn't make it to the fortress. They killed my family." The sob that spilled past his lips flipped Coralie's stomach inside out. "They slaughtered everyone."

His hands slipped from hers, and he collapsed at her feet. Someone rushed to check his pulse, but Coralie remained frozen. How could that have happened? She'd thought she was saving those people by sending them away, but Prolus had somehow known her plan despite her considerable efforts to evade his spies. A tear escaped her eye and trailed over her cheek. She'd believed herself to be Verin's savior, but she had doomed her own people to the grave.

41

MORDON'S BACK WAS damp with sweat when he exited the rumlok cage. The beasts yipped behind him, the long practice apparently not enough for them. He glanced back at the alpha. His black fur and red eyes flashed, and his sharp teeth seemed to grin.

"You look better, *dsell*," Silopar said. He'd been waiting by the gate. The Savorian's lips turned up, but worry creased his eyes.

"Who knew a few hours wrestling rumloks could do a person so much good?"

Silopar's smile dissolved. "I know you are fond of them and they of you, but if someone speaks of it to Prolus? If Winston finds out? What will you do?"

"If Winston hears . . ." He shrugged.

"What can he do? And Prolus . . . He might want me for greater reasons than a Calestor."

"They will use you."

Mordon gripped the Savorian's shoulder. "Don't worry about me. I can look after myself. I always have."

Silopar nodded and stepped back. "The next Handler will take my shift soon. You should go."

After bidding the Savorian farewell, Mordon spotted Chishma Talon hurrying to Winston's tent. Curiosity welled, and he followed. He paused before the tent. Bellowing laughter could be heard from within. The deedan guarding the tent glanced at him, but Mordon ignored him.

"They are fools. What did you expect?" Winston said.

"I hadn't anticipated it would be this easy," Talon replied.

Mordon frowned, edging closer. What were they speaking about?

"The castle will be ours. They lost many in the ambush and have no morale left. It will be effortless."

The words sent shock through him. Had they attacked the group traveling from the castle? When had that happened? And then a name smashed through his mind with the unrelenting pounds of a hammer. *Coralie, Coralie, Coralie.* An image of her sprawled across the ground came unbidden. Her once-warm skin, flush with life, was ashen, and her pink lips were pale. Her eyes lifted to the sky, unseeing. Lifeless.

Mordon pressed a fist to his head, cursing. He tried to remove the image, but it returned to him again and again like a haunting nightmare. She couldn't be dead.

She was alive and well in the castle. She *had* to be. Despite all his plans, all his dreams to build a name for himself, a fearless reputation, and a place to call his, she'd been the one he saw at the center of it all. Something touched his arm, and he jerked upright.

"Calestor?" the deedan asked, concerned.

"Don't touch me," Mordon snarled, stepping away.

A Savorian in his group rushed up to him, heaving quick breaths. "The guards at the prison tent are unconscious."

"Sound the alarm," Mordon ordered. "Now!"

The Savorian sped off, and Mordon said to the deedan, "Let the general know."

Mordon headed toward the prisoner tent, his long strides eating up the ground. His men crept around the tent, surrounding it. He nodded at Silopar, who was closest, signaling him to wait. Mordon unsheathed his sword just as the tent flap moved. A figure stepped out. Mordon closed the distance between them to place his sword at the intruder's throat. Green eyes gleamed at him, widening slightly as they took in his appearance. Mordon stared at the man who'd ruined his life, or rather, tore whatever good remained in it to pieces. He held in the urge to touch his scar and the desire to dig his sword just a little deeper. To sever the skin at Velamir's neck and watch the life drain from his eyes. The impulse to kill him was so strong, it thrummed in his chest.

"Just as expected. Welcome, *Cavalier*."

Velamir met his gaze, holding it with that cursed confident stare. He scanned his uniform, taking in the pin over his chest. "You joined him," he said.

"And you joined Verin. Boltrex told you to infiltrate, didn't he? To save his long-lost wife." Mordon chuckled.

"He believes you are held prisoner here."

"I'm the last thing on his mind." Mordon stepped closer to Velamir. "Check the tent."

His men rushed inside. A woman shouted from within—a young woman, Mordon calculated, by the venom and strength in her voice. Significant thuds sounded, but Mordon retained his focus on Velamir.

"Coralie sent me here."

The words were so unexpected, Mordon froze.

"She sent me here for you."

Mordon dug his blade deeper. "Coralie would never trust you. She's smarter than that."

And yet, even as he said that, Mordon couldn't quite believe it himself. He remembered her on the tower, deflecting Boltrex's blow meant for Velamir. She'd saved him then. Why wouldn't she trust him?

"She may never fully trust me," Velamir said, his probing gaze unsettling. "But she trusted you."

Mordon wanted to shout and throttle Velamir, but he couldn't. He couldn't do anything but stand there with the threat of slitting his throat. *She trusted you.* Past tense. *I betrayed her*, Mordon thought. *Instead of fighting my captors, I allowed Winston to bring me into the fold.* Mordon had never hated himself more than at that moment, and it was all because of a Chishma who had taken everything from him. A Chishma who'd saved him when he'd wanted his life to end the most.

"On the tower," Mordon said, forcing the words past his lips. "Why didn't you let me go?"

"Would you have let me fall?"

"Yes." Mordon didn't hesitate. "I would have."

"It was an instinct." Velamir shrugged. "I saw something in you, a goodness somewhere."

Goodness? What did that even mean? Mordon was corrupted. He didn't have a speck of light in him. Boltrex had done that by raising him. Winston had done that by abandoning him. The world had done that. If he was the way he was, it was because of how he'd been forced to live. And there Velamir was telling him he had something good inside him. He'd never heard anything more absurd.

"Who do you think you are?" Mordon spat, leaning closer. A trickle of blood dripped down Velamir's neck. "Some kind of hero?"

Velamir
Kingdom of Verin
Tariqin War Camp

Some kind of hero? The words hit too close to home, striking Velamir in a vulnerable place. It had been his dream as a child and even up until he'd first arrived in Verintown. He'd wanted to be someone's hero, someone's savior. But that was before everything changed. It hadn't taken Velamir long to realize the world didn't have heroes. They were only myths, people in stories.

"Far from it," he replied. "But I do know that I will not be a pawn again."

Mordon sneered. "You think Boltrex won't use you? You're wrong."

Jax and Lissa stumbled from the tent, with Lissa's mother behind them. Lissa wielded a kilisham, and Jax's hand edged to his belt. Mordon swore. The others neared him just as reinforcements appeared.

"It's not too late," Velamir told Mordon. "You don't have to go down this path."

Something flickered in Mordon's face. Velamir tried to read it. Doubt? Confusion?

"Despite how much you don't want it to be true, we share the same blood," Velamir pressed. "Our mothers were sisters. We are supposed to fight side by side, not on opposing ends."

Mordon hesitated, and Velamir saw the conflict within him. Deedans swarmed closer. Velamir heard a clicking sound and saw Jax pull the metal sphere from his belt. He winked at Velamir and flicked the top of the contraption before flinging it into the air.

"Sedelon!" Jax shouted, much to the confusion of the deedans surrounding them.

A thick cloud of smoke exploded. Velamir blinked, ducking away from Mordon's sword and shoving him hard. He heard a grunt, and curses blasted around him. He could make out only unknown figures in the smoke. Velamir retreated, releasing a stream of coughs. He headed toward the forest on mere instinct and memory, hoping he was going in the right direction. The sizzling of a kilisham startled him and he drew his sword, but it was only Lissa. She dragged her mother with her other arm, her face clenched as she held in coughs. Velamir's lips burned, and spit trailed down his chin. He dragged his hand across his mouth.

"Jax," he sputtered. "Where's Jax?"

"Here," said a labored voice, and Jax stumbled through the mist after them.

Velamir heard shouts and pounding boots. "Move, move!"

Jax and Lissa rushed forward. Her mother cried hysterically as she was shoved along. Mordon stumbled through the fog not far from them and bent on his knees and heaved. Velamir didn't linger. He took off behind the others. They were nearing the trees when they faltered. Velamir peered ahead and saw that Winston stood in their path with a crowd of deedans behind him. Latimus and Finnean were bound and on their knees, swords trained on them.

"Look what I found in the forest." Winston smiled. "More friends."

Velamir gritted his teeth. More deedans and Mordon pulled up the rear behind him.

"If you don't want me to slit their throats, drop your weapons," Winston warned.

Velamir could not surrender, nor could he allow his friends to be slaughtered. He glanced at Lissa and Jax. Lissa held her mother's arm in a death grip. Her purple eyes were wide as she shook her head at him. Jax grimaced, his body tense with evident fear as he took in the state of Latimus and Finnean. Then he met Velamir's gaze, and an unspoken message passed between them. Jax would follow him to the end. Even if it meant certain doom.

Velamir raised his sword.

42

Natassa took Velamir's advice and stayed off the main road. She and Krea cut through the forest and headed toward the slopes. The air grew colder the higher they climbed. They puffed small clouds into the air with each breath. Natassa wrapped arms around herself, earning an angry squeak from the Sirchoba. She loosened her grip and laughed softly.

Krea's head whipped around, and she froze, wide eyes trained on Natassa. "Did you hear that?"

"What?"

Krea tilted her head, motioning. "Listen."

Heavy wind blew over them, unraveling their thick hair into unkept tendrils. Natassa tucked a strand back. A sound, soft as a whisper, brushed her ears. And then it grew louder.

"Help!" The cry was desperate, striking Natassa with panic.

She pressed onward, gripping a towering rock and pulling herself up, with her feet on available footholds. The rock bit into her frozen hands. Below, between stone hills in an open cluster, stood a man wearing thick fur. His hands were outstretched, his face tense with fright. Two men closed him in on either side. They wore sneers as sharp as the blades in their grips.

"Give us the coin, and we will spare you," one said.

He glanced between them, as if searching for an escape route. Natassa had been in such a situation before. She'd hoped for a way out, and it had come in the shape of Velamir. Would he have left that man to fend for himself? The answer thudded in her chest.

Krea hauled herself up beside her. Natassa glanced at her, and Krea shook her head, evaluating the scene. "Don't do what I think you're going to do," she told Natassa, wariness in her tone.

"I can't leave him."

She clambered down from the rock as Krea's sharp whispers faded behind her. The bandits' taunts grew louder as Natassa crept closer, hidden by rocks jutting out in uneven segments. She peeked over the rocks. The furred man grimaced as a bandit pointed his sword closer to his throat.

"Or we can take what we want from your corpse."

Natassa's hand trailed to her belt. She slid a knife loose. The bearded man hissed as blood trickled along his throat. Natassa flung the knife. It impaled the bandit's wrist. He howled, and his weapon slipped from his fingers. Natassa flicked another knife free as the other bandit wheeled around. His eyes grew into saucers at the sight of her. Natassa threw the second knife as he advanced. It smacked into his shoulder. He stumbled back a pace and glanced at his injury. At the sight of the knife, his face darkened, as if he couldn't believe she'd thrown it.

"You little demon," he snarled. "Where did you spawn from?"

She fumbled with another knife. *Focus on the target. Let everything else fade.* Thorsten's words poured into her, instructing her as he'd always done, but she also heard another voice, one full of warmth and promise and daring. It belonged to a face with green eyes and warm skin and a smile so rare that, when revealed, it chased away the darkness. Natassa inhaled. *Focus on the target.*

Time slowed as she lifted her arm. The angry sneer painting the bandit's features spread wider with each nearing step. Natassa's eyes hovered over his heart. She could hit him there as easily as she could hit a tree in the forest. But taking a life was something far different. She adjusted her aim and released. It thumped into his shoulder. But he charged her despite the new damage to his body. A shape fluttered before her. Krea slashed the bandit across the throat in one clean swipe. Blood gushed forth splattering over the rocks. He dropped to his knees, and only then did Natassa notice his fellow bandit's limp body behind him, his neck sliced with a similar cut.

Nausea climbed her throat. She knew it was easier for Krea. Back in the palace, her father would often call for her handmaidens to assist in Savorian executions. To toughen them, he'd said. But Natassa saw a darkness in her eyes, a deep sorrow that was usually hidden behind a bright smile and words of encouragement, and she realized it couldn't be any easier for her.

Krea met her gaze and approached her quickly. After appraising her for injury, she threw her arms around Natassa. Natassa returned the hug, squeezing tight.

"Thank you," she whispered.

Krea had taken the lives that she couldn't. Footsteps neared, and they broke apart. Natassa eyed the furred man, and his face warmed with an uncertain smile.

"You have my thanks," he said. "Khuda lights my way."

"Khuda?"

Only a secretive smile answered her question. "What are two young ladies doing in these parts?"

"I think we should be doing the questioning." Krea crossed her arms. "Seeing as we just saved your life."

He laughed. "Very true. I was heading home when they ambushed me."

"You live near here?" Natassa asked.

"In Sok. It's a few days' walk."

Natassa exchanged a glance with Krea. Sok was the main town in Devorin.

"You have a long way yet. You might need protection," Natassa said.

"Are you offering to help me?"

Krea frowned, but Natassa nodded. "We are going there as well. It's better to travel in numbers."

He shifted his stance, as if weighing her offer. "Certainly, I agree."

Krea sniffed but crouched down to run her hands over the bandits' clothing.

The furred man reached out. "Leave him. I have coin enough for us."

Krea smirked, and she raised her brows. "It seems we've saved a rich man."

He had a pleasant enough face and a well-groomed beard and mustache. The fur he wore was of quality, indicating he was someone of means.

"Are you a merchant?" Natassa asked.

He pursed his lips. "You could say that. My name is Rost."

"This is Krea." Natassa pointed. "And I am Natassa."

Krea's gaze bored into her, but Natassa saw no reason to lie to him. They would part ways in a few days.

"A pleasure." He nodded.

"Let us be on our way." Krea trudged out of the area.

Natassa followed her but peered back at the merchant when she didn't hear his footfalls behind her. His head was lowered and eyes closed. He held out his hands, as if saying a prayer. He glanced up, catching her stare, but Rost didn't seem surprised and only smiled. His smile was unnerving, full of secrets that he seemed content to keep concealed.

They traveled over the slopes, going higher and higher. The trek became relentless, and the merchant soon called for a halt. He didn't have any food, or if he did, he didn't reveal it. They stopped in a cramped spot under a mountain overhang. Natassa and Krea sat close together, conserving heat against the frigid cold. The merchant sat apart from them. His eyes were closed, and he rested his head back, appearing to sleep. A soft gasp escaped Natassa. She hadn't realized it before when they'd been out in the sunlight, but then, with darkness closing over them, she could see it. His skin glowed, not overly so, but a soft light emanated from him.

Natassa glanced at Krea to see if she'd noticed too, but her friend was snoring softly. The Sirchoba pecked at Natassa's side with a whine, and she rose, careful not to disturb Krea. Natassa stepped out from under the shade of the overhang and glanced up at the starry night. She took the Sirchoba from where it clung to her beneath her cloak. It was much bigger than when they'd found it. Natassa's curiosity to communicate with it returned as she settled onto the rocky ledge. She glanced below, peering over the large expanse they'd climbed. Her stomach turned. It was beautiful, but if she slipped, the fall would prove fatal.

Natassa leaned back, holding the Sirchoba in her hands. It squawked while settling into her palms. Her eyes drifted closed, and she saw darkness until a golden barrier emerged—the barricade between her mind and the Sirchoba's. Her shadows' looming presence shuttered on either side of her. Cold lips pressed to both of her ears. The Seer and Lure whispered. She blocked them off, focusing more intently on the barrier. Her brow furrowed as she attempted to break through it. She stroked the Sirchoba's soft head, and sweat drifted down her temple. Finally, she heard another voice. The Sirchoba's voice. The bird dreamed of wings, a blue sky, and freedom in the wind. Natassa leaned forward and kissed the bird's feathered head. It was ready to survive on its own. A rush of warm words came to her.

Fly, phoenix. Spread your wings and soar.

Natassa smiled. Those words had pierced something in her. Velamir had healed the vulnerable part of her that had always been captive. Natassa stood and lifted the Sirchoba.

"Yera," she whispered. It was the last thing she would give the bird. A name of freedom.

She flung the Sirchoba into the air and watched her spin in a flurry of gold and red as she found her wings.

43

Kingdom of Verin
Tariqin War Camp

IT SEEMED AS if everyone's breath halted when Velamir raised his sword. Mordon shot a glance around, and an unexpected smile creased his lips at the shocked faces Winston, the deedans, and Vykus's mercenaries wore. They couldn't believe Velamir was willing to risk death to escape, that he was willing to risk his friends. Mordon's lips turned downward again. They clearly didn't know Velamir, not even the man who'd raised him. Mordon detected the slight tremble in Velamir's sword hand, the darting of his eyes, the hesitance in an otherwise firm stance. Mordon had no doubt that, if he'd been alone, Velamir would have fought with every drop of blood he had. But he wasn't alone. Lives rested on his choice. Although he'd turned down the notion of being a hero, Mordon could see his savior habit kicking in.

The sword hit the ground with a thud, and Velamir's shoulders drooped in resignation. Winston jerked his head, and Mordon stepped forward, placing his sword at Velamir's neck.

"This is getting irritating," Velamir said.

"Don't worry. This will be the last time it happens," Mordon replied. "You'll be dead before you get another chance."

Lissa gave a frustrated scream as she thrust the kilisham to the ground with a vicious swing. Winston ordered a search of their persons. Lissa's knives were taken; the Shadow Manos's belt and hidden vials were removed. Mordon passed Velamir's weapons to a deedan standing nearby. His arm was nearly wrenched from its socket when he held Velamir's sword. He frowned at the blade resting in the deedan's arms, which shook under the weight. *Strange.* It hadn't only been him affected by the weapon. He looked at Velamir and found him staring back, his features blank and stony.

Mordon cracked a smile. "How does it feel to be on the losing side?"

"You would know." Velamir's reply was quick. "That's usually where you are."

Mordon flinched. Winston called for ropes and Mordon lashed the rough bindings around Velamir's wrists as tightly as he could. Then he took up guard behind Velamir, aligned with more than a dozen deedans on either side of him. Winston paced before them.

"I've given you many chances, Chishma Lissa." Winston's voice reminded Mordon of a kind teacher, forgiving and earnest, but his eyes contained a deadly threat. "But you've disregarded them. Again."

Lissa's jaw was set, and her back was straight. Her eyes darted to the prisoner woman beside her.

Winston approached her. "What does Tariqi do with traitors, Chishma? Do we forgive and forget?"

The silence grew overwhelming, and Mordon was almost thankful for the endless shifting of the mercenaries. Lissa remained quiet. Her eyes closed when Winston pulled his sword free from its sheath.

"I intend to show you that I see my threats through. This isn't a place to have fun, Chishma. This is a war camp, and we follow Prolus's rules." He shifted closer, angling the sword so the moonlight gleamed on the metal. "And Prolus . . ."

The next movement was so fast, Mordon had to blink twice to comprehend the scene before him. One moment, Winston was standing before Lissa, and the next, he had shifted to the prisoner woman. There was a squelching sound, and Winston's sword protruded through the woman's chest.

". . . doesn't forgive traitors."

Lissa screamed, a sound so raw and filled with wretched agony that the hairs on Mordon's neck rose. She screamed and screamed, fighting against the deedans holding her bound arms. Winston wrenched the blade free, and the woman crumpled into a heap of blood. He wiped his sword on the woman's clothes before advancing to Velamir.

"And now on to the next traitor." He lifted his blade

to Velamir's chin. A spot of remaining blood flicked from the sword onto Velamir's skin. Mordon attempted to ignore Lissa's wails, but the screeching only grew louder.

"I had so much hope for you, Velamir," Winston said. "But you chose to deny the truth. You chose to follow a dying land, a dying custom. And now . . . you must die." He pulled back his sword, preparing to strike.

Mordon inhaled sharply, words frozen on his tongue. Should he stop it? No, Velamir was his enemy. But the image of Velamir grasping his arm, holding him as he hung from the tower, flashed in his mind. He owed him a life. No matter how much he wanted to deny it, he *owed* him. Mordon's mouth parted just as Winston's sword grazed Velamir's neck. But instead of severing Velamir's skin, Winston flicked out a silver chain from around his neck. A circular pendant hung on the end. Letters in a foreign language formed a word across the pendant.

"How interesting." Winston snatched the chain free. "You're out of my sight for a month and have already found yourself a new faction."

Mordon frowned at Velamir's blank face.

"And a mysterious one at that. So, tell me about the Elders."

Velamir shook his head. "I don't know what you're talking about."

Winston laughed. "Of course you don't. The Velamir I knew wouldn't have given Tariqi's secrets to the Empire even if it cost his life. I suppose I won't be able to learn anything from you without a little motivation."

Winston's attention flitted over Mordon before landing on Vykus.

"You are in charge of interrogation," he told Vykus, and Mordon realized he'd just been passed up. "Secure the prisoners and come to my tent for a discussion."

The mercenaries grumbled, upset by the lack of further bloodshed. Winston strode away with deedans at his back. Vykus met Mordon's gaze.

"Get moving, pup."

Mordon bristled. "What did you call me?"

"You're Winston's dog, aren't you? Or would you prefer being called *his brood*?" Vykus chuckled. "Both mean the same thing." He glanced over his shoulder. "Salvador?"

The giant stiffened. "Yes, Boss. Same thing."

Vykus angled his head, a confident grin emerging to highlight the gold in his teeth. "There you have it."

Mordon pressed closer, seconds from throttling the man. "I'm not one of your slaves for you to order around like vermin. And I won't be leaving until the prisoners are properly secured." Mordon allowed a smirk. "After all, Velamir's escaped you before."

Vykus's grin flickered. "Well, then, get to work, pup."

Mordon gripped Velamir's arm and tugged him forward. The mercenaries did the same to Lissa and the Shadow Manos. Captain Latimus and Galva Finnean were dragged behind them. The prisoner woman's corpse remained on the ground, blood pooling around her body. Lissa's harsh sobs accompanied them to the tent. Mercenaries and deedans surrounded them. Even if Velamir and his accomplices attempted to escape, they wouldn't get far. Velamir seemed to realize that, because he didn't fight Mordon's hold.

Inside the tent, a thick wooden pole stretched up to the top, and connecting logs hung over them like outstretched arms. Mordon chained Velamir to the beam with metal shackles. By the time he stepped back, the others were secured as well. Vykus ordered Salvador to keep the watch doubled until he returned. He brushed past Mordon as he left. Mordon tried to tamp down his annoyance, but then the taunting began. Finnean stared him down—a man he'd once fought alongside in the Borderlands, a man he'd once trusted to have his back.

"You're pathetic," Finnean growled. "Traitor."

Latimus spat at the ground. "May darkness overtake you, you parasite."

"Don't waste your energy." Velamir's voice was enough to fill Mordon's irritation to the brim. "He's not worth it."

Mordon stormed over to him, sensing Salvador tense as he did. He grabbed hold of Velamir's collar and wrenched him close. "I wasn't worth it, not in anyone's eyes in Verin." Chains rattled. "But now I'm starting over, and I couldn't care less what you think." Mordon glanced at Finnean and Latimus before returning his gaze to Velamir. "If I were you, I would consider my options carefully. Tell Winston what you know or die. The way is clear."

Velamir's smile was sad. "If only Coralie could see you now."

He slammed a fist into Velamir's face. Velamir's head snapped back, and blood dribbled from his nostrils. Mordon's lip curled. "That was just the beginning."

44

VOICES PILED OVER each other, growing louder and louder as everyone's fear and anger and confusion mounted. Coralie fought the urge to cover her ears. She had to speak, to calm them down, to do something, but she couldn't move. All those people, the corpses surrounding her, were dead. And so were the civilians she'd sent to the fortress. They were dead. Because of her.

A scream loaded with desperation pierced her ears. Silence followed the sound as all eyes riveted on her. Because the scream had been her own. Even Jovinne stilled where he crouched beside Elwin, fingers freezing over the stable master's neck, where he'd been checking for a pulse.

"My queen?"

Coralie's hand shot out to halt him, and she backed away. She stumbled over a blackened body, bile rising in her throat. She covered her nose and staggered out of view of the soldiers into a burned, partially collapsed building. As soon as she was out of sight, her composure dropped. The walls around her caved inward, their charred edges forming together. The ceiling was gone, leaving the moon in full view. She pressed her head to a wall, and the tears came. Her sobs sounded foreign to her own ears.

She recalled her father's gentle tone. *You will lead our people one day when your mother and I are gone. You will understand then how the choices we make are done out of necessity. Some things we do torture us, haunt us forever, but they must be done. If not by us, then who? Who will take this task?*

Coralie had been angry at her father for a decision he'd made. She'd hid in her chamber and told the maids she didn't want to be seen by anyone. But he'd come and found her skulking in the corner of her chamber. And then he'd lifted her chin and explained the reasoning behind his actions. She hadn't wanted to accept it.

Why do you have to do this? Let's leave this power behind. I don't want to be a princess, and neither does Mother. I see her crying all the time. I know you don't want it either.

Her father had brushed her hair back. *What have I taught you? Cowards retreat. Cowards concede.*

He nodded as she finished for him: *Victors repeat. Victors complete. Victors succeed.*

Know that your father is not a coward. Neither is your mother, and I hope my daughter isn't either.

Coralie lifted her head, face grim. *I'm not.*

A smile cracked her father's serious exterior. *Good. Now remember that this family doesn't give up, no matter how hard the road is or how heavy the crown weighs. You understand?*

Coralie shifted against the charred wall. If her father could've seen her, what would he have thought? His hand came over her shoulder, but Coralie didn't move. She couldn't look at him. She couldn't face his disappointment even if he was just a figment of her imagination. But his grip tightened, and he turned her toward him. Coralie kept her head lowered, unable to meet his gaze.

"Your Majesty?" he said, but it wasn't his voice.

Coralie closed her eyes. Fingers drifted below her chin, lifting her head.

"Coralie."

She opened her eyes, and the face she saw wasn't her father's. Coralie brushed Zenrelius's hand away. His touch was confusing. "I thought I clarified that I needed solitude." She crossed her arms, hoping he would leave.

He didn't. "My men died assisting Verin, more men than I've ever lost."

Coralie clamped her jaw tight. Of course he was concerned about his reputation.

"I've prided myself on being a good general with people who trust me with their lives."

"We both know what happened this time was my fault," Coralie told him.

"I'm not trying to lay blame."

Coralie finally met his swirling black eyes.

"My soldiers are calling for a retreat. Once my

cousin hears of this latest account, he will summon us back to Ondalar."

Coralie laughed, an emotionless wrung-out sound. "Leave. You will face Prolus soon enough. After all of Verin is buried."

"Coralie, the only way I can help you is if you sign an agreement with Ondalar. Make peace between the kingdoms."

"And your king will accept this peace?"

A muffled shout interrupted his reply. It seemed like it was coming from below them. She crouched, and the noise grew louder. She pried at the floorboards with urgency. Zenrelius helped her wrench them from the ground. A young girl stared up at them. She was impossibly thin, and dark spheres circled her eyes. Coralie reached down and hauled the girl up to them. She wrapped her arms around the child, holding her tight.

"You're safe now. You're safe." She hushed the girl, but there was no need. She didn't cry. She didn't make a sound.

When Coralie pulled back, the girl whispered, "My mother."

"Jovinne!" Coralie called.

When her bodyguard entered, Coralie pointed below. "Search for survivors."

Zenrelius jumped down with Jovinne. Minutes later, they hefted a woman as equally disheveled as the girl aboveground. She coughed. Dust coated her clothes and face. When she saw Coralie, her eyes narrowed, anger straightening her posture.

"*You*," she snarled. "You royalty think you're better than the rest of us. You wretched trash!"

"Watch your tone! You are addressing your queen," Jovinne snapped.

"It's all right," Coralie said. "Let her speak."

"You are no queen. You are a murderer! Because of you, my babies are dead! My husband is dead." She lunged at Coralie, nails and fists at the ready.

Coralie didn't stop her, wincing as the woman scratched her. Jovinne stepped forward, but Coralie motioned for him to stay back. The woman's attack halted a second later. She sagged against Coralie, soft sobs racking her bony frame. Coralie wrapped an arm around her and pulled the little girl closer. Coralie didn't retreat or run. She held them—her people. Because she would try again. She would repeat, and she would succeed. For them.

She looked up, meeting Zenrelius's stunned expression. "How soon can I sign the agreement?"

45

VELAMIR
KINGDOM OF VERIN
TARIQIN WAR CAMP

VELAMIR LONGED TO wipe the dried blood coating his lips and chin. His arms had hung suspended above him for hours, and he could no longer feel them. Vykus had left them with one solitary guard and an unfamiliar man chained across from them. Lissa had stopped crying at some point, and the last time Velamir glanced at her, he'd shivered at the frozen look on her face. It appeared as if every bit of warmth had drifted from her, and the only sentience remaining was the cold hate in her eyes.

"Lissa," Jax whispered. There was no response, just like the last twenty times he'd tried. "She's in a better place now. Better than us." Jax chuckled slightly, his chains rattling.

Lissa's head swung in his direction. "And

what do you know? You don't remember your mother. You have no idea what I'm feeling."

Jax said nothing. Velamir shifted, his aching muscles tensing for his friend.

"We may not remember, but we do know loss. We know that hollow feeling very well," Velamir said. "At least you knew your mother, saw her, spoke to her. We never knew ours."

"I wished I hadn't known mine either," she spat. "She didn't even want me."

"You're not the only one to lose someone," Finnean said. "I lost my brother and father."

Latimus nodded. "I lost a distant cousin of mine. He was an irritating chap." After seeing Velamir's sharp look, he added, "Of course, we'd only seen each other one or two times, but . . ."

Lissa huffed, falling silent. Finnean side-eyed the chained man beside him, and Velamir addressed the stranger. "If Vykus put you here to learn information from us, he will be sorely disappointed."

The tent flap was shoved aside, and the man himself breezed in, Salvador at his back. "Nestor is being punished for his mistakes. No need to worry."

The chained man, Nestor, flinched but didn't respond. Vykus smiled widely, showing off all his teeth. "Now that we've given you time to settle in, shall we get some answers?"

Velamir remained silent as Vykus prowled near him. "When did you first communicate with the Elders?"

"I never have."

"How did you find their symbol?"

"It was given to me."

Vykus raised a brow. "By an Elder member?"

"What does it matter? Why does Winston fear them so much? Kill us and get it over with."

"It seems we will have to do this the hard way." Vykus glanced over his shoulder. "Salvador."

The big man unsheathed a dagger and handed it to Vykus. Velamir steeled himself for what was to come. But Vykus turned, nearing Jax instead. He tore the front of Jax's shirt, revealing his pale skin. Jax's eyes widened, and the rise and fall of his chest quickened.

"No," Velamir said. "Whatever you want to do, do it to me."

"We know your weakness, Velamir. Why should I waste time on you when I know of a far more effective method?" He edged closer to Jax and pressed the dagger tip against his skin.

"Stop!" Velamir called.

"Let me give you some motivation." Vykus wheeled around. "Answer correctly, and I will carve Nestor. But if you give me the wrong answer, I cannot spare Jax the same treatment."

Velamir's nostrils flared as he glared at Vykus.

"Now," Vykus said, "how did you get the pendant?"

"From an old man in Castle Verin. He was a prisoner in the dungeon."

Vykus examined him for a long moment before nodding and pulling away from Jax. He strode to Nestor and ripped his shirt. Salvador held the man in place by his chained arms. Vykus dragged the dagger against his flesh, and blood welled along with Nestor's screams.

Vykus examined his bloodstained dagger as he asked his next question. "So, he gave it to you? Did he tell you about the Elders?"

"He told me to find their place and return the pendant to preserve his memory."

Vykus contemplated the answer and faced Nestor, drawing another heart-pounding scream. When he finished, he turned again.

"What was his name?"

"I don't know."

Vykus raised his brows and smirked, striding to Jax.

"Stop!" Velamir shouted.

Vykus pressed the tip into Jax's chest, then cut downward. Jax's jaw clenched, and his hands fisted as he wrenched against the chains. Blood pooled down his friend's chest, and Velamir winced at the pain on his face.

Vykus returned to the center of the tent and eyed Velamir. "Who was in charge of the castle when you were there?"

"Princess Coralie," Velamir said without hesitation.

Vykus smiled. "There, wasn't that easy?"

He dug into Nestor's skin, and Velamir grimaced at the bloody mess.

"Was General Boltrex leading the troops?"

"No," Velamir said. "He was wounded."

Vykus nodded. "Good."

He inflicted another wound on Nestor, and Velamir shook his head. "You knew the answers to those questions. Why would you ask them?"

Vykus laughed. "For Nestor, of course."

Velamir didn't find it amusing.

"Now, tell me where the Elders' base is. Where is the location the old man wanted you to return the pendant to?"

Velamir hesitated. "He died before he could answer."

"Wrong." Vykus wagged the dagger at him.

He marched to Jax, who stared warily, body tense. The dagger fell in swift cuts, over and over. Jax roared. The agony in his voice unbearable. Velamir jerked against his chains, swearing at Vykus. Lissa, Finnean, and even Latimus called for Vykus to stop. But he didn't. Red, so much red, dripped from Jax until Velamir couldn't watch any longer. When Vykus pulled back, he smiled broadly.

"There, now he won't ever forget who I am."

Velamir's gut twisted at the words, and he forced himself to look at Jax. His friend's head hung limply, his cries silenced. Written in brutal cuts across his chest was Vykus's name.

46

Natassa

Outskirts of Devorin

NATASSA PEERED INTO the darkness. Screams met her ears, and the hairs on her arms rose. Instinct told her to run, but despite the foreboding feeling, her feet led her to the tent in the distance. She entered. A man stood shackled to a beam. She approached him. Dark matted hair fell over his lowered head. She stopped before him, and he slowly looked up.

"Velamir," she whispered.

His face was sad, heart-wrenchingly desperate. She wanted to wrap her arms around him, to take the ache away, but her feet were glued to the floor.

"I did it," he said finally. He raised his hands, staring at them with horror. Blood covered his palms. "I killed him."

It was then that Natassa noticed the body lying on the ground. She crouched beside it and turned it over. Empty blue eyes peered back at her. Blood coated his chest and trailed over his face.

Jax.

"No," she said, rising to her feet. "*No.* You didn't do this. I don't believe it."

"I did it," Velamir repeated.

She shook her head. "He was your closest friend. I know you, Velamir."

"Do you?" he whispered, and tears welled in his eyes. "Do *I* know *you*? Do I know you, *Natassa*?"

Natassa gasped. How did he know her name?

His smile was grim. "You lied to me."

A sword burst through his chest. Natassa screamed. A black-haired man emerged from behind him.

"No!"

Her eyes flew open, her heart pumping in rapid beats. She lay on the mountain ledge where she'd released the Sirchoba. It was a nightmare. Just a nightmare. But she couldn't shake the horrible feeling, the betrayal written across Velamir's face, or the agony of seeing that blade pierce his chest.

You left him, one of her shadows said. What if it had been a vision? What if he'd been captured? Natassa stood, then rushed under the overhang. She kneeled beside Krea, shaking her awake. Krea blinked startled eyes.

"What happened?"

"We have to go back," Natassa told her.

"What?"

"I had a vision. We have to go back."

Krea must have recognized the fear on her face, because she scrambled for her pack.

"I take it we are no longer heading to the same destination."

Natassa turned to see Rost watching them, his skin glowing in the darkness.

"We have something urgent to attend to . . ." The explanation was a feeble one.

"I see." He lifted his own pack over his shoulder. "I have a feeling we will meet again in the near future."

"Perhaps."

She and Krea readied fast, and as they went to leave, the man called after them.

"Safe journey, Princess."

Natassa halted halfway down the mountain path and glanced back, watching the man disappear as he walked his own way. He'd known who she was. He'd known the whole time.

MORDON
KINGDOM OF VERIN
TARIQIN WAR CAMP

"Up!" Mordon shouted.

His men jumped to their feet. Sweat lined their skin as they shoved spears into the air. They'd been at it for hours. Mordon wasn't familiar with the Tariqins' style of fighting, but he did know the Imperial way and that was what he would teach them.

"Down."

They dropped to the ground, sinking to their chests before pulling up, their forearms bulging with the weight of their upper bodies.

"Sevelis!" he yelled.

They partnered in swift seconds, the whole of his team, 40 men, forming groups of two. In each duo, the bulkier man squatted, lacing his fingers together, and tossed the other man into the air. The men angled their spears toward the ground as they flew down, smashing them into invisible enemies. Mordon nodded.

"Good work," he said, and the Savorians bumped shoulders. "Again!"

They continued repeating the move as Mordon observed. His eyes glazed over, and the nearest pair transformed into a young man and a woman. Both smiling, both smitten, both compelling the other to strive harder.

Coralie snatched a spear from the weapons rack. Mordon's brows rose as she strode toward him with a smirk. "My trainers taught me a new move today."

"Let's see it."

"I need your help," Coralie told him.

Mordon nodded as she instructed him. He already knew the move but didn't stop her as she explained, enjoying all the little movements she made without realizing—the way she brushed back a flyaway hair and bit the inside of her cheek, the way her fingers tapped the spear as she spoke. She frowned, and Mordon realized he'd missed something.

"You weren't listening," she said, planting a hand on her hip.

"You were talking about Sevelis."

"And?"

"Do you know the history of the move?" he asked in response.

She rolled her eyes. "I assume you do?"

He chuckled. "It's named after twins. Kira and Kerstor Sevelis. When they were children, they loved a certain bakery, but their parents forbade them from buying more treats. They didn't understand their reasoning, so they came up with a plan."

Coralie sighed. "Sounds like someone I know."

Mordon ignored her. "They snuck into the bakery from the second level since they were banned from entering the storefront. Kerstor tossed his sister up, and she would hold a long pole for him to climb up after her. They continued to do that for years, and when they were drafted into the Imperial army against the Savagelanders, they enhanced the move, turning it into a fighting one."

"So, they didn't die of sugar but in combat," Coralie said dryly.

"They survived the war," Mordon replied. "I'm not sure how they died."

He laced his fingers together and nodded for her to try. She took a running start and leaped from his hands. He propelled her higher, and she launched into the air with a piercing yell and a wild swing of the spear. And then she crashed onto the ground. The empty barracks turned silent. The spear rested a short distance from her unmoving form, and Mordon felt a sudden rush of fear. He moved quickly, dropping by her side.

"Coralie!"

He leaned over her, and she whipped the spear back into her fingers, holding it beneath his chin. "I got you."

Mordon held his hands up in surrender, and she lowered the spear. A smile crept across Coralie's lips. He contained his own smile for a moment before breaking into a laugh. Coralie grabbed his shoulder, hefting herself up.

"Do you want to rest? We can practice the move another day."

Coralie shook her head. "Again. Let's do it again."

Mordon's smile faded as Velamir's words rushed to his mind. *You betrayed her.* Guilt swirled in him. Was she safe? Was she alive? Something told him she was, but fear was a powerful emotion he couldn't seem to control.

The moon graced them with its presence, shining over the camp. He dismissed his group. A day had passed since he'd punched Velamir. He'd given the tent a wide berth since then, hating the strong emotions that overcame him every time he looked at it. Although he'd avoided the tent, he had heard the agonized screams from within. Vykus's method of torture was not one he'd want to experience from the sounds of it.

A woman approached him with her head down. She held a tray and wore servant garb. She looked up at him as she came closer. "Where is the prisoner tent?"

He frowned. Something was off about her. "Who are you?"

"I was sent to deliver food to the prisoners. You don't want to interfere with orders."

A strange sensation overcame him, like a sudden

explosion of warmth and comfort he didn't want or need. He couldn't refuse her.

"They're in that tent there."

She nodded and headed in the direction he'd pointed. He shook his head, touching his brow. It wasn't until he was unstrapping his leather chest armor in his tent that he realized what was bothering him. She was wearing servant attire, yes, but *Castle Verin's* servant attire.

47

Jax was a bloodied mess. His torn shirt clung to his gaping wounds, and he practically hung from the chains, his knees bent awkwardly beneath him. Blood leaked from his back and dripped onto the ground. After the carving, Vykus had returned and whipped Jax. Velamir's wrists were chaffed from fighting against his restraints, and slick warmth trailed down his arms as the shackles bit into his skin.

Vykus and Salvador spoke in low tones near the front of the tent. Salvador held a strange contraption Velamir had never seen before. Parts of their conversation drifted over to him.

"Boss, the men are restless. They haven't been paid."

"The general will give a portion of Verin's treasure once we claim the castle."

"What if they are just using us?"

Silence met the question.

"You're wasting your time!" Velamir called to Vykus. "I've told you everything I know."

"Have you now?"

He approached Jax and gripped his chin to lift his face and inspect him. Lissa hissed at him. He ignored her but released Jax's face. Velamir feared if he didn't do something soon, his friend would die of blood loss.

"It seems he's drained. Why don't we start on another prisoner?" He turned to Latimus and Finnean.

Latimus paled, and Finnean swore at him in a way that would have made any hardened warrior flinch. Vykus laughed in response and waved at Salvador to give him the contraption. Vykus wrenched Finnean's chained hand toward him and placed a finger within the contraption.

"Now, Velamir, I will pull every nail off if you don't answer my questions."

Velamir glanced between Finnean's finger and Vykus's merciless grin. "And once you learn what you believe I'm concealing, you'll what? Tell Prolus? Tell Winston? What will you receive in return?"

Vykus shrugged. "What I always get: exactly what I want. I never lose a prize once I have it in my sights."

"Is that why you aren't getting your gold now? Prolus will use Verin's treasury for himself."

Vykus stepped away from Finnean. "If he hasn't given me anything, it's your fault. You ruined my mission."

"Don't blame your problems on someone else. If you

don't act soon, you will lose your reputation, along with your men."

"And what would you suggest I do?"

"Set me free. Help me defend the castle. You have men in the Docks, mercenaries who would come at your call. Help me, and you will receive thrice the amount Prolus has promised you."

Vykus stared at him, appearing speechless for a long moment. Then he burst into laughter. "Thrice as much means nothing if I lose all my men in the battle. You think we can defeat Prolus's forces? You have lost your mind, boy."

But the thought must have unsettled him, because he tossed the contraption back to Salvador and strode out of the tent. His large companion grunted, following him out. Velamir sighed in relief and leaned his head back to relieve his neck of some of the tension. Finnean sent him a nod of wordless thanks.

"Jax," Lissa whispered. "Jax!" she called again, but Jax was still.

"He will wake soon," Velamir said.

Jax would wake up. He had to.

Hours passed, and Vykus didn't return. Jax mumbled a few times, much to Velamir's relief, but didn't raise his head. Latimus had somehow slept standing, while Lissa and Finnean kept quiet but alert. Velamir yanked on his chains repeatedly, hoping to dislodge them from the beam. They didn't budge. He groaned in frustration. Sweat coated his shirt and face. Velamir leaned against the pole, panting. He smashed his head against the wood, and it gave the slightest creak. He did it again and again, faintly hearing Finnean telling him to stop. Blood poured down his face; tears blinded his eyes. His best friend was dying, and he could do nothing. He'd never felt so hopeless. His breath hitched as he tried to contain the unwelcome emotion clogging his throat.

He glanced up at the swish of fabric. Kasdeya stood before him. He must have knocked his head harder than he thought. But he wasn't one to complain. His imagination appeared so real. She stepped closer, wearing an uncertain expression on her face. She carried a tray in her arms, which she set down.

"You're here," Velamir mumbled, his throat raw.

She nodded, and through his blurry vision, he could see the trembling smile on her lips.

"Are you real?"

At those words, she rushed to him. Velamir grunted as she collided with his chest. Her arms wound around his neck, holding him tight. He ducked his head as low as he could to return the embrace. He buried his face in her hair, inhaling her scent.

"Velamir." Her voice broke.

"You're really here," he whispered into her tangled tresses.

"I'm here."

"How?"

She pulled back, eyeing the blood and cuts marking his face. "I had a vision. I couldn't leave you. You promised me you would be safe." She tore part of her dress and dabbed his skin with it.

Velamir's eyes drifted closed. He flinched as she prodded the most tender areas. Blood drifted from the corner of his eye down his cheek. Soft fingers brushed it away, and he opened his eyes, meeting her hazel ones. She leaned over, reaching for something on the tray. When she pulled upright, a gleaming key rested in her palm.

"How did you get the key?" he asked as she slipped it into his chains to unlock them.

"The guard is unconscious behind the tent. I took it from him. We need to move fast. Krea is waiting for us by the forest."

"You knocked him out?"

She nodded and tossed his shackles aside. "We need to go."

As soon as he was loose, Kasdeya darted to the others, unchaining Finnean first, then a startled Latimus. When she got to Jax, she sent Velamir a worried glance. Velamir waited beside them as she unchained him. Jax slumped forward, and Velamir caught him, placing his shoulder under his arm to carry his weight. Finnean and Latimus moved to assist him as Kasdeya freed Lissa.

"I've got you, Jax," Velamir told his friend.

Jax mumbled incoherently, his head falling forward. They headed to the tent entrance and were heartbeats from exiting when the flap opened and Mordon entered. Velamir froze. Mordon glared with a hand on his sword. His eyes roved over them, and then he did something Velamir never would have expected. He moved aside, head high.

"Go," he said.

48

KASDEYA HAD BEEN staring at the knife planted in the carriage seat across from her for hours. Her hands fisted in her skirts to keep from shaking. Vomit covered her dress, but she didn't care. She'd thought the numbness would be enough to give her the strength to slide the blade across her throat and follow in her father's footsteps. But she hadn't realized how much of a coward she was. She hadn't realized how much she feared death.

The carriage came to a halt, and the door opened. Fresh air drifted inside, seeping into her nostrils and replacing the scent of putrid vomit. Her focus on the knife didn't waver. She made out Draven from her peripheral as he stepped inside. His spicy fragrance sank into her senses, and she started to *feel*.

Hurt.

Anger.

Regret.

Her nails dug into her palms. Draven released a fit of uncontrollable coughs.

"What is that stench?"

When she didn't answer, he waved a hand before her face and followed her gaze to the knife. He yanked it free and sat on the seat across from her, forcing her to meet his gaze. His eyes trailed the thin cut along her neck, and a glint of understanding formed over his face.

"You won't go that easily," he said. "Your precious emperor awaits."

He grabbed her arm, wrenching her from the carriage. Another wave of sickness rushed through her, and Kasdeya nearly puked again. She gripped Draven's arm with both of her hands, dragging her feet along the cobblestones in an attempt to slow his bruising pace.

He glanced down at her, and he must have seen something in her expression because he stopped. She leaned against him, pressing her head to his shoulder. A guard rushed to Draven, along with a True Manos.

"Can we be of assistance, Your Majesty?"

Draven muttered something, and the True Manos took her arm, leading her away. As she took slow steps into the palace, Draven told the guard to inform Emperor Malus of their arrival.

Inside, the True Manos gave her a tonic to settle

her nerves and pricked her skin, drawing blood. He collected the drops in a vial and smiled.

"You should be well soon enough, my lady. I suggest rest and some time off your feet."

Kasdeya nodded and was escorted to her chamber. A maid assisted her, and Kasdeya dismissed her after she'd helped her into a new dress. She glanced around the chamber, belatedly realizing that it was Natassa's. The portraits were still there. Natassa's talent for painting was the best Kasdeya had ever seen. It filled the room with life. Kasdeya approached a portrait Natassa had done of the three of them. Natassa's arms were thrown around her and Krea, and they were laughing, with joy evident in their postures.

Tears welled in Kasdeya's eyes. What had she done? She'd destroyed everything. And for what? What did she have? A murderous husband who hated her, no home to speak of, and no hope for all the things she'd wanted. Kasdeya wished she could turn back time and return to those first days after meeting Natassa. When the three of them had enjoyed each other's company before her envy emerged, when her smiles had been genuine.

The door swung open. Kasdeya brushed tears from her cheeks and straightened her gown before turning to face the intruder. Draven halted at the sight of her. He seemed conflicted. Kasdeya's heart cleaved in two as she remembered his harsh words and actions. The struggle on his face cleared, and he held out a hand, giving her the smirk she had seen hundreds of times before. When he'd just been a prince and she'd been a handmaiden.

When she hadn't seen the dark parts of his life. When she hadn't seen *him*.

But he'd become a stranger once again. Kasdeya swallowed the lump in her throat and placed her hand in his. He curled his fingers over hers and accompanied her from the chamber. They moved in silence. Draven had many guards with him, more than necessary for a simple meeting with the emperor. They reached the throne room, and the herald announced their presence. Draven pulled her inside, gripping her hand so tightly, she winced.

"Your Supreme Majesty!" Draven called.

Kasdeya kept her chin raised as they neared. She caught the moment Emperor Malus and Prince Honzio spotted her. They tensed and glanced at each other. They knew she was a fraud.

"As I promised in my letter, I have come. And I brought your princess as well."

Emperor Malus laughed uneasily. "Though, now she is your queen."

Draven's gaze slid over her. "She is."

Kasdeya met Prince Honzio's eyes. He tried to communicate with his face, sending her a question she couldn't decipher.

"Although, she never was your princess, was she?"

Kasdeya stilled at the cold words. A glance behind her revealed Draven's guards inching closer, taking up aggressive stances.

"What are you insinuating? I am not a fan of games, Draven." The emperor's panic revealed itself in the shake of his voice.

Draven wrenched her by the hair, snaring her taut against his chest. "This isn't Natassa." Kasdeya closed her eyes, grimacing as his grip on her hair tightened. "You thought you could dupe me?"

Emperor Malus sputtered, and Draven yelled, "Attack!"

His gaurds raced toward the emperor and prince. Prince Honzio shouted at the people in the room to get to safety. They screamed, fleeing into the hall. The throne room was an instant bloody mess as bodies fell all around. The Cadellion swarmed around Emperor Malus.

Kasdeya attempted to wrench free. She grabbed hold of Draven's dagger and nicked his arm. He wrestled her to the marble floor, knocking the blade from her grasp. He smacked her across the face. Kasdeya cried out, seeing stars. She blinked through tears. When her vision cleared, Draven stood above her, a crazed gleam in his eyes and a large broadsword in his hands. He lifted it. Kasdeya looked past him, past the throng of fighting men, to Prince Honzio. He was fighting alongside his bodyguard, struggling to reach her.

"Tell her!" she screamed with the last of her energy. "Tell Natassa . . ."

Honzio stopped battling to focus solely on her.

"Tell her I'm sorry," she murmured, a tear sliding free and soaking into her hairline.

The sword came down, shrouding her world forever in darkness.

NATASSA
KINGDOM OF VERIN
TARIQIN WAR CAMP

Natassa pulled a knife free, her eyes on the man she'd spoken to in the camp earlier. Since she saw him in better light, she realized he was the man she'd seen in her vision, the one who'd stabbed Velamir. But he wasn't on the offensive. Instead, he stood aside, waiting for them to pass.

"Hurry up," he snapped.

"Why are you doing this?" Velamir asked him.

"For Coralie. Only for her."

"Velamir," Finnean said. "Let's go. We need to get help for Jax."

Velamir glanced at Jax, his face stricken as he nodded. "This better not be a trap."

They rushed from the tent and moved fast. Natassa inhaled the soft night breeze that swept her hair back. Velamir took the lead, leaving Jax in the care of the black-haired girl and Finnean. Leaves and twigs crunched beneath their boots as they entered the heavily wooded forest. And then Natassa crashed to a halt, almost smacking into Velamir's back. A deedan watchman stood in their path, holding a torch. His eyes went wide at the sight of them, and his mouth parted.

"Prisoners escaped!" The two words had barely left his lips when a knife plunged through his neck.

Natassa gasped as he fell to his knees. Velamir caught his torch as the knife was wrenched back, crimson blood appearing black in the night as it streamed across fallen leaves.

"Let's move," Krea said, sliding the knife back into her belt.

Natassa's heart pumped wildly as she quickened her pace. Only seconds later, shouting and pounding footsteps began from what seemed like every direction. Latimus cursed.

"Go, go, go!" Velamir shouted, and Natassa pushed herself forward.

The arrow came from nowhere, straight toward her. Velamir shoved her aside just in time with a grunt. Natassa crashed to the ground, then scrambled right back to her feet. Deedans swarmed around them. Natassa slid her knives free, giving two to Velamir and one to Finnean. They made a protective circle around Jax and the black-haired girl, who was attempting to lift him.

The deedans pressed closer. Natassa flung a knife, and it slammed into an approaching Tariqin. He pressed his hand to his chest, falling back. The deedans closed in as one. Natassa was so entrenched in defending herself that she didn't hear the scream of anguish until the second cry. She turned, spotting deedans dragging the girl and Jax away, back toward the camp.

"Jax!" Velamir shouted, slashing through the swarm of deedans.

"Velamir!" Natassa threw her final knife at an attacker behind him.

A dark flurry stole her focus. A deedan flew toward her too quickly to evade. Then someone jumped in front of her, and a sword pierced flesh. The deedan collapsed with a knife in his throat. Natassa stared at the figure before her.

"Krea?" she whispered.

Her friend turned, her lips parted as she stared down at her middle. Natassa gasped when she saw the sword impaling her. Krea dropped to the ground, veins of red traveling across the fabric of her dress like routes on a map.

"Krea!" Natassa fell beside her handmaiden, her closest friend. "Krea!"

She was faintly aware of the bodies falling around her and then of the sudden stillness. Of Velamir's presence drifting beside her. She heard a harsh breath, and Finnean dropped to his knees at Krea's other side. Latimus stood nearby, holding the bloodied wooden branch he'd been using to fight. His brow creased as sadness coated his features.

"Stay with me," Natassa pleaded, tears making her voice shaky and uneven.

Finnean grabbed hold of Krea's hand. His chest heaved as he pressed her palm to his lips.

"I did my duty . . ." Blood trickled from Krea's mouth. "I kept my promise, Princess."

Natassa shook her head, holding a part of her dress to Krea's chest. Krea lifted her free hand. Her fingers shook as she gripped Natassa's.

"Live the life you want, not the one others want for you."

"Shh," Natassa shushed her.

"Can you forgive her, Natassa?" A tear slipped down Krea's cheek. "Please forgive Deya."

"I forgive her. She's forgiven. Stay with me." Natassa caught Finnean's desperate stare, the tears hanging off the edges of his lashes. "Stay with us."

"I'm always with you." Krea slid her hands from their grasps, pressing one to Finnean's chest and the other to Natassa's. "Here."

Her hands slipped down, soft and slow, and she smiled. She gazed at something not visible to the rest of them. "I see Alaris, Natassa. It's beautiful."

Natassa gasped, biting her hand to hold in the tears.

"Just like the stories you used to tell," Krea mumbled. Blood pooled at her lips, and her body shuddered. Her eyes became glassy, shadowed, *gone*. Natassa cried then, tears of anguish pouring down her cheeks.

"No," she whispered. "Don't go."

Something stiffened beside her, and she glanced at the source. Velamir's face was cold and unreadable. Through her pain, she realized why. He knew who she was. He'd heard everything.

49

HONZIO
KARALIK EMPIRE
HEARCROSS, CAPITAL OF THE EMPIRE
THE GRAND PALACE

BRONUS SHOVED HIM and screamed in his ear, but Honzio was frozen, his feet planted on the floor. Bile slithered up his throat as he stared at Natassa's decoy. At her severed head. Blood coated the tiled floor, filling the thin cracks with rivers of red. Honzio blinked, startled by the wetness clinging to his lashes. A rough hand pushed him, and he stumbled back.

"Get out of here." Bronus held his sword in a white-knuckled grip.

"Honzio." Moralis came to his side, wielding a sword as well. "We must leave."

He tugged him toward one of the many doors lining the grand throne room, along with Aylis. Honzio heard a shout and glanced back. Bronus stood before the door they were escaping through while Draven's guards swept the throne room, eliminating all foes. They began to circle Bronus. Honzio's attention flitted to his father. The Cadellion fought with precision, killing all who came close. But it took one hit, just one, to eliminate a Cadel, and the formation was lost. And they continued losing more members until only his father stood in Draven's path to the throne. Honzio's heart jumped to his throat. His father glanced at him, then watched as he slipped into the hall. His eyes were dark beads of disappointment.

I can't leave, Honzio thought. *No matter who he is, he's still my father. I can't leave him.* But Moralis propelled him into the hall.

A group of guards was gathered there. Moralis called to them just as Honzio noticed their uniforms—Ayleth's guardhouse symbol pinned on their shoulders, purple fabric merging with tan. Honzio cursed under his breath, and Moralis quieted as the guards turned their way. They zeroed in on Honzio with mutters of, "... the prince." They marched their way, swords slipping free from scabbards. Honzio looked back. They were boxed in. The only way out was forward. Aylis seemed to have the same thought, because she snatched Honzio's dagger from his belt and lunged forward, slashing a guard across the throat. Blood spattered over her as he slid to the ground before her. Honzio's mouth hung open, and Moralis appeared equally flabbergasted. The guards swung at Aylis, three at once. She locked in combat with one while avoiding the blows of the others. She glanced at them over her shoulder.

"Get moving!"

Moralis jumped into the fray, and Honzio didn't need further prodding. He crouched by the first man Aylis had killed and pried the sword from his grasp while avoiding looking at the gaping cut in his throat. Honzio stood and raised the sword, a battle cry ready in his throat, only to find the guards already lying in bloody heaps. Honzio was both relieved and a little disappointed that the fight had finished before he could join. Moralis stepped close to Aylis, searching her for injuries.

"We need to go before the next wave," Honzio told them.

Moralis nodded. "But where? Where will we go?"

Honzio led them to his chamber. There was no time to change. They were only able to procure cloaks, and Honzio stuffed as many coin pouches as he could into his pockets. Then they left the castle, heads low.

The sounds of clashing swords echoed behind them as the remaining loyal guards struggled to retain the palace. And he'd left them. Their prince had left them. Honzio stuttered to a stop before the stables, the dark night pulling him into darker thoughts. He couldn't forget the blood, the handmaiden's brutal killing. His father's disappointment . . .

A hand came down on his shoulder, and he glanced at Moralis. "It's not easy, Cousin, I know."

Honzio nodded, his voice brittle. "I'm going back."

Aylis and Moralis stood in his path.

"They are dying in there," Honzio said.

Moralis stopped him with a palm to his chest. "They're dying for you. Are you going to return and let their deaths be meaningless?"

Honzio swallowed. "What can I do? How can I reverse it? How can I stop it?"

Choose wisely. The accented voice drifted to his ears. Moralis searched his gaze.

"I think you know," his cousin said.

"You have to go," Honzio told him, glancing at Aylis. "Take her and go. Hide out somewhere."

"Are you crazy? I'm not leaving you."

"I need to do this part alone. Please, take Aylis. I will call for you."

Moralis considered for a moment, while Aylis shook her head vehemently.

"Swear you won't do anything impulsively reckless?" Moralis said.

A tiny smile quirked the corner of Honzio's lips. "I'm a Hartinza. I think reckless might run in our blood."

"That's not comforting in the least."

"Can you give us a moment?" Aylis asked Moralis, and he nodded, moving a short distance away to give them privacy.

Aylis gripped Honzio's arm. "What about my brother?"

"He might be elsewhere. He might be dead. But if he's in the palace, I will do whatever it takes to free him when I return. I will free him. I will free the Empire."

She nodded, a small smile gracing her features. "Thank you." She reached up and cupped his cheek. Her icy blue eyes glistened. *"Maavalin."* At his confusion, she huffed a laugh. "It's a farewell. One that wills you to return home safely."

Honzio smiled, placing his good hand over hers. "And what should I say in return?"

"*Dracis Soel.* Wings in the water."

"And what does that mean?"

"The unknown. Savorians believe a water dragon accompanies the journeyer into the sea. The dragon helps them or dooms them. You carry the weight of a dragon, Honzio." She held his stare, then slid her hand free and stepped back.

Honzio nodded at her, unsettled by her words. He gave a few pouches of gold to Moralis and watched them set off. It felt strange to be without a bodyguard or his father's orders pressing down on him. He was finally his own man. It was time to make it count.

Honzio stumbled into the stables after glancing back in search of pursuers. He jumped at a sudden thump. Honzio spun toward the sound, holding his good arm forward to ward off any attack, but his fears were unfounded. The noise had simply been a pitchfork clattering to the ground from the hands of an open-mouthed stable boy. Honzio glanced down at himself and grimaced at the state of disarray he was in. Besides his strange appearance with the cloak hiding half his face and form, his run through the palace had torn parts of his clothing and drenched him in sweat and blood. Honzio looked up, and the stable boy had the decency to close his mouth.

"You, boy, saddle a horse for me."

The lad retrieved his pitchfork. "Sorry, sir, but

these horses are only for Their Royal Highnesses and close allies."

"I'm the bloody prince, and I need a horse immediately."

The boy's gaze fell to his misshapen arm. His eyes filled with pity and then disgust as he took in the odd shape of Honzio's wrist and fingers.

"Saddle the horse," Honzio said in a low but demanding tone.

The boy nodded quickly, smart enough to not further anger the agitated prince, and moved to one of the stalls. Honzio waited with growing impatience, his gaze fixed on the stable entryway. At the sound of clomping hooves, Honzio turned to see the boy standing beside a fully tacked lancer horse. He tossed the boy a coin and mounted the horse before shooting out of the stables.

He rode into the city without stopping and halted outside a populated inn. Honzio needed to find the Uluzar. If anyone could help him overthrow Draven, it was them. He dismounted and flipped a coin to the inn's guard to watch over his horse. Inside, he leaned on the bar top and slapped a gold coin onto the surface. That caught the barkeeper's attention quickly enough.

"What would you like?"

"Information." Honzio pulled his cowl farther down.

The barkeeper smiled, revealing yellowed rotten teeth. "That cost a mite more than the average drink."

"It is a fairly simple question. Where are the Savage-landers residing?"

The barkeeper's face paled, and his smile died. "I know next to nothing about 'em. Only that 'em are vicious to their enemies. I heard me one story of 'em cutting a richie man to pieces 'cause he didn't agree with 'em." The barkeeper shook his head and glanced around. Then he scanned Honzio, seemingly attempting to peer past his cover. "Stay way clear of 'em if you know what's good for you."

The barkeeper pushed away to assist another patron. Honzio had learned nothing and parted with a precious coin. His purse was getting lighter and lighter. On the way out, Honzio stumbled into a solid form. The man grabbed him to keep him from falling. Honzio muttered his thanks and tried to pull away, but the man leaned closer.

"I know where they are. Meet me outside."

Moments later, Honzio stood with his reclaimed horse. Just when he thought the man would not come, he stepped out of the inn. He met Honzio's gaze and strode up to him.

"They are in Whispering Woods."

For years, Whispering Woods had been rumored to be home to witches. Tales spread that none who ventured there ever returned. Honzio had planned to take a contingency of soldiers and put an end to the rumors, but it seemed there was some truth to them. Not witches, but Uluzar

"Will you take me?" Honzio asked him.

The man nodded and turned his head to see if anyone was listening, revealing the tattooed runes that decorated his neck and part of his face. Uluzar shamans had those same markings.

"You're one of them."

The shaman grinned. His teeth were coated with something red. Honzio hoped it was not blood and inwardly shuddered. He moved to mount his horse, but the shaman stopped him.

"We go on foot."

Despite his doubt, Honzio followed the shaman out of the city, leaving his horse behind. They traveled for some time until reaching the tree line. The shaman motioned for Honzio to hurry, and an eerie feeling bloomed in his chest as he took his first step into the Woods. Deep in the trees, the shaman paused.

"What is it?" Honzio asked.

The shaman plucked a bunch of red berries from a tree. He held them out to Honzio, but Honzio refused, suspecting they were poisonous. He wasn't about to die at the hands of an Uluzar shaman, from poison berries no less. The shaman shrugged and tossed one into his mouth before continuing forward. They marched on.

Finally, a clearing opened between the trees, where stakes lined up one after another. Disemboweled men hung from the stakes. Honzio gagged, forcing his eyes away from their empty cavities. He peered ahead instead, to where more shamans danced around a crackling fire. Uluzar drank and smeared their faces with what Honzio hoped was paint.

As soon as they noticed him, all action ceased, and they stared at him with murderous intent. Honzio straightened his shoulders. A man emerged from the only tent in the camp—a familiar man with thick braided hair and black eyes. Grongar-ja smiled when he saw Honzio.

The shamans drummed in unison. A quick glance behind him revealed his route out was blocked by more Uluzar.

"Welcome, princeling," Grongar-ja said, spreading his arms wide.

50

WHEN THE SHOUTS began, Mordon knew the alarm had been raised. Deedans rushed into the wooded forest in search of Velamir and the others. Silopar approached him with a look of concern.

"The general is calling for you."

Mordon nodded before navigating to Winston's tent. More guards stood around it than usual. When he entered, Winston was leaning over the table, his shoulders bunched and his face in shadows. Chishma Talon and Quintus stood on either side of him. Both turned to face Mordon, their hands raised as if he'd interrupted them mid-argument. Winston's eyes narrowed.

"Any idea how Velamir escaped?"

Mordon shrugged. "Why don't you ask Vykus? He's the one you put in charge."

"I would . . . if he were here."

"What do you mean?"

"Vykus is gone, Velamir's gone, and even my chest is missing. You wouldn't know anything about that, would you?"

"Chest?"

Winston nodded. "Full of confidential information."

"Perhaps you will find it with Velamir, if you manage to catch him."

Winston stared at him for a long second. Before he could speak, a deedan rushed in.

"General, we've captured two of the escapees. We have more deedans after the rest."

Mordon moved swiftly, grabbing hold of the deedan's collar. "Which ones?"

"The Shadow Manos and Chishma Lissa."

Mordon drew in a relieved breath, then glanced at Winston, hoping he hadn't seen his reaction.

Winston glared at the deedan. "Lissa is stripped of her title." He looked at Quintus. "I want them out of the camp by morning. Deliver them to Devorin. Perhaps they will interest the queen."

Quintus slapped a hand on his forearm. "At your order, General."

He ducked out of the tent, along with the deedan and Chishma Talon, who sent Mordon a warning look as he passed. Mordon brushed it off and focused on Winston, who stroked his chin in a thoughtful gesture. Finally, his cold, searing gaze landed on Mordon.

"Head to Castle Verin. Gather your men and take another Calestor and group. I will march out with the rest of the camp in the morning. I want you to attack from behind the castle while we take the front. We'll crush them between our forces."

Mordon nodded, then backed away as Winston waved him off. He turned, his jaw clenching as he strode out of the tent. He hoped he'd done the right thing by allowing Velamir to escape. He hoped he would advise Coralie to surrender rather than encourage her to retaliate against Prolus. *He hoped.*

CORALIE
KINGDOM OF VERIN
CASTLE VERIN

Coralie steered her horse across the drawbridge and through the gatehouse. The clomping of hundreds more horses followed her. The little girl sat before her, her head bobbing against Coralie's chest. She brushed the girl's hair back. As soon as they entered the courtyard, a man rushed to her—her newly promoted head advisor, Blayton. His clothes were rumpled, and shadows creased the skin beneath his eyes.

"Your Majesty!" he exclaimed. "We thought something terrible had befallen your company."

Coralie motioned to the little girl, and the advisor reached up, grimacing as he lifted her from the saddle.

"Namaar was abandoned. Prolus expected our move." Words caught in her throat, and she had to force them out. "The civilians sent to Fortress Yadigar were slaughtered."

"We heard the news from the soldier you sent ahead. The people need you. We need you."

She dismounted, glancing up at the gatehouse. Watchmen guarded from the walkways above, looking out for newcomers. Their torches flickered and revealed their firm, resigned profiles. They'd almost shot arrows at Coralie and her party when they'd arrived, but they'd held back at the flash of Verin's flag and Ondalar's.

Zenrelius came to stand beside her. "Are you certain you want to continue with the agreement?"

Coralie glanced at the hardened general, then looked away just as fast. She was finding it harder and harder to avoid his penetrating gaze. "Yes."

She had to endure his strange pull for her people, for Verin. Because without Ondalar—without the general—there wouldn't be a place left for her to call home. Galva Blayton frowned, but before he could press her with questions, she tipped her chin forward, and he led them to the keep.

Zenrelius's men stayed behind to tend the horses. Jovinne fell in step behind her. As soon as they entered the keep, a hush fell over the people gathered there. Coralie attempted to keep her face impassive but couldn't hold back a flinch at all the stares. Their faces lit when they saw her—something she hadn't been expecting. They looked at her with hope, like she had the key to save them all. They sank into bows and then rose.

"My people," she called, her voice echoing against the stone walls, reaching every ear. "We've fallen."

That was met with confused glances and disgruntled mutters.

"We've fallen and fallen and fallen. But what happened each time? We stood again. Despite the odds, despite what we had to do, the blood we spent, we rose again and again." She raised a clenched fist. "And we will once more."

Light shone in their eyes. She could feel Zenrelius's gaze boring into her.

"But this time, it won't just be us fighting." She motioned to Zenrelius. "Although years of bitter rivalry have existed between our kingdoms, Ondalar has come to our aid."

"Verin isn't alone in this." Zenrelius's deep voice seemed to quell any remaining doubt in her people. Maybe it instilled in them that strange comfort she felt around him. "We've made a pact. Queen Coralie has allied with Ondalar. We will provide more assistance."

The people cheered, some touching half hearts to their chests.

"Long live Queen Coralie!"

The shout was taken up by the rest of the people. Coralie allowed a small smile of relief at their support, which was a surprising contrast to the hatred she'd expected.

With her people's morale lifted, Coralie left to visit Boltrex. She entered his dark, damp chamber. The smell of sickness permeated the room. Coralie approached the bed and his sleeping form. His dark skin was wan, and perspiration coated his brow. Each breath he took had a long pause before and after it. Coralie fidgeted with her thumb ring. She glanced at the weary-looking True Manos standing beside the bed. He was one of the nine True Manos they had remaining.

"He hasn't gotten better?"

The True Manos shook his head. "It's odd. He should have healed by now, but he only seems to worsen."

Coralie leaned closer. Boltrex's labored breathing reminded her of Mordon when he'd been poisoned.

Poisoned.

"Who else comes into this chamber?"

"Mostly myself, though it's not guarded any longer. Anyone can enter."

"I want everything given to General Boltrex to be tested for poison first. Don't allow entrance to anyone but yourself. I want someone guarding the chamber at all times."

The True Manos peered at her with curious eyes. "You believe he's being poisoned? But who would do such a thing?"

The same person who'd opened the gate for Prolus when he attacked the castle. The same person who knew of their plans to head to Namaar. The snake nestling within them, and she didn't intend for him to remain that way.

51

DRAVEN
KARALIK EMPIRE
HEARCROSS, CAPITAL OF THE EMPIRE
THE GRAND PALACE

"HERE IT IS. Your fountain. The one you made your promises to."

Draven's fingers closed around Malus's collar. The once-proud emperor lay in a bleeding mess at his feet, regal clothes stained a deeper red than the Imperial flag. Draven shoved him forward, holding him closer to the fountain. Misty water spritzed them.

"You should've given me Natassa instead of playing tricks. Maybe then I would've made your death easy." Draven leaned down to whisper in Malus's ear. "I wouldn't have humiliated you."

Malus mumbled, blood spurting from the gash in his lip.

"Shh," Draven said. "Don't worry. I *will* claim her, and I *will* kill your boy. I will end the Hartinza line. What did I tell you? I would make new promises."

He glanced back at the pale-faced servants and his stony guards, their backs ramrod straight as they watched him, their king. Their new *emperor*.

"Malus's reign is over!" he called, lifting Malus by his collar.

Malus snarled, struggling in his grip, and scratched curled fingers down Draven's face. Draven growled and smashed him against the fountain.

"Your! Rule! Is! Over!" he shouted, bashing Malus's head against the fountain with each word.

Blood pooled into the fountain from Malus's cracked skull, staining the once-sacred sight. Malus's eyes were wide and unseeing. Draven stared for a moment, the hush of the people behind him disturbing him. He was suddenly in Ayleth. In the back gardens, stabbing the birds he'd caught. His mother screamed for him to stop.

"Don't hurt them!" she cried, falling beside him. Then she wrapped her arms around him. "Don't do that."

Draven was shaken by the tremor in her voice and the tremble of her arms. He pulled away, looking at her.

"They are alive, like us. Don't hurt them."

"But Father does it. I'm practicing so that when I'm king, I can punish the guards."

"No." She shook her head. "You will be a better king. You will be different."

Draven laughed, rubbing Malus's blood between his fingers in wonder. His mother would have feared him if she saw him then. He'd wished for most of his life that she could still be alive, that he could have her with him, but he'd never been more glad that she was dead. He unsheathed his sword and sliced it through the thick mass of Malus's neck, then released a relieved breath.

He looked up, eyeing each frozen face watching him, and pictured himself through their eyes—a young man covered in blood and gore, eyes crazed, hair wild. He straightened to his full height and tossed the sword aside.

"Put the heads of the false princess and Malus on stakes. Let it be a sign to those who doubt my rule." His voice carried like icy chips in the silence.

The guards saluted him. "Long live the emperor! Long live Emperor Draven!"

The words drifted over him like soothing honey. He spread his arms, letting the feeling seep in.

Finally, he thought.

Draven sprawled across his grand new bed, hair falling in his eyes as he stared into his glass of zat at the swirling liquid within. He should've felt elated and proud, but instead, he felt empty. Normally, he would've pleased himself with women, but he couldn't bring himself to. He'd called for a few of Malus's courtesans, but each woman who entered wore the face he couldn't erase. Natassa's face. *Kasdeya's* face. It made him sick. He couldn't handle the guilt that consumed him.

With a knock on the door, the True Manos who'd greeted him when he first arrived entered. He appeared hesitant.

"Say your piece," Draven muttered.

"Your wife." He paused. "The false princess."

A cough followed, and Draven's eyes narrowed. The True Manos stumbled over his words before expelling them in a sharp exhale.

"She was pregnant."

Draven's breath whooshed out of him like he'd received a punch to the gut. *Pregnant.* Kasdeya had been pregnant. With *his* child. It wasn't the first time he'd received such news. But those had come from courtesans, women he'd dallied with but would never have at his side. He'd ensured none of those pregnancies lasted. Too many little bastards running amok would have been a threat to Ayleth's throne. But Kasdeya . . . Their child would have been different.

Draven stood, slamming his glass against the bedpost. The glass shattered, leaving the sharp stem in his hand. He curled his fist around it. The True Manos flinched and backed away. Draven roared, lunging at the healer and stabbing the glass stem into his throat. The True Manos's eyes bulged, and he sank to his knees. Draven collapsed beside the body and sat there for a long while. He'd killed her. She'd been pregnant. He fisted a hand in his hair and yelled until his throat felt raw. He dragged a hand over his tearstained face.

"What have I done?"

VELAMIR

KINGDOM OF VERIN

Tears streamed down Kasdeya's cheeks. Velamir wanted to wipe them away more than anything, and he would have if he hadn't learned a vital truth in those past minutes. Kasdeya had deceived him. *Natassa* had deceived him. He'd thought she was someone like him—a pawn abused by greater forces. He'd found companionship in her because of that, because something had bound them together. But it was a lie. She stared at him, her glistening eyes wide. She knew she'd been caught.

"Velamir," she whispered, reaching for his sleeve.

He stood before she could touch him. Finnean remained beside Krea's motionless body. Latimus met Velamir's gaze, his expression saying he was waiting to hear their next move. The dark trees created shadowy silhouettes, and he imagined deedans pressing in on them again to avenge their fellow soldiers on the ground around them.

Natassa stood and closed the distance between them. "I wanted to tell you—" Her voice broke. "So many times."

He searched her gaze and the stark pain lingering there. "What's done is done, Princess."

She flinched. "Don't call me that."

He laughed softly. "Is that not who you are? Or is this another game?"

"I had no choice," she said desperately, her fingers digging into his arm.

Footsteps crashed toward them. Velamir gripped a fallen sword and one of Kasdeya's—*Natassa's*—knives in his other hand. He tugged his arm out of her grasp and stepped in front of her. Despite the betrayal carving him, he would fight with every breath to protect her. More deedans entered his line of sight. He tensed, preparing himself for battle. The deedans rushed forward, and before Velamir could inhale, a pickaxe penetrated the skull of the deedan in the lead. A roar echoed from behind him. Velamir turned, and a wave of mercenaries rushed past him. They clashed against the deedans.

Vykus strode up to Velamir and smirked. "That gold in the castle better be worth it, boy."

Velamir stilled at the words, his sword halfway raised. The memory of Jax being scarred for life lingered in his mind.

"What?" Velamir stuttered. "What are you doing?"

"Coming to your rescue," Vykus said, motioning to his men.

The mercenaries had already defeated the deedans and pounded each other on the backs with ruthless strikes. Vykus called to Salvador, and the giant clambered over, along with another mercenary who carried a large chest. Salvador dropped a pile of weapons and belts at Velamir's feet. Velamir glanced down, recognizing his sword and dagger in the mix. The other mercenary extended the chest.

"A token of our goodwill," Vykus said. "Your weapons and the chest containing the names of spies."

Latimus was quick to take the chest and arm himself. Velamir followed suit, relief consuming him when his sword settled in its rightful place at his hip. Natassa lingered near him, but he shrugged off her presence. There were more urgent matters at hand. He turned then, heading back in the direction of the camp. Salvador stepped in his path. Velamir's jaw clenched.

"Call off your lapdog," he told Vykus.

"Where do you think you're going?"

"I need to get my friend."

"Forget the boy," Vykus told him. "He's half-dead, and you *will* be dead if you try to save him."

"Half-dead, thanks to you. Don't think I'm going to forget what you did." Velamir glared at the mercenary.

"But I saved the rest of your lives just now. I've invested too much for you to return. I turned my back on Prolus for that gold, and I plan to get it."

Velamir stared Vykus down. The man's thick arms were crossed, and he seemed determined. Velamir surveyed his surroundings. Mercenaries peered at him everywhere he looked. He was outnumbered. Latimus was the only one he could count on to have his back. Natassa he couldn't trust, and Finnean was still sobbing beside Krea's form, clearly numb to his surroundings. Velamir's fists clenched. He couldn't leave Jax behind when there was a chance he could save him.

A sudden howl snatched his attention, and he turned to where Latimus crouched over the chest. He'd broken the lid and his hand was inside the chest, but acid was filling it and poured over his skin.

Velamir rushed to him and wrenched Latimus's hand out, along with a flutter of stained parchment. He winced at the bubbling blisters forming on Latimus's skin. Velamir grabbed a water flask someone extended and poured it over his fingers. Latimus roared, his body shaking in anguish as he struggled to fight the pain.

Velamir shook his head. "What were you thinking?"

Vykus laughed. "Fool. That needs a special key to open it. Now you've ruined the documents."

Velamir's eyes zeroed in on a piece of parchment with ink still visible in a corner.

"Not all," he whispered, stunned by the name scrawled across. He lifted it with a tentative hand. Latimus scanned it, too, paling and shaking his head. "No. This is fake. He gave us a phony!" He pointed wildly at Vykus.

Vykus seemed amused by Latimus's incredulity. "And what would I gain by giving you a false list of spies?"

"My father isn't a traitor!" Latimus shouted, his voice rattling the leafless branches.

But there was his name in bold ink. *Blayton.*

Velamir should have known. It had been obvious from the start. His friendship with Winston. The reason he'd helped Velamir in Castle Verin. Everything fell into place.

"Latimus . . . I know how it feels to put your trust and belief in someone only for them to crush it." Velamir glanced at Natassa, and she flinched. "Winston did it to me. I couldn't believe it at first, but I learned to accept it."

Latimus's eyes flashed, and spittle escaped his lips as he repeated, "My father isn't a traitor!" He unsheathed his sword with his uninjured hand and swung it at Velamir.

Velamir blocked it in time, and sparks flew as their blades dragged against each other. Velamir shoved Latimus, and he stumbled back a few paces. He heaved harsh breaths, and then his face crumpled and he sank to the ground, resting his head in his palm.

Vykus shrugged. "You know what they say . . . You can't choose your relatives."

Velamir shot him a look. With Latimus subdued, his mind raced for a way back to Jax.

"Don't think about it, boy. I would kill you myself before sending you back. Waste less time that way. You won't be able to save your friend."

Velamir's jaw tensed, and his finger ran across the pommel of his sword.

"You know I'm right." Vykus stepped closer. "Another patrol will come any minute. Right now, we need to think of materials. Weapons, horses, food."

"And I'm sure you know exactly where to find those things."

"Speaking of relatives, there's a small town close by." Vykus chuckled, snatching a glance at Latimus. "It's been a while since I visited my cousin."

52

MORDON
KINGDOM OF VERIN
TARIQIN WAR CAMP

MORDON SHEATHED HIS sharpened sword and tied his hair back with a leather cord, preparing himself to meet Prolus. He'd been surprised when Winston told him. Apparently, it was customary for Calestors to receive the blessing of the Dark Lord before setting off on a mission.

"Are you ready?" came a muffled voice from outside his tent.

Mordon strode out, ducking his head as he moved the tent flap out of the way.

Quintus evaluated him with distaste. "It took *that* long, and you still look terrible."

"I can't blame you for saying that since you can't see my good looks from your height."

"Luckily, I won't have to see your face for

a while." Quintus puffed his chest out. "After escorting you, I will leave on an important mission."

"Why are you here, anyway?" Mordon asked, annoyed by his presence. "Where's Winston?"

"Lord Prolus gave him a task. He asked me to bring you."

"Let's get this over with."

They started toward the pavilion. The morning chill stroked his skin as the last fog of darkness filtered away with the rising of the sun.

"Did they find Velamir?" Mordon asked Quintus, attempting to sound nonchalant.

"The search party we sent out hasn't returned. Velamir is probably long gone by now."

They stopped in front of the pavilion, where two deedans blocked their entry.

Quintus nodded at them. "Lord Prolus is expecting the Calestor."

One of them ducked inside the pavilion. Mordon waited impatiently beside Quintus.

"Try not to speak when you meet him. You appear imposing until words slip out of your mouth. Then you sound absurd." Quintus side-eyed him. Mordon's lips parted to respond, but Quintus raised a hand. "Also, don't smile, or you will look inane as well."

Mordon's brows lowered. "The only thing that will look ridiculous is your face when I pound it into an unfixable shape."

Quintus scoffed as the deedan stepped out of the pavilion. He motioned for Mordon to enter. "Lord Prolus will see you now."

Mordon walked inside, leaving Quintus behind. It was dark. Thin pillars held torches, lighting up the corners. Mordon squinted, making out a figure standing beside what looked like a throne. The figure turned and stepped into the dim light. Mordon's heart jumped when he saw the menacing smile on the man's face. Then he realized it was the mask. Mordon couldn't help being curious about the face beneath it.

"At last, we meet," Prolus whispered in a gravelly voice.

Mordon's brow furrowed. "You've heard of me?"

"Winston tells me many things. He was eager to mention you, his newfound son. Tell me, Calestor, how do you feel being part of the Tariqin army?"

"I would feel more confident if our leader didn't hide behind a mask," Mordon said brashly.

Prolus's head snapped toward him, and a long silence made Mordon wonder if he was deciding how to execute him for his disrespect.

"I am curious to know the reason for the mask. I've heard many rumors about it," Mordon said, pressing closer. "Some say scars or deformity. What is the real reason?"

Prolus held up a hand, and Mordon stopped. "You are very brave to speak to me so openly. I like that about you."

The way Prolus spoke made Mordon think he was trying to hide his voice the same way he hid his face.

"How long have you heard my name?" Prolus asked.

"Since I was born. Everyone knows Prolus."

"But how long have they known my name?" Prolus

pulled back into the shadows and returned with a thick book. He brushed dust off the cover and handed it to Mordon.

Mordon's brow creased as he opened the cracked pages. He stared at the words, and confusion bloomed through him. "But this doesn't make sense."

Prolus settled onto his throne. "And why is that?"

"Because what's written here is something that happened over a hundred years ago." Mordon looked up. "You should be dead. Unless . . . unless you have it. The Golden Crown. The one that was lost in the depths of the Lagrima Sea. That's why you're still alive. The crown is keeping you alive, but you hide your face because it is so old that it's become disfigured." Mordon shook his head, eyes wide.

Prolus nodded slowly. "You've figured it out."

Mordon's mouth turned with distaste. "The rumors aren't even close to the horrifying truth."

Prolus burst out laughing. It was a deep and hearty laugh that proved he otherwise spoke in a low tone on purpose. "Ah, your face was so amusing. If only that were true! If only I had the Golden Crown and were over a hundred years old." Prolus gave another chuckle for good measure. "But the truth is, *that* Prolus—the one mentioned in the book—is dead."

"What?"

"You see, Prolus is just a name, a name that has belonged to several men. After the first Prolus died, his commander assumed his place. He wore a mask and allowed rumors to spread that he had become scarred. That is why people believe Prolus is immortal."

"Which Prolus are you?" Mordon asked. "The ninth? The tenth? What makes you different from the rest?"

"I am the one who will rule the world." Prolus stood from his throne. "Starting with the Karalik Empire. And unlike the others, the ones who waited until the previous Prolus died to take the name, I killed him."

"You killed the Prolus before you?" Mordon said in disbelief.

"He wasn't driven, not like I am."

"Why are you telling me all of this?"

"Because I see potential in you," Prolus said, "to be my first-in-command."

"Aren't you worried I would kill you and take your place?"

"You won't be able to harm me. The Golden Crown is almost within my grasp. After taking the Karalik Empire, I will return my attention to Savoria and continue searching for it. And then I truly shall be immortal, like the legends say."

"And what exactly does first-in-command do?"

Prolus reached up, touching the edge of his mask. "They are the one who keeps the secret of who's behind the mask. If you prove yourself to me, perhaps I shall share it someday."

Honzio
Whispering Forest

"Do you happen to have cutlery?"

The question elicited no response.

Grongar-ja munched on the bloody meat and smiled. Red stained his sharpened teeth, and Honzio shuddered. After he was led into the camp, Grongar-ja had decided to host him in the small confines of his tent, where an Uluzar placed an odd-looking piece of meat before them with nothing to use except their bare hands. Honzio was certain the meat was raw. There was no other explanation for all the blood seeping out.

Honzio struggled to smile back at the Uluzar, his lips freezing in a grimace.

"Eat," Grongar-ja said. It was not a request.

Honzio touched the thick chunk of meat. He attempted to tear off a piece, and squishing noises were the only result. Grongar-ja laughed and unsheathed his dagger. Honzio's eyes fixed on the weapon as Grongar-ja waved the blade in the air. With relative ease, the Uluzar sliced into the meat and handed him a strip. Honzio accepted it, hesitating before he took a bite. The texture was tough and would not break down no matter how many times he chewed it. Blood soaked over his tongue, and he gagged.

"What is it?" Honzio asked after he'd managed to swallow it.

"The leg of my last enemy."

Honzio choked, his stomach twisting. He was sure Grongar-ja's most recent enemy had not been an animal. He rubbed his hand over his tongue, trying to remove the taste. Through his laughter, Grongar-ja nodded at an Uluzar sitting with them. The man pulled a flask from his belt and handed it to Honzio. Honzio drank the water in quick gulps, drowning his disgust with the cold liquid. He nodded his thanks and returned the flask.

"Now," Grongar-ja said, "why are you here?"

"My father was killed by the new king of Ayleth. I need your help removing that madman and reclaiming my throne."

Grongar-ja licked the blood off his lips. "What will we receive in return?"

"I will sign your treaty."

"It is too late for that, princeling. We need something more. The king who killed your father . . . We want his kingdom in return for saving your Empire."

Honzio's jaw slackened. "You want Ayleth?"

Grongar-ja's grin was as sadistic as the tattoo on his hand—the image of a snake curled around a dying rat.

Honzio shook his head. "I cannot accept that."

"Then there is no agreement." Grongar-ja sliced more meat.

Honzio swallowed. It could be his leg next. He had no other options, and no one else could help him. "Fine. You can have Ayleth. Just help me take back my Empire."

Grongar-ja spat in his hand and extended it to Honzio, who stared at the blood-covered palm. The expectation was obvious, so Honzio spat into his own hand and clasped Grongar-ja's. It was a deal.

53

THE SUN BEAT down on them as they dug a large hole. Hours had passed since they'd escaped. Natassa shoved her borrowed pickaxe against the dirt with renewed force, sweat pouring over her face and bloodstained hands. Finnean and Velamir dug beside her and Vykus's men. The mercenaries wore scowls, and Natassa was sure they were only helping to speed the process.

Half of the thirty mercenaries remained behind when they'd left the forest to stall any deedans searching for them. That would buy them some time, but not much. Finnean had carried Krea's body the entire way as they escaped. He'd clearly been strained by distress and the weight of her body as the hours went by, but he hadn't allowed Velamir to carry her when he offered. Natassa understood his reasoning. He felt like he'd failed when Krea died. Natassa felt the same way.

"That's good enough." Vykus peered into the gaping hole.

Natassa approached Krea's still form. She leaned over her friend—her sister. Her skin was smooth, her eyes closed, her expression calm. Even with the blood staining her face and dress, Krea looked like a princess from a children's tale. A tear slipped from Natassa's eye and dripped onto Krea's neck. She wiped it off and brushed a kiss over Krea's forehead.

"Farewell, Sister," she whispered. "Laughter in life, daring in death, a star in Alaris."

She pulled back to allow Finnean his turn. His shoulders shook as he began his farewells. Natassa couldn't bear to watch. When he finished, Velamir and Natassa helped him lift her. They placed Krea inside the grave and cast the dirt back inside. Natassa's lips trembled as her friend's face disappeared under the mound. When they finished, the mercenaries moved to the stream nearby to wash their arms and fill their flasks.

Velamir stared at the ripples in the stream, seemingly unaware of the blood coating his sleeve. Natassa approached but halted before reaching him, not wanting to disturb him. He spoke, filling the space between them with his voice.

"I've failed in everything I set out to do." He didn't turn to meet her gaze as she came to stand beside him. "When I was in Tariqi, I failed as a Chishma. In the Empire, I failed to accomplish the mission I was sent on.

I failed to get Mordon out of the camp. I failed to save Lissa's mother. I failed Jax."

"You did your best, and that's all that matters," she said.

He laughed softly. "And everyone I've cared for has betrayed me."

She winced. *Cared for.* Had everything she felt between them been destroyed?

"You're bleeding," she blurted instead of sharing the feelings threatening to burst past her lips.

He didn't stop her as she touched his arm. She worked fast, knowing Vykus would call to leave any minute. She tore Velamir's sleeve, inhaling at the deep cut in his forearm. She crouched down and washed her hands in the stream. Her hair fell in her eyes, and she reached up with wet fingers, shoving the strands back. She met Velamir's gaze as he settled down beside her, not protesting as she washed the blood from his arm. He was staring at her like he used to, when it had seemed like he wanted to commit every feature of her face to memory.

"Why?" he said.

She held his gaze, knowing he was asking why she'd lied to him. "I was scared you wouldn't look at me the same way. That you would see me as a spoiled princess." He stayed silent, waiting for her to continue. "I had no choice. My handmaiden, Kasdeya, threatened me. She took my place against my will to advance her own plans. She almost killed me." Her voice broke at the memory. She blinked. She'd promised Krea she would forgive her sister, and recalling the bad times wasn't making that an easier thing to do. "My father was forcing me to marry Draven. I couldn't do it."

Velamir broke contact at the mention of Draven, his eyes moving once again to the water. His jaw flexed. "You didn't want to marry a rich prince?"

"He killed my brothers."

Velamir's head whipped back to her, and she nodded. "Thorsten in a jousting match, and Hesten, he had assassinated. It was only a matter of time before he got to Honzio. I was a prize to him. He would have disposed of me eventually. His true goal was the throne."

Velamir's face was stony as he processed the information. Natassa focused on his forearm, wrapping the torn fabric of his sleeve around it. She held it there, her fingers pressing against the wound to keep the blood flow back. She noticed a trail of burn scars marking his skin. Lines crossed into each other, resembling a crown.

"One of the things I regret most," Velamir said, nodding at his arm. "The Chishman mark. The symbol branding me as a servant of Prolus."

"It doesn't define who you are."

She moved one hand to his chest. His heart beat against her hand in fast thumps. She tugged the collar of her dress down so that he could see her shoulder. His eyes narrowed and then flared when he caught sight of her burn.

"I have it too," she said softly.

"Who did this?" he asked, his voice so hoarse and fierce, it sent chills over her.

"My father," she whispered, glancing at the imprint of the crown, remembering her father's maliciousness as he placed his scorching ring into her skin. "A parting gift."

Velamir placed his finger under her chin and lifted her face to meet his eyes. The fury in them nearly undid her. "I won't let anyone hurt you again. Even if it is the emperor himself."

Tears burned her vision, and she blinked quickly.

"Don't be afraid," he said. "Never again, all right?"

"All right." The words slipped out in a soft whisper.

His gaze dropped, settling on her lips, and her stomach swooped.

"Getting a little cozy here, aren't we?" Vykus stepped close to them.

Natassa jerked away from Velamir. She stood, brushing her hands on her skirt. Velamir stood, too, tearing his gaze from her to face Vykus.

"You're the girl I thought was Prolus's spy," Vykus said, a smirk building on his face. "But it seems you were something else entirely."

Natassa wanted to slap him. Salvador appeared behind him, and Natassa had the horrible recollection of him chasing her and Krea.

"I don't know what you mean," she said.

"Careful, Velamir." Vykus laughed. "Dallying with the emperor's daughter is dangerous. In fact, it is against the law for her to marry anyone but royalty."

Velamir stiffened. "I don't see how that concerns you, especially since you're the greatest lawbreaker around."

"It's just a warning, since we're on good terms and all."

"I don't need your advice," Velamir told him. "What I need is for you to send a message to Castle Verin."

Vykus tilted his head. "And what should that message be?"

More mercenaries pressed closer. Two among them, Natassa had learned, were Salvador's younger brothers, Tio and Tyras. They looked identical and were nearly the same size as their older brother.

"It's confidential," Velamir replied. "I need some ink and parchment."

54

T HEY ENTERED THE town. It was small but vivacious, and Prolus's mask adorned banners that covered every available spot. According to Vykus, his cousin was the head of the town and an avid admirer of the Dark Lord. In the town square, tables were filled with people thumping cups.

"Are they celebrating something?" Velamir asked.

"Prolus's victory," Vykus said. "And the yearly tax day, most likely."

"Yearly tax?" Finnean said. "Why would they be celebrating that?"

"Because they're not paying it, of course." Vykus chuckled. "Verin officials are not in the position to collect taxes."

Latimus scoffed. He hadn't said a word since finding out his father was a traitor.

Velamir had hoped he would draw out of his resentful state, but he didn't seem to be lightening up. He couldn't blame him. He'd been in that mood for a long time himself.

Music started up in a corner where a group of minstrels were set up, and hoots flew around. Velamir and the others weaved through the tables. Couples sprang up into the open area, breaking into a confusing dance with practically no rhythm. None of them followed the same pattern, and it took Velamir a moment to realize they were each creating their own dance. Ahead of them, a man sat on the raised podium they were quickly approaching. He wore a gold overcoat, black trousers, and was clearly the best-dressed man in town. A white neckcloth adorned the front of his shirt, and a large hat covered his head. He held a strange-looking staff with a tassel at the end. On his shaved face, a large mole stabbed one cheek, and a dimple adorned the other. His dimple grew wider when he spotted them. His eyes were round and large. A look that should've made him seem innocent somehow made him appear more deceitful. He rose, his voice carrying over to them.

"Vykus!"

"This is your cousin?" Velamir asked. The difference between them was stark.

"Distant cousin." Vykus winced and lowered his voice. "We call everyone *cousin* in the Docks because no one knows who their father is. It's easier to assume we're all related."

"Good to know."

Vykus raised a hand in greeting, and they stopped.

The cousin stepped down from the podium and covered the remaining distance between them.

"Let me do the talking," Vykus muttered under his breath and then, with a classic wide smile, called, "Sim!"

Sim's smile seemed pasted on. "I can't believe you had the guts to return after stealing my gold."

Latimus groaned, and Velamir nearly cursed as well. How were they supposed to get recruits and goods if Vykus wasn't even on good terms with the supposed cousin? Then again, was he on good terms with anyone? Velamir should have known better.

"I had to pay for my new teeth." Vykus extended his arms as if awaiting a hug.

Sim huffed. "That's not my problem."

"Your man knocked mine out."

"Have you forgotten the code?" Sim leaned closer. "We don't steal from brethren."

Vykus dropped his arms. "Bah. You know how hard that is to follow, and besides, we're mercenaries. We gamble for ourselves."

"You have new faces with you." Sim scanned over them. "It's hard to keep your men alive, isn't it?"

"I keep getting new recruits. Many are your men. People like a little adventure with their zat."

"You enjoy stealing from me. It makes me wonder why you're here now."

Velamir exchanged a glance with Finnean. It was not going well.

"Why don't we sit down and have a drink?" Vykus suggested, motioning to a table with empty seats.

Sim raised his brows. "Sounds like you're bribing me."

"Using your own drinks is enough to sway you?"

"I do purchase the best zat," Sim acquiesced as they walked toward the table.

"You will need to let me know where you 'purchase' it." He glanced back at them, mouthing, *Mingle! Try to blend.*

Finnean nudged Velamir and jerked his head to his left. Natassa watched the dancing couples, and the hint of a smile appeared on her lips.

"Go with her," Finnean said. His features were pained. Velamir had caught him watching Natassa at times and knew he was remembering Krea. With faces so similar, it was easy to imagine her in Natassa's place.

Velamir stepped beside Natassa and twined his fingers with hers. She glanced up at him, eyes widening. "Shall we dance?"

She looked down at their linked hands and finally nodded. Velamir pulled her with him until they entered the edge of the square. Natassa laughed, and the sound flooded him with a light that spread through his chest. She wore a large smile—a true smile—and everything around them faded until it was just him and her. No titles, no lies, no secrets, no divisions.

Velamir tugged Natassa to him, and she gasped, losing her balance and stumbling into his arms. He set his hands on her lower back and then peered down at her to ensure she didn't look uncomfortable with the placement. Her arms drew up in response, and she splayed her fingers over his shoulders. They swayed slowly. Velamir watched her cheeks pinken as she avoided his stare and glanced over at the other dancers. She exclaimed softly as one of the couples did a daring lift.

"I always hated dancing," she said. "Back home, it was so rigid, so uniform. A structured set of moves I couldn't deviate from. But this . . . this is different."

Velamir set his chin on top of Natassa's head, closing his eyes as he inhaled her scent. She smelled like grass after a storm, like wind before it rained. As he pressed closer, sudden guilt gripped him. Jax was still suffering in the Tariqin camp. Velamir had no idea if he was even alive, and here he was enjoying a dance with Natassa. The ache in his chest increased, and he swallowed a lump in his throat.

"I'm sorry about Krea," he told her, glancing down at her.

Natassa lowered her head, but not before he saw her distress. She took a moment before responding. "We will save Jax, Velamir. We won't allow him to suffer."

Velamir didn't deserve her comforting words. He still couldn't believe he'd left Jax behind.

"He's like my brother. My only family."

She nodded, sympathy shining in her soft features. "I know the feeling. After my mother's death, I was closest to Thorsten."

"Tell me about her. Your mother."

Natassa stiffened in his arms, but the tension seeped out of her in one breath. "They proclaimed her the most beautiful woman in the Empire. She was sought after by everyone. I believe that's what made my father want her the most."

There was brittleness in her voice, like broken shards

of glass crumbled beneath a boot. He dragged his hand up her back, and she leaned closer, resting her head on his chest. His jaw clenched at the thought of her father. Emperor Malus had been a symbol of the enemy for so long, one he'd disliked but hadn't hated. Knowing Natassa had changed that and made him loathe Malus with a rage he hadn't known he could possess. What kind of man scarred and tortured his own daughter?

"She's the one who inspired me to paint. Despite my father's disapproval, she encouraged me to pursue my passion."

"You like to paint?"

She angled her head to peer up at him. "I painted you once." An endearing blush bloomed across her cheeks.

Velamir couldn't hold back his smile. "When?"

"In the palace."

"How? You didn't know me."

"I saw you," she admitted. "When I was in Verin. It was the day my mother died. I ran from the castle, unwilling to accept what had happened. I climbed a tree and stayed there for hours. Then I saw a little boy around my age. A man was calling to him, asking him to retrieve the trapped fox. The boy looked behind him, and when he saw no one in sight, he opened the trap and let the fox go free. He rebelled. He became an inspiration for me. A hero."

Velamir knew what day she spoke of. The recollection came swiftly. It was before he'd been sent to Tariqi, when he'd stayed with the Blaytons. He hadn't wanted to hurt the creature. That mercy died in him later. He brushed a hand over Natassa's hair, fiddling with the ends.

"I saw you in my visions after that. Little snippets of you. Mostly vague things I couldn't recall. But I remembered your face. Your eyes, your determination. Sometimes, I would think I'd imagined it all, that you'd never existed, but it hurt too much to consider that. You filled the gaping hole left in my chest. And you didn't even know I existed." She chuckled softly.

"I saw you too." At his admission, she leaned back. "I've had strange dreams. You're always calling to me in them."

"When we locked eyes that day," she whispered, "when you rescued me, it was like . . ."

"Like I'd known you forever." He gazed into her hazel eyes. Those exact shades of gold and brown and green were his favorite colors. He wouldn't mind staring into them for the rest of his life. But a muffled shout broke the moment. Velamir acted on instinct and pulled Natassa behind him. Latimus and Finnean stood, their weapons rasping from their sheathes. The town gates slammed open. Men garbed in Prolus's uniform rushed inside.

"Sim!" the leader shouted.

Velamir drew Natassa into the crowd of townspeople, hoping they wouldn't be seen. Vykus's mercenaries seemed to be doing the same thing. Sim stood, placing himself before his cousin.

"Commander Feldon!" Sim replied. "What brings you to my humble town?"

Feldon was a hard man, with lines that grooved deep

into his skin. His eyes were dull, like those of a puppet used to taking orders.

"Lord Prolus believes you may be housing deserters. You know what the cost of betrayal is. You swore obedience to Lord Prolus. Are you going back on your word?"

An inward debate raged across Sim's face before he nodded. "I was just going to send news." Velamir's blood ran cold as Sim stepped away from Vykus, revealing his position. "The traitors thought I would help them."

Vykus brandished his sword. "You slimy bastard."

"I've been called worse."

"Attack!" Feldon yelled.

"Get in one of the buildings! Go!" Velamir ordered Natassa.

"I want to help," she said, though she visibly trembled. Feldon's men roared as they swarmed in.

"Go!" he repeated.

Latimus grabbed Natassa's arm. "I'll keep her safe."

Velamir watched until they entered a shop, then turned, unsheathing his weapon. Feldon had at least forty men with him, vastly outnumbering Velamir and Vykus with his fifteen men, who were too spread out to assist each other. They would be hunted one by one.

"Finnean," Velamir said, and the man drew up beside him, giving him a nod.

The surrounding townspeople moved away. Feldon's men spotted them through the gaps. Velamir heard Vykus curse but kept his focus on the approaching onslaught. A deedan slammed a kilisham at him, and Velamir blocked it with a clang of steel. Finnean fought at his back. They stabbed and slashed, holding off an opposition of ten men. Through the assault, Velamir spotted Feldon racing to the watchtower. A pile of wood, ready to be lit, rested at the top. He was trying to inform Prolus of their location.

Velamir swore under his breath. Something tightened on his wrist, and he glanced down to see a kilisham whip coiled around it. He winced and pulled against it. The deedan tugged, forcing Velamir to drop his sword. He lunged forward and planted a fist in the man's stomach, following the blow with a slash of his dagger. The deedan groaned, collapsing.

"Velamir!" Finnean shouted, motioning to the tower.

Feldon neared the wood pile, and Velamir shot into motion. He had no choice but to leave Finnean to fend for himself as he raced to the tower. Feldon's deedans guarded the stairs. The first deedan sprang at him. Velamir ducked under the blow, then slammed the deedan against the stone wall. The man slumped on the stairs, out cold. Velamir stepped over the body, barely avoiding an arrow flying at him. A second arrow whizzed by. Velamir crossed over the remaining steps, zeroing in on a deedan archer reaching for another arrow. Velamir smacked the bow out of his hands before being yanked back by pursuers, blows pummeling into his sides. His dagger was wrenched away. Feldon lifted a torch, a cynical smile on his lips as he watched Velamir fight desperately to reach him.

Velamir attacked with his bare hands, feeling bones crunch beneath his fists. As soon as the last man dropped, Velamir lifted the bow and nocked an arrow in place. Shock twisted Feldon's face, and it took him a moment to register the weapon aimed at him. A moment was all Velamir needed. He released a breath along with the arrow. It slammed into Feldon, and he stumbled back. The torch dropped from his hands to his clothes. Screams rent the air as he slapped himself.

Velamir heard a grunt and turned. A deedan hissed while staring at the knife planted in his palm, pinning it into a wedge between the stones. His weapon clattered harmlessly at his feet. Velamir searched for the person who'd saved him, although the beating in his heart already told him who it had been.

Natassa stared up at him, her hand outstretched. Their gazes tangled together. Velamir's pulse thudded in his ears as he exhaled with relief. He scanned the struggling men below him. Blood pooled across the cobblestones where, minutes before, he and Natassa had been dancing. Sim watched on with arms crossed, his men standing back as Vykus's mercenaries fell.

"Sim!" Vykus shouted. "Damn you."

Something flickered in Sim's expression. He looked up at Velamir and peered past to Feldon's burning corpse. Then he snapped his fingers. His men jumped into the battle. With help from Sim, Prolus's opposition ended quickly. Velamir finished off a deedan at the bottom of the stairs, then rushed to Natassa, who was standing with Latimus. Blood covered them both.

Latimus scowled. "I tried to stop her."

Velamir paid him no mind, pressing his hands to Natassa's cheeks, uncaring that he was coating her further with blood. "You could have been killed," he said, frustration, concern, and gratefulness at war with each other.

She looked at him seriously. "We're a team, Velamir. If one of us isn't safe, none of us are."

"Thank you," he whispered. "You saved my life."

"If we're keeping a tally," she whispered back, "that means we're no longer even." A smile tilted the corners of her mouth. "You owe me."

He laughed, pressing his forehead to hers. "I didn't plan on getting into so many dangerous situations."

"I don't think you can avoid them," she said, her lashes golden in the sunlight. "They seem to be very fond of you."

For a single moment, they shared the same breath, the same laugh, and Velamir was transfixed. He brushed her hair back, glimpsing the phoenix beneath. He heard Natassa's sharp exhale and witnessed the fear that always accompanied the chance of her shadow mark being revealed. He leaned in, gently kissing the mark.

At the sound of a throat clearing, Velamir pulled away.

Latimus eyed them pointedly. "While watching this is gag-worthy, we have a bigger problem." He tipped his chin.

Velamir followed his motion to the cousins. Vykus and Sim stared each other down. After a long second of silence, Vykus's stony exterior cracked, and he slammed Sim into a hug. "You scumbag. What took you so long?"

Sim coughed as though it were squeezed out of him. "I like to draw things out. Besides, gold is thicker than blood. I only did it for that reward you mentioned."

Velamir's eyes narrowed, and Vykus glanced at him before saying, "Yes, a grand reward. More than half of Verin's treasure trove in exchange for defending the castle."

"That wasn't what was promised," Velamir stated calmly.

"I got you recruits."

Latimus muttered, "Don't press it, Velamir. We can't have them turning on us now. We need them."

"We will discuss the reward once it is rightfully achieved."

"I want the agreement documented and signed," Sim said. "I will have my man prepare the papers. I want it finalized tonight." He glanced around at the wounded. "In the meantime, I suggest you visit my True Manos."

Vykus appeared stunned at the last piece of news. "You have a True Manos?"

55

MORDON

KINGDOM OF VERIN

THEY SURVEILLED THE castle from beneath snow-covered foliage. Mordon's focus lingered on the green flag planted atop the battlements. It waved in the wind, proud and true. Symbolizing the last stand of Verin's people.

"Ten watchmen," Silopar said, his voice low. "Not much of a defense."

"There aren't many people left to spare." Mordon pulled a vial filled with blue powder from his belt. "Put this in the food cauldron."

"What is it?"

Mordon glanced from side to side, lowering his voice. "Enough to make the other group and their Calestor fall asleep for a week."

Silopar's eyes widened. "But why?"

"You value your countrymen, don't you?

Those people in the castle, they're my family. I have to get them out."

Silopar's mouth opened and closed. "*Dsell*," he finally muttered. "How will you manage that?"

That depends on if Coralie can be reasoned with . . . he thought. "Don't worry about my plan. Just focus on yours. Ensure that you and the boys don't eat the food. Once they're unconscious, bind them. Then escape with the men. Wherever you want to go."

"Where will you go?"

"I may not be coming back. If they've learned I'm a traitor, my people might kill me. If Winston figures out I poisoned the troops, he will also kill me. The chances of my surviving are slim." He slapped a hand on Silopar's forearm. "Lead the men. You will be fine."

Silopar shook his head. "We will help you, *dsell*. You cannot do this alone."

Mordon stared at the man earnestly. "I'm not the man of legends, Silopar. I'm not the next Savorian king you're searching for. That's not me."

"We know, *dsell*. But you *are* hope. You gave us a light we thought died long ago."

Mordon felt something hearing those words. He'd always been someone's bane, someone's burden. Never their reason for hope. A swell of emotion filled his chest, and he swallowed.

"I'm not worth it, Silopar. Leave while you can."

Mordon stood and started through the destroyed town toward the castle. Soft wind blew at him, slicing into his hair. Despite the calls to halt, he didn't stop until he reached the gates. The drawbridge was lifted, so he remained there, waiting. The watchmen glanced at each other, paling—a sure sign they recognized him.

Mordon lifted his hands. "I need to speak to the queen."

They lowered their bows, though uncertainty lingered on their faces. After a long moment, the portcullis was raised. The gates swung inward, and the bridge lowered. Mordon walked inside, the walls of the castle closing around him. Despite Verin's flag blowing from the battlements, Mordon was met with a yellow flood of uniforms. A watchman climbed down from the tower and approached him.

"Galva Mordon? How did you escape?" He frowned at Mordon's uniform—Prolus's uniform.

"I stole it," Mordon said quickly. He didn't have time for the truth. "I need to speak to the queen."

The words were slick on his tongue. *Queen.* Coralie was queen. He had always known she would be, but it seemed so strange to be faced with a fact that had once seemed so far in the future.

"She is in the barracks," the man replied. "I will inform her of your presence."

"No need," Mordon told him. "I know the way."

The watchman sputtered as Mordon brushed past him. As he walked toward the barracks, the stone walkway drooped over him, burdening him with the past. He saw himself bleeding, leaning against the wall. Boltrex forced him up, his stern gaze flaring as he took him in.

The weak never make it. The only way to survive the world is to harden yourself.

I don't want to, he'd whispered as Boltrex left him there in disgust.

But he hadn't given up. He'd trained and trained and trained. Practicing until his wooden training sword broke. Punching the practice dummy until his knuckles were swollen and bleeding. Fighting with everything in him to prove he was something. He'd just wanted to be someone. Mordon's heart twisted, and he took a moment before continuing forward.

Laughter flooded through the first door in the barracks. Mordon stopped and straightened, warmth rippling through him. Coralie. He opened the door the slightest bit. She moved into his line of vision, her lips poised in a victorious smirk as she eyed her invisible opponent. He traced her form with his eyes, his heart thumping aching beats against his chest. Life emanated from her. She was vivacious.

Then someone else stepped into view. Tall, although not as tall as him, with gleaming black hair and streaks of gray along the sides, giving him a stylish look rather than aging him. Mordon's fingers fisted. He recognized that face.

General Zenrelius.

The general struck for Coralie's center, and she parried, bringing her sword to his throat. The general could have easily evaded the blow, but he allowed her to close in on him, to hold him mere inches away on the edge of her blade. Zenrelius stared at her, a smile curling lips that Mordon had thought incapable of smiling. Mordon's fury rose, driving to new heights. He took a breath, attempting to rein in the jealous beast roaring to be set loose.

"Very good, Coralie," Zenrelius said, his voice oily and scheming to Mordon's ears.

How dare he address her so personally? Who did he think he was? Mordon's hatred built as the general's hand edged to her hip, his fingers creasing the leather skirt she wore over her trousers. That was it. Mordon thrust the door open. Good reunion be damned. He would not let some old general prey on Coralie.

They jumped apart as the door slammed against the wall. Steel pricked Mordon's throat, and he paused, his fuming breath the only sound in the still chamber.

"Not another step."

Mordon glanced to his left at Jovinne, his childhood nemesis. So he was Coralie's new bodyguard. Mordon had never been lucky. Why not add one more misfortune to the list? Jovinne's eyes gleamed with cold hate, and his hand didn't waver in the slightest, the dagger within his grasp level with Mordon's neck.

A gasp drew his attention to Coralie. "Mordon?"

She sheathed her weapon, her face slack as she stared at him. He stared back, waiting for . . . He didn't even know what he was waiting for.

"Mordon," she said again, that time with a note of pain in her voice.

And then she flew at him. Jovinne barely had time to move before she launched herself at Mordon. She wrapped her arms around his neck, lifting onto her tiptoes. Mordon tugged her close after a shocked second. He lifted her off her feet and buried his face in her hair.

"You came back," she whispered in his ear.

"Always," he said, echoing the time he'd said it years back when he'd returned from the Borderlands. She'd stared at him with those luminous brown eyes then too.

Coralie gripped him tighter, a frantic laugh slipping through. Mordon looked up from her hair at Zenrelius. The general's hand gripped his sword so tightly, his fingers were white. Jovinne fumed just as equally. Coralie pulled away slightly and brushed Mordon's hair back. She beheld his scar, wincing.

"I know," Mordon admitted, suddenly uncertain. He didn't want her to be disgusted by him. "It looks hideous."

She shook her head, trailing a finger over the scar. He closed his eyes, savoring the feeling. "No," she murmured. "You've never looked braver to me than you do now."

A throat cleared, and Mordon tightened his arm around her waist. Coralie stiffened, as if suddenly remembering they had an audience. She tapped Mordon's arm, and he returned her to the ground.

"Tell me what happened," she said, searching his gaze.

"Can we speak alone?" He darted a glance at Jovinne and the general, who were both clearly livid.

"Thank you for the practice, General," Coralie said.

Zenrelius sniffed at the dismissal, and then his signature arctic mask slid across his face. Jovinne raised a brow when Coralie looked pointedly at him.

"My queen, I can't leave you alone with him," he

protested. "For all we know, he's joined Prolus. His uniform alone proves it."

Coralie darted a glance over Mordon's clothes, seeming to notice them for the first time. Zenrelius crossed his arms.

"You know Mordon," she said to Jovinne. "There's no one I trust more than him."

That seemed to slap both men harder than a hand ever could. After a brief bow, Jovinne left the chamber, and Zenrelius followed a moment after. Mordon smiled. It was one of his first genuine smiles in forever. It felt good.

"Now," Coralie said, "tell me what really happened."

56

Honzio clenched the hilt of his sheathed sword. Grongar-ja walked beside him, followed by about thirty Uluzar. Honzio's tension rose as they entered the city. Behind him, Grongar-ja dropped back, his men spreading out to appear less suspicious. More wanted parchments with his face stared at him the farther they went, proving Draven was searching for him. Honzio dragged his cowl low enough that he doubted anyone would recognize him. The night air brought with it a frigid chill as piercing as a knife.

Honzio's blood froze when he caught sight of the long stakes planted in the ground before the palace gates. The heads of his father and Natassa's decoy were embedded on the stakes.

Honzio's gut twisted, and he looked away from the sight. What he'd suspected was true. His father was dead. He'd never held any sort of love for him, but to see him disgraced in such a way angered him. And Natassa's poor decoy. Honzio's worry shifted to his sister. He hoped she was alive, that she was safe.

On the palace's battlements, the braziers were lit and guards walked about on the parapets, but none of them appeared very alert. Draven was hosting a party in celebration of all that he'd attained. Carriages strolled along the cobbled streets toward the palace. Draven would not be expecting a retaliation from Honzio so soon. He signaled for the Uluzar to exit the city.

Grongar-ja emerged beside him again. "Nervous, princeling?'

After arriving at an accord, Grongar-ja had come up with a plan to storm the palace with Honzio's helpful insight. They were going to enter through the secret tunnels. It had pained Honzio to tell Grongar-ja about the tunnels, but he had no choice. They left the city and entered another section of Whispering Woods. Minutes later, Honzio held up a hand.

"The entrance is around here."

Honzio searched for the trapdoor while the Uluzar settled back and waited. Darkness shadowed everything, making it hard to see. Honzio kneeled, feeling along the ground for the metal handle. Despite the many times he'd used the tunnels, they were proving difficult to find. Everything looked different under the shadow of night.

"Hasten, princeling," Grongar-ja urged.

"It would help immensely if I had some light," Honzio muttered.

Grongar-ja barked orders in Savese. The shamans who had accompanied them lit several torches. Grongar-ja took one and leaned over Honzio, casting the glow above him. More time passed, and the Uluzar shifted restlessly, impatient grunts and mutters circling round the group.

"Is it here or not?" Grongar-ja demanded. "We are wasting time."

Honzio grimaced and stood. "I was sure it was. Perhaps it is farther down."

His foot hooked on something, and he tripped. He grumbled as he scrambled up from the thick snow. Chuckles drifted around him.

"Hilarious," he said.

He attempted to free his boot. When it did not budge, he motioned for Grongar-ja to bring the light. A grin stretched over Honzio's face at the sight of the trapdoor handle. He slid his boot free and brushed dried leaves and snow aside. He gripped the handle and heaved the trapdoor open. Honzio reached for a torch from one of the shamans and shone it over the open hole, revealing steep stairs leading down. Honzio turned to the Uluzar and smiled at a surprised Grongar-ja.

"Welcome," Honzio said, "to Karalik Palace."

Honzio descended the stairs with Grongar-ja a step behind. Immediately, his stomach tightened at the darkness that swallowed the path before him. He forced the queasiness aside. He would bear the fear, like all the other times. He held the torch before him. The flickering light bounced off the dark walls, revealing long creatures sliding across the damp ground.

"Be wary of the snakes," Honzio warned.

Grongar-ja chuckled, leaning down and wrapping his fingers around one. It curled around his arm. "They know us," he said quietly.

Grongar-ja smiled, flashing all his sharpened teeth, and proceeded to bite the snake's head. Honzio's lips twisted in disgust, but he was growing used to the Ulu-zar's antics. Saliva mixed with blood dribbled out of Grongar-ja's mouth. Honzio advanced forward, ignoring the crunching haunting him from behind.

Honzio came to a split in the tunnel and racked his brain, trying to remember where each path led. He decided to take the path to the left. Soon after, they came upon another set of stairs, that time leading up. Honzio clambered up and felt above him, touching the cool metal of a trapdoor. He peered at Grongar-ja.

"Be ready to fight as soon as I open this. I don't know which area of the palace is above this door." Honzio handed his torch to Grongar-ja and shoved upward.

The trapdoor opened with a loud groan. Honzio poked his head out and recognized the long hallway. Seeing no guards in sight, he climbed out and motioned for the others to follow. They would be at the throne room entrance in a few more turns.

"Where next?" Grongar-ja asked.

Honzio gestured forward and crept down the hall, but he froze when a guard appeared. Honzio tried to backpedal, but the guard had already seen him. The guard's hand dropped to his sword and then halted when he saw Grongar-ja. Honzio watched in fascination as the guard nodded and revealed a tattooed wrist to Grongar-ja. He was an Uluzar. Honzio glanced at Grongar-ja, who waved at him to continue. The guard joined them. The same thing happened at the next hall, where two more guards merged into the group after showing their tattoos.

"How many?" Honzio bit out.

Grongar-ja looked at him with feigned confusion. "How many what?"

"How many Uluzar are in the palace?"

"You should pay more attention to your own home, princeling."

Honzio sighed. Clearly, the Uluzar had been biding their time, growing larger inside the palace like a swarm of rats. In the next hall, they encountered a guard who wasn't a spy. He was dead moments later. Before entering the next corridor, Honzio paused at the sound of voices. He peered around a corner. There, around fifteen soldiers pulled cloaks over their armor.

"Why do we have to wear these?" one complained as he tied the cloak in place.

"The king"—an older soldier coughed—"ahem, the *emperor* wants to make our entrance more dramatic."

"When are we going in, Domavan?"

"Soon," the older soldier replied.

Alarm seized Honzio when the Uluzar slipped past without his direction.

"No!" he hissed.

But it was too late. Left with no other choice, he crept forward, unsheathing his sword. By the time the soldiers noticed the Uluzar, they were already upon them. Domavan held his ground and took down a few of the Uluzar. Then he tried to call for help, but a sword slashed his throat, silencing his cry. He slumped to the ground, joining the bodies of his comrades. Honzio stood there, shocked by the brutality of the Uluzar in action. Hands, arms, and legs had been severed. Grongar-ja paraded across the bloodstained floor over to Honzio.

He laughed, examining Honzio's bloodless sword. "Too slow, princeling."

Honzio sheathed his blade with a scowl. It was the second time he hadn't participated in a fight. "We need to hide the bodies."

Grongar-ja frowned. "Forget the bodies. Let us surprise the party."

A plan formed in his mind, and he shared it with Grongar-ja. A slow smile spread across the Uluzar's face as he listened. After Honzio finished, they donned the deceased soldiers' cloaks. The Uluzar seemed uncomfortable but didn't complain. They pulled the hoods low over their faces, as Honzio had told them to. A servant entered the corridor with his head lowered, eyes on the floor.

"His Supreme Majesty Emperor Draven bids you to enter," the servant said and then retreated inside the throne room.

Honzio rolled his eyes at the title and led the others into the room. The guests made way for them. Soon, Honzio found himself standing before the throne. Standing before Draven. He glanced up, sighting the false emperor rise unsteadily from his stolen throne through the obscure curtain of his hood.

Draven held up a glass of zat, his eyes unfocused as they raked over them. "These, my good people, are my loyal soldiers." Zat splashed over the rim of his glass as he slurred.

The guests clapped, and then the sound faded to silence. Honzio wondered why it had suddenly become so quiet.

"Kneel," Draven muttered.

Honzio put one leg behind him and settled into a kneeling position. Draven walked up to him on unsteady legs and unsheathed his sword. Honzio was startled. Had he recognized him?

But then Draven said, "My courageous captain, Domavan, rise."

He tapped Honzio's head with the sword before stepping back. Honzio braced himself and took a fortifying breath. He stood, rising to his full height.

"Not Domavan," he said, his voice somehow deeper and chilling to his own ears.

A hush fell over the crowd, and Draven frowned in confusion.

Honzio threw back his hood. "I am Crown Prince Honzio Hartinza! True heir to the throne!"

57

CORALIE
KINGDOM OF VERIN
CASTLE VERIN

THE SHADOWS IN the training chamber couldn't sway Coralie's exuberant mood. Part of her was certain Mordon was a figment of her imagination. "Did Velamir help you escape?"

His smile faded at her question, and he seemed uncomfortable. "So you did send Velamir."

Coralie nodded. "You saw him?" When he didn't respond, a sinking feeling twisted her stomach. "Why *are* you wearing Prolus's uniform?"

The answer was clear in the guilt that set his jaw on edge and the way he wouldn't meet her eyes.

She grabbed his arm. "Don't look away from me. Tell me the truth. Did you join him?"

He remained silent. Coralie shook her head and ran a hand over her mouth, wishing she could take back all the joy she'd showered on him.

"I suffered, Mordon. I spent every moment of every day worrying and thinking about you. And instead of the cramped tortured prisoner I imagined, you *joined* them?"

Something flickered across his face, and a spark burst forth. "Thinking about me until you took a break to laugh with your general?" At her shock, he nodded. "Thinking about me until Zenny came along to make you smile and lighten your load?"

"I can't believe that's what you think of me. My uncle *died*, Mordon. My people were dying. I was alone. I needed all the help I could get. And during that time, you were on my mind constantly. And yet *this* is how you perceive me? As a silly girl joking around?"

"What should I think?" he shot back. "You chose a bully, a boy who tortured me any moment he could for most of my childhood, as your bodyguard!"

She gasped. "Jovinne?"

She'd had no idea he'd bullied Mordon, but as she was about to voice her confusion, Mordon continued. "Yes, Jovinne! The same Jovinne who's been in love with you for years. And now you've put him right beside you, throwing a bone to a dog who will never have the true prize."

Coralie lifted her hands, wanting him to stop. "I can't believe you. You're speaking about something so insignificant compared to what is happening. Lives are at stake."

"Of course, of course. Someone's feelings are insignificant to you. I'm not surprised. Yes, I took Prolus's side. I did it to survive," he spat. "Is that a crime?"

"You sided with a murderous monster."

"The same side my supposed father is on. He took me there, tried to corrupt me, but I was going to leave. I was going to make my own way."

She sighed, a frustrated breath slipping free. "Your father is Boltrex."

"Boltrex will never be my father. That man is a wretch who used me. I should have seen it years ago."

Coralie could hear the anger and pain layered in his tone. "Boltrex is dying," she told him. "He's very sick."

"I don't care!" he shouted. "We aren't talking about him. How is what I did in Prolus's camp any different from you receiving Ondalar's help? General Zenrelius's help?"

Her nostrils flared. "Zenrelius isn't my enemy!"

A broken pause hovered between them before Mordon extended his arms. "It's apparent that I'm the enemy before you. Don't stop." He closed the distance between them, unsheathing his dagger. "Here, ease your conscience and take one of Prolus's minions down."

A sob clutched her, feeling like frozen fingers clawing up her throat. She looked down at the dagger in Mordon's large hand. He extended it farther. She breathed in, and resentment filled her chest.

"Come on, then." Mordon nodded, urging her on.

Coralie snatched the dagger and held it at his neck. She pressed the lethal edge against the delicate skin there and forced him backward with the blade. Each step led him closer and closer to the barrack doors. Her fingers shook around the dagger hilt.

"Look at me when you do it," Mordon murmured.

She gazed instead at his chest, unable to face him, knowing that if she met his eyes, she would crumble.

"Look at me!" he demanded.

Coralie's eyes snapped up to meet his heated stare. Dark strands of hair drifted over his forehead; beads of sweat trailed down his temple. Coralie peered into those eyes that meant everything to her. She couldn't do it. She couldn't hurt him.

"Come on," he whispered.

A smile crept to his lips as he saw the truth in her face and observed the slackness of her grip on the dagger. He flung her wrist away and spun her around, shoving her toward the barrack doors. Her weapon flew from her grasp, clattering in the distance. Her body slammed the doors closed on Jovinne's stunned face. Coralie gasped as she connected with the wood. But Mordon's arms were around her, softening the blow, one hand behind her head and the other pressed to the wall. They panted, their breath mingling in the small space between them. A tear slipped down Coralie's cheek. She cursed softly, and Mordon laughed. His eyes were tender on her. He brushed the tear from her cheek.

"I'm sorry," he said, and Coralie's gaze flicked to his.

"You never apologize."

"It's high time I did," he muttered. "I know I'm not the easiest person to be around, but I want you to know this. I can't hold back with you. I feel like a dragon. I want to burn anyone who comes close. I know it's wrong, but"—Mordon pulled her closer—"I can't help this possessiveness."

There was a bang on the door before he could say more, and he gritted his teeth.

"My queen! Are you all right?" Jovinne called, sounding panicked. "Do you need assistance?"

Coralie stepped out of Mordon's hold and opened the door despite his annoyed grumbles behind her. Jovinne stood in the doorway and slapped a half heart to his chest.

"I'm perfectly fine, Jovinne."

He peered at her and finally nodded. "There is a messenger here to see you, my queen."

"Let him in."

Jovinne gestured to someone in the hall. A man stepped inside. He was tall, with scruffy armor and an axe hanging from his belt.

"You're one of Vykus's men," Mordon said.

Coralie's brows shot up, and she appraised the man. "What do you want?"

"What is General Winston's pet doing here?"

Mordon seethed, advancing a step. Coralie slammed a hand on his chest and gave him a look that told him to back down. Mordon fumed but crossed his arms. Coralie swiveled to face the mercenary.

"What are you doing here?"

"Velamir! Velamir sent me."

Coralie absorbed that information. It was good to know he was alive. She nodded, waiting for the rest of the news.

"He said to tell you that the traitor is within your people."

Coralie's breaths ceased as she waited for an endless moment while the mercenary scratched his head.

"Bortis . . . Blortan." His nose scrunched. "Blyton . . ." He shrugged. "I had a note, but I lost it on the way."

"Blayton," Coralie whispered.

"That's it!"

Coralie brushed past the mercenary. She would deal with him later. Mordon and Jovinne strode along beside her. She saw Lady Blayton on her way and grabbed her by her shoulder. The lady gasped, staring at Coralie with wide eyes.

"Where is your husband?"

"My husband? He . . ." She sent a worried glance over Coralie's shoulder at Mordon and Jovinne. "He said he was going to spend time with General Boltrex."

Coralie released the woman. They moved for Boltrex's chamber at a clipped pace while Lady Blayton protested behind them, demanding to know what was going on.

Coralie thrust open the door to the chamber and stumbled into the room, where Blayton stood over Boltrex's bed, his sword embedded in the general's midsection.

58

NATASSA WAS IMMOBILE in the Stone Chamber, crowded by bodies and paralyzed with fear. The deedan's dark eyes peered at her. She'd killed him. He smiled, as though he enjoyed reminding her. Natassa backed away, but he kept coming nearer until she hit the wall and mere inches separated them. Then he leaned in, breathing on her neck. His lips brushed her ear. Natassa shook, terror creating trails of sweat over her body.

"You can't run from me, Natassa." The voice morphed, first soft, then harsh, familiar. A deep cadence that had always set off warning drums within her. "I won't accept vile trash having my blood."

"No!" Natassa shook her head. She attempted to close her eyes so she wouldn't see her father's twisted face, but they remained fastened open by an unknown force. "No."

"No?" He tilted his head. "I'm coming for you, girl."

He lifted a hand and tugged off the glove covering it. Rings glinted on every finger. Then his fingers grew longer, and the nails sharpened to points. The rings were gone. His face had changed. Brown eyes with a reddish hue regarded her. Thick lips were nestled above a pointed chin. His black hair was sprinkled with so much silver. But the face was young. He couldn't be over thirty years. She'd never seen him before, which made it all the more terrifying when he whispered, "I'm coming for you."

She grabbed his collar, trying to thrust him away. The material felt so real in her hands.

"Natassa." Someone repeated her name, and the man faded until only the twinkle of his eyes remained before vanishing entirely.

Natassa sat up. The chamber Sim had allowed her to stay in came into focus. She was still holding the collar. She shrieked, releasing it, and firm arms locked around her back.

"It's just me. Breathe."

Natassa inhaled, trying to calm her galloping pulse. Velamir nodded, gesturing for her to take another breath. She pressed her head into his shoulder. Her visions were overpowering her. She needed to overcome her shadows, but she wasn't anywhere closer to doing so. Natassa realized with a start that she was on the ground. How had she ended up there? Natassa recalled readying for sleep and the blinding headache that followed. Then her shadows' voices pouring around her like thick clouds of smoke.

Natassa looked over Velamir's shoulder, glancing around the room. It appeared the same as before. A small bed rested in one corner and a table in the other. An empty fireplace took up much of the wall. She shivered at a sudden chill. Velamir must've noticed and started to move, but she clutched his shirt.

"Stay with me," she said. "For a moment. Please."

He settled back down. He didn't ask what had happened, just sat silently as she collected her wits.

"Have you ever seen them?" she asked. "The people you've killed."

He stiffened. "All the time."

"Not only do I see them . . ." She shuddered. "But the visions keep getting worse. That's why I was going to Devorin. I don't have any aunts there."

He laughed softly. "I assumed as much."

"There is an order there, the Elders. I was informed that they can help me."

Velamir nodded against her head. "I've heard of them. I was actually entrusted with returning a pendant to them." He filled her in on the old man who'd passed away before saying, "After we finish this business with Verin, after we stop Prolus and rescue Jax from their clutches, let's go together."

"Thank you, Velamir," Natassa said, feeling calmer, and then she noticed she was practically sitting on his lap and had ordered him to stay that way. A blush rose to her cheeks, and she stood.

"How did you know I was having a vision?"

"I wasn't able to rest and wanted to ensure you were safe. When I knocked, there was no answer. Then I heard thrashing and a few thumps. When I entered, you were lying on the ground."

Velamir headed to the fireplace to stack it with wood. Natassa dipped her hands into the basin on the table and splashed water onto her face. The cold pierced her skin, reviving her. By the time she'd finished, flames were roaring in the fireplace. Velamir stared into the heat, sparks dancing in his green eyes and highlighting the lighter strands in his beard. His hair crept over his ears. Natassa could only imagine what she looked like. She felt like she'd aged years. She grimaced at the thought of her ragged haircut, torn dress, and thin pale skin.

Velamir turned, catching her watching him. Natassa would have been embarrassed to have been caught staring weeks ago. But now . . . She knew him better. There was something there, a spark that had bound them even as children. She smiled, and his mouth tilted in return. In that simple action, she saw how handsome he truly was. Not just outwardly, but the kindness and courage and determination resonating from within. And when he looked at her like that, the opinion she'd formed about her own looks dissipated. Natassa's gaze drifted down to the dried blood and bruises covering his hands. She rushed to him.

"Why didn't you get these examined by the True Manos?"

He was startled, following her gaze to his hands, then shrugged. "It's nothing. I'll be better in a day or so."

Natassa narrowed her eyes and grasped his forearm,

tugging him toward the table. She pulled out a stool. It screeched over the floor.

"Sit," she said.

He indulged her with a slight smile. Natassa placed his hands on the table and grabbed a cloth. After dipping it into the water, she brushed it over his fingers, catching him wince. She froze, but he urged her to continue.

She frowned but persisted, dabbing softly. "You need to take care of yourself. You're throwing your life around recklessly like—" She froze, catching her lip between her teeth. *Like Thorsten*, she'd been about to say. "Let me check the wound on your arm."

He rolled his sleeve up, and she spotted a scar, thin and pink, on his upper arm.

She pointed at it. "What happened here?"

He seemed hesitant to say, so she didn't press for more. Natassa unwrapped the cloth on his forearm to reveal the cut. It was much improved. She cleaned and rewrapped it.

"I got it in Namaar," he said in a low tone. "Vykus was shooting Savorian slaves. I tried to save one."

When he didn't finish, Natassa did for him. "You put yourself in the way." She tugged the sleeve down and traced the scar through the fabric. "You risked yourself to save him, just like you did to save me, to spare the fox, and even now, when you could run away from all of this, you are returning to a war the Empire might not win. That is bravery, Velamir. Despite everything that may go wrong, despite the risk of losing your life, you will do what you believe is right."

He stilled, at first abashed, and then a broad smile

crossed his face. He tugged her close, pressing his head to hers. "Is the Imperial princess showering a lowly soldier with compliments?"

"Yes, she is." She closed her eyes, exhaling softly as he angled his head nearer.

An unexpected knock startled them. Vykus's voice drifted through the door. "Get ready Princess. We're leaving in a few hours."

Natassa shuddered. The fact that Vykus could so easily enter her room if he wanted to frightened her. She looked back at Velamir and saw him watching her with concern. He brushed a hand against her cheek and gifted her a fleeting smile.

"Get some sleep. I'll be by the door. No one will disturb you."

Natassa followed him to the door and closed it softly behind him. She smiled, knowing that when he'd left and no matter where he went, he would be taking her heart with him.

59

Honzio

Karalik Empire
Hearcross, Capital of the Empire
The Grand Palace

D RAVEN STUMBLED BACK onto his rear end. His goblet of zat smacked the marble floor, shattering into an explosion of glass. Gasps from the guests shot around the throne room as Honzio unsheathed his sword and pointed it at Draven's throat.

"Your celebration is over, *Your Majesty*," Honzio sneered.

Draven looked in desperation at the cloaked men behind Honzio. "Kill him! He is not Domavan! Kill him!"

The Uluzar threw off their cloaks with a roar that could incite fear in any capable soldier. They screamed curses in Savese and bared their teeth, along with their gruesome weapons. The guests ran for the doors, but the Uluzar moved quickly, clambering over tables to block their path.

Draven's brows lowered as he rose unsteadily. "How *dare* you?"

The screaming in the throne room increased tenfold, and Honzio glanced back to see the Uluzar stabbing the guests. He shot a look at Grongar-ja.

"Stop them. We only attack Draven's soldiers, not the guests."

Grongar-ja shrugged, snaring a chicken leg from a table. He tore a chunk off with his teeth. "Uluzar aren't ordered. They command." Juice dripped into his braided beard.

Honzio began to shake his head when searing pain struck his shoulder. He spun, his gaze connecting with Draven's as the false emperor twisted the table knife deeper into his shoulder. Honzio hollered, the agony scorching his flesh. His sword clattered from his hand. A crunching noise accompanied Draven's turn of the knife. Honzio slammed his head into Draven's skull, and Draven staggered back, gripping his head in his hands.

Honzio bit into his lip to keep from shouting as he pulled the knife from his shoulder. Blood poured down his arm, soaking his sleeve. Draven swayed and took an unsteady step before charging at him. Honzio lifted his wounded arm, grimacing at the pain, his fingers clenched around the knife. As soon as Draven drew close enough, Honzio kicked him in the stomach. Draven's face turned green, and he clutched his middle. Honzio jumped back, barely avoiding the splatter. He fought the sickness clawing up his throat at the chunks of food in the vomit.

An Uluzar approached Draven from behind and shoved him onto his knees. The guests continued screeching.

"Stop your men!" he ordered Grongar-ja again.

Grongar-ja whipped his sword up to Honzio's throat. "I don't think so, princeling. You are not in command. Kneel beside the maggot." He motioned toward Draven.

"What?" Honzio blurted. "You're making me a prisoner as well? We had a deal!"

Grongar-ja shook his head. "You were always our prisoner, princeling. Now you will just have different accommodations."

Rough hands grabbed Honzio and pushed him down beside Draven. "I gave you Ayleth!"

"You gave them what?" Draven asked groggily.

Grongar-ja dragged a guest out from under a table and slit his throat. "You gave us nothing we didn't already have. If you don't want to be my next meal, I suggest you keep your mouth shut."

Honzio paled, his vision growing dazed as he continued to lose blood.

"You eat . . . humans?" Draven blinked slowly.

Grongar-ja ignored him and ordered his men. "Take them to the dungeons."

Honzio had been duped. He had been so sure of his victory that he hadn't even thought about the Uluzar betraying him. He had no options and no time. His future was a dank dungeon with two impaired arms. Before Grongar-ja's men could heft him up, Honzio swiveled, stabbing Draven's shoulder with the very same knife.

Jax
Devorin

The first thing Jax felt was cold—bitter, aching cold that seeped through his limbs and curled his fingers into fists. He blinked his eyes open and was blinded by the amount of white flurrying around him. He peered through snow-clumped lashes at the figure across from him. She was hazy, but it wasn't hard to decipher her identity. Those deft hands working at the knots binding her wrists. That sleek sheet of black hair that somehow remained shiny and beautiful despite their recent tribulations.

"Lissa," he croaked.

He winced as he attempted to sit up. Lissa's head snapped up, the binds around her wrists dropping off. She scooted beside him. Her booted feet had rope around them too. He craned his neck to peer down at himself and realized he was in the same condition.

"Jax." Lissa's worried eyes scanned over him. "How are you feeling?"

Her teeth chattered, and her lips were a purplish blue. Jax opened his mouth to speak but then clamped his lips together. It hurt to talk, to move.

"At least they gave us warm cloaks," Lissa muttered. "Even if they are handing us over like slaves." She peered ahead. "We're in Devorin. A few more hours and we will enter Sok."

Her fingers trembled as she fumbled with the rope at her boots. Jax turned to examine the road. His body shook with the rickety movement of the cart they'd been tossed into. Two deedans sat in front, driving the horses.

One of them turned slightly, and Jax glimpsed his face. No, not a deedan. *Quintus.*

"The others." He forced the words out. "Velamir? What happened?"

Harsh wind covered their voices, so Lissa didn't bother lowering hers as she spoke. "You were passed out the whole time, and I slept for a while. We might have missed something, but as far as I know, they got away."

Jax's frozen lips cracked into a small smile. "He got away."

"And we will too." Lissa threw the rope off her boots and chanced a glance over her shoulder.

Quintus and the deedan were focused on the path ahead. She reached for Jax's rope.

"Where will we go?"

She paused for a moment. "Wherever we can."

"We'll freeze to death."

"But we might have a chance. If they take us to that queen's castle, we won't live to see another day."

Jax accepted her reasoning. He was too tired and spent to argue.

"I have no desire to be face-to-face with that woman. Apparently, that's where the general gets all his tonics and the Zamanin Sulari you're so fond of." She snatched the ropes off his wrists and crouched by his legs. "There are rumors she killed her husband, but no one knows for certain."

Jax's throat was raw. "Lissa."

She looked up, her purple eyes gleaming, and Jax imagined he saw something else there. A fondness, perhaps?

"I missed you," he admitted.

She smiled. "I can't believe I'm going to say this, but I did too."

He laughed and then coughed. Lissa frowned and reached out, placing an ice-cold hand on his brow. "You're blazing."

She struggled to untie his bonds. Jax coughed again, clutching at the cart to steady himself. The wood trembled against his weight and creaked. Quintus glanced back, eyes widening at the sight of Lissa free and untying Jax.

"Run!" Jax said. "Go, Lissa."

He could see a thousand thoughts racing through her mind. He knew her. She would leave. She had the chance to save herself, and she would take it. But that was the old Lissa.

She rose to her feet as the cart shuddered to a stop. Quintus jumped off and approached the side of the cart, his face thunderous. The deedan dropped down as well, lashing his kilisham. Lissa darted a glance between them and planted her feet firmly as she fell into a defensive stance. She looked like the warrior he'd always known. The proud woman who didn't back down.

"Don't be stupid, Lissa," Quintus snarled. "Be a good girl and allow us to tie you."

"You contain all the stupid, Quintus," Lissa said. "I'm afraid there is none left for me."

He sniffed, covering a dash of anger with a placating smirk. "Come on. We used to be a team." Quintus gestured to her. "All of us."

"We never were," Lissa replied. "We were on our

own paths, every one of us. Because we were selfish." She glanced at Jax. "I'm going to do something right for once. Jax and I are leaving. Either accept that or face the consequences."

Quintus blew out a cloud of air and jerked his head at the deedan. Jax inhaled as the deedan strode closer, angling his blade at Lissa. He sent Quintus an uncertain look before swinging the kilisham at her. She ducked, and the blade smacked into wood. He grunted, attempting to pull it free. Lissa kicked his hand, and he fell back, clutching his fingers to his chest. Lissa snatched the kilisham and pressed the side of the hilt, then flung it toward the deedan. The long sword shifted into a crackling whip and slithered around his neck like a snake. Lissa yanked the deedan closer. His face purpled as he struggled for breath. Meanwhile, Quintus crept nearer.

Jax's heart pounded. "Lissa," he croaked, but his voice was too hoarse for her to hear.

Quintus grabbed her ankle and yanked her back. She flew off the cart, dragging the deedan with her. The whip yanked on his neck, and there was an audible crack as he smacked the ground. Jax's lips parted, and a queasy feeling erupted in his stomach at the awkward position of the deedan's neck. Lissa grunted as she was hauled across the snow. She clawed at Quintus, who released her ankle and drew his sword. Jax leaned over to untie the rope around his feet, wincing at the pain tearing through his body. Blackness covered his vision for a second. He heard a scream and looked up, searching wildly for Lissa. Quintus was kneeling over her, sword drifting closer and closer to her neck. Her hands latched around his wrists, and she resisted with all her might.

"No, no, no." Jax managed to loosen the ropes and rose shakily to his feet.

Lissa smacked her leg up between Quintus's knees. He groaned, collapsing, his sword falling into a tuft of snow. Lissa scrambled for the sword and launched herself at Quintus. Jax stumbled, falling out of the cart onto the snow.

"Jax!" Lissa screamed.

When he lifted his head, she stood staring at him, her arms frozen above her, fingers clenched around the hilt. Jax's gaze slid to Quintus, whose startled face turned to one of determination.

"Lissa," Jax whispered.

Quintus shot to his feet and rushed at her. He wrenched the sword from her grasp and shoved her arms back. Lissa fought him with everything she had. As her kicks grew wilder, Quintus pushed her, and she stumbled back, falling onto a thick, sharp wooden branch sticking out of a log. It speared her through the stomach. Quintus's face went as white as the snow drifting around them, shock plastering across his features.

"Lissa!" Jax shouted, scrambling to his feet. He ran toward her. His eyes raked over the branch protruding from her midsection, coated with blood. She gasped a pained breath.

"It's okay," he whispered. "It's going to be okay."

But it wouldn't be. He didn't have any tonics or anything to assist him. He had nothing. Tears flooded his eyes as Lissa clasped his hand in her trembling one.

"Don't stop—" She gasped. "Don't stop being who you are."

Jax shook his head in denial, the ache in his chest nearly paralyzing him. He gripped her hand in a vicious hold. She closed her eyes, and a wet tear drifted off her lashes. When she opened them, her eyes were purple rays of shining beauty.

"No matter the evil around you . . ." She struggled to say the words, her body tensing as a spasm rocked over her. "Never stop being the hero, Jax."

He swallowed the lump in his throat. She squeezed his hand a final time and then fell still, staring listlessly at the snow drifting above.

"No," he said, sniffing. "Not you too."

He turned toward footsteps muffled by soft snow. Quintus stood there, his forehead creased, true sorrow marking his features.

"I didn't mean to—" he started, but Jax rose, his eyes blocks of ice as he fixed them on Lissa's killer.

"You sick bastard!"

Quintus easily pushed him down. Jax shouted and yelled until he had no air left. He screamed until he felt a burning sensation pulse from his birthmark through his veins. Until he saw his shadow stream from him in a curtain of gray and smoke. He screamed until the world went dark.

60

WINSTON

KINGDOM OF VERIN

WINSTON EXAMINED HIS stomach in the hand mirror. A jagged scar cut across his midsection. It represented his past mistakes. The silence in the tent was deafening. Blayton had sent him a message earlier.

As requested, I will finish him.

Boltrex would die that day. Winston's lips twitched downward. Why then? Why, after all those years, did it still make him pause? Boltrex had stolen everything from him. He shouldn't care. But sometimes, he remembered when they'd trained together, when they'd shared smiles and laughter. He dropped the mirror onto the table covered in strategy notes. Winston recalled the day he'd snuck into the castle, clothed in Chishman robes and face concealed. He'd crept into Boltrex's chamber and stood above him with a dagger over his heart. But he'd hesitated. And he'd suffered for it.

Winston threw a shirt over his shoulders and buttoned the front, his scar fading from view just before Talon entered.

"The men are ready. Formations are in order. Should we march?"

Winston brushed by him on his way out of the tent. The crisp air blew into his face. The deedans saluted him, standing at attention. Winston looked over his army. The whole camp was there, or at least most of it. Winston wouldn't make the mistake of underestimating the Imperials again. Rows and rows of deedans stood in place before him, their backs to him as they faced the opposition. The castle towers rose in the distance. Soldiers stood guard on the parapets. Though they were few, they were brave, and Winston admired that. It was a pity they would die for that bravery.

"Send them out. I want archers at the back and the slaves in the front to absorb the projectiles. Let's finish this."

Talon nodded and sent out the orders to the Calestors. The army advanced, each collective step thunder on the ground. Dusty wind ruffled the command tent behind Winston. He examined the buckets of water slaves brought forth before his attention drifted to the rumlok cage coasting to a stop on rickety wheels. It was filled with the fiercest of beasts. Winston felt a trembling in the earth that came from something besides his army. He squinted ahead, where his men were nearing the castle.

He caught sight of a sudden swarm of birds filling the air above them. Then he swore.

"What is it?" Talon asked.

"Arrows," Winston hissed.

The sharp arrows pierced the exposed side of his army. Shouts broke out, their advance halted as confusion erupted within the ranks. Winston snatched a spyglass from Talon and peered through the magnified lenses. A line of horses appeared over the hill, poles bearing yellow flags wafting in the cold air.

"Ondalarians," Winston spat.

"Again?" Talon said.

The Ondalarians raced down the hill, and as Winston examined the mounted troops, he realized it was none other than the king of Ondalar himself at the front. The cavalry slammed into his men. Endless minutes of chaos ensued as Winston's army retained heavy losses. When he spotted reinforcements leaving the castle, he knew it was time to change tactics.

"Call the men back."

Talon gave him a questioning look, but Winston didn't budge. The Chishma relented and sent out the order. As the Tariqin army fell back, the Ondalarians formed a barricading line before the castle. Winston could hear their cheering from across the distance. His men drifted closer, changing ranks and gasping for the water the slaves were passing to each row. Winston scowled. His army was bleeding blood and fear. He peered at the Ondalarians through the spyglass. They appeared collected and calm, as if they were only toying with Winston, although his army was twice the size of theirs, even with the losses.

"Send them out," Winston growled.

"Now?"

Winston leveled him with a glare, and Talon slapped a palm to his forearm. "At once, General."

The Ondalarian king paced before the line of his cavalry. From the wave of cheers that rose every so often, it appeared he was giving a speech. Winston turned toward the rattling of wheels as the rumlok cage was rolled forward. Winston's army parted for it until it reached the front line. Growls rent the air as the rumloks battled each other for placement upon release. The Ondalarians shifted, perceiving an imminent threat. Handlers threw open the cage door. The rumloks shot forth, eating up the distance to their prey. Winston chuckled as the first rumlok pounced. The Ondalarians rushed to protect their king, but they were too late.

The rumlok lunged forward, snatching the king from his saddle and tearing into his body with large teeth. The other rumloks gained speed, but Winston's focus remained on the Ondalarian king being ravaged to pieces. It was entertaining. Enjoyable, even. But his laughter faded when the rumlok was stabbed through the belly and crumpled in a dying heap. His brows lowered.

He spotted the man who'd killed the rumlok. General Zenrelius. He was calling to his troops, urging them to remain calm. Winston turned the spyglass on the other rumloks. They weren't attacking. They were facing the opposite way. Facing him. Winston's jaw opened, and confusion drifted through him. What was happening?

Through the castle gates, a small army appeared. Winston assumed it was the last of the inhabitants. A solitary figure stood at the front of the army, making his way past the Ondalarians to stand at the very front. It was Blayton. Winston recognized his armor. Blayton signaled a soldier, and they presented a flag of truce. Winston equipped himself with armor and headed forward with a portion of deedans and Chishmans. They stopped with a field of space between them but were still close enough to hear each other.

"What is it?" Winston called.

"Send your champion fighter," Blayton called back.

"What is he doing?" Talon muttered.

"Giving us time," Winston said. "He knows we plan to corner the army from behind. Did you send word to Cselnsor?"

Talon nodded. "Done long ago."

"Good, give Blayton someone to play with. Cselnsor should be here soon."

Talon sent someone out. Winston recognized him as Chishma Jyorm, an experienced combat instructor at the Chishman Academy. Jyorm drew his sword, and both sides of the battleground fell silent as the two men fought. Jyorm was holding back, not using his full strength. But Blayton was moving deadly fast. He seemed intent on injuring Jyorm.

"What is he doing?" Talon grumbled. A soldier appeared by his side, bringing news. Talon paled, eyes wide.

"What happened?" Winston asked.

"Cselnsor . . . The other Calestor's group appears

to be dead, and Cselnsor is nowhere to be found. They were poisoned."

Winston racked his mind. If he wasn't there, then where was he? The answer fell into place as Blayton shoved his sword through Jyrom's stomach. Jyorm coughed blood, shock coating his face. Blayton stepped back, withdrawing his sword. He faced Winston and pulled off his helmet. Black hair clung to a scarred face, and dark eyes leveled on him.

"Cselnsor, my son," Winston called desperately. This couldn't be happening. He couldn't be seeing this.

"My name is Mordon," the traitor said.

The beasts intended for the Dark Army's use prowled closer. The rumloks had chosen their side.

"And I'm no son of yours."

Velamir
Kingdom of Verin

Velamir stroked the borrowed horse's coat. He wished he were with Vandal. His horse had been left behind in Castle Verin. He glanced up at a rustling between the trees. Vykus emerged with Sim. Both were equipped and ready to fight. They strolled past him, Sim giving him a once-over as he went. Velamir could sense he was weighing the costs in his mind. Were the chances of losing so many men worth gold he might or might not receive? Velamir hoped they would agree. He was running out of time. He needed to stop Winston and Prolus, and then he would get Jax. He would rescue his brother.

Natassa stepped beside him.

"Did you get enough sleep?" he asked.

She nodded, though there were circles beneath her eyes. They'd risen early and left Sim's town after another conversation about the amount of gold up for grabs. Velamir looked over Natassa's head at the gathered mercenaries. They were about two hundred men together, a fourth of them injured from the attack back in town. Vykus and Sim stood side by side, delivering an encouraging speech to their men. It seemed they'd chosen to fight.

"You did not sleep at all." Natassa frowned, concern crinkling her eyes.

"Even if I'd had time to sleep, I doubt it would've been good."

Every time Velamir closed his eyes, he saw Jax tortured, bleeding, *gone*. And he couldn't do anything about it. He had nightmares of everything he feared. The men he'd killed, the children he'd left fatherless. Of Winston. He looked at Natassa and saw understanding on her face. She knew what he felt better than anyone. Velamir stroked the stallion's coat again, looking off at Latimus a short distance away. He paced back and forth with restless tension, while Finnean sat on the ground, resting against a tree trunk.

"You couldn't have stopped what happened to Jax," Natassa told him.

"I should have." The words came out sharper than he'd intended. He repeated them, softer that time. "I should have." He leaned against the horse and fisted his mane, pressing his face into the thick strands.

Natassa's hand closed over his. "And I should have stayed at the palace. I should have married Draven. I should have warned Thorsten not to compete in the joust until he listened. I should have never read the books my mother gave me, and maybe she wouldn't have had that argument with my father. Maybe she would still be alive."

"You can't blame yourself for those things."

She stepped closer. "You can't blame yourself either. We had no control over it. All we can do is try. Try to make the right choice. Try to be better." She gently unfolded his fingers until his hand curved against the horse's coat. "This Empire has made too many half-hearted attempts at changing." She pressed her fingers against his, and Velamir smiled at the image she'd created with their hands tucked together. "It's time we act with our whole strength, our whole hearts."

She looked at their hands twined into the shape of a heart while he looked at her. Her hair blew back, revealing the golden phoenix birthmark. She was so beautiful at that moment. Despite all her pain, she was trying to encourage him.

Finnean rose, and he and Latimus approached. "If my father is the traitor," Latimus said, "it is my duty to the Empire to kill him." His expression was resolved, and his fists clenched at his sides.

"It's time to make those bastards pay." Anger flashed in Finnean's eyes. The Tariqins were to blame for his parents and Krea, and even partially responsible for his brother's death.

Vykus called to them, "We will help you."

Velamir nodded, and a chant spread through the mercenaries.

Sim explained, "It's a mercenary thing. *Tila wes rela.*"

Vykus smirked. "Dock language for *gold and glory.*"

61

Mordon surveyed the fury on Winston's face, his eyes angry slits and his mouth a grim line. Fire seemed to shoot out of him as he glared. Mordon received his hatred with an imposing grin of his own. He thought of Blayton and wished he could inform Winston of exactly what he had done with his spy. His grin stretched wider. Maybe he would.

Blayton yanked his weapon from Boltrex's midsection and spun to face them. Mordon drew his sword, hearing Coralie do the same. Blayton's wary eyes flitted between them.

"Jovinne, stay in the hall and keep your eyes on the door," Coralie ordered. "I don't want word of this betrayal to spread."

Jovinne saluted and closed the door behind

him. Mordon wished Coralie had left, too, but he knew no matter the risks, she wouldn't leave. With a roar, Blayton rushed toward him, his sword flying at Mordon's neck. Mordon spun to the side, and Blayton's sword thrust into empty air. Coralie screamed and launched at him. Blayton pivoted, and steel met steel with a clang.

They exchanged blows until Blayton landed a kick to her stomach. Coralie groaned and stumbled back. Mordon took her place, slicing at Blayton with unrelenting fury. Blayton parried his blows, breathing hard. The man was good but he was also old, and no matter how much training he'd had, he wouldn't be able to outlast them.

Blayton grunted. "You're not bad for a little bastard."

Rage coursed through Mordon, and his attacks grew fiercer. When Blayton's sword sliced across his arm, Mordon realized his mistake. Blayton wanted to make him angry so he would lose focus. Mordon breathed through his nose and slowly out through his mouth as he circled Blayton. The Galvasir kept him in sight, sword angled in the Imperial battle stance.

"You snake," Mordon spat. "How long were you in Prolus's pocket?"

"Longer than you were." Blayton laughed. "You had the chance to become something, but you crawled back into this cesspit and will die a little worm."

Mordon kept his anger in check. Just barely. "What did he promise you? A share of the land? Gold? Safety for your family?"

"He promised me more than your small mind could comprehend. All I had to do was live in this corrupt town surrounded by brainless fools and report to him.

Poison a general and ensure his spies weren't spotted." He glanced at Coralie. "My mission will be over once I kill your foolish queen and step over her dead body."

That had been the wrong thing to say.

Mordon roared and lunged forward, attacking Blayton with ferocious blows. Blayton retreated but was forced to still when his back struck the wall. Mordon smacked Blayton's sword from his grasp, and it clattered to the floor. Blayton's throat bobbed as the edge of Mordon's sword pressed into his neck.

"Still think you'll find your way back to Prolus?" Mordon hissed.

Fear drifted across Blayton's features, but still, he had the guts to threaten, "Even if you kill me, it won't end. Prolus will never stop. Not until he has conquered these lands."

Mordon shook his head. "Not while I am alive he won't. You can rest assured that your Dark Lord will be killed. These lands will never fall into shadow and misery. The only death you should worry about is your own."

He heard a pained gasp and his gaze flicked to Boltrex. The general coughed up blood, his hands clenching the gaping wound in his belly.

"Mordon!" Coralie screamed.

A kick to his middle sent him staggering. Blayton picked up his fallen sword with a triumphant shout. He slashed at Mordon. Mordon bent backward, and the sword skimmed a hair's breadth over his face. He retaliated with a swing so brutal that Blayton's sword flew out of his hand for the second time. Mordon slit the Galva's throat in a lightning-fast movement. Blood sprayed onto

Mordon's face as it gushed from Blayton's throat. Blayton clutched at his neck, falling to his knees before collapsing onto the ground. He convulsed and then fell still.

"Boltrex," Mordon said and exchanged a look with Coralie.

He ran to his bedside. Boltrex's mouth was pasted with thick dark blood. Sweat ran down his face, and crimson had saturated the white sheets to such an extent that it dripped onto the floor. Coralie rushed to the door.

"Jovinne, I need a True Manos sent here now!"

Boltrex, the man Mordon had seen as his father for so long, croaked, "It's too late."

Coralie returned to Mordon's side.

"I wrote a letter for Alaric," Boltrex said through labored breaths. "It's on the table."

Coralie reached for the letter and tucked it away. Despite everything, Mordon felt a trickle of jealousy. Boltrex would move mountains for Velamir, and he didn't even know him. But the man was dying. Mordon didn't want that moment to haunt him.

"Fa—Boltrex."

Coralie reached out and took Mordon's hand. She squeezed, giving him courage.

"I'm sorry I could never be the son you wanted." Mordon swallowed. "I could never be him because I'm not him. You hated me for that. I see that now. But you made me who I am."

Boltrex had caused him undeniable pain and anguish, but he had also made him strong.

Boltrex struggled to breathe as he spoke words Mordon would remember for the rest of his life. "I know . . . I know I was never a good father to you. I did not want . . . to care again. I loved my children and wife more than anything . . . and I lost them. It devastated me. That is why I was cruel . . . and kept you at a distance." A spasm rocked Boltrex's chest, and he gasped. "I was . . . wrong. It is better to appreciate what we have in this world while it's there. Because once it's gone, we always regret taking it for granted. And I regret so much . . . not being there . . . for you. But I want you to know, Mordon." He looked steadily at Mordon despite his agony. "I want you to know that you were always my son . . . and you always will be. And I will always be your father." A small smile formed as he exhaled a final time and fell back against the pillow.

A strange wetness slid down Mordon's face. It carved through the blood and dropped onto the once-white sheet. Another tear followed it. Coralie wrapped her arms around him, and Mordon took strength from her embrace. They held each other for endless minutes.

The chamber opened, and Jovinne stepped inside with a True Manos. His eyes widened at all the blood and Blayton's and Boltrex's lifeless forms. The True Manos whispered a prayer at Boltrex's bedside and pulled the sheet over his body.

"My queen, Prolus's soldiers have attacked. Ondalar's forces have arrived, and they are engaged in a fierce battle," Jovinne informed Coralie.

"Gather what is left of our people," she ordered.

As soon as he and the True Manos left, Mordon said, "You're not going out there." When her brows lowered, he added, "You are the queen. You cannot."

"That is exactly why I must."

Mordon sighed. She would go whether he liked it or not. "Stay close to me in the fight." He looked down at Blayton's body and frowned.

"I know that look," Coralie said. "What is your plan, General?"

He raised his brows in surprise. "Are you sure you want me as your general?"

"Without a doubt."

"Cselnsor, after everything I promised you, how could you turn your back on me?" Winston yelled.

"As I said before, it's *Mordon*, and you promised me nothing I want."

"Your choice. Attack!" Winston called to his soldiers.

Mordon pointed his sword forward, and growls entered his mind as the alpha rumlok connected with the others. They tuned in to Mordon and advanced, sharp claws flinging up the earth. Mordon released a war cry of his own and ran toward the enemy. The rumloks pounded forward, running alongside him, their snarls piercing the air.

Silopar had arrived at the castle minutes before they set out for battle with the group of Savorians who'd refused to leave. They said they would rather die fighting the man who'd enslaved them than run. Their fierce battle cries rivaled his own.

"Follow the general!" Zenrelius shouted, rallying the mounted Ondalarians. "Follow Verin's general!"

62

CORALIE WHIRLED AROUND. She'd long forsaken the helmet Mordon had forced her to wear. She slashed an advancing deedan, and he gurgled blood, falling at her feet. She felt a rush of air on her neck and ducked, avoiding the overhead swing. She spun on her knees over the icy snow and gutted the deedan behind her. His sword was raised over his head, his mouth gaping open. She shoved her boot into his chest and pulled her blade free.

The growls and sounds of tearing flesh mingled with shouts of panic and screams. The rumloks were making their way through the Tariqin army. The deedans were in disarray but slowly regaining their footing and pressing back, using nets to catch the rumloks and throwing acidic vials into unsuspecting faces. Coralie's soldiers were falling one by one.

She blocked a strike to her neck and slashed back. More deedans pressed around her, boxing her in. Coralie's eyes flashed between them as she panted. Wisps of hair clung to her forehead, and her braids stuck to her neck. She jumped back just in time to avoid a sizzling kilisham. The air crackled and buzzed in the place she'd just been standing. She waved her sword in a wild arc, scattering the men back. Fear crawled over her like a spider until she heard the voice of her first training instructor, and her desperate slashing ceased.

Feel the air. It's your guide.

Feel your sword. It's your shield.

Feel your breath. It's your pillar.

Coralie's eyes drifted closed. The air shifted around her. The attacks came suddenly, one from the left and the other from the right. She dropped down, sweeping her leg out to trip the first attacker before lifting her weapon and halting the other deedan's strike. She shrieked, shoving his blade away. She fought with all she had until her weapon slammed hard against a grip of iron. She gritted her teeth, glancing at the enemy's face. Mordon's lips spread into a smile.

"You could've killed me," he said, sliding his blade from hers.

"That seems to be a habit of mine." She smirked. "It's quite fun."

Mordon chuckled and spun around, his back pressing against hers. He turned his head to the side to look at her from his peripheral. He nodded, sweat coating his cheekbone. His dark eyes conveyed his devotion. They were in it together.

As one, they launched apart, striking and stabbing the approaching deedans. They defended and protected each other with equal vehemence, but it didn't take long until they were split apart again. Prolus's forces were too strong. Coralie's sweat chilled when she eventually came face-to-face with the Tariqin general in the melee. The man who had betrayed her uncle.

"Winston," she said dryly, adjusting her blade as she faced him.

"Queen Coralie . . . how shall I rid myself of you?"

"You joined a warlord. You betrayed your homeland. For what?"

"The Empire is not my homeland, and I bow to no one," he shot back with a scowl.

Coralie felt the presence of deedans swarming at her back. The Empire wasn't his home? Where had he come from, then?

"Verin will fall, and you along with it."

Coralie smiled grimly in answer. "As long as there is one brave soldier standing, we will never fall. We will always fight you and whatever master you serve."

"We shall see."

He lunged at her, and Coralie ducked under his sword. Winston avoided her riposte. She stabbed toward his midsection, but he brought his blade down onto hers, knocking it out of her grasp. She managed to grab the shield of a fallen soldier as he swung his sword at her. She lifted the shield, blocking the swing, but the force of Winston's blow still sent her staggering backward. Coralie tripped over a corpse and fell onto her back. Winston sneered down at her and raised his sword again.

He smashed blow upon blow against her shield. Over and over and over. Coralie's strength began to waver, and her shield weakened under the pressure until it gave way, splitting in half. Winston raised his sword once again, his eyes alight with the desire to end her life.

A long blade appeared under his sword and thrust it away.

"My queen!" Jovinne yelled as he propelled Winston back with precise attacks. "Get to safety!"

Coralie went to grab her fallen sword. She was unwilling to leave him to fight alone. And then her heart dropped at an unmistakable grunt behind her, and she turned to see Jovinne standing before her. A sword pierced his back, the point emerging from his front. His face whitened under the bloodstains on his skin. He had placed himself in the way of Winston's sword for the second time. Winston snatched his sword free, and Jovinne gasped, falling to his knees.

"No," Coralie whispered as blood spurted from her bodyguard's mouth.

"My queen," he rasped, reaching his hand out to her, and then he crumpled onto the ground.

Wrath burned through her. Winston had her surrounded. His men could have attacked her, but they held back at his command. He wanted to see her reaction to the death of her soldier. He reveled in it.

"You monster." Coralie launched forward.

A deedan intercepted her. She parried his move and spotted more deedans rushing at her in her periphery. An arrow buried into the throat of the deedan she was fighting, and she stilled, glancing in the direction it'd come from. Up on the hill leading down to the open valley they fought in, an army of men on horseback formed a line. She would've recognized the man in front anywhere. He held a bow in his hands and brought his horse into a rearing position. Attention turned to the new arrivals, and Winston spat the man's name as if it were a curse.

"Velamir."

VELAMIR
KINGDOM OF VERIN

Velamir tilted forward in the saddle, his heart pumping in wild beats as the battle loomed closer. The armies below were entangled with each other but had frozen at the sight of them. A dozen archers turned on him. A flurry of arrows flew in the wind, spiraling toward Velamir. He leaned over the saddle sideways. Arrows whizzed past his face. One scraped his arm. Velamir whipped an arrow free from the quiver in his saddle-bag. He bounced against the horse's hindquarters, legs burning as they held him in the saddle. He stared at the world upside down, nocking an arrow onto his bow and pulling back. Moans of pain and thumps accompanied pounding hooves as bodies fell from the horses behind him. Velamir released the arrow, and it struck one of the archers through the heart. He righted himself in the saddle, and a wave of dizziness shot through his head.

They reached the bottom of the hill and entered battle range. Velamir dismounted and returned the bow to his saddlebag. He slapped the horse's rump, sending him off. Velamir drew his sword and threw himself into the fray. The roar of the mercenaries followed him as they, too, launched themselves into action. Velamir spotted a familiar figure fighting nearby. He edged toward the man cutting down deedans around him. They locked eyes. Mordon faltered at the sight of him.

"Velamir," Mordon said above the battle noise.

"Whose side are you on?" Velamir asked, glancing at the limp Tariqins scattered around him.

Mordon's gaze moved to something behind Velamir, and he shoved past him to block a blow that had been aimed at Velamir's back. Mordon dispatched the deedan and turned to face Velamir with a smirk, strands of his dark hair plastered on his face.

"I seem to keep saving lives today. And to answer your question, I'm on Coralie's side, wherever that is." Mordon's eyes roved over the battlefield, lighting when he spotted the queen. "I will offer my assistance where it is appreciated. Watch your back," Mordon called as he moved off.

Velamir launched back into the battle. He dispatched only a handful of deedans before encountering Winston.

"Why, Velamir?" Winston asked, shaking his head. "Why did you not join me?"

Velamir circled him with his bloodstained sword at the ready. "You're better than this." The shouting and screaming around them died away as Velamir focused on the man he'd thought of as a father for most of his life.

"You don't know me, Velamir."

"That is true. You are not the man I believed you to

be all these years. But there is still a chance for you to return, to make the right choice."

"Enough nonsense." Winston slashed at Velamir with surprising speed.

Velamir shoved Winston's sword aside and retaliated with efficient strikes. Winston parried the moves and retreated. His nose twitched, betraying the move he was about to make. Winston switched hands in a lightning-fast movement and slashed toward Velamir's neck. Velamir evaded the blow. The sword skimmed over his head, slicing off a few strands of his hair. Velamir swung his sword into Winston's, seizing on its momentum and knocking it into the dirt near two fighting soldiers. Velamir pointed his sword at Winston's heart, freezing him in his tracks.

Winston's face reddened with rage. "How?" he sputtered in disbelief.

Velamir smiled. "You taught me that move, remember? It was the one I could never get. You don't know me either, Winston. Not anymore."

His old mentor scowled. "Kill me, then."

"I will give you a chance to surrender. You don't have to be a slave to Prolus anymore."

Winston barked a laugh. "I'm afraid that is something I cannot do."

"Why?" Velamir growled.

"Since only one of us will be emerging from this war alive, I see no harm in telling you." Winston leaned closer. "I *am* Prolus."

63

Velamir

Kingdom of Verin

"How?" Velamir asked. His mind was blank. How could Winston be Prolus? It wasn't possible.

Winston smiled. "Think about it."

"All those trips you would take, the reason you were never at the manor, the reason you sent me away to the Chishman academy, why you were so insistent in telling me to destroy Boltrex. He was a threat, someone who could expose your true nature . . . It was because you were Prolus all along."

"Yes, I was gone because I was Prolus. I had to devise my invasion plans and build my army. But telling you about Boltrex had nothing to do with being Prolus. That was for personal gain."

Velamir shook his head, his mouth down-turned. "How could you do all those things? What about the slaves? Bear's family?"

Winston grinned sadistically. "I'm not the only one who needs motivation. I find threatening someone with a loved one works well."

"You are sick."

Winston frowned. "Anyone would do anything for power if given the chance. Anyone. Even you."

"I would never do the things you've done."

"You already have. You left your friend for dead. What was his name? The foolish Shadow Manos? Jaxon." Winston chuckled when he saw the rage that spilled over Velamir's features.

"Where is Jax?"

"Oh, he's a bit battered from your abuse, but overall, he's doing fine in his little cell."

Velamir gritted his teeth and raised his sword, tired of the poisonous words coming from Winston's lips.

"Stop," someone said. "You kill him, and I will kill her."

Velamir turned to see Talon with Natassa pinned in his arms. Her eyes were wide, her face pale, and her hair flew in a wild mess. Velamir's attention caught on the short sword Talon held at her throat. *No.* She was supposed to have gone to the castle and remained within the safety of the stone walls.

"Let her go," Velamir growled.

"Release Winston."

"You first," Velamir ordered. "You know I keep my word, but I cannot trust the same from you."

"You are finally learning, but I'm afraid you're

going to have to trust me." Talon tightened his grip on Natassa. "Drop your sword."

Velamir's sword tip wavered at Winston's throat as he took in Natassa's stricken features. Her hazel eyes were wide and locked with his. They stared at each other for an endless moment. He could not allow anything to happen to her. After everything they'd been through, he could not continue without her. When he thought of a family—of a future—she was the person he saw, and she always would be. She was delicate yet strong in so many ways. Even then, though she was afraid, she did not whimper or cry. There was resilience in her posture as she gave him a subtle nod.

But a hard blow rocketed pain through his head. Velamir stumbled, blinking against the agony. Winston's shout seemed far away.

"Kill the girl!" Winston ordered Talon.

Time seemed to freeze as terror wrapped its fearful hold around Velamir's heart. Natassa threw her head back with a scream. A crack of bone was followed by Talon's roar. Natassa broke out of his grasp, but Talon snatched her wrist and lifted his weapon. Velamir surged forward, swinging his sword as Talon brought his blade down. He blocked it, holding the enemy's sword at bay until Natassa ducked out of harm's way, and then Velamir thrust the blade away.

Talon slashed at Velamir, his yellow teeth showing as he sneered. Velamir twisted abruptly to the side, and Talon surged past him. Talon stopped and spun back in time to be impaled on Velamir's sword. He blanched and looked down at his pierced midsection in horror.

Velamir pulled the blade free, and Talon fell to his knees, his hands covering his wounded abdomen. Hatred darkened his features.

"See you in hell," Talon spat through blood.

Velamir spared him no response and, in one swift movement, sliced the vile man's neck. Talon's body thumped onto the bloody battlefield, joining many other parts of anatomy strewn about the area. Velamir looked up, gaze locking with Winston's. His old mentor retreated, calling back his army, but his brows were drawn as he stared at Velamir. An unspoken message passed between the two men. Winston wanted to kill Velamir. He would be after him, and Velamir would be waiting.

Velamir heaved another body into the large hole. There had been too many dead for them to bury individually, so they placed several bodies into large burrows. He wiped sweat from his forehead and glanced up to see Mordon talking with Latimus. Pain crossed Latimus's face, and he turned away and stormed off. Velamir approached Mordon.

"What happened?"

"I told him about Lord Blayton," Mordon said. "He died."

"In the battle?"

Mordon shook his head. "I killed him before that. Don't tell Latimus, or he'll look to me for revenge."

"I'm sure he'd understand. Eventually." Velamir

scanned around the nearly emptied battlefield. "What about Boltrex? Is he still recovering?"

Mordon faltered and then recovered his composure. "He's dead," he said in a flat voice.

Shock coursed through Velamir. "What? When?"

"Blayton killed him." Mordon turned to walk away. "He wrote a letter for you. Coralie has it," he called over his shoulder.

Velamir stayed rooted in his spot for minutes. He was sure he was supposed to feel something—hurt or anger or *something* at the news—but he felt nothing. A shout of agony echoed across the battlefield, and Velamir's eyes landed on Salvador, who was crumpled on the ground with a body in his arms. One of his brothers. Velamir winced when he saw Salvador's other brother lying near him. Both his brothers dead. That was a big blow.

Vykus approached Salvador. When he moved his hand from his bloody face to pat Salvador's shoulder, Velamir saw that his socket was devoid of an eyeball. The mercenaries had attained heavy losses, and Vykus had suffered just as much as his men. Velamir would need to give them the payment he'd promised them, or they would be bloodthirsty.

Velamir returned to the castle. The day had been one of heartbreak but also victory for the Empire. Winston had been forced back to his camp after heavy losses. Up ahead, Coralie lifted a fallen table with the help of some other women. The Imperials were rebuilding. Everyone was working regardless of their station. He made his way through the halls and entered a room at random.

Coralie had told him to take any room he wished. There were many spares since so many people were dead.

He washed himself with the water in the basin. The day's battle caught up with him, and his tired body collapsed on the bed in the chamber. He reached into his pocket, fingering the thin chain within. The metal was cold against his skin. Despite all the odds, it had remained with him. He sat up, sleep suddenly gone from his mind as he thought of Natassa. He slipped the chain back into his pocket and left the room.

64

NATASSA HAD HELPED as much as she could until darkness covered them and the queen had ordered her to rest. Natassa returned to the room she'd stayed in before. It was empty. So empty. She sank onto the mattress, staring at the bed across from her. Krea's bed. But Krea was gone. A tear slid down her cheek, and she furiously wiped it away. Krea hadn't deserved to die. She'd always seen the beauty in the world, the best in people.

Natassa's breath caught when she realized the day. A gasp ripped through her chest, and she stood, leaning over the table by the boarded window. Her hands clenched the table edges until her fingertips were bloodless. She heard a knock and her door creak open but didn't turn. Bootsteps echoed on the stone floor until she felt his presence behind her.

"Today was my brother's birthday," she whispered. "Thorsten would have turned twenty-five."

He remained silent.

"He used to bring me a flower on this day, a different one every year, even though the day was his. I used to paint for him. Something sentimental. Like a horse he loved or our mother smiling—something he never got to see as much as he wanted. The blue sky. A green forest. People standing together, faceless, with hands clasped together." Natassa's heart ached at the memory. "Those were the things he loved. Things that would mean nothing to someone else but meant the world to him because they symbolized union, joy, peace, love . . . He didn't deserve to die."

Natassa couldn't bear the silence anymore and spun around, but her next words froze in her throat. Velamir peered back at her with unshed tears in his eyes. Dark circles formed crescents beneath his lower lids. He closed the distance between them just as a sob ripped from her. He pulled her roughly into his arms, holding her as she poured her heart out into her tears. Finally, she felt ragged, stripped dry. Her harsh cries settled, but she stayed there within his arms. She felt protected there, like nothing could ever harm her.

A droplet landed on her forehead, and she glanced up. Velamir's expression was pained, his lips pressed together as though he were trying to keep them from trembling. Another tear fell from his lashes onto her cheek. It trailed down her skin. She could tell he was trying to stay strong, but his shield was cracked, the lines slowly widening. Natassa stood on her tiptoes and wrapped her arms around his neck.

"Don't hold it back any longer," she whispered.

He leaned into her, his arms enfolded her and his face buried in her hair.

"My whole life has been a lie," he mumbled. "I had hope that Winston could return, that he wasn't as lost as it seemed." He hesitated. "He's Prolus, Natassa. *Prolus.*"

She stiffened, shock pouring through her. "I'm sorry, Velamir," she said, her hand tightening on the back of his neck in silent support.

"I draw comfort in knowing I'm no longer lost, blindly following his wicked path." He cupped her face, his green eyes glossy with a teary sheen. "You are my solace in this darkness, my hope in this mess of lies."

Natassa's stomach fluttered like a thousand butterflies had found their home there. Velamir reached into his pocket and pulled out a bracelet. A black stone rested in the center. He took her hand gently, and his warm fingers caressed her wrist. He looked into her eyes, seeking her permission. Natassa didn't stop him as he brought the bracelet closer. The cold metal slid around her wrist above the one Thorsten had given her.

"I may not be able to compare to your brother"—his fingers drifted over the bracelet—"but this one symbolizes a pledge."

"What are you pledging?" she asked softly.

"My heart." He placed his head against hers, peering into her eyes. "My heart to be yours forever."

Emotion burned her throat, and she looked at the

bracelet, blinking in shock when the black stone turned as red as the blood running through her veins.

"The stone remains unchanged if unfulfilled, but red if the vow is true."

Natassa felt shy under his warm gaze. "How long have you had this bracelet?"

"I wanted to give it to you so many times. I could never give you a palace or riches or provide you with a proper home, but—"

Natassa shushed him, placing a finger to his lips. "The things you just described to me are the least of my concerns. A palace is a prison to me. Riches are chains. Anywhere we live, it will be home as long as you're there."

His eyes crinkled, and he kissed her finger before grasping her hand, bringing it to his lips, and placing a kiss on the back of her wrist too. A flutter of warmth traveled up her arm. Natassa had hope. The future looked brighter than it ever had before.

CORALIE
KINGDOM OF VERIN
CASTLE VERIN

Coralie double-checked the drawbridge and castle guards, ensuring there were enough soldiers on watch. Moonlight shone on the stone walls of the keep behind her, giving her home a silvery glow. Coralie exhaled a peaceful breath for the first time in what felt like forever.

"I did it, Uncle," she said. "I defended our home."

Just then, the wooden archway leading to the gardens collapsed. Coralie sighed. Of course, they still had to rebuild and stay armed. Prolus had withdrawn, but he was far from defeated. Coralie walked to the archway, then crouched and lifted the wood. She tried to fit it back, but the wood was cracked. She gingerly managed to adjust the long pieces above her head and slowly lowered her hands, smiling at her achievement. Her smile faded when the wood cracked further, and heavy chunks crumbled down onto her. She covered her head, then blinked in surprise when nothing else fell on top of her.

"Still working?" Mordon asked, his expression dark. A large piece of wood hung in the air above her head, held in his strong grasp. Coralie's gaze drifted from his hand to his face. His brows were lowered. "That's enough. You were out here the whole day. Get some rest."

Coralie smirked. "Since when did you start mothering me?"

"You sent everyone to bed. No one except the watch is out here."

"It's different for me, Mordon. I'm their queen. I can't stop just because I want to."

"You look after them . . ." he said, stepping closer. "But who will look after you?"

Coralie sucked in a breath at his closeness. She braced herself, holding eye contact. "I don't need anyone."

He smirked, his teeth shining white in the darkness. "Clearly," he said, and the wood piece he'd caught clattered across the stone as he threw it.

"We will have a council meeting in a few hours." Coralie grasped for a serious conversation. "There's so much to do."

"Let me help you." Mordon reached out, brushing her arm. His touch pierced through the fabric of her sleeve, and she shivered. His eyes narrowed with concern.

"I'm cold," she said sharply, pulling away.

He followed her. "Why do you keep retreating? What are you running from?"

She ignored him and kept walking until she entered the damaged stables. Mordon reached out again, grabbing her arm and pulling her to him. Coralie flew around, gasping at the lack of distance between them.

"You've been fighting alone for too long," Mordon said. "Both of us have. Let's stand together."

"I can't."

"Why?" he said, his voice bitter.

"Because I'm afraid!" Her shout echoed in the night.

Mordon's face relaxed. "You don't have to be. I'm here with you."

"*That's* the reason. What if one day you're gone? What if one day you leave?" Just like her parents, her uncle, all her loved ones. "I'm better alone."

Mordon scoffed. "Do you hear yourself? Why would I ever leave you?"

"You have big dreams, Mordon. You will never be content with me. You won't be happy." She lifted a hand, touching his cheek.

A thousand emotions ran through his eyes, emotions she couldn't bear to read. She dropped her hand

and moved past him. She'd nearly reached the doorway when she heard the whisper.

"I love you."

The three broken words froze her in place. She felt his stare burning into her back. Her heart clenched, then lurched against her chest. No one had ever said those words to her.

"The whole damn world could burn, and I would still love you. When everything dissipates, you're the only thing I see. You've always been." His voice sent chills over her.

Mordon came up behind her, his breath ruffling her hair. He reached around and hugged her from behind. It was then that she realized she was shaking. His fingers drifted over her hand, and he twined their fingers together. He brushed his thumb over hers where the ring rested.

"Since the day I saw your fierce spirit, I knew you could end me," he whispered. "Don't end me, Coralie. Don't leave me without you."

He turned her until she met his eyes. The burning devotion she saw there nearly unraveled her. Coralie tried to inhale, but she couldn't breathe around him.

She stepped out of his arms.

"Give me time," she said. "I can't think about us right now. We have the citizens of Verin, the war. I must focus on that." Not whatever was passing between them. Not the strange emotion she could almost see, like a rope stretched across, tethering them to each other.

"I can wait," Mordon said. "I *will* wait for you. Always."

That word—*always*—brought a sense of security to her. Because it meant his return. It meant seeing him again, no matter how fleeting. She left then, unable to contain all her feelings. She moved within the castle halls, thinking over his words and smiling. Velamir stepped out of a room ahead of her. He hadn't seen her yet, his gaze still so focused on someone within the chamber. Coralie heard soft laughter, and Velamir grinned as the door shut. He leaned against the door then, his forehead pressed to the wood.

"She's beautiful," Coralie said.

Velamir snapped up, wide eyes settling on her. He rubbed his neck before allowing a smile. "She is."

"I'm happy for you." She stepped closer, taking the letter from her pocket. She extended it to him. "I meant to give this to you earlier."

Velamir stared at it, then took it reluctantly.

"Boltrex wanted you to have it. I'm sorry you only knew him as an enemy. I wish things had been different." She paused. "I wish you and Mordon could've experienced his love, not his loss."

Velamir flinched at the words. "It was Verin's loss, no matter his hatred for certain things. He was a good general."

"We will have a council meeting at first light. You've proven yourself loyal to the Empire. Join us. Help us fight for a greater cause."

His jaw clenched, and Coralie wondered what she'd said that had bothered him. She had just accepted him.

"Bring Natassa too."

At that, his attention snapped back to her. "You knew?"

"I guessed." She smiled. "Now I know." She examined his troubled face. "Your secret is safe with me."

He nodded, but his smile didn't return. Velamir turned away, and Coralie stayed put until he disappeared down the hall, giving him privacy to battle the demons he so clearly carried.

65

Jax
Devorin

Ice-cold water splashed over him. Jax gasped, trickles falling into his mouth and dampening his hair. His wet curls pressed into his eyes, impairing his vision. He shook his head to move the strands and tried to sit up, but his arms were restrained, bound to a table by metal cuffs. So were his legs. Shelves upon shelves decorated the walls of the circular chamber and were lined with equipment and tonics. The chamber was dark and condensed, with only a few candles here and there. It resembled a torture chamber.

"The queen will be here soon."

Quintus stood above him, bucket in hand. He didn't meet Jax's gaze. At the sight of him, Jax's anger returned, and he fought against the bonds.

"You left her there? You left Lissa?" His shouts turned hoarse.

Jax sank against the hard table when the fight in him was gone. He felt vacant, so completely vacant, like a part of him was missing. He couldn't remember how he'd gotten there, only glimpses: snow, a narrow path, a familiar town, the spiral castle that appeared more like a winding tower, the stairs. Jax's gaze shot to the side. The top of the stairs was just ten feet away.

Heels clicked, and his pulse thudded. Quintus shifted beside the table, but Jax remained focused on the stairs until a head came into view. Hair nearly as white as snow cascaded in thick locks around a face with cold blue eyes set above prominent cheekbones and lips painted red. The woman was beautiful. Then the rest of her emerged. She wore a white dress paler than her skin and fitted to her form. The dress ended above what appeared to be shoes made of glass. Jax had heard of the invention. Shadow Manos created it with . . . A spurt of panic spread through him. The materials he'd been grasping for were gone. He couldn't remember them. He racked his mind. His panic grew as he realized he couldn't remember how to make any of the tonics. It was as if his mind had been wiped.

The click of heels drew nearer, and he turned again to the approaching queen. A maid lingered behind her.

"And what has Prolus sent me this time?" Her voice was like snow and ice, soft yet sharp, trickling down his back with shivers.

"Your Majesty." Quintus bowed. "Lord Prolus bestows a Shadow Manos as a gift for you."

"Shadow Manos?" A thin brow arched.

Quintus nodded. "If you want to be sure, his mark is on his arm."

She closed the remaining distance until she stood above him. Jax was struck with fear. She was beautiful but in a haunting way. Up close, her face appeared stretched so lines wouldn't show. Her veins were visible beneath her skin, and her form was so thin, he could see the bones in her neck. But the worst part was her eyes. He'd thought them blue, but he could see they were white. She was blind yet staring at him with such an intensity that he couldn't be sure.

The queen lifted his sleeve with sharp nails. She hissed, and Jax looked down at his arm to see what had caused such alarm. It took him a moment to realize. His birthmark was gone. In its place was a thin line, like a healed scar. The phoenix had disappeared. His shadow had left. But that was impossible . . .

The queen seethed, spinning around. "Is this a joke?" "Return to Prolus and tell him I demand compensation for this. This boy is no Shadow Manos."

"But—" Quintus sputtered.

"Go. Before I kill you." Her tone left no room for argument.

Quintus ducked away, and the queen turned to her maid. An unspoken conversation seemed to pass between them, and then the maid walked toward the shelves to retrieve a vial. When she returned to give it to the queen, Jax saw her face clearly for the first time, and his body went numb.

"No," he whispered.

The girl who used to smile, who used to dance,

who'd taken care of him. She lifted her head when he spoke, and horror shot through him. Her eyes were dull. Her lips were sewn shut with thick black cord.

"Lilly. Lilly, please."

His cousin. He'd hoped she would be safe, but he'd had no idea her fate had been so much worse than he could have guessed. The queen's hand shot out, long skeletal fingers gripping Jax's face and wrenching it away from Lilly. Jax fought against her hold. Her nails dug into his cheeks.

"Lilly," he managed.

"Don't worry about her." The queen leaned over him as she uncorked the vial with a flick. "Soon, you will forget everything. Just like her, you will be at peace."

What was she saying? The rumors of her killing her spouse must've been true. She was mad. The vial inched closer, and Jax's heart raced. He fought against the chains. Slick blood slid down his wrists as the metal cut into him.

"Yes," she said. "I killed him. He kept getting in my way."

Jax stopped struggling. "You can read my mind?"

"Shh," she said instead of answering. "You'll be fine now." She pried his mouth open and shoved the vial into it.

He gasped as the liquid burned down his throat. She held his mouth closed, forcing him to swallow it. He heard her voice again, but as he stared at her blurring image, her lips didn't appear to move.

You will be reborn again, Jaxon, as my loyal warrior.

No, he thought. *No!* He struggled to keep his eyes

open and on Lilly, trying to reach out to her. But she only stared at him with empty eyes until his own fell shut.

MORDON
KINGDOM OF VERIN
CASTLE VERIN

Weary faces stared at each other around the circular table. Dark circles dug beneath tired eyes. Mordon glanced at Coralie, who sat in the high seat. Her spine was stiff and chin lifted proudly. A crown studded with green jewels nestled in the intricate braids woven into a bun behind her head. Mordon hated the bun. He wanted to remove the pins binding her hair and watch the braids fall into their usual position. Coralie wasn't meant to be calm and demure; she was wild, and he loved that about her. She glanced at him, raising a brow and tilting her head. *What?* her expression seemed to say.

Give me time, she'd said the night before. He would give her as long as she needed. Until then, he would be at her side, helping her in any way he could. Mordon shot her a wink, smiling slowly. A throat cleared loudly, and Coralie tore her gaze away. General Zenrelius, the source of the noise, sat across from him.

"Your Majesty, would you like to start the meeting?" Advisor Alesto asked.

Coralie nodded. "Thank you for joining me so early. I know we've had a brutal week, but it's time for us to rebuild and prepare."

Another advisor leaned forward. "Many valuable

council members have passed on and been so quickly replaced." He glanced over at Velamir and the woman beside him. They'd taken Blayton's chair and another council member's.

"The *valuable* people you speak of were traitors," another councilman said. "I'm glad we're rid of them."

"And yet traitors remain," someone else said, eyes narrowing at Mordon and then drifting to Velamir.

Coralie stood. "That's enough." She sliced through the heated conversation with two brisk words. All eyes returned to her. "Every person in this room has the right to be here. They have my full trust. Velamir and his accomplices are hereby pardoned for any crimes. They are Imperials now and will be treated as such."

Her attention drifted to Mordon. "Mordon is my general. His strength and valor were prized before and should remain that way."

The others nodded, grudging respect filling their gazes. Only Zenrelius remained cold, his features sharp as he blatantly examined Mordon.

"You wanted to announce something, General?" Coralie said to him, retaking her seat.

Mordon stood and nodded to the guard. The doors swung open. Silopar entered first, followed by his ragtag team.

"These Savorians will now be part of Verin's army. They will be my personal force."

Gasps echoed around the table.

"You cannot be serious?"

"But they are Savorians."

"They are people," Mordon said. "We won't have

slaves in Verin any longer. These men are free, and they're choosing to fight with us. I have Savorian blood in me as well, and I'm proud of it. Those rumloks in the battle followed my orders because of my Savorian heritage. That's the reason all of you are currently intact. My Savorian blood saved you from being mauled to pieces."

Zenrelius spoke for the first time. "It was quite a surprise, I must say. I thought you'd used some sort of witchcraft. After all, you were in that camp for a long time."

Mordon pinned him with a glare, preparing a retort. A hand slid into his, and he glanced at Coralie. She shook her head, and he contained the angry words he wanted to launch at the Ondalarian general. Mordon retook his seat. He glanced back at the Savorians and nodded at them to leave. They began to shuffle out, but one of them remained frozen in place, staring. Mordon frowned, following his gaze. Velamir slowly rose.

"Bear?" His voice was layered with uncertainty.

The Savorian nodded. "It's me, lad."

"You know each other?" Mordon asked.

66

VELAMIR RUSHED TO the older man and crushed him in a hug. Coralie could have sworn she saw a tear fall from the Savorian's eye.

"He was my mentor when I was a child. I learned much from him," Velamir explained to the council.

The doors to the chamber flew open, and a messenger bearing the emperor's seal rushed inside. The council stood, alarm on every face. The messenger bowed his head to Coralie, slapping a half heart to his chest before unrolling a scroll and clearing his throat.

"Addressed to the queen of Verin. The old empire is gone, and a new one will rise, thanks to me. We no longer fear Prolus or any other force. Join me at the palace as soon as you receive this missive. I've longed to see my sister. His Royal Majesty, Emperor Draven."

First, the room was stunned into silence. Then the shouts rang out like hammers clanging against Coralie's ears. She sank into her chair, lips opening and closing, but she was unable to voice her panic, her shock, or formulate words to calm the room. Questions were thrown at the messenger, and his responses came quick.

Emperor Malus was dead. The false Princess Natassa was dead. They were searching for Prince Honzio, and Draven planned to execute him. But there was one unanswered question: Who was his sister? Coralie's heart jumped in ragged beats until it caught in her throat, and she had to swallow it back. Draven couldn't be her brother. But what if he was? All the fears she'd had, the parchment Welix had shown her . . .

But she'd drunk from the chalice, and it had remained the correct color. Unless, it had recognized her as royal blood. Could it be that she *was* a princess, just not of Verin?

"Coralie?" A hand touched her shoulder, jerking her out of her trance. Mordon peered at her with concern. "What's wrong?"

She shook her head, feeling sick. Draven Valent couldn't be her brother. Not that sick, twisted, perverted maniac. Natassa rushed from the room, a hand clasped over her mouth. Velamir stood, hurrying to follow her, but his path was blocked when Vykus took that moment to enter.

"What is this, some kind of barn?" Advisor Alesto snapped, tired of the interruptions.

"I want the pay the boy promised me," Vykus said. "Now.

Honzio
The Grand Palace

Honzio held his breath. The dungeon was damp and dark, reflecting his inner feelings, and he couldn't tell if the horrible smell came from the filth strewn across the floor or his own sweat and blood. Perhaps it was the strange cream the Uluzar had applied to his and Draven's shoulders that reeked. After all, it had healed their wounds too quickly to be natural. Or maybe the smell came from the false emperor himself, who was reclining on a metal bunk, his clothes stained with his vomit.

Honzio glared at him, but Draven stared listlessly at the top bunk above. Apparently, he had a terrible headache, a side effect from all the zat he'd drunk the day before.

"I can't believe you were foolish enough to offer the Savagelanders my kingdom!" Draven sat up and looked at Honzio.

"Shut up," Honzio muttered.

He peered through the bars. The sight across from him was another cell filled with unscrupulous robbers and a noble Honzio had sent to the dungeons himself a month before.

"Your Highness." Lord Jasper showed his contempt by bowing so deeply, his head almost touched the dirt-encrusted floor.

"I have never heard a sentence more loaded with

sarcasm than that." Draven chuckled. "What have you done with your subjects, Your Supreme Majesty?"

"Let's dispense with the barbed words, Draven. We are both in the same predicament. We should focus on finding a way out. We can kill each other after."

Lord Jasper said, "There isn't a way out. Trust me, I've tried."

Draven shrugged. "Well, there you are."

"You haven't even made an attempt." Honzio tapped his head thoughtfully. "We can try bribing the guards."

"Why don't we offer to scrub the dungeon with our tongues while we're at it?"

Honzio crossed his arms. "That's brilliant!"

"You're kidding?"

"Of course I am, you idiot."

Draven pulled himself off the bed. "You're the only idiot around here. You gave the Savagelanders the Empire on a silver platter."

Honzio glared. "I wouldn't have resorted to such drastic measures if you'd stayed in Ayleth like you were supposed to!"

They fumed at each other, faces mere inches apart.

"I had to do something for the Empire. A change in leadership was needed, and the perfect man was available."

"You?" Honzio said incredulously. "Look at yourself."

A deep accented voice cut through their conversation. "Quit prattling like chickens! A man can't get any sleep with you lot around."

A blond head popped into view on the bunk above the one Draven had been resting on. A young man with chiseled features and piercing eyes jumped over the bunk onto the ground. He was of average height and loaded with muscles. Honzio unconsciously flexed his arm to present a more intimidating appearance.

"Who are you?" Draven asked the man.

"Svorgin, son of Barin," the man said. His blond hair was fastened into a thick braid.

"You're Savorian," Honzio stated.

"Yes, what of it?"

"You were the new slave that had been brought to the palace. The rebellious one. The one my father said knew the location of the Golden Crown. I thought he had you killed."

"I am no slave," Svorgin snarled. "I never will be. I was taken to the torture chambers every week until the new emperor came." He tugged his shirt off and turned, displaying hundreds of crisscrossing scars across his back. Some were recent and inflamed. Repulsion twisted Honzio's stomach. "They tried, but I never give in." Svorgin shrugged his shirt back on. "They were to rip my teeth next." He smiled, revealing surprisingly white teeth.

Svorgin. Honzio rolled the name around in his mind.

"Do you have a sister?" he asked, and the man's body went rigid.

"Why do you ask?"

"Aylis, is she your sister?"

One moment, Honzio was standing still, and the next, he was flung against the wall and pinned by the Savorian's powerful forearm cutting into his throat.

Honzio gasped for breath, his toes struggling to touch the ground.

"What did you do to her?" Svorgin growled, his eyes flashing with a barely contained storm.

457

67

NATASSA LEANED AGAINST the tree. Her tears had long since dried onto her cheeks, and the sting of cold burned her skin. She glanced at the castle in the distance. She had to return soon. Soon, but not yet. She couldn't believe her father was gone. A part of her had believed he would live and torture forever. But he was dead. She thought she would be happy, but his death didn't satisfy her. Only worry for Honzio filled her thoughts. And Kasdeya . . . She was dead too. Draven had gotten what he wanted. He was emperor. Natassa laughed—a broken laugh that carried with the wind.

Natassa closed her eyes, leaning her head against the tree trunk. She inhaled air. The tang of metal and blood tainted it as a reminder of the vicious battle that had taken place on the long expanse of land stretching to the castle.

"What have we here?"

Natassa was startled and looked up. A

tall, thin man leaned over her. His face was narrow and stubbled; his chin jutted into a point. Natassa's heart pounded as she took in his other features: a young face but hair mixed with gray, the ends falling onto his forehead in a V shape; full black brows and a smirk that tugged at his thick lips.

I'm coming for you.

He'd spoken those words in her vision. Natassa scrambled to her feet, putting distance between them. "Stay back," she said, her hand dropping to her belt, fingers grasping the edge of a knife.

He chuckled, the eerie sound sending shivers down her back. "I won't hurt you."

Natassa glanced behind her. There was no one in sight. Just empty land. She heard quick steps and returned her attention to the man. He was too close. She whipped the knife, but he grabbed her arm and wrenched the blade from her grasp. She grimaced, fighting his hold. He yanked her into his chest, and she screamed as loud as she could. He muffled the noise with a thick gloved hand over her mouth.

"Shh," he whispered.

Natassa tried to knee him, but he angled his body farther back. He chuckled at her attempts to free herself and called over his shoulder, "Sovor-ja! I found a girl here."

At his words, a rough-looking Savagelander walked up to them, holding a thick rope in his hands. "She will be a fine addition to the lot."

Natassa's heart jumped to her throat when she realized what he meant. She pulled out another knife and sliced her captor's arm. The man cursed and released her.

Natassa ran as fast as she could. But it wasn't fast enough. He caught up in moments, throwing his arms around her and caging her in his harsh hold. He shook her until she couldn't see straight. Her head pounded, and she saw stars. She felt her knife belt being unhooked, and then ropes lashed around her wrists. Sovor-ja appeared as a blur before her as he tightened her bonds.

She was turned around, and the sinister man stared at her, his lips curled upward. He ran a hand down her face. Natassa jerked her head away, and he laughed.

The Savagelander inspected her belt and knives with a nod. "Good steel. Could get us some coin."

Natassa's captor yanked her toward Sovor-ja. She dragged her feet to slow the process, and he growled, shoving her forward. Natassa stumbled and glanced at his hip, where a large broadsword was sheathed. If only she could grab it.

"Get a move on. We need to arrive on time for market day," Sovor-ja told her captor.

They placed a gag in her mouth, and tears burned her eyes as her horror fully sank in. They were planning to sell her as a slave.

VELAMIR
KINGDOM OF VERIN
CASTLE VERIN

Vykus and his mercenaries left the castle. With no choice but to give them their reward, Coralie had emptied more than half of the treasury. Velamir appreciated her sacrifice. He no longer owed them anything. Bear stood beside him, gazing out at the drawbridge.

"Did you know Winston's plan when he took us from the academy?"

Bear lowered his head as if the shame had been weighing him down. "Aye, lad. There's nothing I regret more than keeping you in the dark."

Velamir had already braced himself for that. He'd known he wouldn't like what Bear would say. But it shouldn't matter anymore. Bear had chosen to go against Prolus.

"And Prolus? Did you know he was Prolus?"

Bear's head shot up, and his red-rimmed eyes widened. That answered Velamir's question.

"That blighted bast—" Bear said a few choice words before turning to Velamir. "I didn't know. I was close to him, and he managed to keep it even from me. I suspected something, but not that. I never wanted to help the Tariqins. Winston convinced me that if I didn't, Prolus would murder my family."

"I'm not surprised he used that tactic."

"But my family might already be long gone. He may have been dangling that sliver of hope just so I continued to work my best. I'm done with that life. If you plan to finish him, lad, I'm with you to the end."

Velamir clapped a hand on his shoulder. "Thank you, Bear."

The older man grunted, and Velamir stepped away. He wondered where Natassa had gone. He'd wanted to follow her, knowing the heartache she must've been suffering at the news the messenger had delivered, but

Vykus had detained him. Velamir asked around for her, but no one had seen her. Finally, he circled back to the drawbridge, and a guard posted there said he'd seen her leaving. Velamir set out, trying to quell his growing alarm as he walked through the burned town and crossed the barren battlefield. She was nowhere in sight.

"Natassa!"

No response. Dread trickled over his neck, making the hairs there stand on end. Where was she? A terrible feeling settled in the pit of his stomach. He'd just passed a large tree when he saw something glitter in the light. Velamir kneeled, reaching for it. His hand froze around the thin bracelet with a black pearl at its center. His heart beat in his ears, and terror clutched him.

"Natassa," he whispered.

A twig snapped, and Velamir whirled, unsheathing his sword. He dropped the tip of his sword to the ground when he saw an old woman. Her hands were pressed to her heart, and her eyes were wide with panic.

"I apologize," Velamir said.

She took a few breaths to steady herself. "I thought you were one of *them*."

"Who?" Velamir asked.

"They raided the nearby town, kidnapped my daughter and her intended. They were to be married in a week." The woman broke into sobs, and tears left clear trails on her dirt-stained face. "I followed them. I thought I could save my child, but instead, I watched as they captured another poor soul."

"You saw them take someone? Here?"

"The girl resisted, but they took her." Her voice broke. "And I was too scared, too useless to do anything."

"Who were they?" Velamir asked again.

The woman glanced around as if something would jump out at her and whispered, "Savagelanders."

EPILOGUE

T HROUGH THE SANDY dunes, a lone man walked at a clipped pace and didn't stop moving until he reached his destination. He strode through the camp of restless Uluzar, glancing at his surroundings from under the fold of his hood. Countless tribes filled the area, symbols of every kind marking each section. The man inhaled, and the familiar scents made him realize how much he'd missed his home. He navigated through the camp to the section he'd been searching for. The man stopped before the main tent when two Uluzar blocked his path. A golden eagle tethered to a tall perch shrieked at the movement of the guards. The hood covering its wide eyes was studded with decorative points and rare feathers.

"Where did you come from?" the Uluzar barked in Savese.

"I need to speak with the chief," he replied.

They glanced at each other.

"Let him come," a deep voice within the tent called.

The guards moved out of the man's way, and he ducked inside the tent. Chief Jinong-ja sat cross-legged on the floor. His head was lowered, eyes closed in meditation. Then the chief lifted his head and leveled a dark gaze at the newcomer.

"Who are you?"

Instead of answering, the newcomer said, "How does the world unite?"

Recognition dawned in the chief's eyes, and he stood, replying, "With justice."

"Where is the justice?"

"With courage."

"Where is courage?"

"In the heart," Jinong-ja finished.

The newcomer threw back his cloak.

The chief laughed when he saw him. "Koseer-ja! I should have known you joined the Elders."

Koseer-ja cracked a grin. "It's good to see you."

"What news do you bring?"

Koseer-ja ensured they were alone, then leaned forward. "We found him. We found *the one*."

If you enjoyed this book, please consider leaving a review. Reviews are so crucial in helping spread awareness about the book.

ACKNOWLEDGMENTS

I cannot believe I am typing these words. We have made it to the end of book two. This story started with a spark of an idea that grew into an adventure I didn't even see coming. That spark would have fizzled without the support of so many people. I must first thank my parents. My dad for working harder than anyone I know and asking me every day, When's the next book coming? My mom for pushing me forward anytime I was down, never allowing me to give up. I couldn't have gone this far without you, Mom. I'm grateful for my siblings, for being amongst their chaotic group gave me inspiration and my best work seemed to happen when they were around. To my other family members, for cheering me on and telling me how proud they were. As always, much appreciation for my developmental editor, Tanya Oemig; you are a treasure. Thank you for all that you do. The team at Enchanted Ink never ceases to amaze me. Thank you, Chelsea; your line editing astounded me, and I was laughing around three in the morning at some comments you left on the manuscript. Lisa, you continue to be an outstanding editor, thank you for your hard work and talent. Loads of gratitude to my proof-reader, Jenny; you didn't miss a thing. Special thanks to Damonza for another gorgeous cover. Elena, you grow dearer to me with every year. I know you will accomplish everything you set your mind to. Thank you for being the best beta reader I could ask for. My cousins, Neela and Mina, thank you for rooting for me and being there for me. To my grandparents. I love you all so much. To the bookstagram community and the booklovers who connected with me and my book, you all mean so much, and I appreciate your love and support. And to *you*, dear reader, this book wouldn't be here without you.

ABOUT THE AUTHOR

Israh Azizi resides in the land of ten thousand lakes with her family and five cats. Since she was a little girl, she has been a lover of words and fanciful tales. It was her dream to one day share a story of her own with the world. With sheer determination, lots of love, and a decent amount of caffeine, she managed to make that dream come true. Besides reading and writing, she has a dizzying number of hobbies, some of which include bossing around her younger siblings, experimenting with new baking recipes, and playing board games with her family and close friends. When life's plot twists don't cross her path and her fingers aren't dancing across the keyboard building a fantastical adventure, she can usually be found in a quiet corner with a good book and a steaming cup of coffee.

www.ingramcontent.com/pod-product-compliance
Lightning Source LLC
Chambersburg PA
CBHW030142200726
48285CB00004BC/1264